FORTRESS OF THE SUN

A NOVEL OF ANCIENT GREECE

BY E.M. THOMAS

ALSO BY E.M. THOMAS

The Bulls of War (Book I of the epic fantasy series Chronicles of the Andervold Thrones)

* * *

As an author, I highly appreciate the feedback I get from my readers. It not only helps me, but also helps others make an informed decision before buying my book. So after you've had a chance to read the novel, please consider leaving me a short review on its Amazon page: https://www.amazon.com/dp/B07MN3DYTR.

FORTRESS OF THE SUN

Maps by E.M. Thomas
Cover designed by E.M. Thomas

ISBN: 0-578-43785-6
ISBN-13: 978-0-578-43785-9

www.emthomas.com

TABLE OF CONTENTS

MAP OF MACEDONIA AND GREECE

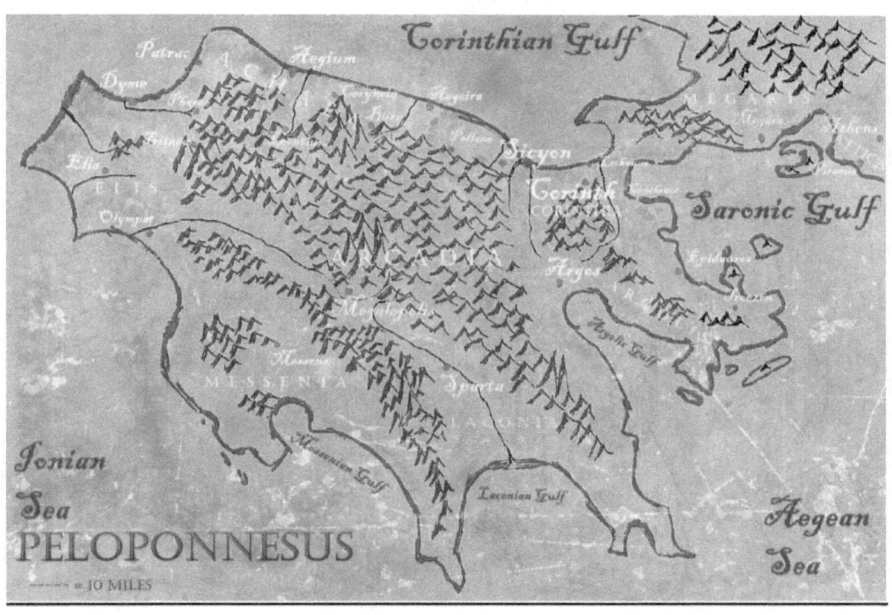

HISTORICAL NOTE

*B*y 243 B.C., Alexander the Great had been dead for eighty years, but the effects of his reign still resonated throughout Greece. Indeed, it is oft forgotten that en route to subjugating the known world, the Macedonian's conquests began with the free cities of Greece. And from the moment he cemented that hegemony in 335 B.C., the dominance of Alexander and his successors would go challenged but unbroken for almost a century.

Three cities were the keys to Greece in those days: Demetrias in the north, Chalcis in the east, and the great trade and fortress city of Corinth in the south—the "shackles of Greece," as Macedonian kings would come to call them. Possession of them meant command of Greece, and command of Greece was a near obsession with the Macedonians. Thus, they ferociously guarded possession of those cities like a bear to her cubs; the current king, Antigonus II, was no exception.

For all of Macedon's power, however, not all Greeks went willingly or quietly. Nowhere was this truer than in the northern Peloponnesian region of Achaea, where ten small towns expelled their Macedonian garrisons and formed the Achaean League—a democratic confederacy united against the monarchs of the north. Per Polybius, the League had "the same laws, weights, measures and coinage, as well as the same magistrates, council-members and judges"; one "could not find a political system and principle so favorable to equality and freedom of speech, in a word so sincerely democratic."

Though born of a noble cause, the League long awaited a statesman ambitious enough to take its reins—and that man was Aratus of Sicyon. Born in 271 B.C. in a city wedged between the League's eastern edge and Corinth, Aratus was forced to flee as a boy following his father's murder—a murder orchestrated by a Macedonian-installed tyrant. Although he flourished in his adopted city of Argos, he never forgot his home or lost his hatred for tyranny, returning to Sicyon in 251 B.C. with a stunning—critics would say suicidal—coup against the reigning dictator. He restored democracy to the city before merging it with the Achaean League, assuming leadership of both; to Macedon's chagrin, he would not look far for his next target.

Aratus's rise had been warily monitored by the old but powerful King Antigonus. The third ruler of the Antigonid dynasty, grandson of one of Alexander's generals, he'd sat upon the Macedonian throne for more than thirty years; he was no stranger to Greek war and politics. He had already slain the infamous King Pyrrhus of Epirus—he of the "Pyrrhic victories" against Rome; smashed a rebellion by erstwhile rivals Athens and Sparta; and ruthlessly put down betrayals by any of his puppet-tyrants. He more than anyone knew the importance of the "Shackles," of keeping them strong, making Greeks see them as invincible. And perhaps they did seem that way... to most.

But to Aratus, they were simply shackles meant to be broken.

I swear by Zeus Homarius, Athena Homaria, Aphrodite and by all the gods, that I will in all things abide by (the terms of) the stele, the agreement and the decree passed by the League of the Achaeans; and if anyone shall not abide thereby, I will resist them to the best of my ability; and may prosperity be mine if I keep my oath, but the reverse if I should break it.

OATH UPON JOINING THE ACHAEAN LEAGUE

. . . Aratus governed the Achaean nation, with his whole policy directed to one end alone: the expulsion of the Macedonians from the Peloponnese, the destruction of the tyrants, and the re-establishment in every state of the freedom their ancestors had long known.

POLYBIUS, *HISTORIES*

He that is possessed of Corinth is master of all Greece . . . Hence, the place was always much contended for, particularly by kings and princes. [King] Antigonus' passion for it was not less than that of love, in its greatest madness.

PLUTARCH, *LIFE OF ARATUS*

PROLOGUE

7th Day of Phoinikaios, Year 1 of the 129th Olympiad
(August 28, 264 B.C.)

It sounded like a thunderclap.

With a start, the boy shot up from a bed soaked in sweat, his room sweltering from the summer heat. His heart raced, a fear of thunder compounded by the midnight hour. To his confusion, however, he found moonlight shining unvexed through his open window. No wind could be felt, no scent of rain.

Did I imagine it? he asked himself, still groggy. *Must have... never heard Zeus so angry under calm skies...*

"Papa?" the boy called out quietly, though he knew full well his father, Clenias, slept in chambers two doors down from him.

BOOM.

Another thunderclap made him jump, no less confused at the source.

"Papa?" he called out again, feeling the corners of his eyes begin to well. With fidgeting hands, the naked lad tiptoed to his window, its panels open wide toward Sicyon's dusty streets.

He didn't see them at first. He looked up and down the street of packed houses from his second-floor perch, seeing them as barren as they typically were this time of night, when even the mutts had settled down for a slumber. But then—

"*Shhh!*" a man hissed, and the boy's eyes were drawn to the home's street entrance below. Pressed against the wall of the house were at least a dozen men in sleeveless tunics, some with daggers in hand, some with blades even longer. One looked to have shoved his through the slit in the double doors.

"*Bloody thing is loosenin' but it won't budge!*"

"*Upward! Swipe it upward, damn—*"

BOOM!

The man's shoulder launched into it again.

The doors crackled, its bracelock weakening.

The boy watched in horror as the lead man laughed. "*Did it! Ha! By the gods, it's splintering!*"

"*Again! Go on, go!*"

Rearing back, he crashed into it again, and all of a sudden, he was gone from view.

He's inside.

Paralyzed, the boy watched the men pour into his home like water to a drain.

They're all inside!

His imagination ran rampant as an excruciating silence took hold. He tried to scream but his voice was lost. His mouth was dry as the floor itself, his—

"*Clenias!*"

The house erupted in clamor and violence, the shrill cry of their slave's warning drowned out by men's bellowing, blades unsheathing. He heard noises like he'd never heard before in the room below him, surely that of weapons finding flesh. The uproar kept him locked in place, warily watching his bedroom door… waiting for the men with daggers and swords to come through.

Footsteps approached.

He screamed a piercing, terrible sound as his entryway flung open, hands covering wet eyes, urine soaking his legs.

"Aratus!"

He couldn't stop.

"*Aratus!*" a man yelled again, barely audible beyond the scrap downstairs.

Hands gripped his shoulders. Shook him violently.

"Oh my gods, my gods!" a woman's voice cried, which he finally recognized as his mother's. "My boy!"

"Close his door and block it!" his father barked at her, calloused hand now gripping his son's cheek. "Now!"

Sobbing, the boy finally looked around and found his father as naked as he but with knife in free hand, dark eyes wide in terror, face in torrential perspiration. His mother bawled in her own right, her small frame weighing as best she could against the door.

"I wanna sleep, Papa!" Aratus mewled helplessly.

"I know, lad, I know," his father said briskly, stroking the boy's curly hair as he frantically looked about for something. "You're gonna get back to sleep, I promise—"

More screams from below. Steps up their stairwell.

"Who is screaming? *Who is scream—*"

"Aratus, there are some bad people here right now, aye?" Clenias said as he dashed toward his son's bed and grabbed his sheet.

"Why?"

"There just are, *huios*, so we're all going to get out of here for a wee bit, all three of us, you understand me?"

"What about—"

"Quiet now, lad!" his father said, pressing a finger to his lips before quickly wrapping the sheet around the boy's bony waist.

"*Clenias!*" came a shout down the hall.

"*Check every room, quickly!*" answered another.

A tear fell from his father's eye, which frightened him further; he'd never seen him cry before. "Papa?"

"We have to leave through the window, so I'm going to lower you down, aye?"

"I don't want to, I don't want to!"

"*You have to!* Close your eyes and you'll be down in a moment!"

"No, no—"

3

But his father's powerful arms yanked his squirming body from the ground, and in seconds he was through his window, suspended in midair over the twilight street.

"*Mama!*"

"*I love you*, huios!"

"*Mama—*"

"*Aratus, when you hit the ground, you run!*" Clenias said, head looking down on him from the window above as he lowered the sheet. "*To Timanthes's or to—*"

He stopped, head jerked back, and in a flash let go of the sheet. Aratus screamed as he plummeted the final five feet onto the gritty road. The crash knocked the wind out of him, scraped his bare buttocks, but his eyes still vacantly searched his bedroom window; his ears heard the awful shouts of his father and mother, but he was grateful to hear them at all.

Because it was horror when they ceased.

"*Mama?*" he mouthed silently. "*Papa?*"

"*Get 'em all?*"

"*Aye... aye, I think so...*"

"*He had a boy, didn't he?*"

"*Uh...*"

"*He did! The bloody boy's dead too, no? Abantidas said get 'em all!*"

"*I'm not sure!*"

"*Well, make sure, dammit!*"

A head appeared at the window, shadowed eyes finding his.

He ran.

He'd never run so fast in his life. Down the desolation of narrow, dusty streets, afraid to look back because when he did—

* * *

"*Dammit, Aratus, wake up already!*"

His eyes sprang open. "Huh?"

"Gods save us from your wailing," he heard his friend Timanthes groan in the cot next to his. "Drivin' me bloody crazy..."

Suddenly, he was back in Bura, a small Achaean city where they'd slumbered in anticipation of arriving in Aegium later that day. Even as his senses awakened, his nightmare of two decades prior still seemed as vivid as the night it happened.

"Last time I bunk with you anywhere, honestly," Timanthes muttered further. "I've said it before, but I mean it now. Even on the high seas, you didn't bleat so bad..."

Aratus sat up on the edge of his cot, running a hand over his eyes and stubbly beard. Ever since it happened, he'd dreamt the nightmare from time to time, but lately it had been happening more and more. And it always struck him that all these years later, he never dreamt about the rest of his escape; perhaps because for years he didn't remember himself. It was only in hindsight that he learned his Aunt Soso had seen him running wildly through the streets of Sicyon, snatching him inside her home to hide him from his parents' murderers; only later that he learned those men worked on behalf of Abantidas, a vicious warlord who'd crowned himself a despot by slaughtering his father, the city's beloved and duly elected leader. No, he learned of all this only after he'd been living in Argos for years, safely shipped there by his brave aunt shortly after the bloodletting. By the time he'd returned to liberate Sicyon some thirteen years later, Abantidas had long been slain, done in by a tyrant in his own right.

"You want to get walking?" he asked hoarsely.

Timanthes barely stirred. "Not even first light yet…"

"Yes, it is."

"Mmph… *barely* even first light then…"

"Get up, you lazy bastard. Not much walkin' left to do anyhow."

He stretched his tired limbs, donning a woolen tunic before throwing open the inn's door to enjoy the brief respite of cool air they were likely to see that day. He stood quietly in the doorway, eyeing the brightening sky as he recalled the dream yet again. The screams of that summer night had followed him for a lifetime, screams that fed an insatiable vendetta against tyrants ever since; an obsession, even. He'd never have the pleasure of killing the man responsible for his parents' murder, for subjecting his homeland to more than a decade of violent oppression, but so long as he breathed, he'd be damned before he'd see it succumb to another in Abantidas's mold; he'd be damned before he'd let *any* other city of Hellas suffer the same fate or ignore their cries for liberation.

And as they set out for Aegium, his eyes were fixed on Antigonus II Gonatus, King of Macedon—the greatest tyrant of them all.

PART I
AEGIUM

CHAPTER 1

*18ᵗʰ Day of Panamos, Year 2 of the 134ᵗʰ Olympiad
(July 11, 243 B.C.)*

A fire burned within him.

A furious, maddening burn. The kind that surged from the belly straight up the back, setting hairs on end; the kind that could only be born from witnessing the absolute worst kinds of men, the worst kinds of things, the worst kinds of *acts*—and surviving.

It had burned for a lifetime, really; certainly as long as Aratus could remember. But now, as he neared the meeting that was sure to set the final course for his life—for all of Greece, gods willing—the flame burned ever brighter. His lifetime of rage and fury and sorrow had at last bred with a dash of optimism, and it scared him as much as it excited him.

He tried to squelch all the emotions, push them down and expect the worst, but how could he? How could he not embrace what was now so near? Now that the showdown he'd been brooding over for nearly a decade was at his doorstep, with just one meeting with the Council left to go? One more damn meeting.

The time was right. The gods had spoken to him. The people had elected him. The King was unawares. Yes, the time was right and it would never be better and surely no good and honest Councilman of the Achaean League would feel otherwise.

"Chances like this come but once in a lifetime," Aratus uttered finally, triumphantly, a welling in his gut. "You know it. I know it." He smiled. "*They'll* know it."

He fixed his gaze on his shorter friend as they walked, tan eyes aflame as they squinted against the high sun. "A chance for *freedom*," he repeated, hawkish face wincing with each word. "By the gods, how can we not take it?"

"Do you really wish me to answer that?" Timanthes replied calmly, almost irreverently, as if he'd heard the question too many times already. "Because it's quite simple to me really."

"Oh?"

"Aye. You see the freedom. I see the war to achieve it."

"And?" Aratus scoffed, thick black eyebrows plunging. "All ends demand means," he growled, noticing the heat again. The red-roofed white houses on either side of them provided no respite from the scorch, the pebbly street leading to Aegium's marketplace a veritable oven.

"And yours consist of war."

"After all this time, all we've done, war scares you? Freedom's not worth a war?"

"Does it matter what *I* say?" Timanthes challenged. "You want the *League's* armies, do you not? To 'liberate' Corinth from the Macedonians? From the King?"

Aratus nodded. "Aye?"

"The wealthiest, the largest city in southern Greece? The King's bloody crown jewel?"

Only a shrug this time. "Aye, and what of it?"

Timanthes sighed and looked away, light brown curls masking the sweat beading underneath; like Aratus, he baked in his ivory tunic and it showed. "Maybe it's worth it, maybe it isn't, but the fact is you have the people's favor, not the Council's, and that Council will *never* support breaching the peace."

"The 'peace' is a façade, a blind man can see that," Aratus said dismissively.

"Isn't any peace?" Timanthes quipped. "Yet peace is peace."

Aratus avoided Timanthes's searching eyes, avoided the onslaught of calculated logic, avoided anything that would chip away at his enthusiasm, his certainty. Yet it pained him not to have his friend's support. He was a good man, this Timanthes. Loved his wife, his sons. Was loyal to a fault, just as his father had been to Aratus's father. Unlike his own, however, Timanthes's family escaped to Argos unharmed by Abantidas's slaughter. Ever since, the two had done almost everything together—trained at the *palaestra*, sailed the high seas, gone to battle, freed Sicyon. But Timanthes was a cautious one; perhaps not compared to the everyday Greek, but against Aratus's vision, Aratus's ambition, he was a veritable hermit. His concerns as to Corinth and the latent furor of the Macedonian king were nothing out of character and certainly nothing that Timanthes hadn't repeatedly conveyed in the prior weeks.

So yes, Aratus knew the magnitude of what he planned to ask of the Achaean League's Council, knew Timanthes's opposition—he just no longer cared and grew weary of explaining why. "Peace may be peace, but it's time to act. The gods have spoken to me on this."

"Aye, well for your sake, hopefully the gods saved some words for the Council."

Aratus chortled, slapping Timanthes's back through the sweat. "If only they have. If only the gods would have *told* me they have and spared me some sleepless nights." His relationship with the other ten Council members was fraught with tension, no doubt; his city of Sicyon was larger, wealthier, and of different ethnicity than any other in the League when it joined. As a result, some of the League's erstwhile power brokers feared its domination—indeed, fear of dominant powers was what led to the League's creation in the first place. Aratus's steadfast dedication and sacrifice over the last decade had done nothing to convince them otherwise, despite his exceeding popularity among the Achaean people at large who'd elected him Strategos.

Timanthes smiled weakly but then fell quiet, a silence Aratus knew all too well. "Now's the time to say it, my friend," Aratus probed as they reached the open-air marketplace of the agora, its vendors and patrons bustling amongst the columned *stoas* that formed its rectangular outline. "One way or another, nothing will be the same once this meeting is over, so if you've something left to say, then say it."

"Aye, well that's just it," Timanthes grunted, the underbite of his stocky face becoming more pronounced. "Whatever clout or goodwill you've garnered to this point, be it for you, for Sicyon, it all hinges on what you say in there today, and—"

"*Listen to me*," Aratus commanded as he stopped walking to grip his friend's shoulders, ignoring the ruckus of the market crowds behind them. "I've always listened to you, have I not? Doesn't mean I've always taken your views, but I've always heard you out, you'll give me that much, aye?"

Timanthes sighed as Aratus's eyes bored in on him. "You have."

"Then know that I've heard you now, just as I've heard any and everyone else, and—" Aratus paused as he let a smile cross a long face normally creased in a contemplative frown. "And you're wrong on this. On Corinth."

"I'm not."

"I think you are, Timanthes," Aratus replied softly but firmly, his eyes never leaving his friend's. "The gods have spoken to me, and despite everything that's transpired, I'm confident the Council will agree. This is my chance, this is *our* chance, and it's one that we may never get again. If I'm right, if-if the Council lets me take our troops to the walls of Corinth, we can win; I know it in my *bones* we can win."

Timanthes shook his head incredulously. "Aratus, even—"

"We can *take Corinth!* And when we take Corinth, we'll have broken Antigonus's hold over southern Greece! Then it will be *he* who must dislodge *us.*"

Eyes nearly watering, Aratus gave a final squeeze of his friend's shoulders, then turned for the *Bouleuterium*, the meeting hall adjacent to the agora's colonnades where the Council awaited him. Timanthes stood silently in place for a moment, the crunching sounds of Aratus's sandals against the dry, sun-drenched street almost lost amid the frenetic din of the agora. Finally, he offered, "Well, just remember…"

Aratus paused and turned toward his friend, pushing wavy dark brown hair away from his sweaty forehead.

"You'll lose nothing if you simply bide your time; if the sign you received in Isthmia was truly from the gods, then surely it's fated and can be done at your whim. But if you go ahead with this and I'm right, you'll never recover your status in the eyes of the Council. You'll never even get the chance."

"Lose nothing by doing nothing," Aratus repeated to himself, baring another smile. "On *that* we may agree, my friend."

Timanthes didn't return the grin. "The League will be all but finished with you."

Aratus chuckled. "If I fail, I'll be all but finished with the League."

CHAPTER 2

18th Day of Panamos, Year 2 of the 134th Olympiad
(July 11, 243 B.C.)

His heart quickened as he moved behind the stone podium.

Now, Aratus thought, eyeing the musty squared confines of the *Bouleuterium.* Eyeing the Council. *Just say it and be done with it.* Say *it.*

There were ten of them. Ten Councilmen, ten of the League's most powerful men, the men upon whose decisions the League withered or thrived. After a customary splash of wine upon Zeus's altar began the day's meeting, they'd proceeded at their own leisurely pace, casually reclined upon cascading tiers of benches, dressed in chitons of every pastel shade and pattern. They chatted politics, they chatted women, they chatted family and friends, only every so often turning to the reason they'd been called together—the League's affairs.

The leisurely mood was lost on Aratus. For one thing, these men didn't like him—most of them, anyway—but then, he'd known that for years. His more immediate concern was the knot in his stomach; it'd cinched the moment he walked through the chamber doors, growing ever tighter as he saw his moment draw closer and closer. Timanthes was right, in a sense: everything depended upon today. True, the League met for three days and only the first was the Council meeting; true, lesser delegates of the League would meet on the second day, the grand assembly of all League men on the third. But it was a secret to nobody that these meetings lived and died by the decisions made by the Council on that first day. Whatever a Councilman wished to see supported, his message had to succeed *that* day; it had to be perfect *that* day. Months' worth of angling and maneuvering could be wasted in an instant.

Hence the knots.

The gods are with you, so say it now! he told himself again, yet still his voice failed, dry mouth refusing to open, eyes scanning the Councilmen with even greater pace.

He wasn't afraid of them; not even the ones of greater renown who'd drawn in other cities to their side. Surely it was inevitable that power brokers would emerge in this League of "equals," that alliances would arise. Chilon of Patrae led the bloc of the League's western cities, for instance, while old Ladas of Aegium led an eastern bloc; the three mountain cities in between were led by the venerable Margos of Ceryneia, one of the longest-tenured leaders of the League, a former strategos, and a living legend for a lifetime of feats.

But no, he didn't fear these men per se—he feared what they could do to his plans, his goals, his dreams, with Margos chief among them. While an unquestioned patriot for the League, and in many respects its father, his stature and brashness led him to dominate these meetings regardless of who the current Strategos happened to be. It was this bald-headed figure whose brown eyes had fallen upon Aratus.

"Are you ill, Aratus?" Margos asked without expression, the men behind him finally quieting. "You've hardly said a word, yet there you are at the podium."

"No, certainly not," the Strategos replied with cracked voice, a weak smile. He glanced around the room. "The air in here, it's stale, is it not?" he said, a cough escaping him. "Irritates the throat."

"Ah, terrible timing then—a podium's wasted on a speaker who can't speak," Margos said, smiling now as snickers spread. "Perhaps some honey water when we finish, no? Or shall we fetch it now?"

Aratus's neck burned in sudden embarrassment. "No. . but thank you," he said with a deliberately acid tongue.

The Ceryneian blinked slowly, victoriously. "Well, it's your call to make, but might I suggest we turn to military affairs?"

Aratus's stomach quivered. "Indeed, and in fact I—"

"Good, and this year's campaigns appear to be straightforward anyway, no?" Margos proceeded, not missing a beat. "Perhaps Chilon could begin so we can hear out the west's concerns."

"Very well," Aratus said as graciously as he could muster, though his irritation swelled despite himself. *Don't let him goad you into this again, not today. There's no need for us to fall further at odds, so don't give him a reason; don't give anyone a reason. You need them, all of them. Patience… patience.*

"My thanks, Margos, Aratus," Chilon replied with a saccharine grin. He was a heavyset, middle-aged man whose smile never left his face, even when bearing the gravest of news. He rose now in a light blue chiton with intricate patterns along its edges, light brown curls spilling almost to his eyebrows and the tops of his ears, his hair almost blond compared to his colleagues'. He represented Patrae, a western city nestled between two bountiful rivers, and one of the few League cities that could claim a truly bustling port due to a fortuitous bend in its coastline. Aratus had always found him easy enough to get on with, but like any man whose expression rarely changed, he was nearly impossible to read, let alone trust.

"And agreed, let's get on with it—too much bloody wine awaits us today to waste time in this sweatbox, no?" he boomed, drawing laughs from around the room. He chuckled to himself before his smile contracted ever so slightly. "Aye, I've had a chance to talk with my colleagues in the west, gods bless them," he said, glancing to Pataikos, his ally from Dyme. "And according to their border spies, the Eleans are thriving on their support from Aetolia. They've been moving troops across the Larisos and back, threatening Dyme's farmlands, maybe even the League's mint. Aetolians litter their ranks, and it seems clear to me—clear enough, anyway—that they're preparing for a raid in force, maybe an occupation of the borderlands outright." He looked back at Pataikos for a moment. "And we've nothing out there to resist it with—at least

13

nothing compared to what Elis can field, 'specially with Aetolia's backing. Word is that the Messenians back the Eleans as well."

Eleans, Aetolians… nothing, Aratus sighed to himself, trying to maintain a concerned façade. Residing just across the Larisos River, the League's western border, the Eleans had always been a mere annoyance, always full of bluster, far too enthralled with maintaining their position as caretaker of the Olympic Games to offer any true threat. As for the Aetolians, the League's rival alliance lurking across the Corinthian Gulf, Aratus regarded them as little more than a union of slavers, raiders, and related backwater filth, and needed to be treated as such; fearsome pirates to be sure, but pirates nonetheless. *Mere distractions from what's important.*

To Aratus's right, elderly Ladas of Aegium arose. "Let's talk plainly—the Eleans haven't put an army in the field in years and the Messenians wouldn't risk angering the Spartans," he barked gruffly, his outward frailness betraying the fire that still burned within. "Neither compares to what we're facing here in Aegium."

"But Sparta is said to be in growing turmoil," Chilon immediately retorted, every word laced through a gritted smile. "Their two kings are at odds and unlikely to concur on any campaign, let alone bringing Messenia into line. And with due respect, Ladas, I'm aware of what the Eleans have done in the past, and this time *is* diff—"

"Bah! Same as they ever were!"

Chilon shot eyes toward Margos then Aratus before relaxing his face. "So what is this greater, more urgent threat that Aegium faces then? Indulge us, please."

Ladas glared at the silver-tongued Patraean, before a hand began scratching angrily at the tufts of gray ringing his hairless dome. "Aegium's helpless should the Aetolians choose to attack her—her temples even more so! My city's proud enough to host the League but its defense should be the first to be resolved, a point I've made year after year, time and again, but this time we simply can't ignore it!"

"Why this year?" Margos asked. "They'd be better suited to guard against the raids we'll be launching rather than sailing to—"

"'Better suited,'" Ladas mocked contemptuously. "When've the Aetolians ever done what's 'better suited' for themselves? Never! When've they done a single bloody logical thing? Never!"

"Yet you speak their minds so clearly today…" Pataikos remarked drolly, eyes avoiding Ladas's.

"Their motives are simple enough to understand, doesn't mean they're logical," Ladas snorted. "Slaves, treasure, and revenge, that's what they exist for. Must our farms burn before we'll act? Our temples too? Must *I* be made a slave? My wife? They're smarting from Aratus's raids the last go-round and they haven't launched a large-scale campaign since—since..." the Councilman stuttered in frustration, memory failing. "They're building toward an attack!"

Chilon smirked. "And from that you conclude that Aegium of all places is their target?"

"Aegium more than fits the bill."

"They wouldn't risk it."

"Wouldn't they? Pellene's halfway to Mount Cyllene yet they made a run at her not long ago. *They want revenge!*"

Aratus's optimism wavered, stomach sinking the more he listened to the Councilmen's bickering. It was radical enough what he planned to propose, but the mood was plummeting into partisanship—as it usually did when it came time to divvy up defense allotments. He tried to shake off his doubts, yet...

Margos stood again, hands raised deferentially toward Ladas, whose bluster left him red-faced and winded. "I see no reason why we can't provide for both cities' concerns. May pare back the forces we can send on our raids into Aetolia, but perhaps that's what circumstances demand this year, no?"

"There are no 'circumstances' in the west," Ladas grumbled hoarsely. "Only Pataikos's fantasy and Chilon's indulgence in it."

Pataikos immediately rose to rebut but Margos smiled and extended a calming hand. "Nevertheless, we're a league of equals, are we not? His word's as valid as yours. So we'll purchase a few hundred mercenaries for the acropolis here, a few hundred more to guard the Larisos valley, and send the rest for attacks along Aetolia's shoreline." Margos looked around, nodding his head approvingly until he seemed to catch himself and turned toward Aratus. "Assuming you agree, of course?"

You son of a whore, the Strategos thought, failing to restrain his stare of daggers. *Offer me your scraps, will you? Treat me like a whelp?* "I'm the Strategos," he said with a bite. "I'll put into action whatever plan garners consensus here, as I've *always* done."

"Aye, but surely you have an *opinion* on the plan?" Chaeron of Pellene suddenly asked, his squat figure still seated as faces turned to him. "You certainly haven't spoken out in favor it."

"No, I haven't, have I?" Aratus remarked coolly, meeting the baby-faced Councilman's eyes straight on. Chaeron's city had traditionally been a stalwart ally of Aegium at these meetings, but had drifted ever closer to Sicyon over the years—partly by luck, partly by design.

Chaeron snickered. "Quite serious today, Aratus. What've you been up to that's made you so?"

Aratus could see Margos shuffle uncomfortably as Chaeron presented him with an outlet to reclaim the meeting. "Actually, I traveled to Corinthia, not long after our last meeting."

"To what end?"

"Well, Isthmia, really. Traveled there for the games."

Heads around the room nodded in approval. Isthmia was a sanctuary due east of Corinth proper, host of one of the other great athletic games of Hellas every two years. As an athlete and champion of some repute in the Peloponnesus, traveling to the Isthmian Games had always been of great interest to Aratus.

"Ah, and what'd you see there?"

"Too many Athenians," Aratus said drily, drawing laughter from the crowd; he was only half-joking.

"As always, I hear!" Lykos of Pharae chimed in to more laughter, only to be met by a rebuking look from Chilon.

"So the proposal, then..." Margos said loudly enough to quiet the crowd. "You agree with it or no?"

Aratus's heart immediately resumed pounding, and he barely flicked eyes upon Margos before finding the ground in front of his podium. *Gods give me my voice, my strength to say it right.*

"My time in Isthmia was remarkable, it really was. The pageantry, the athletes, the beautiful music, the deference to Poseidon; all quite an experience. But it was the people..." He licked his lips nervously. "It was the people I spoke with that made the trip feel ordained by the gods. Poseidon himself, even."

"Quite a statement," Chilon offered with dubious sincerity. "What's that to do—"

"What people?" Chaeron asked with furrowed brow. "Who?"

Aratus's eyes never lifted from his feet; he almost smiled. "Corinthians."

Margos sighed audibly. "Aratus, we've given you a very *simple* proposal to consider so let's address that before we move on to your conversations with—"

"I reject it," Aratus declared bluntly, locking eyes with the Ceryneian, fire ascendant. "I reject it outright, fully aware I'm just one voice among many... but I have a far bolder proposition for the Council and it has everything to do with those conversations with Corinthians."

Margos mirrored the group's surprise and confusion as he looked from them back to Aratus. "Well then, pray tell us your wiser, bolder plan."

Aratus looked away for a moment, breathing deep, basking in the awed silence. "He found me in the seats ringing the stadium for the chariot races," he said at last, envisioning the oval arena once again. "I don't know how he found me and I didn't know who he was, but he found me. The beasts and men hadn't yet taken off when he plopped down next to me in his dirty white tunic, and I barely noticed him until I felt his hand on my shoulder. I turned to look at him but he immediately said not to; he said to fake interest in the riders instead. And that was easy, I said, since that's what I'd come there to do."

A couple Councilmen snickered as the rest hung on his every word.

"'My name is Timodemus,' he said to me. He said he came from Corinth with important things to tell me about the city if only I'd give him the time to do it. Though I'd no idea what *I* had to do with Corinth, I'd no reason to turn the man down, so… I heard him out."

He licked dry lips once again. "'The city's chafing,' the man told me. Chafing under Macedonian rule and the fact that for almost a century Corinth's citizens haven't tasted freedom—not true freedom. Not without the sight of Macedonian boots or Antigonus's men planted throughout the city to keep watch. Not without the King's ships bobbing in their ports at Lechaeum and Cenchreae. I asked him bluntly what that had to do with me…"

Aratus paused and relived the chills that seized his body with the man's next words, uttered precisely as the chariot riders lined up at the starting blocks. "'Everything or nothing,' he said."

Margos sighed audibly. "And what are we to take from that?"

"I'll tell you, Margos, just as he told me: The people of Corinth have had enough of Antigonus, the Macedonians, all of them. *All* of them. More and more of the citizens have secretly rallied behind this cause but it's an endeavor fraught with danger given the King's spies. And despite the swell of support, they still fear to gather arms in such a way as to overthrow the garrison on the Acrocorinth; many are still afraid to commit to an uprising while so many uncertainties remain."

Old Ladas let out a hacking cough before turning bloodshot eyes upon the Sicyonian. "The Corinthians have cried for their independence since the moment Alexander squashed it. Every ten years we hear these wafts of rebellion and resistance—"

"No, not like this."

"—and every time it amounts to *nothing*. They're—"

"Not like this, Ladas, I swear to you."

Exasperated, the old man stopped and grunted. "How is it any diff—"

"He said that if we attack, the city will rise up."

A weight seemingly lifted from his chest as the words left his mouth, limbs felt light as air, toes tingled, and try as he might to resist it, a smile crept across his face as he saw the wide eyes all around him. He cleared his throat to break a deafening silence.

"They just want support and he said that if we give it to them then—"

"'*We*?'" Margos echoed, jaw slack with shock, forehead reddening. "By 'we' you mean the League?"

Aratus nodded.

"He realizes that he's asking us to go to *war* with Antigonus? To-to-to *attack* one of the most impregnable pieces of rock in all of Hellas and…" Margos's voice trailed off, as a new revelation seemingly struck him. "Tell us this isn't the 'bold proposition' you were referring to…"

Aratus's eyes danced around the room for a moment before finding Margos again. "It is, and with all my heart, I think it's time. They're waiting for us, my friends. The whole of Corinth, they're simply waiting for us to give them an excuse to expel the Macedonians, but not only that—Timodemus swears the city would join our union thereafter. Do you have any *idea* what that would mean? Sixty thousand Corinthians, the ports, the—"

"Zeus, make him hear himself!" Margos finally yelled as he looked to the ceiling, silencing the Strategos. "I'm not sure where to even begin, but I will say Ceryneia absolutely opposes any proposal that means breaching the peace with Macedon; or should I say going to *war* with Macedon, which is exactly what this is!"

"We don't know that. Your're—"

"But if it did, Aratus," a wide-eyed Pataikos added quietly, "you can't possibly argue that our troops are capable of squaring off against the King's, can you? With our best muster, we can field ten thousand men and horses; their standing army *alone* is said to be more than twenty thousand! And they can be on the march any day of the year, not like ours. And their armor, their pikes, their horses, I mean..." The Councilman simply shook his head without finishing.

Stay strong. Stay calm. Stay with me, gods. "We don't *need* to match their numbers. The actual soldiers in the fortress are nowhere near that much, precisely because they don't *expect* to be attacked."

"And what of the walls of Corinth itself?" Chilon asked with a disbelieving smile. "You can't very well strike at the keep before scaling the walls of Corinth proper."

"Ladders, Chilon," Aratus said sarcastically. "Just like any other city assault—"

"Don't mock me. You know as well as any that the League's never attacked walls like Corinth's."

"I took Sicyon's with only a handful of men, it's not—"

"*Sicyon is not Corinth!*" Margos raged, voice amplified by the enclosure. "And even if by Tyche's grace we scale those walls and take the Acrocorinth, what then? We'll have the whole of the Macedonian army bearing down on us within a year's time, if that long. What then, Aratus?"

"Then we'll have the most valuable city in southern Hellas in the fold to help fight them off, that's what!"

"But Corinth aside, what about the rest of the League?" Chilon said. "You think Antigonus won't hesitate to ravage every farm and valley in Achaea?"

"I think he'd be delighted to do so, but again—the Corinthian Isthmus is the *gateway* to southern Greece and Achaea within it. So the only way he gets to those farms and valleys is if he breaks through Corinth's fortress which we would *fully* garrison; not even he is up for that scrum. And if what Timodemus tells me is—"

"Who *is* Timodemus?" Margos demanded. "I've never heard that to be a name of any repute or power, so please tell us what authority he possesses to promise us the King's finest jewel in the south."

Aratus sighed. "I don't know what his authority is, but—"

"Then he could very well have *no* authority. By the gods, he could be an agent of the King for all you know!"

"I don't believe that to be true," Aratus shot back sharply, weariness creeping in despite his efforts, his faith. "But we could find out soon enough; he offered to meet with the Council as a whole to lay out his proposal. He said he'd gladly travel day and night to make it to Aegium, we just have to give him the word."

Margos furiously rubbed his eyes. "I cannot believe what we're even discussing. We've gone from protecting our farms, our valleys, our citizens, our shores to *this* bloody nonsense! To *war* with Macedon, this is absurd!"

"You forget that Antigonus has barbarians on his northern frontier, hostile Illyrians to his west; Thracians in the east and gods curse them, Aetolians in the south. So there may be a scrap for the fort, but you *don't know* there'll be war! It's not that simple, not for him, not for us!"

"Oh, it's not?" Ladas asked in a mocking tone, his sneer revealing browning teeth. "Well, I'll forgive you for forgetting this since you were just a boy, but that same Antigonus crushed an alliance of Spartans and Athenians twenty years ago when they rose to assert their 'independence' against him. We supported the alliance by word but thankfully not by deed, because the Spartans were humiliated at Corinth's walls before they'd even come within eyeshot of aiding Athens. Against Athens, he unleashed a fleet of pirates to raid her ships and harbors; he threw the city itself under siege for *years* until she was starved into surrender. And now? Now, Macedonian troops man Athens's harbors and forts to this day." The old man looked disdainfully at the men surrounding him. "I mean you no offense, but that alliance was far more threatening than what this League can muster."

"Thank you, Ladas," Aratus said with a sneer of his own. "Twenty years ago I was fleeing for my life after my parents were murdered by a tyrant that *Antigonus* endorsed. So I appreciate your forgiveness, *oh I do!*"

Ladas's expression softened. "Clenias was a good man for Sicyon and the League, even before the city was a member. Your mother too. Believe me when I tell you we mourned their losses, but my point is that we've been down this path before. Six years ago, we supported a usurper against the King in Corinth; still the result was the same. Two years ago, the King smashed the Ptolemies' fleet at the Battle of Andros. Whether army or navy, these are trained, professional warriors, and they're stronger than they've *ever* been in the League's history; we're *not equipped* to face them head-on, and we'll only end up with an occupation to show for—"

"*What are we doing here?*" Aratus demanded, patience exhausted, the gods' hold over him lost. "Anyone? Why was the League formed?"

Pataikos rose to answer. "Aratus, we—"

"It was formed because our fathers and grandfathers and some of those in this very room were fed up with the shadow of Macedon's occupation! We'd had enough of bowing to a self-appointed emperor hundreds of miles north in Pella! So what did we do? *What did we do!*" Aratus yelled, throwing his arms out wide, face flushed. "We rose up and threw their garrisons from our towns, and when we'd finished with our own we helped others expel theirs. We declared Achaea to be a *free* land and *dared* the Macedonian kings to stop us! And with what result? Almost four decades since and our League is still free."

He paused, and looked from face to face before him. "Friends, we've fallen away from what bound us together. We're too intent on keeping what we have instead of giving others what they deserve! We waste time scrapping with Aetolian filth who aren't even worth the effort of cursing their name." He fixed his glare on Margos. "*That's* what's absurd, Margos."

Chilon calmly intervened, lips curving ever upward. "Absurd or not, you overlook *real Aetolian* threats to the League for *dormant* Macedonian ones. You're more concerned about poking the sleeping bear than the snarling wolf at your doorstep."

"With Corinth in the fold, Chilon, *we become the wolf!* We *become* the bear! You know the Aetolians respect one thing: power. Until they see us as too strong to attack, they'll never cease their raids, regardless of what damage we can inflict in one measly campaign season. But with Corinth and her riches at our disposal?"

Chilon avoided Aratus's gaze now and the Sicyonian's stomach fluttered anew at the prospect of a breakthrough with the influential western Councilman. *How can they* not *see what I'm saying!* "Brothers, you *know* me—I'm not one to put the League at risk. And you *know* I've never shied away from any campaign or battle this League has seen in the eight years Sicyon's been a part of it. I've never questioned my orders, my assignments, not even for a moment. Now I'm asking you to look within yourselves and take a chance with me on this. This is our chance to rid the Peloponnesus of Macedon's blight. It's our *duty* to do so."

After a quiet pause, Chaeron of Pellene stood with a nod toward Aratus. "The people of Achaea elected Aratus to draw the League's path for the coming year. Aye, there are risks with the path he recommends, but there are just as many if we stop taking measures to strengthen our alliance. Everything we're told is that the Kingdom grows stronger and stronger, so we should too. If what the Corinthian told him is correct, we have a massive chance to do that, so I support at least bringing him here to speak."

Aratus nodded back at the man in appreciation, his hopes raised momentarily until he saw no other Councilmen offering their agreement. His gaze bounced from Margos to Chilon to Ladas, all seemingly content with letting an awkward silence linger.

"Margos?" Aratus finally said almost ruefully, immediately regretting it.

The Ceryneian had calmed a bit and seemed like he genuinely contemplated the proposal. But finally, he said, "It'd be suicide, Aratus. There's no other way to see it. It's one thing to give words of support to a rebel, but quite another to wield a spear at his side; the former's noble, the latter's reckless… at least in this case. Even were our men able to dislodge the Macedonians from Corinth, which I am convinced is impossible, we still aren't guaranteed Corinth would join the League. And even if she joined, how do we know she'll take our direction when her numbers match the entire League's man for man?" He shrugged. "We don't, and we can't take a chance that would leave our shores and borders defenseless against Aetolian raids."

Aratus scowled, voice and words nearly failing him again, both swept away in a crushing wave of frustration. "Well, if you bridge enough assumptions together," he muttered, "I agree you can arrive at that conclusion."

Margos wouldn't take the bait, victoriously remarking, "Troops for the west, troops for Aegium, and the rest we'll send with you into Aetolia—that's the plan I proposed, and that's the plan I stand by."

As if on cue, Chilon shook his head and looked from the floor to the Strategos. "Apologies, but I cannot support you on this, Aratus; truthfully, it smacks of your own desire for vengeance, not sound strategy for the League."

You have no idea what my vengeance would look like, were I to have it, Aratus burned.

"It's a bold plan, lad," Ladas added gruffly. "But it's not the right one. And frankly, we must be very careful that not even a word of this proposal go beyond the four corners of this room, lest it get back to Antigonus."

A nauseating feeling seized Aratus's stomach as his eyes glazed over and his attention drifted, defying a pounding that had overtaken his head. "*Gods know I didn't vie for this position, I didn't bind my city to the League only to bow to that man,*" he whispered distantly as he pictured Antigonus on his throne. "*Never did I think this Council would fall so madly in love with the status quo… to be so confined by imagined limitations.*"

"Do you have something else you'd like to say, Aratus?" Margos asked pointedly.

"No," he said, barely beyond a murmur. "No, forgive me."

Aratus left the podium to take a seat on the benches, not needing to hear any more to know what would happen. The western towns would fall in line behind Chilon, the mountain towns behind Margos, and the Aetolian proposal would carry the day. They'd offer him patronizing platitudes as they set to work drafting points to hand off to the *Boule* the next day. As that precise scenario played out before him, his mind drifted again, his body, his soul utterly drained; he suddenly wanted to be anywhere but Aegium; he longed for the streets of Sicyon again, even his days in Argos when there was such promise in the air, a promise that was his and his alone to fulfill. His eyes finally landed on Zeus's altar to which he shook his head plaintively, searching his thoughts for some unintended slight toward the king of the gods or his kin.

What have I done to deserve this? How can I lead men so afraid to be led?

* * *

"There's no polite way to gloat, Timanthes, so just get on with it."

Timanthes looked sharply at the Strategos, perhaps surprised that he finally broke his silence after two hours of brisk walking from Aegium. Aratus had no desire to meet his gaze, fixing his eyes instead upon the Corinthian Gulf's crystal blue waves lapping at the rocky coast a few hundred yards north from their path. The late day's sun speckled the water with red and orange, and even in the fading light he could make out the ruins of Helice beneath the murky surface, the once mighty city brought low by Poseidon almost a century and a half prior.

"You know I wouldn't gloat," Timanthes replied quietly, before looking away. He probably meant it or he wouldn't have mirrored Aratus's silence for so long.

"It amazes me that the Aegians have this testament to Poseidon's wrath less than a day's march from their walls," Aratus said, head shaking as he recalled Ladas's final rebuff in the *Bouleuterium*. "Yet still be foolish enough to ignore the sign he gave me at the Games."

"Did they not believe you?"

"Believe what?"

"That the Corinthian's message was a sign from Poseidon?"

Aratus sighed with exasperation. "Well, I didn't say it explicitly, but then how else could they have taken what I said? I attend the games hosted in Poseidon's honor on an utter whim; a man who I've never heard of nor laid eyes on before finds me in a sea of people to tell me Corinth is ready to throw out the Macedonians, and all within a few *weeks* of when I was to travel to Aegium to discuss the coming campaigns…" His head resumed its shaking. "I mean how else could that be construed?"

"I'd say that's a sign to attack the Aetolians," Timanthes replied in joking tone, a sentiment Aratus couldn't indulge.

"Aetolians," he muttered with a snort. "Another season of burning farms while their 'soldiers' flee."

"They might fight. Their ties with the Eleans and the—"

"Aye, and the Messenians, I know, but so what? So what if they fought? What's it change in the end? It only suits Antigonus's purposes to have all of us fighting each other, anyway. That's what they don't understand; that's what they don't *want* to understand."

Timanthes remained silent for a few moments. "It's not too late to turn back, you know."

Aratus looked at his friend in disbelief. "To do what?"

"You know what. Return to Aegium."

"It was too late to turn back the moment I stood down from the podium today. We're going to Sicyon."

"You really want to leave this way?"

"I didn't leave on bad terms, there was just nothing left to be said; there was no reason to stay. They drew up their proposal for the *Boule* tomorrow and that was that. I found you and now here we are."

"The Councilmen never leave before the three days are over, let alone the Strategos. There are gatherings, there are meetings, there are other deals that will be made. You're not concerned about being there the next two days to defend your name? You know they'll run it through the mud over your proposal; you knew that before you proposed it."

Aratus could only shrug. "They'll do what they're inclined to do whether I'm there or not, my friend. Aegium has plenty of back alleys and dark rooms for that. They'll say what they're going to say, though not all of them were against me; the Pellenean for one…"

"So you'll leave your fate in that babe's hands?"

"A babe has more sense than half the men on the Council anymore— maybe myself included," Aratus remarked with an empty dryness, eliciting a chuckle from Timanthes.

They both fell quiet again, the only sounds being sandals against the dirt path amidst a rising chorus of crickets and distant waves.

"This can't be the end of it," Aratus offered finally.

"No, you won't *let* it be the end, that's your problem," Timanthes replied with tired eyes and a half-smile.

Aratus had to smirk. "That's true too."

"And that's precisely why I didn't bother gloating."

PART II
SICYON

CHAPTER 3

20th Day of Panamos, Year 2 of the 134th Olympiad
(July 13, 243 B.C.)

The wine burned just right as it flowed down Aratus's throat. Watery but sweet, a peppery nip at the end of it. It wasn't much and it wasn't his favorite vintage, but it helped, every drop of it.

Helped forget the disaster at Aegium.

A stack of League scrolls lay on a table next to the backless couch on which he now reclined, begging him for their attention, taunting him. But he gazed distantly instead upon the columns of his moonlit courtyard, desperately hoping his mind would tire and let him rest. Though the travel had drained him, though the Council crushed him, sleep eluded him all the same. He felt as though he dwelled in a place beyond defeat; he felt soulless.

Given the circumstances, wine in his own abode became a pleasure beyond compare, especially when enjoyed in the *andron*. Though just one of eight small rooms among the house's two floors, the *andron* had always been his favorite to retire to, in good times and in bad. The couches lining its walls had countless stories to tell, bearing witness to the many jovial drinking galas the room had played host to.

Still a fine home, he thought to himself, eyes now drifting around the dark room, the walls' red paint barely visible, patterns even less so. When he returned from his exile in Argos to liberate Sicyon, many citizens encouraged him to construct a house in the luxurious style becoming popular among the Hellenic elite. "Tall, opulent, spacious," they told him. He spurned their suggestions with haste; he opted instead for this simple house off a crowded city street east of the agora, and on nights like tonight, he was glad he did. Thinking about his fellow Councilmen, especially Chilon, in their gaudy homes made his stomach turn.

"A palace for Chilon and a palace for the tyrant Antigonus," he said aloud, his thoughts sour. "How noble. How far the League's men have come since the days when they cared only to fight Macedon, not fight for riches, for living space, for... for nothing."

A long gulp of wine, then a second, eyes closing. *Eight years, has it truly been that long?*

At the time, it seemed like the perfect match, his city and the League. Surely, they were both forged from the same fire, that great hatred of tyrants and their sponsor in Macedon, were they not? For Aratus, at least, that fire had raged for years, driving him forward, inspiring him, ever since his teachers' first lessons on the history of Hellas; ever since he learned how his nightmare came to be, why he screamed unhinged nearly every night as a lad, why he cried out for a mother and father who would never again answer his call.

They told him of the turbulent years of the League's founding, the years of the 125th Olympiad (280–276 B.C.), when the dust from decades of

Succession Wars had begun to settle. Those were the wars that had exploded with the death of Alexander the Great, who'd by then created an empire spanning from Greece in the west to Egypt in the south and to the borders of India in the east. Regency of the empire had fallen to Perdiccas, one of Alexander's leading commanders, who quickly divvied up the realm among a dozen other officers and generals; Ptolemy, for instance, got Egypt, while Antipater got Macedon and Hellas. The latter had already ruled his realm by any means necessary prior to Alexander's death, destroying resistance while seeding the region with tyrants loyal to the throne.

Soon Antipater found himself embroiled in the civil war that convulsed Alexander's empire upon his death, first against Perdiccas the Regent, joined by Ptolemy and Antigonus "the One-Eyed," another formidable general of Alexander. Perdiccas's efforts came to an abrupt end when he was murdered by his own soldier Seleucus, one more captain of the late king. As spoils for his treachery, Seleucus inherited the vast territory of Babylon.

It wasn't long before the conflict reached the Macedonian heartland, triggered this time by the Antipater's succession. He'd left his realm to his younger son upon his death, passing over the elder Cassander. With Ptolemaic backing, however, Cassander triumphed in the showdown for control of the kingdom, following which he slaughtered all of Alexander the Great's remaining blood ties to the Macedonian throne—Olympias, his mother; Alexander IV, his teenage son; and Roxana, his son's mother. In so doing, the Argead Dynasty, which had ruled Macedon for centuries, came to an unceremonious end.

The kings' cannibalization of one another always appalled Aratus, always made him detest the autocratic form of rule even more. There was nothing altruistic about the wars, no greater purpose than simple greed and conquest. Indeed, it wasn't long before the myriad Successor powers had been boiled down to just five men: Cassander, Lysimachus, Antigonus, Ptolemy, and Seleucus. The latter three busily expanded their realms—Antigonus in Asia Minor; Ptolemy in Gaza and Cyrene; Seleucus in Arabia, Persia, and as far east as the Indus River—all in anticipation of the next war, the next battle, neither of which was ever far off. Tens of thousands fought and died in the wars of the five kings, none of them able to secure that decisive advantage.

His teachers told him that Hellas bore the brunt of several royal campaigns; they said the worst had been led by Demetrius "the Besieger," an expert siegemaster and the son of Antigonus I. On the sails of a massive fleet, he invaded Cyprus and Rhodes, before storming into Athens, Corinth, and the Peloponnesus; Achaea suffered greatly in these invasions and thereafter, where city after city was placed under Macedonian garrison. Aratus wept when told that Demetrius had punished Sicyon with particular severity; he destroyed everything. Razed it to the ground, building in its stead a monument to the young conqueror's hubris—a new city founded as Demetrias.

Fate intervened, of course, as it's wont to do; the remaining kings united against the father and son, with Antigonus I meeting his fate at the Battle of Ipsus. Demetrius proved a trickier vermin to kill; in fact, not only did he survive his father, but he gradually broke out from his Peloponnesian base to conquer all of Macedon. It wasn't until the 124th Olympiad (284–280 B.C.)—some forty years following Alexander's death—that he was finally defeated by Lysimachus. Left in the wake was Demetrius's son, clinging desperately to the rump of his father's kingdom in Thessaly.

Fortune would continue having its way—Lysimachus was soon crushed by Seleucus, who in turn was done in by an exiled royal from Ptolemy's court, who *in turn* was overrun by a sudden onset of barbarian invasions, when tens of thousands of Gauls poured into Macedon and Hellas in the largest such wave a Greek had ever seen or ever wished to see. Shockingly, it was that lonely, vulnerable son of Demetrius in Thessaly who made a stand and stopped the barbarians; it was that son who then claimed the throne of Macedon, taking his seat against the two remaining powers of Alexander's Successors, the House of Seleucus in Asia and Syria, and the House of Ptolemy in Egypt.

That son was Antigonus II Gonatus.

It was that Antigonus who had led his father's campaign of populating Greece with tyrants. It was that Antigonus who created an artifice of freedom among those states. And it was against that Antigonus whom the league of Achaean states finally declared they'd had enough. In short order, they ejected their garrisons, ejected their rulers, then bound together in a union which Antigonus had expressly forbidden. It was a bold step, stunning even, one that most poleis had grown too fearful to take while the great monarchs battled over the corpse of Alexander's empire. And perhaps had Antigonus not been so preoccupied with clawing back his realm, he would have brought the full might of his forces down upon them in punishment. Nevertheless, the moves had been made, *in spite of* what consequences may come.

The lessons about the Achaean League had given Aratus hope, he remembered. It had captivated him, even. That story of the undermanned and underarmed making a statement against the most powerful man for a thousand miles; aye, it was the very essence of Greece. In Achaea, he found his inspiration; in Achaea, he saw the mechanism for hammering the chains that bound the Peloponnesus.

He saw salvation.

So what's happened to them since then, since those early years when ramifications were but secondary concerns? Aratus wondered, spiraling deeper in thought. *Is complacency the natural order of things? Is the natural result of profound revolution an ignorance of the past, the sacrifice?* Indeed, many of the League's founders had long since passed on, leaving their legacy in the hands of their offspring. *But it's all so precarious, don't they see that? All so fragile, yet they act as if the progress we've made will persist in perpetuity. As if a kingdom which considers the whole of Greece to be its ward will simply leave them be if it was treated in kind; as if they wouldn't roll back every sniff of freedom, every inch of territory gained at their expense.*

A darker thought sent chills through his body. *Will Sicyon fail to remember their oppression forty years from now? How they broke free? It's not possible, is it?*

In the wake of Demetrius's destruction and rebuilding of Sicyon, his son installed a tyrant faithful to their house. Between that man, the tyrants before him and the tyrants after him, there had spanned more than a fifty-year stretch of tyrannical rule over Sicyon, ending only when the people expelled the tyrants in favor of Aratus's beloved father; they elected him to return democracy to the state at last. That his father's magistracy would prove to be just a brief aberration in the tide of tyranny was a pain Aratus knew all too well; the dictatorship had returned and remained until Aratus's liberation in the second year of the 132nd Olympiad (251 B.C.).

A slender silhouette suddenly appeared in the doorway. "You're home?"

His wife's smoky voice startled him from his ponderings. "Aye," he said with a clear of his throat, wiping away wine that spilled on his hand as he sat up. "Only for a moment."

"Don't rise on my account, I didn't mean to bother you."

"It's no bother... just didn't expect you'd be awake. Not at this hour."

"I heard noises," she offered, defense in her tone. "And I wasn't expecting *you* for several more days..."

"Hmph," Aratus grunted, his eyes finding the pebble mosaics beneath his feet in the darkness.

"I just thought your meetings usually last for three days... did this one—"

"Telesilla, I'd rather not discuss it," he said, head turning sharply in her direction.

"Very well," she said quietly, shadowed face turning from his. As she retreated from the doorway, she paused and turned back to him, blackish brown tresses and pale sleeveless chiton illuminated by the moonlight. "I can summon Sekis to pour your wine, you know. You needn't do your slave's work."

"Don't bother her at this hour," he said with a shake of his head and a sigh. "Just... just don't bother."

She looked at him for a moment without comment, then turned to leave again, not unfamiliar with her husband's moods. This time, however, he scolded himself for being so short with her—she was, after all, the daughter of the man who saved his life.

He was only seven years old when he lost his parents. After all the screams and cries of that horrible night had died, after he'd wandered naked and terrified through Sicyon's streets, he found himself living in Argos, a city that felt like a month's ride away from his homeland, rather than the day or two it actually was. He was more terrified by his new surroundings than awed by its legend, its history—that birthplace of Perseus, son of Zeus; that site of settlement for as far back as the Greeks could count. Nevertheless, he was sent there for good reason.

Respected in Sicyon as he was, his father kept many friends in Argos, one of whom was Telesilla's father, Naukydes. Defying any fear of retribution, he took Aratus in and raised him as his own son. He spared the broken lad no expense, educating him in the finest liberal institutions, striving to make Aratus the embodiment of *paideia*, that peculiarly Hellenistic approach to educating young males such that they were the epitome of self-fulfillment, that they were *kalos kagothos*—"beautiful and good." They should be well-rounded in their being—skilled in history and mathematics, fluent in philosophy and rhetoric, impressive in their physical build and athleticism. Aratus took readily to the teaching, his mind swelling, body molding into a champion wrestler on the sands of the *palaestra*, an Olympic pentathlete, and a horse rider of considerable renown. To his instructors' chagrin, however, it appeared that for all his talent, enthusiasm, and acumen, it was rage that pushed Aratus forward, that seemed to drive every grapple, every punch, every spur of the horse; in other words, the very antithesis of the balance the ideal Greek should strive for. When asked, Aratus wouldn't deny it; hell, he reveled in it.

When he came of age, Naukydes never spoke against his audacious plan to free Sicyon; indeed, he facilitated the process by providing fora for his fellow exiles to meet in. Taking such a risk was incredibly dangerous on two fronts: not only was the Sicyonian tyranny he sought to overthrow sponsored by Antigonus, but Argos too was run by a tyrant—Aristomachus the Elder, his family longtime friends of the King. Though Aristomachus ruled with a relatively light hand, he still would broach no hint of revolt or rebellion, be it within his walls or beyond. The debt Aratus owed Naukydes was thus beyond measure, and he vowed before he left that he would one day also restore democracy to Argos, his adopted home.

He made another vow. Although Telesilla was just a child when he set off on his venture, Aratus promised Naukydes that he would marry her as recompense for supporting his coup, support he still sorely needed as a man of only twenty years. Marriage amongst citizens of different Greek cities typically meant an absence of rights not only for the non-resident spouse, but also their offspring. Aratus's father, however, had long ago arranged an *epigamia*—a contract permitting just such intermarriage—between Sicyon and Naukydes, for an occasion such as this.

When he returned to Argos to fulfill his promise only two years ago, he found a bride who had developed a woman's figure even if she was rather plain otherwise. Romantic feelings had been slow to develop since they'd wed, partly because he saw her only a handful of weeks during that time due to his constant travels, but mainly because neither really expected them to bloom in the first place. The marriage had been born out of respect for her now-deceased father, to bear heirs that could claim the blood of two noble houses. If his ardor needed quenching, there were plenty of courtesans in town for the task—as were his unquestioned right to visit—though Aratus found himself so preoccupied with the League's affairs or Sicyon's that he spared little time to indulge in the flesh, be it Telesilla's or anyone else's.

As he looked at her tonight, however, he *did* want to talk to her, and it wasn't just a result of the ample wine he'd consumed. He respected her. Admired her. And he knew as soon as she assumed her responsibilities for running their house that she burned with her father's considerable intellect. Slight as she was, the house slaves quickly realized she was not to be lied to or trifled with, as she adeptly saw through any stories they tried to tell; she had a knack for boiling exchanges down to their inherent logic or illogic. These qualities drew him to her even if her physical features did not, and they so echoed Naukydes that he wanted her take on state matters even though they weren't the province of women—let alone women barely into their eighteenth year.

"Tell me something, will you?" Aratus called after his wife, emboldened now.

She stopped and shot him a look of confusion. "Aye?"

"Did your father ever tell you about your name? Its legend? About the famous Telesilla of Argos?"

"No," she replied. "But then I rarely saw him; you probably did more than me."

Her comment rang of bitterness and he shook his head. "That's a pity. He adored you, you know. And you're his mirror image in so many ways."

She blanched, hands suddenly fidgeting, clearly disarmed. "Well, I should be so lucky." At length, she shrugged, cleared her throat. "But my name? My mother might've told me about it once or twice when I was little but I've forgotten now. I know Argos still celebrates 'Telesilla'—*that* Telesilla—with a festival; it's a silly scene, men dressing as women, women as men," she said, her normally pursed lips arcing into a smile. "I've missed that since coming to Sicyon."

Aratus smiled back. "Aye, it's quite a show, I must confess. Her tale is even greater, though; as someone who carries her name, you should know it."

She stepped back into the doorway and gently leaned her head against its framework, body relaxed now. "So tell me."

He nodded as he sipped his wine. "Lived hundreds of years ago, had to be during the Sixty-seventh or Sixty-eighth Olympiad at least. She was renowned as a poet, but it was her stand against Sparta that made her the legend that she is—the reason your people throw that festival," he said with a shared laugh. "See, the Argive army had suffered a disastrous defeat in the field against the Spartans; so bad that even the survivors that took refuge in a grove nearby were burned alive when one of the Spartan kings set fire to it. Telesilla realized that

31

with the city's fighting men all but annihilated, the city itself would be ripe for conquest, so what did she do?"

"What?" she asked lightly.

"She gathered every weapon the city had left; she placed them in the hands of every boy and slave for manning the walls and then armed every *woman* she could find and set them directly in the path of any Spartans that managed to breach the walls. Poor bastards." He smiled further, relishing the thought of the incorrigible Argives standing up to the Spartans. "So when the Spartans arrived with their other king, they were stunned by the array of fighters along the walls, but of course they didn't shy from battle. The King quickly breached the gates but Telesilla wouldn't let her women be swayed by the Spartan war cry. No, they stood with Athena's courage and fought with Ares's fury, to the extent that the King had to beat a hasty retreat if he didn't want to be left in ruin. The Spartans fell back from the Argive plains, with Telesilla lauded for preventing her collapse."

He sipped his wine again and looked to his wife. "So that's the legend of your name. Strong with the spoken word, endowed with bravery beyond measure; selfless to a fault. More the ideal Greek than a thousand men I know."

"I suddenly feel a great burden, husband," she said without expression. "So much to live up to with that name."

Aratus twitched his lips. "I feel the same about my own at the moment, I assure you."

Her head never left the doorframe, calmly offering, "I'm happy to keep listening if it'll help."

His eyes narrowed upon her, considering her offer. He wasn't sure he wanted another honest take, but at last he relented. "I never told you what happened when I went to Isthmia for the Games, did I?"

"No."

"A Corinthian approached me. Approached me right in the middle of thousands of people at the races to tell me that his city is ready to throw off Macedon's chains, can you believe this?" He chuckled to himself, still disbelieving the exchange with Timodemus. "And he said, Telesilla... he said that the city would do so if only the League would come to its aid; to show the Corinthians that they would be welcomed into the community of free Hellenes. So I took that proposal and I threw it before the Council in Aegium—thinking as Strategos it was my power to do so and as my Council their duty to give it weight—and to what end?"

His wife's brow furrowed and her arms crossed her chest, as she took soft steps into the andron.

"Well, I was humiliated, that's the long and the short of it. The Council argued their way around offending the King in Pella and instead will be sending me to Aetolian backwaters yet again."

He gulped down the wine remaining in his chalice before looking blankly at the courtyard behind Telesilla. "But here I sit *knowing* I'm right on this. *Knowing* the gods have gifted us this chance to make things right in Corinth, yet I'm *bound* to follow the Council's directive... so what to do?"

His eyes bounced up to hers. "What to do?" he repeated in a near whisper.

She stared silently at him as she took a seat at his side on the couch, her hands icy cold as they squeezed his. Her nearness brought the smell of the flowery oil perfumes rubbed into her skin, a whiff of honey perhaps. "I had a dream," she said, lips in a frown. He could see none of her hazel eyes in the darkness, though they were wide with concern. "A *horrible* dream, the very night after you left for Aegium. I woke terrified from it."

Aratus looked at her in confusion. "What of this dream?"

"I can barely recall the specifics—nor do I wish to—but you were being tortured, unbearably so, at times by the Furies but at times by those whom I was convinced were the men you were going to see in Aegium. I wouldn't have told you this, but when I hear what you're telling me tonight..."

He sighed and looked away from her.

"You're trying to find a reason to do what's in your heart and not what you've been told, I know it," she said with surprising conviction.

"Sicyon has her own troops," he said quietly, frightening yet exciting himself for giving voice to a scenario he'd hitherto confined to his thoughts. "I could take them and just do it on my own. Damn the cowards...*damn* them."

His wife squeezed his hands harder. "I think you should be very careful right now, Aratus. I think that if the Corinthian man really was a sign of the gods then they will surely send you another and remove all doubt. But for now, what the Council said to you and what my dream said to me is that you should be patient."

"Aye, you and Timanthes," he grunted.

"At *least* for now..."

"You give your dreams too much weight. Some may foretell the future, but some are just a result of a busy mind. And for that matter, what of mine? What of those dreams that have haunted me for the last twenty years, seeing those assassins over and over—"

"I know, Aratus, I know," she said sternly. "But the last time *I* had such a dream—"

"You can't keep returning to that!"

"No, the last time I had such a *horrific* dream of torture was days before our child was lost; our *son*," she said in a rising tone that betrayed raw emotion, betrayed her pain; Aratus winced and teared at the remembrance of their first son, born alive and well only to perish within a week. "It was the *same* dream, just with you in place of my—"

"Well, then your dream says my fate is already sealed, regardless of what I do," Aratus said. "But *I* don't believe that."

33

Telesilla sniffed repeatedly, fighting back tears. "You've asked me what I thought and I'm telling you," she said as she released his hands and stood up. "And I don't want to consider what else my dream could mean because… because I'm with child again."

Aratus's head shot up, looking from his wife's face to her belly then face again, his heart suddenly lifting. "Are you?"

She nodded with welling eyes. When his first child perished, he'd sunk deep into despair. The babe had looked strong and healthy and perfect; a clean slate of life that only redoubled Aratus's dreams of an end to the Macedonian tyranny. Alas, it was not to be. And though it was hardly uncommon to lose a newborn among his community, he was haunted nonetheless by the worst expectations, the worst fears—among them, the fear that they'd never conceive again, let alone birth a son.

"Then I don't want to hear any more talk of these horrible dreams, am I clear?" he commanded. "Never again. We won't speak of them, not to anyone."

She nodded again.

"We'll give extra thanks and offerings and we'll—we'll make sure the mistakes we made last time aren't repeated, whatever they may have been."

Telesilla wiped the wetness from her eyes. "Will you promise me you won't do anything until we're certain you have an heir?"

Aratus sighed again, his exhaustion suddenly resurgent. He resented the question yet understood it all the same. "Do not ask me that. Not now."

"*Please.*"

"Nothing will happen to this child, I promise you that; it will be born and thrive regardless of whatever happens to me," he said firmly. "But it's a conversation for another night."

He could feel her plaintive stare. "I'm going to raise this with you on another night, then… *I* promise *you* that."

Aratus nodded. "And I'll welcome the talk. But you should head off to sleep for now. Gods willing, I will too."

She at last relinquished her gaze and retired, her tiny steps barely echoing as she crossed the courtyard's pebbles to the stairway. Aratus listened to them until he was alone with the night's still silence again. Inevitably, his eyes were drawn to the scrolls upon the table in front of him, leaving him more conflicted than ever now. Half his heart soared with the thought of an heir, yet Corinth's allure pulled at the other. And what of his wife's dream? He was no fool to the gods speaking through dreams, but then what to make of the man in Corinth? Was he no less a sign of divine will?

He groaned as he reclined back onto the couch and closed his eyes.

What to do?

CHAPTER 4

*24th Day of Panamos, Year 2 of the 134th Olympiad
(July 17, 243 B.C.)*

"Sire?"

By the gods, who bothers me at this hour of the night?

"*Sire?*"

Aratus's eyes opened slowly 'til the morning brightness slammed them shut. The man prodding him didn't help. He brought a forearm to block out the ubiquitous light, his body still supine upon the couch where he'd slumbered through the night. His other arm lazily hit the empty chalice lying on the floor beside him.

"Too bloody early..." Aratus groaned. "What do you want with me this early?"

"The birds crowed hours ago, sire," the man offered.

The Strategos's brow furrowed underneath his arm, the wine-induced fog in his head slow to clear. "So?"

"Sire?"

"*What is it*, Technon?" Aratus replied more forcefully, irritated by his servant's hovering, poking. "Do I have affairs today that I'm not aware of? No one in Sicyon expected me back for another few days at the earliest. No one should even know I'm here."

"I'm sure not many *do* know you're here... but—"

"But what? Who's come asking for me?"

"Come now... you know who."

A pause before Aratus peeked out from under his arm. "Ecdelus?"

The silver-haired, middle-aged man nodded with a knowing grin, creases appearing at the corners of his eyes. "That's the one."

Aratus sighed as he finally threw his legs over the side of the couch and sat up, running hands through unkempt locks. *Ecdelus*, he repeated to himself with a scowl.

By any measure, Ecdelus was one of the most feared and polarizing figures in the entire Peloponnesus, an incendiary famed for fomenting rebellions against tyrants all over the Greek-speaking world. The very mention of his name could get one gutted in some cities, and rightfully so. Aratus met him in Argos not long after his father's assassination, and once he came of age, the old radical was more than willing to help him fight the tyranny that had overtaken Sicyon; help him take the city back. Indeed, he wanted to be the first one over the walls on the night of the attack. In any event, the Sicyonian liberation left them forever intertwined, and from then on, he had Aratus's ear, free to lend his insight on the politics of the day in Sicyon or the League or beyond—whether requested or not. Ecdelus was without question the best and worst thing to ever happen to him.

The results of the last two weeks left him feeling like the latter.

"How'd he know?" he asked, already knowing the answer.

"His servant didn't say, but uh... well, you know him."

"Aye, but by the gods, it had to be halfway to sunrise by the time I arrived last night. Doesn't that old bastard ever sleep?"

"Probably. But his slaves don't."

The Strategos nodded. "Aye."

"And I catch them watching your movements around the city like hawks, day or night," Technon said with a chuckle.

Aratus shook his head again. "He's insane, that man. He really is. Top to bottom mad." His eyes drifted out the door to the slave women bustling between the courtyard's white pillars and the portico's red walls. Some balanced black water jars atop their heads, others carried sand-colored mortars and pestles. Telesilla stood in the middle of it all, calmly directing traffic with points to one area of the house, then another. Her eyes briefly met his, smiling at him as she saw his gaze fall on her belly. Her hand came up to it for a moment, before she turned and disappeared into one of the lower floor's storage rooms.

"Seems better now... she was a little put off this morning, sire," Technon said casually, noticing the spouses' silent exchange.

"Aye?" Aratus muttered distantly, expressionless.

"A little abrupt, aye... everything well?"

"I've been gone a couple weeks, so you'd know better than I," his master said briskly. "Probably disturbed her with my late arrival last night." He began recalling their conversation from the night prior and a weariness came rushing back. The pregnancy, the dreams, and now Ecdelus's calling—it was all too much, especially with an aching head. He closed his eyes, rubbed them. "So our Arcadian friend—what's he want?"

"Only an audience. Plans to be in the agora by high sun," Technon said, before quietly adding, "I wouldn't have disturbed you this morning otherwise, I know you must be exhausted."

"I know you wouldn't," he replied gruffly, but he meant it. Technon had served him well ever since Argos; he valued his opinion more than those of many free men. He'd been at his side when they stormed Sicyon, set sail with Timanthes and Aratus on their voyage to King Ptolemy's court in Egypt, acted as a faithful liaison for all his dealings with the League. His loyalty and courage were beyond dispute, which Aratus rewarded at every opportunity.

So the curtness in Aratus's tone didn't spawn from irritation with Technon, but the thought and mention of Ecdelus—the man Aratus blamed at least in part for the Aegium debacle. He shook his head. "Well, should be an interesting chat," he said as he arose, feeling an orneriness he'd be hard-pressed to quell.

Technon bowed his head deferentially and with a sympathetic smile. Thankfully, he forewent any questioning about Aegium; his ability to read Aratus's moods, to sense when to probe and when to let him be was one of the qualities his master valued most in him. Though he'd often discussed League affairs with the servant, this morning wouldn't be one of them.

"I'll meet you outside in a moment," Aratus said as he clapped Technon on his bare shoulder; its clamminess suggested the summer heat was already in evidence, to say nothing of the sweat-darkened swathes of his chiton. "Never keep a madman waiting."

* * *

The agora was packed during the high sun hours. It was a horde of patrons, vendors, pack mules; music, smells, and noise aroused every sense. Having muscled through the crowds, he now leaned against a stoa's pillar at the far eastern side of the marketplace and looked back whence he came, Technon's arrival with Ecdelus imminent. He was grateful to have escaped the attention of his colleagues thus far, a difficult feat given his stature and fame among the cityfolk—it was *his* statue in the agora, after all, erected in honor of his daring liberation.

Sicyon's agora bore the same rectangular shape as Aegium's, but at three hundred yards long from west to east, it was far larger to accommodate a population almost three times the size of the League's capital. The portico under which Aratus took shade marked the agora's southern edge, and was mirrored by another row of red-roofed stoas across the plaza. Tucked inside were galleries holding priceless works of art, Sicyon's reputation as a center of Greek painting and sculpting still alive and well after all these years. At the far western end of the market, he could see the beige Temple of Apollo, six columns across its entrance beneath a colorful triangular pediment; the temple was renowned for harboring Meleager's spear, the same that was used to slay the mighty Calydonian boar sent by the goddess Artemis to terrorize Aetolia.

Between him and the temple ran the expanse of the market, magnificent bronze and gray marble statues rising above vendors peddling every ware and service one could hope for. Potters and lamp-makers sold goods beneath makeshift stands with green awnings. Farmers of all types laid olives, figs, cheeses, and honey across wooden tables. Artisans showed rolled-up bundles of blankets or pairs of sandals while fishermen hung dried fish from their stalls. Other men volunteered their services as officers of the law, offering to serve court summonses upon the accused. Indeed, no skill was left unspoken for.

On the far eastern side, closest to Aratus, stood a raised platform for slave auctions. Three pieces of such chattel stood there this day. His eyes were drawn to the smallest of the lot, a brown-haired boy who couldn't have been past his sixth or seventh year; he looked scared as the auctioneer pulled him around the block by the arm, touting his perks to passersby. Aratus became lost in thought as he watched him, and for a moment, Aratus felt his aunt dragging him inside her house twenty years ago, crying hysterically, his parents' murderers giving chase with—

"Well?"

Aratus heard the question right before a fig seed hit him in the face. He blanched as a lanky man with wild silvery black hair came into view. He wore a faded yellow himation, large cloak wrapped around his waist, legs, and left arm, gray-haired chest exposed. With a wide crooked smile under a spotty black beard covered in fig juices, he carried the face of a man decades older than his forty-four years, crevassed with wrinkles around a thick, prominent nose.

Striding toward Aratus with Technon in tow, his gait betrayed the slightest limp, albeit one that didn't stop another seed from flying at Aratus.

"Well?"

"What's the matter with you?" Aratus scolded, looking around in embarrassment, already regretting his decision to meet in public.

"Nothing that I'm aware of," Ecdelus replied as he eyed the Strategos head to toe before launching a hand at his groin. "Cock's still there, so what's the matter with you?"

Aratus angrily swatted the man's hand away. Technon couldn't stifle a laugh in time to avoid his master's glare. "Find something else to do while we talk," Aratus said sharply.

Technon nodded back and disappeared into the crowd.

"Well?" Ecdelus asked again as he threw the fig remnants to the ground, leaning against the pillar to face Aratus, licking fingers clean.

"By the gods, well *what?*"

"Well, what's the matter with you?"

"Nothing's the matter with me."

"Then why didn't you pay a visit when you got back? Why am I just seeing you now, along with the rest of bloody Sicyon?"

Aratus met the man's eyes—odd-looking orbs of deep brown speckled with blue—in disbelief. "Why should I have paid a visit? You want to discuss politics in the middle of the night?"

"Aye. I did."

"Well, nothing's changed since then, so you lost nothing, I assure you."

Ecdelus shook his head as if he heard none of it. "You should've stopped by, no excuses."

"I'd likely have strangled you if I did," Aratus said under his breath as he looked away. "So you're carrying a limp, I see," he remarked after a pause, drawing an immediate scoff. "Did the tyrant-killer finally meet his match?"

He came by his moniker honestly, at least, though perhaps "lawgiver" was fair as well. Years ago, Ecdelus and a cohort had been invited to Cyrene, that territory west of Egypt, in order to establish a constitution for a burgeoning republic there. The kingship that preceded the republic was one that died out under suspicious circumstances, an assassination that Ecdelus had never owned up to even if it bore all of his handprints. He did, however, speak proudly of his hand in bringing down Aristodamus, a long-tenured tyrant and Macedonian ally in Ecdelus's home city of Megalopolis.

39

Was it poison that time, or was that one a knife in his sleep? Eck had overseen so much death, lives big and small, that Aratus could never keep their fates straight. The Megalopolitan's legend spread quickly—in some circles as an unflinching freedom fighter, in others as a cursed menace, a scourge of tyrants, one who struck fear and loathing like a plague; either way, he embraced them all, and his full-blooded, unpredictable passion meant there was no middle ground in one's opinion of Ecdelus, and indeed, there was no middle ground in his opinion of them. This was his concept of *arête*: a man's commitment to justice, excellence, bravery, and, above all, resourcefulness—his ability to use mind, body, and soul to achieve his ends. It was a dangerous *arête* when applied to Ecdelus, but *arête* nonetheless.

To Aratus, the Megalopolitan's volatility was worth the risk and political capital of befriending him. Too many men in this day and age were nothing but words and platitudes, leaving actions to those of years past or bemoaning the efforts of taking them now. Ecdelus acted first and let everyone else try to catch up. Unfortunately, his reputation and personality meant he was ill fit to actually lead or resolve the fractious politics of a city, which ultimately kept the tantalizing fruit of Megalopolis outside the Achaean League's fold. An equal fear of Sparta and Macedon left the southern Arcadian city paralyzed in neutrality, wedded to no one. Not openly, at least.

The downsides of the Tyrant Scourge.

"I've no tyrant to kill in Sicyon, more's the pity," Ecdelus said, before jabbing a finger into Aratus's chest. "That's your job. Did you get me one to fight?"

"You think I'd already be back if I did?"

Ecdelus's stare fell away from the Strategos. "So it went well?"

"No, it didn't go well."

"Did you make the comparison to Sicy—"

"Of course I did. They didn't consider attacking Corinth and attacking Sicyon even remotely similar."

The radical wore a mask of utter shock. "And you told them Corinth was certain to join if we succeeded?"

"They didn't care. Apparently threats from Elis on the western border and fears of Aetolian invasions take precedence. Only Pellene stood with me."

Ecdelus fell silent for a few moments. "I guess they're not ready, then," he finally offered with a thoughtful frown.

He made the comment so matter-of-factly that Aratus's jaw dropped, his temper barely restrained. "Not ready? For a solid month after I returned from Isthmia, you told me they *were* ready! That *now* was the time to make the push! That I shouldn't hesitate, that I should—that they were *ready!*"

"I told you I *thought* they were ready. So did my sources."

"You said it with a little more certainty than that. You *knew*. You said I should *act*."

"What did I teach you about assuming a man can ever *know* anything?"

"Oh, spare me Arcesilaus's proverbs, I beg you."

"Never assume, that's all I'm saying," Ecdelus said, shaking his finger in his friend's face.

Aratus looked around again, finding their conversation drawing looks from others gathered underneath the portico; he nodded at them so they would look away. "Stand on the other side of the pillar, will you?"

"Why?"

"For impression's sake. It's just best that we're not seen too closely in league with each other right now." After all, he accepted the risks of Eck's friendship, but he didn't necessarily have to embrace them... not all the time.

Ecdelus stared at him for a moment before moving a few feet around the circumference of the pillar, such that both looked northward into the agora. "I think people can still tell that you're talking to me—either that or that you're a madman."

"That I'll live with."

"So one stumble in Aegium, and now you're scared of speaking to me all of a sudden? What's behind that, after all these years—"

"Just a sense I've gotten lately," Aratus said briskly.

"A sense of what?"

"A sense that your views are somehow driving my decisions."

Ecdelus sneered. "You'd be better off for it, if so."

"Aye, well, your name is what it is. And my association with it is hurting my power with the League." His frustration made him say it, even if he only half believed it.

His counterpart peered around the pillar at him. "*Who* is saying this?"

"Timanthes for one, but there are others—and with the disrespect I received in Aegium, I am inclined to believe him... er, believe *all* of them."

With a groan, Ecdelus returned to staring at the agora. "You don't believe me, but that boy is the one holding you back, not me. I swear it to you."

"Holding me back?" Aratus said, recognizing the use of "boy" as the radical's favorite term for chiding Timanthes, a man his polar opposite in nearly every respect. "Of the two of you, he was the only person who predicted the Council's response—almost down to the snicker!"

"Well, now you know the Council's temperament on the proposal. You'll ask again the next time you're Strategos."

"I can't imagine there's a next time, and even if there is, how could the circumstances possibly be better than they are now?" The Sicyonian's hands flopped in the air. "I spent eight years of good will on that pitch; eight years, only to be labeled reckless, vengeful."

"So you've spent the power they think you have—so be it. There are many forms of power."

"Meaning what?"

"Meaning you can still exercise the power they think you *don't* have. Did people think we had the power to do what we did here? Did people think I had the power to do what I did in Megalopolis? In Cyrene? No. People don't know what power you have until you show it to them; *you* don't know what power you have until you show *yourself*. Don't let those crones in Aegium dictate what you do."

Despite his aggravation, Aratus recalled the option he considered last night—about going it alone with Sicyon's troops—before shaking his head. "I can't attack without the League's support. If not politically, it'd be militarily imp—"

"No, you can't attack without the League's support."

"So then how are the 'crones' not dictating what I'm doing?"

"They are if you let them."

Aratus sighed and looked to the ground. "I don't know what you're talking about half the time, I really don't."

"Half is good, half is very good. Probably used to be only a quarter," Ecdelus said in complete seriousness.

The two men fell silent for a bit, taking in the sights and sounds of the busy marketplace. Aratus searched for the little boy on the slave block again but he was nowhere to be found. For some reason, a pang shot through his stomach at his disappearance.

"Timanthes worries I'm a target for assassination now," Aratus said to finally break the silence, not wanting to stay, but now not wanting to leave.

"At whose direction?"

"The League's, the Macedonians'." Aratus shrugged. "Who knows, maybe both."

Ecdelus gave this a thoughtful pause. "I'd kill you if I were them."

Aratus let out an unexpected chuckle. "Would you now?"

"Aye. And in fairness, I'd kill me too. Neither Councilman nor Macedonian wants the status quo challenged apparently, and that's precisely what you proposed to do; it's what I propose to do, what I spent my *life* doing. You know the typical reaction chair-sitting politicians have to that."

"If Ecdelus of Megalopolis would kill me, then I should sleep with an eye open, I suppose," Aratus said half-jokingly.

"As it happens," Ecdelus began, a hint of uncharacteristic hesitation in his voice, "Megalopolis has called on me again."

"Who has?"

"Cleandor."

The name had a distant familiarity. "A man of some repute, is he not?"

"Indeed he is."

"What's a highborn man like him want with you?"

"Apparently, I'm old enough and wise enough to be the subject of highborn children's admiration. He says he has a pupil named Philopoemen who's become infatuated with tales of my deeds and has personally asked if I would return home to be his tutor."

"Aye?"

"Aye. Sounds like a special one, this boy. Only ten and he's said to work the family's farm like a common farmhand, tends the herd, Lves sparingly. And if there's not a sword in his hand, there's a book of tactics."

"Sounds like quite an honor," Aratus said, before he looked at Ecdelus with a knowing grin. "It's a long endeavor to teach a boy, are you prepared to sit in one place for that long?"

But his friend only scowled. "Ah, I'd be going for more than just the boy. The city's fallen to chaos again. A man named Lydiades seized power and in no time declared himself tyrant…"

Aratus leaned back, stomach sinking. "When? I hadn't heard—"

"Several months ago, actually, but I only learned of it in the last few days. It was a coup, like they always are, though this one wasn't even by a Megalopolitan by birth, only raised there. Rose high through the city's military along with some other bastard, Leocydes. Then, when the moment was right, he struck. Seized control, seized everything; kept it quiet though. Killed a good many that tried to get word out."

It was sobering news, to say the least. A step back from the progress they'd made. "Another tyrant in Megalopolis?" Aratus muttered rhetorically. "Not seven years after…"

"Another man of Antigonus, no less."

The revelation confirmed his assumption, making him curse the Macedonian name even more. At length, he could only sigh in frustration. "If all that's true, Lydiades is never going to let you inside the gates; or let you stay if you did."

Ecdelus grunted. "I can get in—I can *always* get in—it's getting out that might be the problem. Even for me, killing two tyrants in the same city is going to be a feat."

"Then if you're so inclined to 'get in,' maybe it's best you stay quiet, leave the citizens to their own devices, focus your efforts on the boy if you can do it without notice. Help protect him, help make him and those around him strong enough to stand up to these men of Antigonus, since there's no one else in your city that seems willing." To Aratus's surprise, Ecdelus held his response. "You agree?"

"If I return to Megalopolis, Lydiades has to die," the older man finally said with typical bluntness.

"But you tried it that way already. You killed Aristomachus after he'd been in power for almost twenty years but then you just left and now Antigonus filled the void all over again, don't you see that? If you kill Lydiades, and *if* you survive, it'll just repeat itself unless you take action to break the cycle."

It felt odd giving Ecdelus counsel after so many years of the opposite, but frankly, it was nice having someone else's problems to take Aratus's mind off his own for once. Whether the years of constant intrigue or instigation were finally catching up to Eck or not, it was clear that this decision vexed him, despite his intentions toward Lydiades.

"If you leave here, leave with the right intent, Ecdelus," Aratus said. "When you helped me return, I knew I was coming back to stay and to make sure the tyranny of years' past could never come back. That has to be your vision for Megalopolis, too."

"Ah, you just want to be rid of me," Ecdelus said drily. "Can't even stand on the same side of a damn pillar with ya anymore."

"No one'd dare blame me for that."

Ecdelus rolled away from the pillar and grabbed Aratus's shoulder. "Well, as for you, keep your spirits up about the League, lad. You know what has to eventually happen at Corinth, but only you can say how long that eventuality will take to arrive. You, of course, have my support."

Aratus rolled his eyes. "I'm sure I do, that's part of the problem."

"Good. Then be well and give thanks," Ecdelus said as he turned to walk away. "We'll talk again soon."

"You'll tell me, of course, whether the Tyrant Scourge is bound for Megalopolis?" Aratus called after him with a teasing grin. "Whether he's bound to play teacher?"

"Maybe," he replied with a dismissive wave before venturing off toward the heart of the agora.

Aratus followed the man's yellow himation as far as he could before the crowd's mass swallowed him up. In an instant, a large stray dog was at his feet, gobbling up the remains of the fig Ecdelus had tossed away. Aratus could only smile—the hound's size and coloring reminded him of the guard dogs he'd had to avoid the night of his twilight raid on Sicyon.

"If only we'd thought to bring some figs that night, we wouldn't have had to worry about them at all," Aratus said to himself.

He sat down on one of the stoa's steps and stroked the dirty animal's head, intending only to ponder Ecdelus's comment on the "eventuality of Corinth" for a few moments.

By the time he left hours later, the dog had long since departed.

CHAPTER 5

27th Day of Panamos, Year 2 of the 134th Olympiad
(July 20, 243 B.C.)

In two weeks, six thousand soldiers were due to muster outside Sicyon's walls.

One thousand mercenaries were still left to be purchased.

Ten warships and another twenty for transport still had to be outfitted with supplies and reviewed for seaworthiness.

A day's worth of sailing lay between the city's harbor and the Aetolian coast on the far side of the Corinthian Gulf.

And one man had to coordinate all of this.

Such were the logistics thrust upon Aratus, Strategos of this grand flotilla and army—logistics that cared not for his dissatisfaction with the Council's orders. In truth, after three days back, good nights' sleep, and ample time for reflection, the sting of Aegium had begun to wane—only waned, of course, not disappeared. Nonetheless, he'd resolved in the stoa three days ago not to wallow any further on his misfortune, instead throwing himself into planning the campaign, running over the numbers he'd have to make work with his customary precision. Anything to avoid the agony of an idle mind.

The order crafted by the *Boule* after he'd left Aegium called for an invasion of the Locrian shores, a fertile stretch of land bearing many of Aetolia's farms. Aratus knew the area all too well from his first term as Strategos two years ago, when he led an even larger army to ravage those lands in support of their Boeotian allies attacking Aetolia from the east. Boeotia, those bountiful tracts southeast of Thessaly and northwest of Attica, had never been the same since Alexander III destroyed their great city of Thebes. Nevertheless, they had recovered a modicum of power in the decades since, which Aratus was quick to cultivate—much to the antagonism of the Aetolians lurking to the west.

The campaign's results were the source of discord among the Councilmen. While Aetolian croplands were devastated as planned, Aratus's army was more enthused about gathering loot than making haste to link up with the Boeotians. The result was the utter destruction of their allies at the Battle of Chaeronea, a battlefield that had already seen its fair share of death over the years; indeed, Chaeronea was the very site where Philip II had annihilated the combined might of the Athenian-Theban army some hundred years prior, the prelude to Macedonian domination in southern Hellas. The field's latest victim saw a Boeotian army surprised near the lakeside town by a swift Aetolian vanguard, and by the time Aratus arrived with the Achaean army to help, the disastrous battle had already come to pass; Aboeocritus, leader of the Boeotians, lay martyred with a thousand of his comrades along the banks of the great Lake Copais, armaments spread asunder, the ground a gruesome mix of mud and blood and much, much worse. Under a brutal sun, somber Chaeroneans were still going about the task of retrieving the bloated bodies of soldiers who'd been cut down in flight; far fewer had died during the battle itself.

Thus, Boeotia was effectively conquered, its holdings annexed to the Aetolian League, leaving the victor even more dominant across the center of Greece. Meanwhile, the Achaean League was left with little to show for their efforts and nothing to do but beat a humiliating retreat back to the Locrian shores where they'd disembarked.

None of the Councilmen predicted the Aetolians' swift reaction against Boeotia. Regardless, they were horrified by the result, while Aratus swore that he would never again run a campaign with so little focus, or at least so little focus on the things that mattered. Ever since, the tension with the Council was palpable, their blame obvious, fires stoked with particular vigor by Chilon and Margos; after all, they said, it was Aratus who encouraged the Boeotians to go to war as much as anyone. It was almost as if they'd been waiting for Aratus's first taste of failure with the League, more than eager to muddy his name. His standing with the Achaean people as a whole was still largely in its ascendancy, but he knew he could ill afford to have anything go awry in future missions under his command; not if he wished to have a third shot at being Strategos, that is.

"'The powerful few know too well how to manipulate the weak masses,'" Aratus said to himself, recalling a typically acerbic and straightforward maxim of Telesilla's father as he stepped out onto a Sicyonian street bustling with people.

He used to resent those same people that he passed so pleasantly now. The whole lot of them, bitterly so. He'd harbored so much anger as he came of age in his Argive home, an anger that swelled the more he learned about his family's fate. Anger toward his father for failing to protect their house, for letting him and his mother to be slain. Anger toward King Antigonus for installing his puppets across Hellas, playing her *poleis* off of one another like a game of knucklebones. A vehement anger, however, was reserved for Sicyon's people, for allowing Abantidas to seize power in the first place; for allowing that nightmarish night to unfold.

But Aratus remembered the summer eve that changed his perspective on everything. He was in his fifteenth year. The day was done but as usual, he couldn't sleep, and Naukydes found him sitting on the moonlit stones of the home's courtyard, fists and face raw from a hard day of brawling in the gymnasium. With a groan, the corpulent man plopped down alongside the teenager in his himation, saying nothing for a while except for a comforting hand on Aratus's shoulder.

"Trouble sleepin', lad?" he had finally asked in the resonating baritone he was known for. "Sore?"

"No," Aratus lied with a shrug.

"Trouble stayin' awake?" he said with an easy smile.

"No."

"Gotta be one of 'em."

Aratus shook his head as he played with the straps of his well-worn sandals.

Naukydes eyed the boy's fingers. "Looks like you could use a cobbler on those. We'll take 'em down to the agora tom—"

"Why didn't anyone stop what happened to my parents?"

The older man looked at Aratus's face for a moment before looking away. "Your father did everything he could, lad."

"I don't mean him... I don't mean *only* him. I mean the people in Sicyon. Why didn't they do anything? You tell me they respected my father, loved my father, elected him, yet they stood by and did *nothing*, nothing at the time, nothing before, nothing after... they just sat there. Like sheep, like bloody sheep. They *still* just sit there."

"I don't think anyone knew something was afoot that night save for Abantidas himself and those that were in league with him—and they certainly weren't talking."

"But *no one* else knew? How is that possible? We know the details of every single thing someone does on this street, from the meals they eat to the wine they drink to the gods they favor to the—to the—" he stuttered frustratedly before shaking his head again. "Is Argos so different from Sicyon?"

"It's not," Naukydes said thoughtfully. "But I mean it when I say your father was as well connected and well respected as anyone in Sicyon. *I* wouldn't align myself with someone who wasn't. So if he didn't know about the plot, it's unlikely anyone knew."

"And it's not just Sicyon," Aratus continued, as if he'd barely heard Naukydes. "The tutors speak of tyrants seizing power in poleis near and far from here and that King Antigonus helps 'em do it. Been happening for years, decades it sounds like. But why do those cities let that happen?"

Naukydes was slow to answer. "I can't tell you that, Aratus. I can only tell you that more damage is done when good men do nothing than when bad men do anything."

"Why? Seems like an even trade to me."

"Because it takes no effort to give in to or go along with the bad," Naukydes replied, gesturing with his hands. "Doing right takes effort. It takes courage. Resolve."

"So Sicyon's full of cowards, then."

"Not saying that. But you can't begrudge the people for their fears."

"Why not? Aren't they the same good people doing nothing that you're talking about?"

Naukydes smiled. "Because not all good men have courage, and even those that do may not *realize* they have it. He may be a skilled baker, a smith, a poet, a priest—but not a *leader*. So those strong, those realized few must make every effort in their power to lead the weak… that's how good lives or dies. That's how the gods willed it."

Their conversation was in many ways a lifetime ago, but Aratus could still remember the chills that ran through his body as he heard Naukydes's last observation. It gave him a moment of clarity, a maxim he'd sworn by ever since; it let him release the anger that had pent up within him, at least that which was directed at Sicyon's people. He told himself that while it is easier to succumb to the wicked, people *do* want to do right if only someone would lead them.

And as long as he so breathed and a tyrant so ruled, that someone would be him.

* * *

Helios had nearly completed his chariot's trek across the sky as Aratus headed south toward the agora. The fading daylight barely climbed over the city's semicircular theater rising on the hill to the west, his own body casting shadows twice as tall as he, the stony street burning fiery orange. He passed well-kept white plaster houses on either side of him, while to the far southeast he could see the red-tiled roof of the Temple of Artemis peeking out. The street itself was "paved" with little more than weathered earth and crushed stone and could hardly be considered spacious, especially with the stream of foot traffic steadily increasing the closer he came to market. Nevertheless, he'd always preferred to deal with issues of finance when the agora's daily frenzy had begun to wane and Selene took her brother's place in the heavens.

The day's vendors had all but vanished by the time he reached the agora's rectangle, leaving the statues silent watchers over the few still packing up their kiosks and goods. Aratus cared little for the traders this evening, instead quickly veering off into a small stoa at the northwest corner of the market. It was an isolated strip nearly hidden altogether by Apollo's temple in front of it, and if it weren't for a well-lit room at the rear of the colonnade, he would have been in total darkness. There was a reason this room was still alight at this hour, the banker within well aware of Aratus's preferences.

To Aratus's surprise, however, voices already emanated from the room. They were hushed voices, but echoed all the same through the cavernous stoa. Brow furrowed, he slowed as he neared the entrance; sure enough, he saw the back of a tall, broad-shouldered man standing before Aegias the banker. Stringy coal black hair descended down his neck, the skin uncovered by his chiton a lighter shade than the typical bronze of the southern Hellenes.

Aratus's eyes met Aegias's over the man's shoulder, the unintelligible whispers ceasing. Aegias, an elderly man who'd survived the tyranny of Abantidas despite close ties to Aratus's father, smiled at his long-time patron. Shifty looks to the black-haired man betrayed his unease, however.

"Evening, Aegias," Aratus said, trying to keep a tone that hid his curiosity. "And you as well."

The other man kept his back to him, even as Aratus entered the small room, one bearing nothing but a counter and chests stacked along the white walls. Open-shuttered windows allowed dwindling daylight to filter in, aided by oil lamps burning at either end of the counter.

Aratus eyed a small brown bag on the table's center that Aegias smoothly moved to hide. "Have I come at a bad time, my friend?"

The banker's eyes again bounced from man to man. "I'm here at your service, there's never a bad time. My business with… this man kept me longer than I'd planned. You'd have my thanks if we had a moment to finish."

Though intrigued at the mysterious man's silence, Aratus only shrugged and smiled. "Certainly."

Aegias replied with a grateful nod. Aratus turned to leave before he caught himself in the doorway and looked back. "I must ask, does 'this man' have a name?"

The silent man finally turned, revealing large hazel eyes above a beak-like nose and a heavy black beard that nearly swallowed his lips. "Erginus."

"Erginus," the Strategos echoed, mirroring the man's unflinching stare as his hands locked with one another behind his back. "Well, I'm Aratus, son of Clenias."

The man replied with nothing more than a respectful tilt of his head. Aratus shot another look at Aegias. "I'll leave you to your business, then."

He wasn't a step out of the room before Erginus's whispers resumed— whispers that Aratus tried unsuccessfully to ignore. Something didn't feel right. Moreover, Aegias had to *know* something didn't feel right. He had worked intimately with Aegias for the eight years he'd been back in Sicyon, and in all that time, Aratus had never seen him so uncomfortable. And in eight years, he'd never arrived for a meeting when the banker was not at his disposal—let alone asked to wait outside.

And that accent, he thought to himself, recalling Erginus's peculiar dialect even from only hearing his name. *Odd… sounded a bit Macedonian but not—*

"…*Corinth.*"

Aratus's head shot up at hearing the word, and he immediately stormed back into the room.

"What of Corinth?" he demanded to the other men's shock. "What about it?"

Erginus now shifted his eyes away from the Strategos, as if he awaited Aegias's counsel.

"You said something about Corinth," he barked with a finger jabbed in Erginus's direction. "So what is it?"

Aegias sighed, then lifted the brown sack up by the closed end, letting a cascade of gold coins spill across the table. Erginus's hands quickly guarded them from the table's edge.

"From Corinth," Aegias finally said.

"That must be more than a hundred drachmae," Aratus said, flickering lamplight bouncing off the gold coins. "What are a hundred Corinthian drachmae doing in Sicyon?"

"He is—"

"If it's all the same, I'd rather he answer me, Aegias," the Strategos said curtly, eyes falling on the black-haired man again. "Will you tell me?"

After pushing the coins into a disorderly pile, Erginus faced him, expressionless. "I'm *from* Corinth, but—"

"Not with that accent, you aren't. Where are you really from?"

The "Corinthian" looked back to Aegias for a moment. "Doesn't matter where I've been… I'm there now."

"It matters to me. Any Corinthian man carrying a hundred Corinthian drachmae into my city matters a great deal to me."

"Is a hundred days' pay that suspicious?"

What the hell is going on here?

"Is this his first deposit with you, Aegias?" Aratus said, eyes fixed on Erginus.

Aegias nervously cleared his throat. "It is not."

Aratus nodded his head. "How many times, then?" The banker was slow to answer. "How many times has he come here in the last year, Aegias?"

"Seven… perhaps eight?"

"Eight, then. Always with a hundred Corinthian drachmae?"

"Yes…"

"So eight hundred days' pay, then. Do you rule Corinth in Antigonus's stead, Erginus?"

At this, Erginus grinned wide, revealing gaps throughout his teeth. "I'd have every whore in Corinth with me if I did."

"But you don't."

"Not *every* whore…"

"Then what else pays you so well in only seven months?"

A lengthy silence. Aratus's heart quickened, eyes narrowed.

"Just tell him, Erginus," Aegias finally urged.

"I don't know this man," the Corinthian shot back defensively, losing his smile. "All I do know is he means to take my gold."

"I can promise you I don't."

"I know it when I see it," Erginus growled.

"By the gods, Erginus, I do *not*. But I do have questions; and I *do* have to have them answered."

Erginus eyed the Strategos from head to toe. "You swear you'll keep your hands off these coins?"

"Put them back in the satchel and hold them in your own hands if you'd like. I want nothing to do with your money; I want to know how you came by it."

The answer seemed to relax Erginus, his hands finally moving away from the table. "It's a mercenary's wages."

"You're a mercenary?"

"No… but my brother is."

"There's nowhere in Hellas paying eight hundred drachmae for seven months of mercenary work. Your brother'd be lucky to see a fraction of that, even with the King's coffers; but let's say that's the truth—*why* is it here?"

"'Cause Corinth's a dangerous place to carry that coin…"

"Any polis would be a dangerous place to carry that much coin," Aratus said, drawing an amused grin from Erginus.

"No," the Corinthian replied with a raspy laugh. "*That* coin…"

"And why is that?"

"Because that's the *King's* coin."

A chill ran through his spine. Aratus looked at the sparkling gold, meeting Aegias's eyes for a moment before back to Erginus. "You don't mean wages, do you?"

The Corinthian shook his head, baring his gap-toothed smile again.

"You steal from the King of Macedon?"

Erginus nodded.

"How? Why?"

The foreigner's hand came up to stroke his beard. "My family's from Macedon but not for several generations. My grandfather settled in Antioch as a mercenary, right after Seleucus founded it—Alexander's Seleucus, you remember this name?"

"Of course," Aratus said with a nod, well taught about Seleucus's empire and imperial capital. He'd never seen Antioch in the flesh, but he'd heard it was as magnificent as any city in the known world, its palaces, gardens, and colonnaded streets rivaling even those of mighty Alexandria, its peoples numbering in the hundreds of thousands. After Seleucus was assassinated in the fourth year of the 125th Olympiad (281 B.C.), his progeny allied with one Successor power in Macedon, so as to war with the other, King Ptolemy in Egypt.

"My father fought as a mercenary as well, but under Seleucus's son, Antiochus. He died with the King, fightin' at the battle of Sardis just before I's born."

"You're barely more than a boy, aren't you?"

Erginus smiled. "I've always passed for older."

"I can see that. You look well beyond your years."

"You learn quick in Antioch; it's unforgiving. Mother's a Syrian, but she didn't survive my birth, I'm told; to this day, I don't know who nursed me. M'brothers and I scraped by on the city's streets, because there was no one to take us in or show us otherwise. Eventually, we fell in with a mercenary troop in Antioch and learned the battle's trade. The Seleucus on the throne now is desperate for any troops with Macedonian blood in 'em, so we were fetching a high price fightin' on his account."

"That king hasn't seen a day's peace since he took power."

"Aye. That's why we left."

"Ptolemy?"

Erginus nodded. "Bastard brought his whole army from Egypt and there was nothing Seleucus could do 'gainst it. He'd promise us all the gold in Syria if we'd stay, but he had nothing. Nothing to pay us with, nothing but promises. Once we got word that Ptolemy was closing in on Antioch, we grabbed what little we had and fled. By the time we reached Macedonian lands, we were told King Antigonus needed mercenaries of his own for his garrison in Corinth so…"

"So?"

"So here I am."

"Yet you're stealing from him?"

Another nod.

"Why?"

"Because it pays better."

"Aye, but the risks are far worse. Why not just work the garrison shift, no one's daring to attack it…"

"Ah, they didn't want me, only my brother. The King's a fanatic about the garrison he's put in there, whether anyone's plannin' to attack it or not. Some bastards named Persaeus and Theophrastus command the fortress and harbor tight as a wine barrel, and an even bigger bastard named Archelaus roams the city proper with patrols night and day."

"And through all that, you still manage to sneak hundreds of drachmae out of the King's coffers."

"We didn't survive on the streets of Antioch through others' charity," Erginus said with a sneer. "Not willing charity, anyhow."

"A noble man, you are."

"The King left us little choice," the Corinthian fired back defensively. "We'd risked everything to leave Syria, only to find there was nothing for us here either. Diocles earns enough coin to feed himself, but not the rest of us; I wasn't a beggar as a boy, and I won't be one now."

Aratus nodded in agreement as he looked away from Erginus, his gaze drawn to the table's oil lamps. He'd been rendered speechless for the moment, overtaken by the feelings he'd tried to put aside in the agora just three days ago.

Corinth. Again.

"So you wanted this knowledge, what will you do with it?"

"I did, you're right," Aratus said, eyes becoming lost in the lamp's flame. "But I don't know what I should do with it. Part of me asks whether to believe you at all; part of me asks what any of it matters…"

"Then I'll be on my way—"

"…but then another part, the strongest part, tells me I can't let you continue doing this out of Sicyon."

Erginus scowled. "Since when's a man of Sicyon been known to be lookin' out for Macedon?"

"Since I swore not to embroil Sicyon or her allies in Macedonian affairs," he replied, every word of the sentence more agonizing than the last. "And that's precisely what you're doing; it's a matter of time before the King's men realize eight hundred drachmae are missing, and I don't want to give him any excuse to send a guard here."

He let his eyes finally return to the Corinthian's. "I can *assure* you it's not out of love for Macedon."

Erginus grunted. "Result's the same."

"I need this gone from Sicyon, my friend. By the end of the campaign season, it has to be—"

"Aratus, there's more," Aegias suddenly chimed in, drawing his patron's glare. "Maybe an arrangement could be made where his gold *could* stay…"

Aratus stared hard at Aegias. It was a statement the old man wouldn't dare make without purpose, but it was also a statement beyond his station to make. "What terms could excuse this?" Aratus asked, growing increasingly annoyed. "What more I should know?"

The old banker glanced at Erginus with a wrinkled smile. "It's your choice… may I tell him?"

The Corinthian looked long at Aratus before back to Aegias. "That information's more valuable than that entire stack of coins. I told you that as a sign of my good faith."

"I haven't said a thing yet, have I, boy?"

"And I'd ask that you not until I have your word," he started, then turned his attention to Aratus. "*His* word that my money can stay here."

"That's a tall request to make when I haven't the slightest idea of what you're talking about," Aratus scoffed. "I can promise you a fair deal if what I hear is worth what you say it is."

Erginus's eyes danced between the two men. "No," he declared, quickly turning to shovel the coins back into the brown sack. "As you asked, I'll have all of it out by the end of the season."

Aratus nearly laughed out loud at the man's gumption, this man who would trade the security of eight hundred drachmae for a secret. *Is he bloody bluffing? Trying to pique my interest to its breaking point?* He looked again to Aegias, who'd simply folded his hands on the table and shook his head.

After Erginus frantically finished filling the bag, he shot a finger toward the banker. "By Nemesis's grace, I'll kill you with my own two hands if you share what I've told you. You should never even have hinted about it."

"Only trying to help you, boy," Aegias replied calmly.

With a brusque about-face, the Corinthian stormed toward the exit.

"Leave it here."

Erginus stopped.

"Leave it," Aratus repeated, throwing his hands up helplessly. "You've broken me, I want to hear—"

"Promise me," Erginus said, back still to the men.

Aratus chuckled again, still dumbfounded. "Promised."

A long pause followed, until finally, "Tell him."

Aegias cleared his throat as a relaxed smile crossed his face. "Well then... I've been doing business with the good Syrian for some time now, as he said. In one of our conversations I simply had to know how he pulled off his pilfering of the King, as he so proudly told me Macedon's treasury there stays locked within the bowels of the Acrocorinth. So what does he tell me? Why, 'walked right up to the fortress gates,' he said! Proves the most obvious route is oft the most neglected, doesn't it?" he said, weathered eyes looking to Aratus as he laughed. "So then he tells me, by accident or otherwise, that... the great Acrocorinth, that beating heart of Corinth... it isn't the impervious monolith we mortals give it credit for..."

Eyes widening, Aratus's heart immediately began to race even faster. He crossed his arms over his chest as he listened intently. "How do you mean?"

"It's a steep, windy road that leads from Corinth proper to its fortress, he told me. The mountain that it sits upon, shaped like a bean—"

"A *gigantes* bean..." Erginus interjected.

"—a massive bean indeed, broad from east to west, the perimeter lined by walls well over twenty feet high. The main path up to the mountaintop is on the west, he tells me, and it ends in a gateway guarded by massive towers that sweep any approach; any other route is suicide, and the Macedonians know it, he says. All other routes are nearly impossible to scale..."

Aratus felt himself deflating the more Aegias went on. "Then why—"

"All but one," the banker added, grinning wide.

"One?"

A nod. "Just before you round the mountain path's final bend leading to the gateway is another, smaller path cut in the rock, whether by Corinthians long ago or by the hand of time, but it's a path nonetheless that splinters off, snakes its way up to a spot in the walls about ten, twenty yards south of the gateway... a spot where the wall's not even fifteen feet high and often deserted."

Aratus's mouth smacked dry as the summer air, his mind sent racing. "But the men of the towers, they—"

"For the life of them, they can't see it," Erginus said, drawing the incredulous stare of the Strategos. "Can't see a thing."

"This is all true?"

"It is."

Aratus shook his head. "The Macedonians, their—their planning, their organization down to the finest detail—they've really left such a simple flaw overlooked?"

"I hardly noticed the path myself until the fifth or sixth time I'd made the climb. Tufts of grass here and there make it even harder to see, let alone where it leads to."

"And the path is scalable?"

The Corinthian shrugged. "Looks to be…"

"So I said to him," Aegias continued casually, "'why would you, my good friend, steal the King's treasures for this paltry sum, risking life and limb time and again, when you might treat yourself to a lifetime of opulence by one hour spent guiding an army to the walls? After all, you surely know that if your thievery's discovered, you'll as certainly be put to death as if you'd betrayed the fort?'"

A white-toothed grin emerged from the black of Erginus's beard. "I can't say I've climbed the wall myself, but I'm sure men of your abilities could—"

"Mind yourself," Aratus snapped. "I've never said a thing about wanting anything to do with Corinth and nothing should make you think otherwise."

Erginus's eyes jumped curiously from Aratus to the banker and back. "You seemed interested enough."

"I was interested in what bit of information you'd bartered with my friend here that would make him comply with a scheme against the strongest man in Hellas," Aratus said, hardly believing his own bluster.

"Well… even if the knowledge wasn't for your own use, I'm sure it'd be valuable to somebody," Erginus replied, smile fading into a sly grin.

The three men stood in silence for a bit, Aratus's mind racing faster than he could articulate. The setting sun outside meant the room was increasingly kept alight by the lamps alone, sending flickering shadows dancing around the room. His stomach, meanwhile, twisted like a vine as he recalled his pledge to the League, the mandate they'd handed down; the prophetic counsel from Timanthes. He *couldn't* engage in this conversation any longer. No, he couldn't even *entertain* it. Yet…

"So what was your answer to Aegias's question, then?"

"Oh, I never gave it much thought."

"And why's that?"

"Because I took it in jest, of course…" Erginus chimed in hardly disguised innocence. "Just as he intended it."

"But if you took it seriously," Aratus said, gritting his teeth. "If someone were to ask you to show them this path, this low-flung part of the wall beyond the tower's watch… what would you say?"

The Corinthian thoughtfully stroked his beard again. "Depends on what that someone would do with the knowledge… what's your end, Aratus, son of Clenus?"

"*Clenias*. And that's not your business."

"I think it is," Erginus replied quickly, eyes locked on the Strategos. "Because if you're plannin' to do what I think you are, you might put my brothers and I out of business... and back on the streets of yet another rat-strewn city."

"Then what—"

"And I can't have that," Erginus said with a grin.

Aratus stifled an irritated sigh. "Then let's speak plainly: what do you want as compensation should you choose to help... whoever it is that wishes to use you."

"Now we're progressing. Well, for starters, we'd have to involve Diocles, my brother serving in the fort; we'd have to have his agreement to assist first, and I can't promise that."

"Why? Knowledge of this should be kept to as few people as possible."

"Ah, but getting to the path's only the first step. You'll need Diocles to shepherd away any soldiers patrolling the ramparts of that part of the wall, no? Your banker friend is correct, there aren't many, but what if there happened to be th'night you wish to take 'em? You do want to *take* the fort, don't you?"

Aratus could tell the Corinthian was well aware of his bargaining power, and wasn't shy in wielding it. Nevertheless...

"Okay then, you and Diocles. And your other two brothers?"

Erginus gave a dismissive wave. "The one's a cripple now and Dionysius is an even bigger rogue than I... only Diocles can be trusted."

"You mean trust the man betraying the very king he swears fealty to, correct?"

The Corinthian let out a hearty guffaw. "I hadn't considered it that way... Opportunity makes for strange bedfellows, no?"

"Maybe it does," Aratus said softly. "So all told, then—your guidance to the wall itself and his diligence to clear the guards on the inside; how much?"

"A hundred talents."

Aratus blanched, face quickly turning to a scowl. "A *hundred* talents?"

"A hundred talents. That's what I make stealing, and that's what you say you'd replace. Not to mention my brother will be out of work, don't forget."

"Either you're a terrible liar or poor with numbers, but what you've stolen thus far amounts to a few years' pay; a hundred talents is a few *hundred* years' pay!"

Erginus looked away with a shrug. "Aye, I was never one with numbers."

"A hundred talents is more than half the League's *cities* take in a year!"

"The squalid towns of the League, maybe. But a hundred talents is barely a fraction of what Corinth brings in, I'm sure. Corinth'd do that in a month perhaps; a couple weeks, even. You should see the ships come and go, the convoys. Reminds me of Antioch, that way."

"I should just do it myself at that price. I know the path exists now, I'll find it."

"You won't. Especially not if you tried to find it by night, but as you wish. Even if you did, the wall guards will catch wind of you, even if the towermen don't. And maybe I'd alert them as well."

Aratus's hands balled into fists as his contempt rose. This was a devil he bargained with; a devil indeed. He turned away at last, angrily mounting hands on hips.

"You either do it with me, Strategos, or you don't do it at all."

"A moment ago you just wanted a safe haven for your spoils."

Erginus snickered. "A moment ago you weren't asking me t'lead you and I both to certain death."

Aratus watched the flickering lamp flame in silence for a few moments before his eyes found Aegias's.

"For only a few days' worth of trading in Corinth, you'll have paid for the venture," the banker said quietly, opening his clasped hands toward the Strategos. "All while holding the most valuable polis and ports in southern Hellas."

Aratus gave a subtle nod as the old man smiled at him. He was almost amused at the quaint, docile perception people had of Aegias in his advanced age; as a youth, there'd been no fiercer man in Sicyon, Timanthes's father once told him. His mind was sharp as a dagger and he never met a bold adventure he didn't embrace wholeheartedly.

"Sixty talents," Aratus said finally, drawing Aegias's deferential nod. "And *only* if we're successful."

"Seventy-five."

"*Sixty.*"

"Sixty but with *some* collateral *before* we leave."

"*Some.*"

"Done."

Aratus wheeled about to face the grinning Corinthian, the men's hands clasping each other's with conviction. "How soon can you get agreement from your brother? The trustworthy one?"

"Nine, ten days? Maybe more?"

"Seven or less, understand me?"

"For an extra talent I'll get here in—"

"By the gods, just get here in seven days. If I end up doing this, then I'll need to move quickly, I won't be able to dither about waiting for you. Get me an answer beyond seven days and the entire venture is *off.*"

"I'll do my best, then. I don't want to be known as the Syrian bastard who lost out on sixty talents."

"Nor I," Aratus said gruffly, darting for the door.

"And if we fail, Strategos?"

Aratus stopped. "If we fail? If we fail, then you're dead and longing in Hades, anyway. And me along with you."

Erginus laughed. "Who'll pay the Boatman, then?"

Even Aratus had to smirk.

"But if I *do* survive a failure—"

Aratus sighed. "If I fail and you survive, you'll be paid a talent along with a house in Sicyon for your troubles and safekeeping, to be used as you see fit. You won't be returned to rat-strewn streets, I promise you that. You and your brothers."

Erginus's grin slowly faded, betraying a sense of genuine gratitude. "Very generous," he mumbled. "I'll get you your answer soon."

"You have my thanks," Aratus said, heading back out the door into the blackness of the stoa.

Once outside, he stopped, stood there. Motionless, speechless. He blanched, mouth ajar, nose crinkled. *Was that real? Did I really just...*

By the gods, what am I doing?

CHAPTER 6

28th Day of Panamos, Year 2 of the 134th Olympiad
(July 21, 243 B.C.)

Sicyon's acropolis loomed nearly nine hundred feet high over the populace below, the highest point of the city's triangular plateau. Though he hadn't climbed all the way to the fortified summit, his mountainside stopping point gave Aratus magnificent views of the settlement below and its checkered streets. Nearest to him was the theater and a long, U-shaped stadium carved into the side of the acropolis's hill; further east sprawled red-roofed homes and temples, clustered around the agora's rectangle with green cypresses and kermes oaks peppered throughout dusty yellow streets. Still further, one could see to the coastal plains northeast of the Sicyonian plateau, where roads snaked through farms and olive groves toward a bustling harbor, white-sailed ships bobbing in crystal blue waters.

The hillside's vantages to the south and west were perhaps more important, providing sightlines with strategically placed towers in the villages ringing Sicyon proper. The network of towers, some as far as ten miles away, could quickly use different patterns of torch lightings to relay the proximity and severity of any approaching danger. With a territory of almost two hundred fifty square miles, the towers were crucial to Sicyon's defense, and Aratus kept them manned day and night.

Despite these vistas, Aratus's gaze was drawn elsewhere, locking on the 1,900-foot beige crag dominating the southeastern horizon. Sitting in the shade of a gnarled oak, he squinted against a persistent breeze, eyes already sweeping the roads leading to Corinth for the scoundrel he'd seemingly latched his hopes—his *livelihood*—to. As he looked at it now, the mountaintop fortress may as well have been a stone's throw away instead of the twenty miles in reality.

Corinth and Sicyon… he thought to himself with fidgeting fingers. *Always so near to each other, yet…*

He'd learned early on that even before the Macedonian destruction, Sicyon had never been like Corinth, not in power, not in wealth, not in population. Aye, both cities were ethnically Dorian, both were centuries old, both were inclined to fight for the same side in the many wars of the Greeks—when they weren't fighting each other, that is. To a greater extent, however, they differed. Corinth would always have that position on the Isthmus that let it dominate shipping and trade routes, that let it establish colonies throughout the lands bordering the Middle Sea, like mighty Syracuse. It would always have more people drawn to it as a result, people from across the known world; it would always have that seemingly impossible fortress, taller and larger than Sicyon's by a substantial measure—all the things that made the King declare Corinth to be the "passion of his life."

But then, Sicyon never wanted *to be like Corinth*, Aratus found. Perhaps that was because she *couldn't* be, perhaps not, but regardless, Sicyon instead lent itself out to Greece as a bastion for the enlightened, a place where the greatest musicians, potters, artists, and sculptors of the day could come and mingle among each other, inspire one another. There was Lysippus the infamous sculptor, the only man Alexander III deemed worthy of depicting him; Apelles the master painter, another man "worthy" of the great Macedonian king, author of a treatise on the subject that was second to none; Pamphilus, Apelles's teacher and head of the Sicyonian school of art. Then there was Melanthius the drawer; Epigenes, Sicyon's tragic poet; Epigonus the musician, a man so brilliant as to create his own instrument of forty strings, strings which he plucked using bare fingers, a first for any Greek. Thus, Sicyon's legacy grew self-perpetuating, not unlike that of Olympus in relation to its Games; through force of culture, not force of arms, Sicyon maintained its own form of preeminence, one that demanded recognition by other city-states of repute, even if Sicyon itself preferred distance from the dangerous games of Hellenic politics.

Alas, Hellenic politics found Sicyon, Aratus thought bitterly. It found her in the form of Macedon's rise a hundred years ago, capped when Demetrius "the Besieger" conquered her outright; ironically, some say the conquest was made to flatter Lamia, his wife, a flute player of some repute who'd fallen in love with Sicyon. She found its master artists to be her kindred spirits, but was greatly concerned that the defenses of the city were ill equipped to protect such treasures. When she repeatedly expressed that concern to her husband, he reacted with barbaric brutality—he torched the city so as to rebuild it upon the plateau which it currently resides, renamed Demetrias in his own honor.

That's Macedon. That's King Antigonus's father. Just like that, centuries of history destroyed, done in by the very "culture" and reputation the city thought was its shield.

Ah, but I would have liked to have seen that old city, Aratus thought. *That Sicyon before it burned.* His father was a boy when it happened, but he fondly recalled its beauty as far as Aratus could remember, Naukydes and others corroborating the assessment. As he looked out onto the plain now, remnants of the old settlement still beckoned, all these Olympiads later. The occasional charred stone and other ruins marred otherwise pristine groves and farms, their ugliness a permanent totem to Demetrius in a way that his short-lived renaming was not. Even the gridded pattern of the new city's streets paid homage to the late king, who left the scrambled style of ancient streets behind in favor of the more modern checkerboard layout.

Sicyon was reborn in a king's image with its body bruised, but its soul persisted—through the monarchs, through their tyrants, through the wreckage they left in their wake. Indeed, she rose ascendant from the ashes, like the Phoenix of lore, regenerate and free.

But for how long? Aratus wondered, more than usual lately. *When would it happen again? The next tyrant, the next assault? People think it can't happen—well, so did the Sicyonians of sixty years ago!*

"You can't just duck your head and expect peace from these bastards," he said aloud in frustration, thinking again of the Council's stubbornness, the plan he'd set in motion the day prior. "You can't live in gratitude that today's not the day they'll attack us, that they won't raze everything to the ground again!" There was time for the cities of the Peloponnesus to unite against Demetrius before his atrocity, against the monarchs that sought their servitude. And in fairness, some did, but not enough... not nearly enough. The majority sat and waited for the threat to pass, like lambs among wolves. "We needed them all," he said with a tired sigh. "We *need* them all."

He'd hardly slept the night before. No, it hadn't been a dream—he really had shaken hands with a thief of the most powerful man in Greece; he really had agreed to terms he'd no authority to agree to. And after a sobering day to think about the chance meeting with Erginus, he was as terrified as he was enthralled. The opportunity he'd forsaken was now tantalizingly close, yet he felt an anxiety overwhelming his being, straight to the bone. That he was anxious vexed him further—was this venture so different from the one to free Sicyon?

The Sicyon campaign had started out quite similarly, in fact. The colony of Sicyonian exiles in Argos were fearful but too proud to say no to his plan of liberation, his intention for a midnight sneak attack. In fact, he learned that many had joined to convince the brash twenty-year-old to reconsider. Every step of the way they resisted, from the timing of the attack, to the fear of guard dogs giving them away before they'd scaled the walls, down to the people's rejection should they ultimately make it in. Every step he'd led them kicking and screaming, and it wasn't until the tyrant's palace was aflame that they breathed a sigh of relief; only then did they embrace him. All of a sudden he was their hero, when not one day prior he was the reckless Sicyonian too young to know any better.

So why did Corinth give him so much pause now?

"This *is* what I wanted, is it not?" he asked himself aloud.

* * *

Quick footsteps crunched along the path that zigzagged up the acropolis's hill. Just before reaching the summit's flat top, the path went through a line of scattered oaks. It was a steady climb that would leave even the fort's soldiers winded, but Timanthes practically sprinted his way to the tree line. Finding Aratus reclined against one of the trees, he answered a wave with one of his own and made his way toward him.

"This seems a bit ridiculous," Timanthes said with a grin, his short-sleeved beige chiton dark with sweat. "There a reason Technon has me meeting you halfway up the acropolis? Should I ask?"

Aratus smiled without comment and looked to the dry rocky soil beneath his legs.

"You okay?" his friend said as he reclined in the shade.

"Your little ones... they're well?"

Timanthes looked away from him as he winged a few pebbles down the slope. "Rambunctious. Mischievous. At each other's throats," Timanthes said, mouth curving. "Two good sons."

Aratus chuckled. Timanthes was nothing if not a man wedded to his family, committed to his boys, his wife. He came by that fidelity honestly, one of five children—a large number as Greek families went—of a noble house, the patriarch of which was one of the kindest souls Aratus had ever met. The Sicyonian woman Timanthes married was a daughter of Sosicles, a magistrate during the brief leadership of Aratus's father. Though both Sosicles and Clenias were fervently anti-tyrant, their camps were rivals in the election, an old contention which made Aratus somewhat awkward with Praxilla, Timanthes's wife. It was even more awkward for Aratus to watch the two of them embrace, see the love in their eyes for one another, feeling how foreign that sentiment was in his own household. At times, he wondered if it was even a good thing, to love someone that much; wouldn't it be a hindrance? A weakness? A distraction from the greater good that they were supposed to have at the forefront of their minds? In fairness, Timanthes's bravery had been reaffirmed with every venture they took—and they'd taken their fair share.

"Happy to have their father back, I'm sure," he said lightly.

"Of course. Just learned I've another on the way, in fact."

"You and I both, then."

Timanthes glanced up with a smile. "Artemis received our wives' offerings, it sounds."

"No better explanation," Aratus said with a shrug.

The men fell quiet for a few moments, gazing out across the miles of soil and sea before them. Aratus could see his friend sneaking glances, his dark brown eyes giving away his curiosity.

"Technon didn't tell me much, but you didn't call me here to discuss children. At least I hope not."

Aratus shook his head. "Do you still remember when we left here? Setting sail for Egypt after the liberation?"

Timanthes looked askance at him, brow furrowing. "Of course I remember. I can't believe I've gotten on a ship since."

Aratus laughed tensely as he pictured the vessel shoving off from the harbor of Methana, a port city at the end of the Argolid peninsula protected by Ptolemy's navy. "Didn't start out so treacherous."

"Starts rarely do," Timanthes said, laughing some more.

The euphoria over the city's freedom had been short-lived. A scrap soon erupted when the exiles he'd brought back tried reclaiming properties which had been taken over by the Sicyonians they'd left behind. The exiles demanded the properties as their lawful right, but demands were all they had; they had little coin to offer. Needless to say, they were rebuffed with increasing rancor and violence, with Aratus left watching his hard-won gamble at risk of imploding. He needed coin and quickly, but he could think of no source in the Peloponnesus that could provide such a sum; thus, his thoughts turned toward the only friendly source he could recall—King Ptolemy of Egypt.

Ptolemy was a monarch of the Macedonian lineage who ruled over Egypt following Alexander's death. He'd been a kind one to the Peloponnesians, but perhaps most importantly, he utterly despised King Antigonus. As such, he sent a huge amount of coin into the Greek peninsula for combatting Antigonus's tyrants. The Achaean League was among the beneficiaries, and though Aratus greatly preferred not to befriend any monarch, Ptolemy's support came without ever seeking Peloponnesian conquests of his own. Surely then, if the means of dealing with Antigonus could be justified by the ends of preserving or expanding Achaean freedom, it was all worth it, was it not? At the sole cost of opposing a king they already were?

In truth, Ptolemy did make one other demand: art. The old pharaoh-king had a voracious appetite for Sicyon's works of art, and Aratus gladly indulged it. So pleased was Ptolemy, in fact, that upon Sicyon's recapture, the King delivered more than a thousand pounds of silver as a gift. A generous gesture to be sure, but it paled in comparison to what he needed to resolve the exile crisis—*nine* thousand pounds of silver, a sum he felt he could only request in person at Alexandria.

The plan then had been simple: head to Methana, charter a ship to sail him and his small guard to Alexandria, and make a heartfelt plea before Ptolemy—with a few paintings in stow for good measure. Once at sea, he just needed the ship to avoid the Macedonian-controlled Aegean Islands by sailing due south past the Malean promontory to the west and eventually Crete's shoreline to the east. The path had to be precise, because if Antigonus merely disliked the Achaeans, he loathed Ptolemy; discovery of his plan could have Aratus and his party in chains, if the Macedonians let him live at all.

As the gods would have it, the "plan" lasted all of a few hours. Almost immediately, the winds betrayed them, sending ship and cargo more than a hundred miles east into Andros, precisely one of the isles he meant to avoid. Even now, Aratus grimaced when thinking about the lurching of the massive ship, port to starboard, starboard to port, waves pouring over the bow, steersman in an utter panic. "Poseidon's blessing we landed that damn ship at all," he muttered, picturing the rocky shore it slammed into.

"At Andros?"

"Aye."

Timanthes smiled. "I'd say the blessing was more that we made hiding within eyeshot of the fort without detection… and still kept some of those cursed paintings dry."

"Blessings come in all sizes, don't they?"

To this day, he didn't know how he'd avoided the King's garrison. The island itself was fiercely defended by Antigonus following a hard fought campaign against Ptolemy not long ago. Worse still was that the polis they'd crash-landed near had a clear view of the coastal rocks, so surely the Macedonians would see some two hundred crew and passengers scurrying ashore; surely, it was just a matter of time before they came to inspect the wreckage.

It wasn't long before his premonition proved correct.

A handful of his brave servants stayed with the wreckage to allay the soldiers' suspicion while Aratus led the rest into a thicket nearby. He remembered watching with bated breath as the soldiers grilled the servants, close enough from his hiding spot in the trees to see their light tunics and bronze helmets, hands gripping spears as short swords dangled around their waists. But despite the Macedonians' gruff tone and aggressive shoves, the servants succeeded in their ruse, and though the men were taken captive along with the ship's ruins, it bought him a precious few days to find a way out of his predicament.

His savior appeared in the form of a large flat-sterned ship of square sails that he spied coming into a nearby port. By its bizarre shape, he knew it wasn't Macedonian, which was all he needed to see before sprinting toward the harbor when it later prepared to disembark. The vessel's master was a Latin-tongued merchant having set sail from Rome to Syria, but the barbarian thankfully spoke enough Greek to let him barter a ride as far as Asia Minor. Though it would be many weeks still before he'd finally arrive at Ptolemy's capital—a crowded yet exquisite display of Greek architecture, gardens, and broad boulevards—the worst of his trip's dangers had passed, and he remembered feeling no greater peace than he did when that Roman ship pulled away from Andros.

Aratus rubbed his chin in thoughtful anxiety. "You know, when Ptolemy handed us those chests of silver, it seemed like an afterthought. Given what we'd been through just to get to make the request, given what we'd survived... aye, just being able to take a free breath was all the reward we needed. The problems here seemed so far away."

"Hm, perhaps. Truthfully, I just remember wanting to be home again... and to never set sail again."

"But think back on it now, Timanthes—it was all worth it in the end. Sicyon as we know it wouldn't exist if we didn't make it back with that silver. There's a damn good chance the city would have collapsed by year's end." He swallowed hard. "And a damn good chance that another tyrant would have risen."

He felt his friend sneak another suspicious stare at him, but offered no response.

His fingers shook. "That's why we do the things we do; that's why we've done the things we've done: it's that mysterious end result we chase, isn't it?

66

That thing that intoxicates us the most, that thing we cannot know. The thing that makes us blind to the dangers and sacrifices that stand between us and what we aim to do..."

"And why are you telling me this, brother?" Timanthes asked quietly, almost mournfully.

Aratus wasn't quick to reply. Nerves stayed his tongue, but beyond that, he felt almost guilty for what Timanthes was about to hear. Just as he found his voice, though, he heard new footsteps heading toward their spot in the grove. Hobbling steps, muffled only by the curses of an ornery old man.

"... I'll throw the fool from the top of this hill, making me walk all the way up here!"

Timanthes looked up sharply to see the silver-haired firebrand from Megalopolis en route, assisted all the way by Aratus's ever faithful Technon. "Oh by the gods, Aratus!" Timanthes groaned.

For his part, Ecdelus froze in place upon seeing Timanthes—all but his eyes, that is, which locked bitterly on Aratus. "So ya make me traipse all the way up this bloody mountain, ya obviously have no wine on ya, only to have me make company with this ingrate?"

"The pleasure's mine, I assure you," Timanthes muttered.

"Ah, piss on this," Ecdelus said, briskly showing the men his back to leave.

"Stay here," Aratus ordered sharply. "I didn't call you both without reason; you should know that by now."

"I should smack the boy and give him some sense, but I'd rather not do him the favor," the old man said without breaking stride away from them.

"You'd do well to try!" Timanthes barked back as he leapt to his feet.

"Oh? I'll be in the agora in short order, you can find—"

"Ecdelus, stop!"

"You heard me—"

"This is about Corinth, dammit!"

Finally, Ecdelus paused. His head turned back with a look of shock, at last sharing sentiment with Timanthes. "Well, what of Corinth? Its food? Its whores? The color of its bloody banners? I mean what, Aratus?"

The Sicyonian clenched his jaw. "It's about an opportunity."

"Am I mistaken here?" Timanthes's face bore a look of worried confusion. "Has the Council changed its directive to you?"

"No."

"Then why..." But Timanthes let his sentence die off with a shake of his head.

"I met someone yesterday, someone in the agora," Aratus said with a voice that suddenly felt hoarse. "His name's Erginus, a Syrian man, and he told me he's fetching work in Corinth at the moment."

"So what's his business here?" Timanthes said cautiously.

"I saw him as he was visiting Aegias."

His friend's brow wrinkled. "The banker?"

A nod. "He's been leaving his coin with the old man for months now."

"The hell kind of work is he fetching that would make him travel all day to store his coin here?"

Aratus cringed, eyes meeting those of the quietly intrigued Ecdelus. "His business there doesn't go beyond thievery, I'm afraid. He does so with the help of his brothers, one of whom works the garrison at the Acrocorinth…"

"I see," Timanthes said with hands on hips, looking away from his friend. "So you've brought us to these lovely trees on this lovely day to discuss a common thief?"

"There's nothing common about him," Aratus said quickly. "He steals from the King of Macedon."

Timanthes glanced at him with a look of surprise. "So a common thief with a terrible deathwish."

"Perhaps… but in the course of his vices he's learned some invaluable secrets about that mountain of Corinth, about some invaluable vulnerabilities… about an invaluable path hidden even to the fort's garrison…"

"Has he?" Timanthes asked quietly after a pause.

His friend nodded. "And he's offered to show me the—"

"Oh damn it all, Aratus!" Timanthes exclaimed, hands aflail. "Truly, this again? The Council said *no!*"

"I understand that…"

"So you'll defy them? That Council is the people, like it or not! So the *people* have spoken—"

"I pray for anyone who believes that dithering bag of eunuchs represents the people," Ecdelus offered bitterly, breaking his silence. "The true 'people' elected Aratus!"

"Oh, I can't imagine you wouldn't condone this!" Timanthes barked in response.

"And I can't imagine you'd be willing to keep trading your pride for the pathetic façade of freedom you delude yourself with!"

"I've done plenty to see that—"

"Brothers…" Aratus pleaded as Ecdelus raged on.

"No, there are those that light the tinder, and those that tend the fire. Men that shape the world, and men the world shapes!"

"Oh, tell me how you've shaped the world, Ecdelus," Timanthes snapped, dripping in scorn. "You move city to city, you work your mischief, then leave the rebuilding—the *real* work—to the rest of us! Look at what's become of Megalopolis! Look at Cyrene, collapsed on itself within an Olympiad!"

The old man's fists clenched at his city's mention. "You're a lichen on a stone," he growled with pointed finger.

"Brothers," Aratus said with greater force. "I understand your 'love' for one another and that's precisely why I called you both here. I value *both* your counsel so I need you to get all of this out now. I *need* your input, your *backing*, on whatever I decide to do with this information…"

Timanthes let out a long exhale, chin dropped almost to his chest. "Tell me honestly that a decision has yet to be made."

"Nothing's been committed to yet…"

"How long, Aratus?"

Aratus looked back in Corinth's direction. "I told him to be back within a week's time…"

"To do what?"

"To let me know if his brother would agree to assist with any uh… any plans we create. We couldn't do it without him."

"A decision *has* been made," Timanthes said with a dark chuckle.

"Proud of you, lad," Ecdelus said, smile spreading wide to reveal his missing teeth. "I told you to keep your spirits up; told you something would reveal itself to you."

"Nothing's in place yet," Aratus said sheepishly, trying to hide the fact that he devoured Ecdelus's sentiment; he relished it, even if it pained him to see Timanthes. "His brother *has* to agree, or nothing's even considerable… but if he does, and we do decide to act on it, we'll have to move extremely fast."

"Offer him whatever he wants!" Ecdelus declared with a wave of his hand. "Life's made of precious few moments like this, you *cannot* afford to miss them!"

Timanthes rolled his eyes. "So there's a path on the Acrocorinth, is that the extent of your 'plan'? And you'd storm its walls with what, your personal guard? A pack of dogs?"

"Ha!" Ecdelus cried. "No dogs for this. Give you right away."

"I wasn't serious, you imbecile."

"I'll know more once I've seen it—*if* I see it," Aratus said, ignoring their banter. "But as Erginus tells it, it's just a matter of getting to the Acrocorinth's path. To do that, we'll have to breach the walls of Corinth itself, then move quickly as possible to pick up the mountain's trail. From there, it's a brisk climb, but before the final turn toward the summit gates, there's a path in the rockface leading to a low point in the wall… scale that, and the fort's ours."

"Scale that, and the fort's ours? Scale it, and the fight begins, it sounds like," Timanthes said, staring long at his friend before shaking his head. "And the troops for this venture? The money?"

"That's in my hands. It won't be cheap, but then how many coins do I really need for the Boatman?"

"Comforting."

"As for troops, I'll need at least a thousand. The Acrocorinth itself is not supposed to have much more than that, plus we'll have them by surprise."

"You hope."

"I pray," Aratus replied, hint of a smile.

"They'll never expect it," Ecdelus declared. "That's the thing you've never understood about these tyrants, Timanthes, they're simply bullies at heart. Arrogant, weak-minded men that squeal when someone pops them back."

Timanthes didn't bother responding to the Megalopolitan, instead sending his hands over his sweaty face and through his hair. "By the gods, what's it all been for? The League, the campaigns, the—well, what of your legacy? Your name? Your power with the League—"

"Aegium proved I have little reach beyond these walls, Timanthes."

"But all this—you'll throw it all away on the word of a Syrian thief?"

"His word's still to be proven, but I do think it takes courage to steal from the most powerful man in Hellas."

"Oh, a courageous thief, then? If he were courageous, he wouldn't be a thief. That you'd betray the League—"

"Betray the League to free a people!" Ecdelus interrupted. "To strengthen it!"

"Timanthes, the League offered and I agreed to bring Sicyon into this alliance on the *understanding* that it would go after the tyrants of Hellas, as it was born to do; that it would fight to *free* people," Aratus said as calmly as he could muster. "That promise has not been fulfilled, and the reason for that is *fear*. I'd much, *much* prefer this with the League's backing, and I pray for it still. But… in the end, freeing Corinth—freeing Antigonus's *jewel in the south*!—will send a message far beyond the League. It will tell all the people suffering under tyrants that there *is* another way, that there *are* men of honor, men of righteous stock that will stand with them if they rise up! So if the League wants to cut off Sicyon for honoring the League's purpose, if they want to banish me from the Council, then so be it! I cannot pass up this chance… I have to at least try."

Timanthes stared off toward the Corinthian Gulf in silence for a bit. Aratus could see the distress in his face and felt even worse for causing it. He knew Timanthes wasn't the same man that set off without a care with him to Egypt. But it was that very caution he'd developed over the years that Aratus relied upon to maintain balance in his ventures, be it political or military. He *needed* Timanthes.

"Aratus," his friend finally offered, gaze still afar, "I've lived the life of ten men to this point, and you probably twenty. If I protest the things you do, it's out of my love for you, my love for my family, the fact that I care for both of your well-being probably more than my own." He paused and looked at Aratus. "But I also do so out of fear that perhaps we're spitting on the gods for not standing back to appreciate our good fortune or this time of peace we've been privy to—whether you call it real or not. I see you picking a *war*—not just a battle—with this gamble of yours, with your plan of invading the strongest fortress in Hellas with a paltry thousand men."

"Timanthes, listen to me—"

"I *do* want to see my children grow well, my friend," he continued, voice anguished. "Before my sight leaves me or my hearing fails or the plague begins anew. I want to tell them what I've done, tell them of their forefathers, their house, their place in a long line of honorable Sicyonians; teach them to pick up the mantle when I fade away, give them *reason* to keep my memory alive. I do. That's selfish of me, I know, but I want that for you too."

"Timanthes, I beg of you to listen to me," Aratus ordered with a deep frown and intense tan eyes. "If twenty years ago the League had done at Sicyon what I'm proposing we do at Corinth, my father and mother might still be alive. And to point that out is selfish of *me*, but remember it anyway—and remember that my father was *your* age when he was murdered by a tyrant, and I your oldest son's. *The strong must stand for the weak.*"

"I know," Timanthes replied with a quiet nod and sad eyes. "And I'll be at your side for this raid like every one we've done, but I want your pledge that you'll not ask me again if we make it back. I want this to be it for me."

The request made Aratus pause, mostly due to its impossibility. He couldn't fathom a campaign without Timanthes; didn't want to. Nevertheless, he softened. "You've my word… but I'll ask the League to rename Corinth in your honor either way," Aratus said with a straight face, eliciting an eye roll. Aratus looked between both of his colleagues. "Goes without saying word of this stays between us. If the answer comes back in the affirmative, we're going to be mobilizing and on the move within a week or two at the most. As far as you're concerned, I'm still prepping for the raid into the Aetolian backwaters. The people that know differently will be kept to a minimum."

"You know enough of my deeds to keep me honest, I promise you," Ecdelus said as he casually wiped a prominent nose. "More worried you'll sell me off and use the bounty to pay for this bloody idea."

"A thousand bloody men…" Timanthes muttered. "Who'd have thought immortality could come at such a measly price?"

"Measly? You're not the one trying to find the coin to pay them," Aratus replied darkly, answered by a smirk. "*And* you're not the one that has to tell Telesilla about any of this."

"Gods protect you… or gods make her force you to change your mind."

CHAPTER 7

28th Day of Panamos, Year 2 of the 134th Olympiad
(July 21, 243 B.C.)

He remembered the day he'd resolved to take Corinth.

It was the day Antigonus II Gonatas, King of the Macedonian Empire, hegemon of all Hellas, extended his gilded hand in friendship.

Friendship was the King's favored approach when dealing with the Greeks in the first instance, rarely the sword. He much preferred to lure them into his orbit with promises of favor and fortune, to lull them into complacency before launching his coups. The sword he reserved for enemies he believed to be his equals: other kings; the kings of Epirus, the kings of the Seleucids, the kings of Ptolemy. It was the rare exception that would make him bring military might to bear against his Greek subjects, but one exception was when those subjects aligned with the Ptolemies of Egypt. Antigonus *hated* Ptolemy.

It was a rivalry born the moment Alexander the Great died in that magnificent palace in Babylon eighty years prior. From there, Ptolemy I, his son, and now his grandson would spar with the Macedonian kings for domination of the eastern Mediterranean Sea—first, against his grandfather Antigonus I "the One-Eyed," then his father Demetrius "the Besieger." But it was the Ptolemaic push for influence on Hellas itself that sent Antigonus into a state of madness.

Aratus knew all about this loathing for Ptolemy. He craved all such information about Antigonus Gonatas, obsessed over it. He wanted to know what shaped the man who meant to lord over Greece, who filled her cities with puppets, his to control. He wanted to know his enemy, the man he held responsible for his grief.

Antigonus was the epitome of the Macedonian elite—grandson of two of the most powerful men in Alexander the Great's inner circle; his namesake grandfather came closer to reunifying the empire than any of the Successors. As to his father Demetrius, Antigonus II would fight side by side with him in their "liberation" of Greece, a term Macedonians were all too fond of in describing their conquests. This was a task often deadly for the Macks, even if Demetrius treated the danger with irreverence—it was at the siege of Thebes, for instance, where a young Antigonus, distraught at seeing their men fall in great numbers as they launched themselves against the walls, begged of his father, "Why should we see these lives sacrificed so needlessly?" In response, his irate father was said to have barked, "Why should that disturb you? The dead cost us no coin or rations!"

The Macedonian mind, Aratus thought when he'd learned of this.

But then, a series of catastrophes struck the Royal House of Antigonid. First, his father's rival kings united against him to bring about a swift collapse. Antigonus's beloved mother was said to be so crestfallen by the disaster that she immediately took to the poison, ensuring some degree of honor in her

73

death. His equally beloved father, meanwhile, was imprisoned by Seleucus in Syria, a place where he would die only three years later. Though the Seleucid king had refused Antigonus's offer to switch places with his father before his death, he did have Demetrius's ashes delivered in an urn of gold, adorned in royal purple and a diadem, royal crown of the kings. It is said that an honor guard protected the urn until its interment in Thessaly, a master flutist playing his most mournful song as Antigonus II wept uncontrollably.

Thus, within a span of three years, Antigonus went from heir to a kingdom to an orphaned prince, a man without a homeland, and a man whose bases of control were now pitifully few and tenuous. Even when he did muster an army, his first attempt at seizing back his throne was thrown aside in bloody repulse. They were circumstances that would have broken many men or gotten them killed in the process, and Aratus often wondered what Greece's landscape would be today had Antigonus indeed wilted.

But he didn't wilt. No, he scratched and clawed and fought for every moment of his waking life thereafter, igniting a resurgence that Aratus both surprised and hated himself for admiring. It started bizarrely enough through a fortuitous bit of romance. The same Seleucid king that had imprisoned Antigonus's father also had a son—his heir and future king, Antiochus. Antiochus had fallen madly in love with his young stepmother, Stratonice, who happened to be the sister of Antigonus. The Seleucid king, keen to maintain peace among his royal house, relinquished his bride to his son, although not before Stratonice bore him a daughter named Phila. That daughter found a willing husband and suitor in her uncle—Antigonus. Thus were the Houses of Seleucus and Antigonus made harmonious; and thus would Antigonus secure his eastern borders as compensation for the inglorious fate of his father.

But if his kingdom was earned with fortuitous matrimony, so too was it earned with fortuitous blood and steel, as about the same time as his nuptials, a scourge of Gallic barbarians under the monstrous warlord Brennus poured into Macedon from the north. Ptolemy Ceraunus, the man who'd seized the Macedonian throne for himself after Demetrius's ouster, was hopelessly overrun and burned alive with great ceremony, with many more put to the sword, children among them. When the Gauls resumed their rampage south into Greece proper, it was Antigonus who summoned his ragtag force of loyalists in alliance with the Aetolians and checked the barbarian advance.

Victory in hand, more Macedonian lords rallied to his banners and pursued the Gauls all the way into Thrace, ambushing them by the sea at Lysimachia. So many Gauls were said to have died there that the beaches stayed blood red for the better part of a decade. After such a triumph, he had no trouble getting noble support for his claim to the throne, immediately setting off for the capital of Pella to secure just that. So it was that in the fourth year of the 125th Olympiad (277 B.C.), the Antigonid crown was restored; privately, the King was said to have given thanks to the gods for sending the barbarians; for although they pillaged and slaughtered many of his Macedonian subjects, so too did they drive off the usurper Ptolemy, and so too did they let him make his own claim as lord and protector of Greece.

His reign was not marked by immediate good fortune. He was instantly thrust into a grueling struggle with the kings of Epirus, a fight that grew so desperate that he briefly lost his royal seat altogether at one point—aye, never had a king's fortune ebbed and flowed the way it did for King Antigonus II Gonatas. But for every setback, he always managed to return, always came back stronger, wiser, and more ruthless. Every time, he grew his web of vassal tyrants and spies, further entrenching Antigonid roots in Macedon and throughout Greece. Some points, like Corinth, he deemed too important to entrust to a vassal, opting instead for a full garrison and direct control. Slowly but surely then, did he constrict Hellas like a python to its prey, Sicyon no exception. And indeed, the Epirotes learned this the hard way, as the Macedonian king and his son triumphantly stormed into Epirus itself.

Naturally, the Ptolemies of Egypt were none too pleased with the restoration and expansion of the Antigonid realm, made worse through her Seleucid alliance. Ergo, the Egyptian king put his bottomless coin to work with renewed vigor in support of anti-Antigonus poleis, finding many receptive audiences. First and foremost were the restless and chafing states of Sparta and Athens, their primacy in the region eclipsed decades prior by the monarchs of the north. They readily picked up the mantle of resistance with Ptolemy II's backing, but alas, both monarch and poleis were in for a shock—King Antigonus was more than prepared for battle no matter the terrain, humiliating the Spartans on land at Corinth, the Egyptians and Athenians by sea at Cos. They were victories so resounding throughout Greece that they paralyzed the Achaean League's Council to this day, some eighteen years later.

For his part, Aratus wasn't put off by the disasters, and thankfully, neither was Ptolemy II or his son, Ptolemy III. Even after the younger Ptolemy suffered his own naval disaster at Andros not two years ago—and even after Antigonus inaugurated festivals to Zeus, Athena, and much-revered Pan in celebration—Egyptian gold flowed unvexed into the Peloponnesus, to those still brave enough to take it and risk Macedonian wrath.

Yet from the time he'd retaken Sicyon from the tyrants, Aratus hid from no one that his city—if not the Achaean League—would resume the policy set forth by his father years prior and remain open recipients of Egyptian favor. He'd use every damn weapon he had to fight back; he had to. He knew he'd be under Antigonus's watch after his stunning coup in Sicyon, anyway; he knew the League's borders now abutted Corinthia, the King's doorstep. All the same, it wasn't until he and Timanthes had returned home from Egypt with Ptolemy's silver that he realized the extent of Antigonus's awareness.

Macedon's charm campaign toward Aratus started innocuously enough: invitations to the Royal Court in Pella; gifts delivered to his abode; offers to strengthen Sicyon—if only the King's soldiers and engineers could enter the city's gates and have a look. The Macedonian message was clear: *You may have overthrown one of my tyrants, but you can have my blessing as the next... or else.* Yet with each pretentious and patronizing "offer" of aid, Aratus grew more and more repulsed, more and more weary; he wasn't fooled in any event. The reality was that a friend of the Ptolemies was a day's march from Corinth, the King's most fanatically prized possession in the south.

But that reality didn't deter the King from espousing otherwise. With the Antigonid invitation to dine in Corinth itself rejected, the Macedonian's true nature emerged. He held the feast anyway, a lavish, lively gathering of the city's elite, at which he proudly lied that Aratus had forsaken King Ptolemy upon return from his Egyptian trip; that he now bowed to the Pellan throne and called Antigonus his friend. Some of the King's lingering allies in Sicyonia quickly spread the lies as fact, ensuring that Achaeans and Egyptians alike were made privy to them. By the time they'd filtered back to Aratus, he'd become swept with rage and embarrassment, ultimately forced to repledge his friendship before a visiting envoy from Ptolemy's court.

He'd never met Antigonus in person, but he'd heard tales of glowing praise—that he was a lover of poetry and a pupil of Zeno the Stoic, whose philosophy required one to live a virtuous life; that he considered kingship above all things to be a "kind of glorious servitude" to his subjects, deliberately hailing the bygone era of Alexander's Argead monarchy through construction of massive monuments in the old capital of Aegae. He'd heard Antigonus was humane and modest, one who rejected flattery, loved his children, yet was quick-witted in even the most dire of circumstances; he quipped once upon retreat that he "was not fleeing, only seizing an advantage that lay behind" him. He was said to promote chivalry in all matters of the court, advancing his officers only on merit, never lineage. He was said to be a handsome man, even in his advanced years.

But whatever he was or was said to be, and for as much as his near miraculous rise demanded respect, he was now simply an object of Aratus's loathing. An inhuman barbarian who was as ugly in his mind as he was heartless. If any of what he'd heard was ever true, it was a lie now, as far as Aratus was concerned. He was a tyrant, plain and simple, irrespective of any benevolent or regal trappings, and tyrannies were by their very definition antithetical to the poleis way of life; the dictation of one could never replace the dictation of many.

In that sense, everything about the King and what he stood for was a lie, just like the stories of Aratus forsaking Ptolemy's favor for his own. Even now, he could see the image of the aged Ptolemaic emissary walking away after their talk in Sicyon's agora, Aratus forced to make amends. His eyes had turned eastward toward the Corinthian crag, where they almost watered in anger, teeth grinding painfully as he sought to keep his calm.

And that's when it struck him. That's when it all became clear.

He'd already known his life's calling was to hunt down and destroy every tyrant in Hellas; he already knew he would do it or die trying. And after Sicyon, it was supposed to be about moving on to the next city, and the next city after that. But it took Antigonus's slander to make him realize he was ignoring the greatest tyrant of them all: Antigonus himself. A tyrant of tyrants that beget others in his mold, most far more depraved and cruel from intoxication with the power he permitted them to wield.

It was then that he no longer saw Corinth as the jewel of southern Hellas, or a trading city wealthier than the whole of Achaea. Until it was freed, he could only see it as a conduit of tyranny, a spigot of oppression flowing into the Peloponnesus. And he saw that for every city he freed, two more would be blackened with Macedon's shadow, like the heads of the Lernaean Hydra.

Yes, it was then he knew—Corinth had to fall.

* * *

But money, Aratus thought jadedly as he threw open chest after chest in his sweltering bedroom. *Does it always have to be about gods-forsaken money?*

It was a truth that had galled him since he was young: spirit, courage, honor, pride—they only carried one so far against Antigonus. Because regardless of those intangibles, at a single muster, the Macedonian could call tens of thousands of spearmen and sailors to his banners, a force easily funded by the tributes of mainland towns and isles alike, silver mines churning out precious metals in Thrace, and the abundant timber of the lands north of Aetolia. The gears of the war machine.

Since Aratus had left Argos, it had been much the same. It took money to fund the venture, money to quell the resettled exiles in Sicyon, money to buy mercenaries. Today was no exception; indeed, Erginus was a soldier of fortune, and it was a fortune he had to come up with. He couldn't dare summon the amounts from the bankers of Sicyonia, lest their suspicion find its way directly to the King's agents, and maybe the League's. So instead, here he was, desperately seeking something to give as collateral for a man who expected a city's ransom in due time.

The problem was that all the coin he'd saved was still a relative pittance; his power and nobility in Sicyon by far outweighed the income he derived from them, and it had been his choice to reject a gaudy lifestyle in any event.

"Shouldn't bloody have to be this way," he muttered in frustration. His goal was so honorable, so noble; the execution so base, so lowly. "Honor's not compensation enough for him? Redemption? Better deed than the rest of that bastard's life combined, I bet." But he shook his head for the umpteenth time as he finally found what he'd been searching for—a chest full of the jewelry and ornaments Telesilla had amassed since she was a girl, from her earliest days in Argos through their wedding. As he ran his hands through a shimmering pile of golden earrings and bracelets inlaid with gems, he smiled, albeit guiltily. "But I do *need* that bastard."

"That you making all that racket up here?"

He turned suddenly, finding his wife in the doorway with a stack of neatly folded laundry. He was certain she'd be downstairs for at least another hour or so. "Oh, I…"

But she paid him no attention, nonchalantly setting her stack at the foot of their bed, refolding an already perfectly folded tunic; perfect by anyone else's standards, that is. "Sweltering in here," she said, forearm wiping away her brow.

Aratus remained in an awkward crouch with his back to her, hands still buried in the chest. "Have you finished downstairs already?"

"Downstairs is in good enough hands, wanted to make sure these were properly creased," she said with a pat of the tunics. "Didn't look their best when I saw them on you earlier."

"Oh… well, thank you, then."

"Out of the way with you, now," she said as she came up behind him. "Let me put them away."

The Sicyonian gritted his teeth. "Just leave it be for the time being, will you? Something you have to do now?"

"Why? I've a half dozen other things that need doing, so I'd just as soon get this done and I'll be out of—" She stopped as her head craned over his shoulder. "What've you got there?"

"Nothing, Tele. I'm just—"

"That my chest?" she asked in an amused tone, before turning confused. "Is that my jewelry?"

"Aye," he said, rising to his feet in embarrassed annoyance. Above hot red cheeks, his wife's dark eyes locked on him.

"And what's your fancy with that?"

"I, uh… I want to bring it to Aegias's place, safer keeping there…" he offered weakly, terrible at spinning the lies that came so easily to men like Ecdelus in their trade. Unsurprisingly, Telesilla's face morphed into a scowl.

"Since when's Aegias made a business of storing jewelry?" she demanded. "And for that matter, safe from whom?"

Sweat dripped into Aratus's eyes, prompting a blanch. "I just prefer it this way, aye? Never mind the reasons for it—"

"I think I will mind the reasons, thank you!"

"You haven't worn a strand of this in ages, what's the difference to you?" he barked sharply. "And when've you been one so consumed with trinkets and the like? What would your father—"

"*My father* would probably be asking why I'm so keen to get rid of the first bit of jewelry he'd ever had made for me!" she fired back, black hairs falling across her forehead. "Some of that I've had since I was a toddler, some of it's all I have left of him and Argos."

"And it's not going away, Tele, it'll just be kept there for safekeeping. I'm moving most of our coin over there as well, it's not just your jewels."

She scoffed. "'Our coin' is a fraction of what's in that chest and you know it. Maybe if you'd been *more* consumed with 'trinkets and the like,' you wouldn't be reduced to raiding your wife's riches instead."

She knew how to sting him in their bickerings, always had. And it worked yet again. His narrowed eyes or clenching jaw must have told her as much as she looked away from him.

"I'm sorry I said that," she said quickly, as poor with apologies as he was with lies.

"Are you?" he asked in darkened tone.

"Aye. But you *know* I don't like being lied to and you're lying to me right now."

"I'm not lying to you! And how's it lying if I'm not obligated to tell ya in the first place?"

"So your 'obligations' place me beyond the courtesy of the truth?"

"It's the League, Telesilla. Aye? That's all it is, just the bloody League a-and—"

She shook her head in even more confusion. "What's the League want with *my* jewelry? The towns' coffers aren't enough? The people have to empty their personal fortunes now as well?"

"The *League* doesn't want anything with your jewelry, but bankers aren't lending it money to pay our mercenaries for the Aetolian campaign without some bit of security! So that's what the jewelry's for, nothing more to it!"

"Bank-*ers*?" she asked, darkened eyebrow in an arch. "So you're spreading this among several now or is it still just Aegias?"

He cursed himself silently, caught again by his wife's perceptiveness. "Aegi—"

"Just stop it," she commanded, disappointed eyes searching his face. "Why are you lying over jewelry of all silly things? 'The League,' 'safekeeping,' why? Why say these things?"

He was slow to respond, pondering his words and approach more carefully as he let his anger wane. "Because I don't want you worrying about anything you don't need to be," he said calmly, a sweaty hand moving to her belly. "And this is one of those things, I promise you."

Her eyes turned softer but no less determined. "What's going on, Aratus? Dishonesty's unbecoming of you; it's beneath you, that's why you're no good at it."

The irony of her comment wasn't lost on him as he considered all the different ways he was trying to screen his intentions from the League's Council as well.

"Is that funny?"

"No."

"Then what's—"

"I received another sign, Tele," he said before a loud sigh.

She shook her head. "What—"

"You told me, remember?" he asked quietly, hand rising to her cheek. "You said to me that if the Corinthian man I met at the Games—"

"Oh no…"

"*You said* if the Corinthian man I met at the Games was a sign of the gods then they would send me another!" he said passionately.

"No…"

"You did. And they have," he said, smile breaking out across his face, eyes almost watering. "Everything I wondered since I met him, every question I had since—"

"Aratus, please no!" she pleaded, balled up fists pounding his muscled chest. "You promised me!"

"Telesilla, it's a sign of the gods! It's a sign of Poseidon! Of Apollo!"

"What's the sign! Tell me with an honest heart that it's not you making up a reason to believe it's so!"

His anger flashed back but he restrained himself. "It's a *sign of the gods*! One of the King's own mercenaries in Corinth—*in Corinth!*—has offered to lead us by the hand, lead the *League* to the gates of the city!"

She shook her head. "The League or you?"

His eyes danced. "The League or me," he parroted, best answer he could manage.

"And it never struck you that the 'King's own mercenary' is in fact *working* for the King in this? You told me yourself Antigonus has long since fallen out with you!"

"I have ways of proving this one's loyalty and I intend to—"

"Mm-hmm, and where's this man to lead you that's so safe from failure?"

"The fortress."

"The fortress?"

"Up a path unseen to sack that bloody fortress that's mocked every free Achaean, every free Hellene of this land for a hundred years! And for this sign to come not three days after you told me to wait for one, not two months after the Games, I mean I, I—" He lost his words as he saw Telesilla look to her feet, hands cupped over her eyes. *How could she not see it? It was precisely as she said it would happen!*

"Hear me, I know what I told you before, but there's no guarantee I'd survive again in Aetolia any more than I'd survive attacking Corinth. The gods could take our ships, they could let an Aetolian rat's arrow find my chest. It doesn't mean I can shirk my duties as the leader of the League—"

"So I ask you again—you plan to tell the League of this 'sign'?"

"Well… no."

She nodded mournfully.

"Wouldn't do much good, and we don't have the time in any event."

Finally, she turned away from him, walking softly toward the door.

"Tele, your father told me that the strong have to lead the weak; those that can see must lead the blind, and that's what's happening here! They're blind, they don't see it! They don't see the most powerful ally we could *imagine* extending its hand to us, opening its door to us—not once, but *twice now*! I can't begrudge the Council for that, but neither can I magnify its folly! *I* can show them the way! *Your* father said—"

"Please," she said firmly, back still to him, body conveying sheer brokenness. "*Please* don't invoke his name any further in this. Just take his bloody jewels and be done with it." She sniffled loudly then sighed, bloodshot eyes looking back to him. "Have I so failed you as a wife that it's really this over me? Over our child? Have we so failed each other?"

It struck him hard, stomach knotting at their marriage's mention, a topic they rarely discussed, rarely acknowledged. His gaze fell away from her for a moment, swallowing hard, feeling every bit like the jewel-stealing scoundrel he appeared to be in that moment. But finally, he offered the only bit that he could. "I don't know... but I do know our child deserves a shot at living in freedom."

With that, her lip quivered again and she was out the door, the Strategos left staring at the void left in her wake. Eventually, his head fell toward the jewelry again, troubled that her father would essentially be funding something that brought his child so much pain.

"I don't mean to hurt her, good Naukydes, I truly don't. And the jewelry, I promise you it's only temporary... she'll get it back with interest; on my life, I swear it." The longer the gold and gems sparkled before him, though, the more his thoughts transcended the roof of his Sicyonian abode or his own petty concerns. "But if that bastard from Corinth comes back, if he tells me there's a way, *you have to know* it's my calling in this life to take up that challenge... Surely, your grandchild deserves to live free? Surely, *that* tyrant's fall is worth a sack of jewels?" He sighed.

"It's worth my life."

CHAPTER 8

*5th Day of Apellaios, Year 2 of the 134th Olympiad
(July 27, 243 B.C.)*

Another *bouleuterium*. This one twice the size of Aegium's but just as hot, just as stifling. At least this time there was only a fraction of the people, before whom there was no question as to who was in charge.

Gathered around him in the squared confines of Sicyon's Council chamber were the League's *Navarch, Hipparch,* and *Hypostrategos*—its master of ships, master of horse, and lieutenant general. Their voices echoed in the vast emptiness, interspersed with the clamor of the daylight agora just outside the chamber's door. The chamber anchored the western end of the agora's long south stoa, the colonnade ending just before its porched entrance.

The persons chosen for the positions left no mystery as to their sponsors. With Mnaseus of Patrae as Navarch and Agonippos of Dyme as Hypostrategos, two of the three highest ranking junior officers in the League fell under the influence of Chilon's powerful western bloc. Though young, it was beyond dispute Agonippos was a brave warrior; Aratus saw him fight well as a spearman in the Peloponnesian mountains when the Aetolians invaded a couple years back. The problem was that he knew he was good, knew he had the romanticized looks of a god with long waves of hair that framed a chiseled face; and if what Aratus heard was correct, Chilon's bloc was already championing him as their "Aratus of the West," likely with a mind for a future run at the Strategos office outright.

Mnaseus was a man he'd met plenty of times, someone who'd logged more days on the seas than dozens of others combined; the "son of Poseidon" his sailors called him. He lived for his ships, and at forty-four years was zealous as a youth for his craft, even if the gods had weathered his face and taken his hair. It was Mnaseus, in fact, whom Aratus had turned to for advice before setting sail for Egypt. Though he was a close friend and ally of Chilon, Aratus knew he avoided the League's politics, even if fully aware of its machinations.

He was most surprised to see Cratinus of Aegeira, his Hipparch. Cratinus was a squat, powerful man, who had been a wrestling champion at the Olympic Games some seventeen years prior. Aratus knew him well, training with him at the Argive palestra, later riding with him in the League's cavalry; he'd always seen him as a man of honor, though one content to keep to himself and follow the group, rather than lead it. Therein lay the surprise, then, not to mention he wasn't a particularly good rider with his stubby physique. He was surely a choice made at the behest of Margos, seeking another set of eyes and ears to add to Chilon's.

Forgoing his choice of officers was the price he paid for leaving Aegium early, though he allowed himself to wonder all the same. *Who would I have picked among those of Sicyon? Those beyond? Lysistratos, perhaps? Promachus of Pellene?* Timanthes, of course, could have had the choicest of positions, but he and

Aratus had always preferred that he stay closer and act as the eyes in the back of his head, rather than inject himself into the highly political positions of League officers.

Regardless of their sponsors, it was League law that these officers took orders from their Strategos. While the Council knew how to wedge themselves into the Strategos's duties as war planner, politicians' hands stayed far away from the spears, swords, and weaponry of the wars they'd chosen, to say nothing of the war's execution—all the better for sniping at the results afterward. But whether there was or wasn't any hostility or distrust among his officer corps, today's meeting brought only one *true* problem for Aratus...

It had been seven days.

Seven days of silence.

Seven days of waiting for word, a signal, anything...

Seven days of watching those dusty roads that meandered off toward Corinthia.

And now hours of pretending that wasn't the case.

In the interim, his wife barely spoke to him. His closest friend was glum and brisk in his own right. Aratus himself barely slept. And it was all for what? So far, nothing. He tried to keep his spirits high, but his anxiety grew with each day that passed. How could it not? In his mind, he'd crossed the point of no return, he was irrevocably committed, and as such, he was infected by the idea; Corinth consumed him, his every thought, every conversation. He second-guessed every word of the conversation he'd had with Erginus that night in Aegias's candlelit room, to the extent the whole interaction seemed like a dream now.

I told him seven days, didn't I? I said no more than seven days... has he been found out? How will I deny it, if so? Maybe I should check again with Aegias... aye, I'll check again. Then again, maybe he very well was a Macedonian agent... maybe he's reported every—

"Aratus?"

His glazed eyes refocused on Mnaseus's wrinkled face. "Aye?"

"The ships should be in port within a week, so will we have ample space or not? It's jammed bow to stern out there right now and the men at the wharf said they aren't—"

"It'll be cleared, it'll be cleared," the Strategos said briskly, tiredly running a hand over his eyes. "Same as it was two years ago, just takes a lot to put six thousand men in the field."

"They're not going to get a chance to see the field unless the port is—"

"Mnaseus, I'm aware, I promise you."

The older man's light brown eyes lingered on him for a moment before darting away. "And how are we on that score, anyway? Patrae's contingent should be here before the ships, I'm told."

"Good, then. No issues with the levy?"

"May be a little bit light—little less than six hundred men?"

"Six hundred?" Aratus said with a look of surprise. "I was expecting at least seven hundred from you, where's the rest?"

"Preference was to hold them back closer to home, keep watch for any Elean movements near Dyme."

"Whose preference?" he asked irritably. It wasn't even the campaign he was interested in, yet still the gamesmanship out west annoyed him.

"The League's, I hear," Agonippos chimed in with a smug smile. "Elean bastards have been dancing across the Larisos without a care in the world; I'd almost hoped to stay behind to give them a whack."

"Well, you're Hypostrategos here, so here you'll stay—"

"I know that, I was—"

"—and we need seven hundred from Patrae, not 'less than six.' I want you to send again for the full levy, Mnaseus."

The Navarch demurred as Agonippos's hands fidgeted, both men avoiding Aratus's gaze. "I'm just saying, I could have helped against the Eleans," the Hypostrategos muttered.

"Instead of worrying about them, you can help *me* by providing numbers for the rest of the West—should be around two hundred fifty each from Pharae, Tritaea, and Leontium, another six hundred from Dyme; are we still on target there?"

The young upstart was slow to answer as he flexed his jaw. "On target. Aegium's going to be light."

"Following Patrae's lead, no doubt," Aratus said with a shake of head. "Sicyon's two thousand will be ready, of course, so with Bura, Ceryneia, Aegeira, and Pellene we should be close to the six thousand I was promised."

"And the mercenaries?" Mnaseus asked.

"All but final. Have a few of the units in town already, the rest of the thousand shouldn't be long in waiting."

"Purchased them again through Xenophilus, I presume?" the Navarch asked, smacking of disapproval.

"Indeed I did. Served me well enough before, no reason to deny him now."

"Has he? Seems to me he's more the villain every day that goes—"

"It's a villain's game, mercenary work, so it takes one to find them," Aratus said curtly, defensive over the broker who'd been supplying him with mercenaries since his days in Argos. Notwithstanding, Aratus was no fool to Xeno's more clandestine activities when the brokering business was slow— leading predatory raids on the clients of the Macedonian king in the Peloponnesus, targets so selected because where the King went, so did his wealth. Old-timers like Mnaseus were especially unsettled by the raids, given how fearful they'd grown of Antigonus. "Awfully brave for a villain, too, raiding the King's lands like he does."

"Ah, your favorite kind of Hellene?" the Navarch quipped pointedly.

"They're in short supply these days," Aratus shot back, thinking at one time, he was *everyone's* favorite kind of Hellene. "Besides, idle mercenaries are bound to create mischief, so better Xeno direct them toward the King than us," he continued, forcing a begrudging nod from Mnaseus. He sighed and looked to his quiet Hipparch. "Cratinus? Anything to add about the horse?"

The wrestler's dark eyes surveyed his colleagues, mouth a serious thin line. "They've been summoned."

Aratus waited for more until it was obvious it wasn't coming. "And their status?"

"Three hundred summoned, but a good fifty have caught the fever I hear."

"The western horse, I take it?"

Cratinus looked to a glaring Agonippos before giving a silent nod.

"Then we'll just have to make do with two hundred fifty."

"Less fodder to store on the transports, anyway," Mnaseus added.

"If I might add something, Strategos," Agonippos interjected, drawing the leader's eyes. "You didn't ask me earlier, but several cities are complaining of worn weaponry, worn usage. They want replacements for their contributions."

"Then those cities need to look to their own coffers to do so, that's the pledge we've all made to each other," Aratus said sternly.

"And I think they will, Strategos... eventually. But I also think there's some hope that Sicyon will help fill the void in the meantime."

Taken in isolation, the request would have been neither surprising nor objectionable. In context, however, he knew it was yet another way for the elder statesmen of the League to make a point to Aratus. They knew full well that Aratus needed success in his next venture if he wished to regain the political capital he'd spent in Aegium, so of course he would foot the bill on the campaign's eve to do so. Nevertheless, it was especially irksome given that some of the better wood for spears and shields alike resided in the western Peloponnesus, not the east, and the equipment wasn't complicated to manufacture in any event.

Spearmen typically carried a light, oval-shaped shield called a *thureos* that covered about two-thirds of the carrier's body while their weapons of choice were a two-meter spear of ash, a few small javelins, and a sword as a last resort. These *thureophoroi*, as they were called, were rarely armored with anything more than linen at best and a helmet of bronze; indeed, they were meant to be light on their feet—slower than true skirmishers but faster than the heavy phalanx of the Macedonians. Aratus kept his Sicyonian thureophoroi among the best armed of the League, in part because they were most likely to see combat, but in part simply from a sense of obligation. He also kept an elite branch of thureophoroi for the heaviest combat known as the *thorakitai*, who were armed in similar fashion but with advanced reps on the training grounds and a shirt of chain mail to boot.

Sicyon's penchant for equipment excellence meant that today wasn't the first time it had been asked to help arm the other poleis, but that didn't make it any more palatable. "I'll check our stores," he grumbled.

Agonippos smiled, shades of Chilon's sincerity. "I'm sure I can offer thanks on their behalf."

"I'm sure you can. Next on our agenda, is—"

"Beg your pardon again, sire, but Pataikos sent me along with some other suggestions about the raid itself, specially drafted by Margos from his campaigns."

Aratus's neck burned red. "You have my thanks, but we're well-versed on that end. I'll welcome your questions on the specifics when I'm done."

"You don't want to hear what he's to say?" Agonippos asked with a look of confusion that made Aratus even angrier.

"No."

"Why? He had some concerns about the last—"

"Dammit, Ago, I'm the bloody Strategos, that's why and it's the only reason you need! Do we understand each other? *Do* we—"

"Aratus..." Mnaseus intervened with furrowed brow in the Strategos's direction. "He understands... don't you, Agonippos?"

"Only trying to relay what I've been told," the young man said with a shrug. "Meant no offense..."

"Well, it's—"

A cough at the doorway.

Heads turned to find Technon silhouetted against the opening.

Agonnipos looked back and forth between Strategos and servant, but it was Mnaseus who finally broke the silence. "Aye, Technon?"

Tech's hands hung at his sides, nervous tongue licking lips. Aratus knew it hadn't been just any cough.

"Aratus, I uh... you're needed."

The Strategos could barely stifle a grin, fatigue melting away. "Oh?"

Nods.

"Is it urgent, friend?" Mnaseus asked.

Technon's eyes were locked on Aratus. "It is, in fact. Issues with some of the mercenaries need sorting. They're threatening to leave."

"What issues?" Agonippos chimed in.

"Payment," Technon said with a shake of his head. "Are there any other kinds of issues with mercenaries?"

"Not in my experience," Aratus said, slapping Mnaseus on the shoulder as he rose to his feet. To his surprise, his knees felt wobbly... he knew where he was headed, whom he was headed to meet. "Forgive me, lads, let me see to this business and we'll wrap up afterward."

"They're threatening to leave right this instant?" Agonippos asked, still transfixed on Technon.

"So they say, I'm just a messenger."

"Who's their commander?"

Aratus could see his servant freeze as he headed toward him. "A Syrian no doubt. Xeno's dealt with them more and more but he's quick to say how impatient they are," he said, winking at his servant. Technon gave a pursed grin.

"Maybe so, but—"

"We'll cover your questions when I get back, Ago," he said as he urged Technon out the door.

Now my destiny awaits.

* * *

Sandaled feet floated across hot stone. Heart pounded as Aratus weaved through the agora's crowds and carts, statues and stalls.

"You're certain?" he called back to Technon, following close on his heels.

"That it's him? No question."

"Did he say—did he accept?"

"He wasn't letting on."

Has to accept… not the type of man who'd risk his life just to tell me no in person… is he? Or is he here to kill me in person?

"I have him at Aegias's, but are you sure that's best? I can—"

"His collateral's there. If he's saying yes, he'll want to see it… has Aegias's been—"

"Cleared out? Of course… best we can this time of day, anyway…"

"Good," Aratus said, closing fast on the western stoa room he'd been looking for. He barely felt the cool shade of its portico, barely looked at the city denizens loitering about so as not to draw attention. If anyone had called his name he pretended not to hear it and pressed on. "Watch the door, but don't make it obvious. Look for followers."

Into Aegias's. The door closed behind him, bar lock slamming soon after. Window flaps had been closed, leaving him in the cramped little room with the scent and light of burning lamps. Aegias eyed him blankly from across his table. Aratus turned…

"Greetings, Strategos."

Erginus grinned a hideously beautiful grin, one that Aratus couldn't help but echo. "Greetings, indeed," he said, extending a hand. "You traveled well?"

"No," the big Syrian said, smile fading into his bushy beard ever so slightly as he walked toward Aegias. "It's been a busy week, Strategos. To do so much moving, to do so much running in seven days' time… it isn't much time at all. Hard to do *anything* in seven days' time."

Aratus's heart sank just a bit. "Gods know it's not much."

"Don't need the gods to tell me that," he said gruffly, eyeing filthy fingernails. Sweaty black hair spilled over his face before he looked up with hazel eyes. "I needed more time, like I told you in the first place… but I made a promise to respond to ya, didn't I?"

Aratus nodded. "And you'd be a good man to keep it."

Erginus laughed. "A good man? I don't know that the things you asked me to do are the things of a good man or not."

"A brave man, then?" Aratus said, anxiety chewing at him.

"I'll take that."

"Good... so..."

"So?"

"So you'll forgive my bluntness, but I have three League officials waiting on me to return—"

"And you left them for me?" Erginus chimed mockingly.

"I did—so what's your answer?"

The Syrian chewed the inside of his mouth as he eyed the tall Sicyonian. "You have something for me?" he finally asked.

Aratus looked to Aegias with a nod, who pulled a small chest from below his counter. Its hinges groaned as he opened it wide, laying bare a stash of Aratus's coin and Telesilla's jewelry; the latter was still hard to look at.

Erginus moved toward it, dipping grimy hands into the pile of gold and silver, scowl on his face. He bit one piece, let a few more trickle through his hands. He looked to Aratus. "The King would piss on this."

"I'm no king, you knew that from the start," Aratus said, impatience growing. "The reward's in taking Corinth."

"You promised me a talent and a house if you fail and I live."

"And by the gods, I meant it."

"Not by the looks of this."

"By the looks of things, I'm still alive and we haven't failed. *That chest* is a sign of good faith."

"I would say it's—"

"You've had seven days, Erginus," Aratus barked, temper withering. "Seven days and you're back now. You see what I have to offer, jewels and coin taken from the most private stocks of my personal fortune. You knew the deal when you left, so by the gods, spare me your agony and give me an answer. I have a campaign across the Gulf to plan which launches in a matter of weeks if not, so—"

"Aye."

Aratus froze as Erginus's face turned stone serious. "I'm putting my life in your hands, Strategos. My brother's too. We know damn well we won't survive a failed attack on the fort; bloody thing's monstrous when you see it up close, path or no path. The Macedonians there are warriors through and through, so're their men in the city below, the ports too. So—so, I—"

"You're a damn brave man, I told you that and now I really mean it."

"A damn fool is what I am."

"Nothing foolish in fighting for this cause, I promise you."

"Ah, curse your causes, Aratus. You don't fear the Styx, that's your problem."

"I do."

"Well, you don't fear it enough then. You don't realize what you're asking for here. I've seen these bastards fight, seen 'em train. And Antigonus is ready to build a seat next to Zeus himself the way the men talk about him there."

"Aye, and Alexander conquered the world but a simple fever brought him low," Aratus said, confidence swelling as he said it, extending a hand to Erginus again. "Now tell me an orphan from Syria and an orphan from Sicyon can't humble the man who inherited his kingdom?"

Erginus finally conceded a grunting laugh, clasping hands with the Strategos. "I think *you* could use a humbling. *I* just want good money, good drink, a pretty face to look at."

"Only one face now?"

"Aye."

"Well, if you're the man you say are and you do what you say you're going to do, you're worth far more than whores and drink," Aratus replied with a tight smile. He toyed with the idea of telling the brute that he was a sign from the gods, that he was the fulfillment of a vision, but he decided to hold his tongue; no way he'd believe it anyway. "But as to your wishes, base as they are—gods willing."

The big man nodded with a loud exhale, flapping his chiton to relieve himself of the heat. "So what now? Do we have a day?"

"I have to see it first."

"You've never been to Cor—"

"Not like this, my friend," Aratus said quickly. "I need to study it, get a long view at it. Map it. In another seven days we'll meet; I'll bring Timanthes, one of my dearest friends, a soldier without peer. And you'll arrange for your brother to meet us."

"We'll meet at the Ornis, then."

"Which is where?"

"Just to the west of the city walls; there's a beaten path up a hill that heads south off the road to Sicyon. At the top you'll see a grove—that's the Ornis. It'll provide good cover, but good vantages all the same."

"The Ornis, then. Don't come out together; don't even tell your brother where we're meeting, just tell him to head out of the gates and start walking. I'll have Technon fetch him."

"Aye, well, tell this Technon that my brother's of darker hue than me; beardless. Scar running ear to mouth on the left side. Look for it."

"Understood," Aratus said, plotting mind already fast at work with a surge running through his body. "'Tween now and then I'm going about recruiting the army I'll need—all while prepping for a campaign across the seas..." He gave a terse laugh.

"I'd not much like to be a Strategos, I think," Erginus said with his gapped grin.

"Nor I at times, but then chances like these come along."

Erginus nodded. "All the same..."

"It goes without saying, I hope, that you're sworn by your life and honor to secrecy on this. Not a word of it to anybody—not your brothers, not—"

"M'brothers are bastards or useless, I told ya that; just as soon sell me off if it meant another sack of gold. Diocles is the only one I'm trusting with a whiff of this... don't have much choice on that one, but at least he's as much to lose as me."

"Very well..." he said, looking around the room before finding Erginus's eyes one last time. "Seven days, then. Highest sun at the Ornis, agreed?"

"Agreed."

Aratus sighed. "Wait here a few moments before you leave," he said, turning for the door before he stopped.

"And thank you."

* * *

Aratus's mind raced faster than he could put into words as he made his way back across the agora. After all, he'd said yes—yes!—but now the true work would begin. Now he had to put together a secret operation; now he had to find the hundreds of warriors necessary to pull it off without detection; now—

"Did the crisis pass, Strategos?"

The leader paused upon hearing his title, glancing to his right and finding the columned backside of the palestra, the gymnasium his father built in his day.

"To your left," the voice called again over the market's din. To his surprise, it was his lieutenant, approaching him in his light blue cloak, nonchalantly chewing on some kind of nuts. He wore a bemused smile.

"What are you doing out here?" Aratus demanded. "I told you I'd be but a moment."

"Aye, we heard you. Mnaseus was feeling a bit weary in there, thought some fresh air would help... not sure he's right in this kind of heat, though. The man needs the seas!"

Aratus tried to hide his annoyance. "Well, gather them up, I'm ready to continue."

"So it's been resolved?"

"What?"

"The mercenaries—you've gotten them to take the campaign free of charge?" Agonippos said with a laugh at his own quip.

"In so many words, aye," Aratus said with a placating smile.

"What a statesman you are to juggle the planning of an overseas invasion with the petty details of a *misthios*'s wages."

His tone smacked of arrogance. "Nothing's petty about it; one man isn't paid, that one man isn't fighting and the rest'll soon—"

"Did you really say what they say you said? In Aegium?"

The Strategos looked back at him, dumbfounded as his voice escaped him. *By the gods, who does he think he is?* "What's said in the *Boule*'s chambers remains within the *Boule*'s chambers," he said finally, enunciating every word. "Those that haven't honored that maxim have broken their oaths."

"I know that's the practice, but—"

"It's not a 'practice,' it's an *oath!*"

"Agreed, but it's not reality," the young man shot back, wiping his hands clean of nutshells. "And what you proposed was so far beyond anything I've been raised to expect from the League that I—" Ago's eyes fell away as he shook his head with open mouth. "You asked for *war* against Macedon, no? You asked to march on Pella—"

"I never said a thing about Pella," Aratus said, gritting his teeth. "The capital means nothing to me, I only said Corinth—"

"It's the same thing, then."

The Strategos looked around him, suddenly suspicious of the market crowd. "I'm through talking about this with you, Ago. It's beyond your rank, in any event."

"It certainly is, but if I may say—"

"You may *not.*"

"I think you were bloody right."

Aratus's tan eyes narrowed on the upstart's. "Pardon?"

"I do," he said with fading smile. "I know you don't like me, I'm not sure why, but I'd just as soon go after the King as you, Aratus. What are we doing in those Aetolian swamps? What are we accomplishing?"

The lieutenant spoke well, spoke forcefully, but the Strategos still searched for signs of sincerity—and he couldn't find one, perhaps *because* he didn't like him. "Ago, I'll tell you one last time on this," he said in a low growl, grunting sounds of the palestra wrestlers ringing out to their right. "It's a dead... issue."

"Is it?" the younger man said, unbowed as he leaned in close to Aratus's ear. "I'll be honest with you, Strategos—I've been told to keep eyes on you."

A chill ran up his spine. "Have you?"

"Aye."

"By whom?"

"Who else? Your friends in—"

"I assumed."

Agonippos put hands on his hips. "They're worried you won't let it go. Not that they think you would, uh... well, they're worried."

Aratus looked east into the market place, far enough to find the Temple of Artemis. "Why are you telling me this, lad?"

"Because I mean it—I wanna take on Antigonus with you... so if there was something to be done..."

"There isn't."

"But if there was?"

Aratus fell quiet, gaze still locked on the Temple, studying its pillars and painted, sculpted pediment. At last, he sighed. "All right, well if there was, there might be meeting about it soon. A private meeting."

Agonippos blanched, face a mask of shock. "There is?"

"There might be."

The Hypostrategos looked side to side. "Where? When?"

"Three days, around sundown."

"Where—"

"The west gate. About two hundred meters north of the Theater."

"Who—"

"That's all I'm saying. If you want what you say you want, you'll find it then and there—but tell *no one*."

"Of course not," Ago said, grin returning.

"Then we're clear. Now gather Mnaseus and Cratinus and let's finish up."

The younger man looked like a miner who'd struck gold, turning slowly to quickstep his way back toward the *Bouleuterium*. As he made distance, he shot a glance back at Aratus.

Aratus could only smile.

CHAPTER 9

8th Day of Apellaios, Year 2 of the 134th Olympiad
(July 30, 243 B.C.)

It was almost dark as Aratus leaned against the door of his abode. The evening air still burned hot in his lungs, no doubt thanks to a street that had baked all day. Even still, he kept himself wrapped in a faded blue cloak over his himation, brown satchel in hand—the accoutrements of a man set to attend a secret meeting in short order.

The Strategos's eyes tracked his servant approaching from the west, the city's checkered pattern making him easy to spot from several blocks away, even in the twilight. Technon had developed a distinctive hobble the older he'd gotten, and no matter the temperature, his chiton always seemed to be a sweaty mess. Today was no exception.

"So? He's still there?"

"He is. Milling around the gate like a lost calf."

Aratus chuckled darkly. "Well said."

"Waiting on you, no doubt."

"Of course—anyone else?"

"Aye. The other's a block away, if that. Staying in the shadows… but as obvious as he thinks he's hidden."

The Strategos nodded in satisfaction. "Well, good. It's a long enough wait, let's pay them a visit."

* * *

The ashlar slabs of the city wall were stacked twelve feet high in perfect succession, one row on top of the next. Blocky crenellations girded the top, with a walkway thick enough for at least two soldiers to stand side by side. Almost precisely where a north-south street intersected with its east-west counterpart, the walls gave way to a small brown-leafed gate, beyond which a path sloped down to the Helisson River. Flanking the gate were two twenty-foot towers, manned this evening by a handful of spearmen keeping watch amidst a chorus of frogs and crickets.

Aratus returned their waves as he approached. "*Khaírete*, my friends!"

"*Khaíre*, Aratus!"

Agonippos emerged by a house catercorner to the gateway.

"Lad's been trolling around here for some time," the guard called down in amusement.

"Oh, this man's no troll, friends!" Aratus replied with a tone of dubious sincerity. "He's the Lieutenant Strategos of the Achaean League… this man's to be honored!"

The "lieutenant" looked back and forth between the Strategos and the soldiers, hands out before him. "Have you dropped all pretense of this being a private affair?" he demanded in hushed tone, clearly perturbed.

"It'd be rude not to return their greetings, would it not?"

"In light of the circumstances? I suppose it begs the question why you'd arrange a meeting within eyeshot of two bloody towers!"

"That's my business," Aratus said calmly. "You'd do well to follow."

"Well, should I yell to them that we're conspiring together too? Unless those guardsmen are part and parcel of what you've hinted at, then—"

"Maybe they are. And that's why you'd do well to follow," the Strategos said, a bit sterner.

Ago's eyes lingered on him for a moment before he sighed and looking around him. "Well, who else are you expecting? It's bloody dark out now, I've been here for quite a while."

So the guardsmen said. Aratus grinned to himself. "My apologies if you've been put out, that wasn't my intent."

"Well, you said *sundown*. Not sure what that means in Sicyon, but in Dyme, it means—"

"Earlier?"

The prickly upstart huffed. "Aye."

"I'll remember that next time, then."

Agonippos glanced back at the towermen again. "So? What is it then, this plot of yours? Something with Corinth, I'm presuming?"

Butterflies flitted about in Aratus's stomach at the question. "Shall we talk now?"

"Are you expecting anyone else?"

"Hm," Aratus said, with a scratch of his chin. "No, I s'pose."

Ago's brow furrowed in confusion. "What do you mean?"

"I mean exactly as I said—I came here to see you, Agonippos, and you alone."

"Me?"

The Strategos moved in close, close enough to know the young man felt his breath. "*You.* Because I want to tell you a story," he said, in a low, threatening tone.

"About—"

"*About* a man whose blood runs through these streets, Agonippos. About a man who spent his waking hours seeking freedom for this city, freedom from the bloody tyrants that had infected Sicyon for decades. He did it for no man's bounty, no reward or public adulation; he did it because it was bloody right and because *Sicyon deserved better than it was getting!*"

"Aratus, I—"

"His name was Clenias," the Strategos declared through gritted teeth. "He was my father."

"I know your father's tale, Ara—"

"Well, in case you've forgotten, then!" Aratus snarled. "Because look around you! These walls, these buildings, the gym," he said, pointing to all sides. "They're my father's work, and men like him. He poured his soul into this city helping make it what it is, only to see his chest stabbed seven times by a fresh tyrant. He bled the grounds here, and my mother along with him. I never had the chance to see to their funerary rites, to see them off, to even kiss their hands farewell. And when I fought my way back here, I *knew* I'd never be but a pale shadow of that man's greatness."

Agonnipos finally ceased protesting, cheeks flushed with embarrassment at the older man's dressing down, undoubtedly loud enough for others nearby to hear. "Why are you telling me this?"

Aratus's eyebrows peaked. "Because I wanted you to know, why else? Because there I found myself three days ago, being questioned by a junior as if I was his slave. Imagine that! In front of my father's gymnasium, not a block away from where I torched the tyrant's home!" He grunted. "Well, you'll never speak that way to me again."

The younger man's petulance started to return, but Aratus had none of it as he pushed his nose almost to Ago's. "Look at me—*look at me!* If you learn nothing the rest of your life, learn this—*never* disrespect a man in his city again."

"I didn't!"

"You did. I told you there was nothing. I told you to drop it. I told you it was a dead issue. You didn't listen."

"I—"

"I *am Strategos*. And I am the proudest Sicyonian you'll ever lay eyes on, so it *angers* me when I'm disrespected within my own gates. *Never. Do it. Again.*"

Ago's lips quivered in restrained fury but his eyes fell away from his superior's in silence. Aratus stepped back, wiping a sweaty brow with the back of his hand, glancing up to find the tower guards fixated on the exchange. He sighed. "You may or may not be the man you think are, Agonippos, or the one others say you are—for the League's sake, by gods, I hope you *are*. But you've gotta *earn it*," he said, punctuating his last words with a point into the brawny young man's chest.

Still avoiding eye contact, Ago turned to walk away, but Aratus only smiled as he called after him. "Now you're to the pillow early tonight, because tomorrow I want you up and counting inventory of every spear, shield, and linen the city's stocks will provide."

The lieutenant whirled back in one final show of defiance. "What? Why?"

"Why, because as you'd have me believe, other League cities need Sicyon's wares," Aratus replied calmly as he recalled the discussion in the bouleuterium. "So you need make sure their efforts aren't in vain."

Frozen in place for a moment, Agonippos finally balled his hands into fists, looking hard at the Strategos. "You betrayed me tonight."

Aratus was unmoved. "Off you go, now," he offered coldly, which had its desired effect.

As he watched Ago disappear down an easterly street, he heard footsteps slowly crunching up behind him. He didn't even need to look. "Find your way out of the shadows, Mnaseus?"

"Was that necessary?" a gravelly voice asked in return, seemingly not in pursuit of an answer.

"If Dyme would tame their dogs, I wouldn't have to. You think I like playing the boy's mother?"

"You demand a lot of respect for someone who simply walked out on the *Boule* last month. He emulates you more than you realize."

Aratus bristled, shooting a glare back at the grizzled Navarch. "He's got immense talents, I never denied him that. But he needs to learn *humility*."

"Believe what you will, but you're better than what you showed tonight."

"As are you, hiding like you were," Aratus scoffed.

Mnaseus shrugged. "When I'm told our Strategos has secret designs on Corinth, I'll listen. You'd do the same."

"Not the point—the point is that the mere fact that you're here right now means he shared a 'secret' which I told him not to; it means he has a while to go before he earns whatever trust he believes he's due."

"Well, in any event, he comes from a good house; he's a good man, all in all, a strong—"

"Aye, and an honest one too, I see."

The older man paused and locked on the Strategos. "Aratus, do you really want more people irritated with you in the west?"

Aratus was slow to respond. "No…"

"Then give the lad a break, because they like him; it'll save yourself some troubles, anyhow. Boy's like a lion when put off."

Aratus rolled his eyes away from the wrinkled warrior. "I hope he's good, Mnaseus. For the good of the League, if nothing else."

"Speaking beyond your years again?" the Navarch asked with a mouth curving upward.

"Haven't I earned that right?"

The men fell silent for a moment as the evening's wildlife took precedence once again.

"You really had mind to attack the fort, did you?" Mnaseus finally asked.

The question surprised Aratus more than it should have, especially given the context of their meeting. He looked to the Navarch briefly before shrugging. "What's it matter?"

"It doesn't," Mnaseus said with a frown, before eyeing the Strategos. "But the King's fleet alone should have given you pause, anyhow."

Aratus groaned. "Oh, I'm well aware of the many, many things that should give me pause, old friend."

The Navarch let out a gritty chuckle. "Enough of the midnight watch. Gonna go chase down that wine I spotted back near that beautiful theater of yours. Maybe catch a performance if there is one."

"There's always one in Sicyon."

"Well, will you join?"

"You have my thanks, but no. Do enjoy it, though."

With a whack of Aratus's shoulder, the old man was off to find his wine. The Strategos, of course, had no time for such indulgences.

No, he still had a secret meeting to attend.

CHAPTER 10

9th Day of Apellaios, Year 2 of the 134th Olympiad
(July 31, 243 B.C.)

The valley looked like a canyon under a blanket of moonlit mist.

Writhing through the earth like a serpent, the River Asopos clove the landscape in two, throwing up the Sicyonian plateau to the northwest, an even higher ridge to the southeast. The further southwest one followed the river, the steeper the cliffs became on either side. In the winter months, the river stormed toward the sea like a rushing bull, water afoam with rapids; in the summer heat, however, the river was gentle as a lamb, coursing calmly and peacefully through banks lined with stones and brush. Closer to Sicyon, those banks were lined with fecund olive trees, but after a few hours out, pines, willows, and red-berried strawberry trees took their place.

Sicyonians believed that the Asopos was born not of their land or even the Peloponnesus as a whole, but was a continuation of the River Maeander, a mighty run that emptied into the Aegean hundreds of miles east off the Ionian coast. The Maeander's twists and turns were the stuff of legend, and though Aratus hadn't seen it for himself, he had no doubt the stories were true and that the river rose anew in Sicyonia. How else to explain the Asopos's vicious curves? More than once during this midnight trek, it felt like he'd made a complete circle, or surely gotten sidetracked by an errant tributary. Thankfully, this wasn't the first time he'd taken the river path, and in fact, he knew just about every bend by heart. But that provided his companion little comfort by the time they'd been at their brisk pace for several hours…

"It was a few hundred yards back," Timanthes urged, serenaded by babbling water and a chorus of owls near and far. "We should have headed west at that gully."

"That wasn't it, I told you; Titane's still a bit further south before we bear west."

Timanthes scoffed. "As the gods watch us now, you'll have us end up in Phlious. You watch. Bloody Phlious."

Aratus couldn't help but chuckle. "So much the better, then. Couldn't hurt to pitch the campaign to them as well. Get a skin of their wine, perhaps?"

"You're not serious."

Aratus looked back at him in the dark with wide eyes. "Why can't I be?"

"You're a dead man if you are."

"The Phlians can't fight."

"Piss on the Phlians; *I'll* gut you."

In truth, he knew Timanthes's agitation stemmed from more than a wrong turn. They'd left Sicyon hours earlier through the city's lesser traveled southeastern gate, a simple, two-towered passage with a path that descended immediately down to the Asopos. Timanthes agreed to come with Aratus as protection in his journey to the far reaches of Sicyonia, because lauded or not, everyone was a target for bandits outside the walls in the midnight hours; what Aratus had neglected to tell him, however, was his plan to "teach" Agonippos a lesson before they left. The Strategos knew it would gain no approval, so why bother? Nevertheless, his friend had grown increasingly ill at ease the farther they marched into the vale, hands constantly rolling over the handle of a perfectly sharpened dagger.

"Should have bloody gone back," Timanthes muttered, forearm swiping sweat from his brow.

"By the gods, I told you it's only a bit further," Aratus replied, pointing down the path. "You can see the fork up ahead."

"Not that, not that," his friend grumbled. "I mean at Aegium."

Aratus grimaced. "What about Aegium?"

"I told you to go back, remember? Not to leave it like you did."

"Ah, come now, what's done is done. What's it serve raising it again at this point?"

"It didn't serve anything, apparently, that's the problem. Neither did learning they'd sent Agonippos to keep watch on you. By the gods, you'd angered the Council enough; you couldn't have just placated the boy to relieve their suspicions? You had to pick a fight with him?"

"I'm not delving into this again," Aratus said with an annoyed shake of his head.

"Aye, well, you're a fool if you think he's going to let it go at this, you should have seen that. Everything you want to do has been put at needless risk."

"You wouldn't have forgiven his tone so easily had it been you, I assure you."

"Maybe not... just one more thing to worry about with him running around though..."

"Then let him run, he's in fit health it appears," he said dismissively. After a quiet spell, he asked, "Have you told your wife yet?"

"No, I've not," Timanthes sighed. "And I doubt I'd take your suggestions on my approach."

The jab was enough to make Aratus pause, knowing he need do nothing more to tell Timanthes a line was being approached.

"Apologies, didn't mean to be—"

"No need," Aratus said with a wave of his hand. "I hate what I've done to her," he offered, a vision of Tele's distraught face filling his thoughts. "She's done nothing to warrant the grief, nor did her father... but I can't, I-I can't *not* do this..."

Timanthes was slow to respond. "Before the day you'd even met her, your heart was already taken with this fight of yours. Deep down, I bet she knows that as well as I do. As well as *you* do," to which Aratus could only grunt in response. "You've always had two wives."

The thought unexpectedly made him chuckle. "Only barbarians have two wives… and gods tell me, I don't know how they do it."

Timanthes snickered behind him as they finally arrived at the fork they'd been seeking—indeed, it was unmistakable, eyes rising 1,500 feet up a western path toward a hill's peak. At the summit, he saw the shadowed outline of a wall dotted with two soaring towers, their small windows bearing only the faintest hint of light from this distance. Beyond the simple walls rose the front of an ancient Doric temple, its pillars kept aglow by the radiance of countless torches surrounding it.

Titane.

Named for the brother of Helios, Titane was the last and most important bastion of Sicyonia's southern border, where soldiers and mercenaries maintained a year-round vigil within. A village supporting the fort had arisen on the summit just south of the walls. Far beyond a mere village or fort, however, Titane held immensely holy sanctuaries to mighty Athena and Asclepius, both having been founded centuries prior. They were still exceptionally maintained, the Asclepius with an immaculate courtyard of cypresses surrounded by a stoa filled with statues; indeed, it was a place of profound healing for the sick and wounded, and one that Aratus himself had visited more than once upon his return from summer campaigns. A bit farther north and down from the summit was the Altar of the Winds, upon which priests would offer sacrifices one night a year, praying that the slaughtered beasts would tame the fierceness of the gusts. The chanting of the priests could be heard for miles around in the valleys below.

From the conqueror's perspective, Titane would make for a daunting assault. Sheer cliffs guarded the southern and eastern faces, to say nothing of the steep climb just to reach it. It was this that made Aratus look to Timanthes once again. "Ready?"

"Aye… set to be a hearty stroll," his friend replied tiredly.

"Off we go, then," Aratus sighed as fatigued legs took their first steps up the shrub-lined slope. When he looked back for the light of the familiar temple, however, it was nowhere to be found.

Footsteps.

Figures descending from the path above blotted out the light behind them. Aratus froze at once, hand drifting to the dagger at his waist. Tim moved quickly to his side.

"*Khaire,*" he called warily.

He moved slowly back toward the riverbank, ever facing forward.

Is it him?

"*Khaire?*" a man between two others replied. As he stepped onto the fork, Selene's glow revealed a slight man that made his tunic look hopelessly oversized; on his flanks were men of more solid stock, though perhaps they just looked that way by comparison. The small man fearlessly marched straight up to Aratus, barely meeting the Strategos's chin, pushing wavy receding hair behind his head in annoyance. Narrow eyes shifted over Aratus's.

"You come here with a fucking *'khaire'*?"

Aratus's tension eased. "What greeting would you prefer?"

"I'd prefer no greeting at all."

"After all the business we've done, Xeno?" he said teasingly.

The man scowled. "Our business is finished for the season. If the men you've bought for Aetolia are giving you issues, *that's not my fucking problem.*"

The Strategos looked back in surprise. "Oh, there's no issue—"

"Let alone a problem that need be dealt with at this bloody hour."

What the man lacked in size, he made up for with the fury in his voice and eyes, the latter nothing more than black pools in the darkness. No matter how much Aratus towered over him, he'd always felt they looked eye to eye.

"I didn't mean to be a bother," the Strategos replied calmly. "I'm not here to—"

"Aratus, let me be clear—I don't *want* you here."

"No?"

"No. You bring me attention I don't need; you bring me attention I don't *want.*"

Aratus held his tongue as he surveyed the men to either side of Xenophilus, shamelessly brandishing curved *kopis* blades around their waists. Neither gave a semblance of a greeting.

"Look at me," the man demanded, as Aratus obeyed. "Why? Why right now? I *told* you never to travel the Asopos path at night—you're lucky you weren't bloody *killed.* You know how many raiders stalk the waterway?"

Aratus nodded toward Timanthes. "Which is why—"

"His throat'd be cut before he even saw 'em," Xeno said with scorn.

"Aye?" Timanthes challenged back, hand on his dagger.

Xeno didn't even dignify him with a glare. "Gods save me, *my* men might have killed you without knowing it, and where'd that leave me? Hm? You're the first to tell me that the League and bloody Sicyon itself wouldn't be so keen on working with me without your word," he said, eyes drifting for a moment before glowering anew. "*I* may not be so keen on working with *them* without your word."

"All right, well, here I am alive and well, aye?" Aratus finally barked, tiring of the rant. "And you've said—"

"There's a *war* going on, Aratus," Xeno growled, revealing signs of a deeper frustration.

The Strategos grimaced as he instinctively looked around him. "Among whom?"

"Cimon—"

"*Don't say his name!*" Xeno snarled at his guard, who sheepishly looked away.

But as soon as Aratus heard mention of "Cimon," Xeno's agitation became easier to grasp. Some fifteen years ago, Xenophilus was establishing himself as a leader of a band of mercenaries before the gods cursed him with a crippling affliction in his legs. Bent by the misfortune, he proved far from broken, instead cashing in the good will he'd fostered among captains of influence and turning his wits toward brokering deals for other soldiers of fortune. It wasn't long before he'd developed a network of informants and connections—some called them spies—in cities throughout the northeastern Peloponnesus and a reputation as a ruthless dealmaker for the mercenaries and purchasers alike. His grip soon came to dominate the region's supply of Hellenes plying their trade of war.

Like most of the Argolid, Aratus had heard of Xenophilus and the quality of "stock" he dealt in by the time he'd resolved to storm Sicyon. Xeno in turn was only too happy to accommodate Aratus's demand for warriors, even if the future Strategos could only afford a paltry few. Those he'd bought fought as hard as any free soldiers he'd ever met, to the extent that Aratus had gone back to Xeno exclusively for supplementing the League's armies.

After Sicyon fell, Aratus allowed him to take up residence near Titane—albeit on three conditions: one, that he cease brokering deals with enemies of the Achaean League; two, that he keep his "clients" from preying upon the lands of Achaea when no campaigns kept them busy; and three, that for any raids undertook or tribute sought, they target the lands of Macedonian allies. While not all of Aratus's contemporaries in the League sanctioned placing trust in a man whom many saw as a professional criminal, the Strategos felt it was the least he could do in repayment for his assistance at Sicyon.

There were others not as adulatory toward Xeno's efforts, least of all Cimon. Little was known about Cimon; even his name was a pseudonym taken from an infamous painter who lived some four hundred years prior. Nevertheless, Cimon had tried to match Xeno's rise stride for stride, eventually coming to base his operations out of Cleonae, an ancient crossroads town on the route between Corinth and Argos. Thus, at the same time Aratus learned of Xenophilus, he learned of his bloody feud for influence with his archrival broker in the region. Once Xeno settled in Sicyonia, the rivalry died down a bit, aided in part by Cimon filling the void left by the former's departure and alliance with the League; Macedonian kings, for instance, routinely used mercenaries to maintain their grasp on their conquered regions, and Antigonus was no exception. For eight years, then, Cimon had been a prime supplier of Macedonian garrisons, which kept the brokers from each other's throats.

Until now, apparently.

"Your Cleonan friend has tired of his patron king, I sense?" Aratus asked.

"You've it precisely backward, in fact."

"Why, what's happened?"

"What's happened? Bloody hell would I know about it?"

105

Aratus's eyes narrowed on the small man. "There's no end to the list of things you know about, let alone things in your backyard."

"All the same, my 'whispers' in Corinth haven't told me why he's fallen out. Some say it's because the King is bringing down more heavy troops from the north, some say that the Cleonan simply overplayed his hand, tried to extort Pella, but no one *really* knows," Xeno said as he turned and paced away in his awkward gait. "I can tell when a whisper simply feeds me words just to collect his coin. Tastes rotten."

The thought of more Macedonian regulars in the area caused him concern. "You need to get confirmation on these rumors, then... quickly."

"What's it matter in the end?"

"It matters to *me*," Aratus snapped, but Xeno's furious look said he'd have none of it.

"I have bigger issues to deal with than some bastard on his throne hundreds of miles away! Cimon isn't simply whimpering to the gods about his change of fortune, Aratus, he's bloody taken to raiding King lands you told me were *mine* and mine alone! He's murdered five soldiers I'd arranged to send to Sparta; sent a bloody knife back with a survivor! You know how long that'll keep me in business? If I have a whole bunch of idle spears and shields with no enemy lands to take tribute from? Or if merc captains see that son of a whore as the new power here? It's a lie, but even a lie becomes truth if told enough times!"

"Your name carries more weight than any lie he wants to peddle."

"So your suggestion's to wait and hope he tires himself out?" Xeno asked sarcastically. "Duck indoors, weather the storm?"

"No..." Aratus muttered, but in truth, the news had surprised him and complicated things at a time when he barely had capacity to plot out his own stratagem. Now, one of the key components of his plan—certainly the most clandestine—was suddenly vulnerable—

"Well, if that *is* your advice, then maybe I should talk to the King; see if *he* could use my services again..."

It was a comment meant to enrage him, but instead, Aratus's eyes lit up and locked on the man. "Why would Cimon's men follow him?"

"What?"

"You heard me—why? Why've they been loyal, why are they loyal to him now, why would they stay that way, Xeno?"

"Spare me your children's riddles—men of that ilk, men of my ilk follow the coin, you know very well that's true."

"*Why are they loyal to him?*"

Xeno looked about in annoyed wonder. "I don't have time for this— they're fucking loyal because he *gives* them the coin, why else? Paid by the King, paid by his raids, why—"

"Aye," Aratus said in a satisfied tone. "And what if I had them all working through you?"

"By which god's magic would that occur?"

"Oh, it's not magic."

"Then how?"

"By taking Corinth."

Xenophilus stared blankly at the Strategos for a moment, eyes shifting from him to Timanthes, then to either of his guards at his side. "What do you mean 'take'? You mean take up residence there?"

Aratus chuckled. "No, I mean to *take* it. That's why I'm here to see you in the gods-forsaken dead of night."

The bandit's mouth formed words but his voice eluded him. "I-I have no more soldiers to sell you... every unit I'm in contact with h-has..."

"That's fine, I'm not asking you for that."

"By the gods among us, what are you bloody talking about?"

"What's important to you is my taking Corinth—if I take it, if Corinth joins the Achaean League as I'm led to believe, if—"

"And why would I want that?" Xeno offered, seemingly coming to grips with the Strategos's surprise. "The King's lands don't provide much coin, though it's something I can promise my captains... aye, Cimon's challenging me for them at the moment, but, but—"

"You help me take Corinth, Xeno, and as Titane watches me now, I'll see to it you're given first priority in supplying all the extra warriors we'll need thereafter. Then you'll see how loyal those men of Cimon are; he'll wither to the point of irrelevance, you watch, and I'll let you deal with him at your leisure."

Xeno's eyebrow peaked, the closest he ever came to a smile.

"Have I not been loyal to you before? Have I not given you sanctuary for nearly a decade on that mount?" Aratus asked, pointing toward the temple hill.

"We've both benefitted," the bandit offered meekly.

"*Nevertheless.*"

Xenophilus looked at the ground for a moment before shaking his head. "But you'd need a hundred men like me to round up enough soldiers to take those walls. Siege men, bowmen, slingers—even if you used the men I thought were for Aetolia—"

"I don't want any of your men."

"—it wouldn't be enough. And I couldn't allow it, anyway, it's suicide—"

"*Listen to me:* I don't want them, I said. I'm taking Corinth with Achaeans or not at all. Achaeans of the *League*, not those that we purchase. Not for this..."

Xeno finally threw his hands out to his sides. "So then what the hell do you want from me? To trade secrets in the middle of the night? Secrets I could probably sell to Antigonus and live as a god the rest of my life?"

Aratus glared at him. "If you can make a lifetime's sum of gold off this information, then by all means, do so."

"I wouldn't... I'm just..."

"Never mind it, then. I only need two things of you: the first is Timodemus."

The bandit's brow furrowed. "Which is whom?"

"That's what I need you to tell me. Or more precisely, that's the man I need you to find in Corinth."

"Timodemus of where? You have nothing else to tell me about him?"

"I do not... though he carried himself as though he'd be easy to find."

"Sixty thousand souls in Corinth, you know how many Timo—"

"I don't need excuses, I just need you find him. Don't pretend like you don't have a web throughout that city."

"As do you, I reckon."

"Fewer allies there than you realize since the King purged it. Those that I have now are needed for other purposes. I have to stay as far detached from the city as possible. I need people that won't make a scene, won't draw attention."

Xeno's eyebrows shot up again. "So I find this needle among needles somehow—you want him killed, I presume?"

"Gods, no," Aratus scoffed. "You won't kill him, you'll say one simple phrase to him—'the man from the Games chooses everything,'" he said, replaying his departure with the mysterious Corinthian in his head yet again. *"Everything or nothing..."*

"'The man from the Games chooses everything.'"

"Aye. He'll either think you're a madman or he'll understand you precisely—and that's how you'll know you found the right needle."

"How much time do I have?"

"Seven days."

"Seven days?" Xeno cried in echo.

"Aye, so bloody make your contacts at first light."

"Even so, there's no way I'll have the orders given and an answer returned in seven days' time..."

"If that's the case, so be it."

Xeno looked to Timanthes before back to Aratus. "You'll march blind? You'll march on a whim?"

The Strategos smiled calmly. "I've received far too many signs from the gods to think there's any whim about this."

"You've a far different read on the gods than I do."

"Perhaps I do. But I also trust that your men are capable—*especially* so given what's at stake for *you*."

Xeno would only offer a grunt in assent. "So you said you had two demands of me. Your second? Hopefully sounder than the first..."

Aratus glanced at the broker's guards for a second. "We launch in seven days, but in seven days my city will be awash in troops from across the League. Dyme, Patras, Aegium, all of them. To say nothing of your mercenaries. And that's fine, but certain of the Western officers disapprove of my venture."

Xeno scoffed. "The sensible ones."

"Well, I'll need their senses distracted if this is to work, you understand?"

"So what's that to me?"

"Because you're to be the distraction."

"Aye?" Xeno said with a groan as his eyes fell away.

"Aye."

"How, pray tell? I'm bloody hobbled if you haven't noticed."

"You don't need to step foot near Sicyon, and I'd prefer you didn't, in fact. What I need are these trusted men of yours to give heart to a rumor that will begin to spread that very same night—a rumor that Aetolians have landed near *our* shores."

"Aetolians?"

"Aye, the League fears them like no other."

"Of course, but no commander in his right mind will believe they'd landed without sight of their ships, your towers would see to that, no? Are you to have them believe the Aetolians swam the sea?" Xenophilus asked with another eyebrow peak.

"Certainly not," Aratus barked back. "And in any event, I don't need them to believe it for long, just a moment or two. When the rumor's been spread, your men are to be in position well beyond the walls, across the Helisson. From there, you'll light fires, torches, raise a clamor, what have you—just so long as it bloody looks like there's a danger to investigate… then an order will be given."

"An order… to investigate?"

"To investigate. One group to the west of the city, one group—*my group*—to the east. Once I'm outside the walls and the men have mustered, I'm off to Corinth."

Aratus finished with arms crossed over his chest, letting his plan sink in on the broker. He was happy with it, especially as it came out sounding far more plausible to his ears than he might have expected. Xeno's face, however, contorted like he chewed a rotten fig.

Xeno's eyes locked on Timanthes. "I don't like this."

Timanthes only shrugged.

"You're telling me you like this idea? This plot?"

Aratus's friend was slow to respond. "I support the Strategos," he said carefully.

"Some counsel you are," Xeno grunted. "You make it sound like he's got the League's backing."

"What do you care if the League backs this or not?" Aratus asked, annoyed. "Coming from a man who would just as soon raid that League's farms if he could."

Xenophilus scowled. "Don't pretend like your motives are any nobler than mine."

"I act for the League's own good, that's all you need to worry about. Now will you help me or not?"

The broker fixed on the Strategos again with shadowed eyes, but seemingly softened. "Lad, don't do this."

But Aratus only glared back, eyes wide. "You gambled on me with Sicyon. Not ten years ago, you did, and I was no one then."

Xeno's face contorted further. "Sicyon is *Sicyon*. Corinth is *Corinth*. Macedon's a fucking giant, are you mad?"

"And a giant's gentle as a lamb when asleep, no?"

"But I had nothing to lose back then, what about now? What bloody happens to me when your head's mounted from the walls of Corinth when you fail?"

"Then I promise to bear you no ill will, in this world or the next, should you choose to do business with Antigonus again."

"I don't like that either, even if he would do business with me," Xeno said as he ran a hand through thinning hair. "You can't just leave well enough alone?"

"You've known me since Argos, Xeno. *This* is who I am. This is what the gods have told me to do."

"Aye, but—"

"I didn't come here to debate this," Aratus said, irritation rising. "Whether you assist me or not, I am going forward, but if you're concerned about keeping my head intact, then bloody give me the answer I need—that you'll help me."

Xenophilus paced along the riverbank, showing Aratus his back. With a lurch, he skipped a few stones across the churning waters, following their hops as an awkward silence set in.

"And my payment for this endeavor?" he finally asked.

Aratus rolled his eyes. *Coin... always the bloody coin.* "Xeno, I can't pay you anything... it's an investment for you, just like at Sicyon, and that worked out fairly well for you, I'd say."

"So *nothing* up front?" he asked with surprise in his voice. "You do know you need me more than I need you, aye?"

"Aratus, enough with this," Timanthes interjected. "Save your dignity and let's find another way, this is—"

"Oh, now you give him counsel!" the broker suddenly raged.

"He does and as usual, he's right," Aratus said quietly, with a nod toward Tim. "I knew I was asking a great deal of you, but I'm not here to browbeat you into it."

Xeno looked away again, hands on hips in silence. The Strategos started back northward along the river path. "We've a long journey back, though, so forgive us if we take our leave. I wish you good fortune with Ci—"

"You promise I'll still maintain League favor if you fail?"

Aratus smiled to himself. "If?"

Xeno glared anew. "*When.*"

"So long as Sicyon backs you, you're safe."

"Then that's your upfront payment—your guarantee among the powers of your city that I'm not to be forgotten in the event of your—your capture, your torture, the gods know what else."

Aratus frowned in thought. "The Sicyonians will certainly lend me a friendlier ear on this than the rest of the League, but I have to be careful not to lead on too much. Obviously, we're keeping the world of people aware of this to a minimum."

"That's your business, which I don't want to know any more than you want to know mine. Just get me bloody confirmation."

"On my word," Aratus said with a nod. After a pause, he extended a hand toward the broker, whose own still glistened from the river water. "So?"

With a sigh, Xenophilus took the Strategos's hand. "So at least do me the courtesy of taking the ridge path back to Sicyon," he muttered as he turned to stomp back up the hill toward Titane. "Be losin' your head before you take a fucking step toward Corinth the way you prance along the river."

Aratus smiled. "Your concern's appreciated—by your leave, then."

CHAPTER 11

13th Day of Apellaios, Year 2 of the 134th Olympiad
(August 4, 243 B.C.)

Is this my Siren?

This city, this temptation, Aratus thought as he gazed upon the sprawling expanse of Corinth's gray walls. *Is this what Odysseus felt as he passed the songstresses' isle? When their songs so tortured him that he made his men tie him to the mast and keep him bound, lest he steer them toward the beautiful melodies… steer them all toward certain death?*

Should I be so bound? Tied to the mast of my life's vessel, so I can calmly pass it by? At length, he grunted.

"No," he said softly, smiling despite himself. *Let the Siren beckon. So be it.*

For there was his prize, plain as day.

Surely, plenty had looked upon this massive circuit of walls and trembled. Walls that had overseen wars with Athens, then Sparta, then Thebes. Their twenty-five-foot height, their rectangular interspersed towers soaring higher still, their guards pacing ominously behind stony ramparts—to say nothing of the gargantuan crag of the Acrocorinth looming in the background like a titan, among the most awe-inspiring in Greece. *Surely*, this sight had intimidated brave warriors over the centuries, had stared down her fair share of conquerors. How could it not? Aratus himself could barely find the words to describe the view.

He also knew the Macedonian kings were nothing if not fastidious about their fortifications. Even ancient poleis like Corinth, a city that had been enclosed in stone for hundreds of years by the time Alexander the Great added her to his realm, weren't spared enhancement. Towers were strengthened, heightened. Toothy crenellations were patched up where the ravages of time had worn them down. The huge wooden gateways replaced and barred with iron. The Royal treasury was damn near bottomless for linchpins like Corinth.

The stamps of the kings were everywhere to be seen, and Aratus's view atop the Ornis hill let him see just about all of them. Perhaps none was more important than the line of parallel walls branching northward from the city to the Gulf, securing the tradeway of Lechaeum, one of Corinth's two fabulously wealthy ports. For time immemorial, this Lechaeum Road had been lined with shrines, tombs, and monuments, some painted, some bare; the structures of man interwoven among pillars of green cypresses, before it finally ended in a harbor overwhelmed with commerce from across the known world. Ships of all sizes, sailors of all tongues, all of them gathered there to seek their fortune or spend it just as fast. Corinth could famously sate any desire.

Including the King's, as it turned out. For the deepwater harbor was also lined with ship-sheds, roofed structures more than a hundred feet long whose purpose was to hold and guard the Royal fleet. A fitting honor for the city that had invented the trireme, the battleship upon which all seaborne Greeks went to war. At a moment's notice, the oars of two dozen ships could be launched, serving as constant reminders that Macedon's domain didn't stop where Peloponnesian soil met the blue waters beyond.

Totems to the bondage of the Hellenes, Aratus thought bitterly, squinting hard at the port as he rose from his squat. "Chains."

"Chains?" Timanthes asked lazily, leaning calmly against a tree with arms crossed.

"You want to know what the chains of sixty thousand people look like? Hell, chains of the whole Peloponnesus? There it is," the Strategos said with a nod. "The ships, the walls. All of it."

Timanthes sighed. "I worried that you were looking at the walls with a sense of encouragement. You've been too quiet."

"Your concern is well placed, then."

"And so my last hope for your good sense is truly gone," his friend muttered, a statement as honest as it was sardonic.

Aratus sneered in reply, eyes finding his servant heading toward the Sicyon Road. Just as he'd discussed with Erginus, they'd veered south when they neared the city, finding the shady copse upon the hill of Ornis. They weren't waiting long before the smaller of the two wallgates had opened, and a tall, dark-complected man marched out behind a group of traders pushing carts. He couldn't be certain from as far off as they were, but his gut told him it was him—it *had* to be him, the Syrian they'd been waiting on.

"Now," he'd said to Technon. "Scar ear to mouth, remember that. Beardless, Erginus said."

"Aye, scarred and beardless."

"*Supposed* to be beardless. And you're not there to chat with him; you just make contact and bring him here at once, understood? Then we should be seeing his brother not long after that."

"Understood, my lord. I'll fetch him." Technon rarely addressed him as "my lord" unless his orders began to annoy him with their precision, their repetition.

And so they waited, but even in the brief interlude, it was hard for his mind not to wander at the sight before him. It was the closest he'd been to Corinth proper in some time, ever since his formal breach with the King. Beyond that, it'd been more than a decade from the last—and only—time he'd ventured inside, but the red-roofed temples and buildings peeking out over the city walls brought back the sights and sounds of his youth in a hurry. Indeed, they could never be forgotten, on one of the favorite days of his life.

It was a dozen years since he'd arrived at the city's gates with Telesilla's father. Naukydes had business to complete there, though it was hard to remember anymore what that business was. Whatever it was, Naukydes demanded that Aratus come with him, despite the young man's fear of leaving Argos's protective shell. To that point, he'd rarely left his adopted city, save to compete in the Games.

But his first steps into Corinth changed his worldview forever—this is a city favored by the gods, he remembered thinking. The city of marble around him looked beautiful enough, but a descending evening sun cast a magical sheen across the stone buildings, bathing them in palettes of orange and red as if they were a painting. Against that backdrop, they'd entered through a southeastern portal on the Argolid road, one of the six major arteries feeding into the city. The arteries eventually met at the city's center, but not before winding through a labyrinth of homes, temples, and pillared buildings in between. Unlike the orderly grid of streets that Sicyon received upon its refounding, Corinth's pattern followed that of all the oldest and most powerful Hellenic cities—in other words, a pattern of total chaos, where thoroughfares snaked their way through, seeking to establish order amidst masses of crowded houses.

He remembered trying to make sense of what he saw by comparing it to Argos or what little he remembered of Sicyon at the time, but he just couldn't. Everything about Corinth just seemed… bigger. The acropolis higher. The buildings gaudier, statues gilded and immaculate.

And the people—the *constant* stream of people moving throughout, from grimy sailors who hadn't seen land in days to refined statesmen, all of them drinking, laughing, singing, becoming more and more hemmed in the closer one came to the agora. The women, some of them anyway, were unlike anything he'd ever seen: freely walking about the city more so than he'd ever known in Argos, beautiful faces made up in all shades, hair pinned with only wavy strands descending, tunics so teasingly angled across supple bodies to make even a eunuch blush. Indeed, he later learned these were the famous *hetairai* of Corinth, courtesans sought by men from poleis far and wide with talents just as vast; or at least that's how they advertised themselves. The truly famed—and exceedingly pricey—*hetairai* of Corinth resided in the Temple of Aphrodite atop the Acrocorinth, descending to the city below only for the wealthiest merchants and officials; but that didn't keep others from plying their trade in mimic.

His trek toward the city center brought him first past the Sanctuary of Demeter and Persephone, sprawled out over three receding terraces above the city proper, linked by ornate stairs. Like much of Corinth, it had been a religious complex in use for centuries by the time Aratus came to lay eyes on it, all in celebration of the great goddess of the harvest and her daughter. The lowest terrace had dozens of square rooms for Corinthians to feast in during the lively festivals, some with stew pots for preparing *maza*, a bread of boiled barley and milk, others with casseroles and hearths for roasting fish. After following the stairs up through the pediment and four columns of the sanctuary's *propylon*, one entered the broad middle terrace where pilgrims brought votive cakes and offerings in sacrifice to the goddesses, and where priests slaughtered pigs in the fire pits of the holy structures. At the highest terrace, Corinthian officials enjoyed the proceedings from the finest vantages in their specialized viewing seats.

No sooner had he finished gawking at the Sanctuary than their arrival in the agora proper was hearkened by a colossal stoa on his right. Naukydes heard his shocked gasp and snickered.

"I've traveled from Olympia to Athens, lad. You won't find a bigger stoa in all of Hellas, I promise you."

There couldn't *be a bigger stoa, could there?* he'd wondered at the time. This one stood two stories high, over five hundred feet long and eighty feet wide; more than seventy columns lined its portico, limestone pillars painted white with stucco.

"What's it for?" he mumbled, wide-eyed.

"It's a stoa, boy," Naukydes laughed. "What do you think it's for?"

"I *know* it's a stoa," he said, embarrassed. And he really did, but… but this one's sheer size made his mind race with its purpose. A divine purpose, perhaps?

"Mostly places to eat, as I recall, maybe grab a night of sleep in the rooms overhead," Naukydes said, eyeing the structure. "Macedonians built it some time ago now, but they've kept adding to it, I see. Even since the last time I was here, they have."

Did he mean the stone reliefs? Everywhere he looked, he saw them—carvings, one of Asclepius, an old man reclining leisurely on a couch, known to bring good health; another of his daughter, Hygieia, leaning against a pillar; a third of Pan, god of the wild, born with the legs and horns of a goat, body of a man, with a catskin thrown over his back. Or did Naukydes mean the statues? Dozens of them; scores, even, all arrayed precisely in front of the portico—a bronze Athena, helmet resting cautiously atop her head, right arm raised, left arm extended in greeting; another large bronze, this one of a man wearing a cuirass, his leg forward as if ready to sprint, head twisted backward as if watching a pursuer. The shadows cast by the day's setting sun made them appear even larger than life than they already were.

Despite his wonder, they kept up a brisk pace amidst the river of people, soon passing a racecourse as long as the stoa they'd just left behind. The finish line of the *dromos* was right before them, the starting line far down at the eastern end, and in between busy workers sprinkled the grounds with water in preparation for footraces to come. Aratus knew from his own training that the track's crushed limestone was nearly impossible to sprint on after baking under Helios all day long; the water would give them grip. He saw the monuments and bronze statues honoring past victors—some by the legendary Sicyonian sculptor, Lysippos—ringing the horseshoe of the course, none more impressive than the four horses of a *tethrippon,* beasts frozen in strain against their charioteer's bridle. Seats of honor were adjacent to the chariot, reserved for the prestigious judges of the races.

"This way, boy," Naukydes's voice boomed over the din, finger pointing northeast toward the other end of the course. They turned right onto a smaller road parallel to the great track, fighting lesser crowds until they turned left onto a broad thoroughfare sloping north toward a gate along the northern wall. "You follow that all the way down, through the gate, you'll be at Lechaeum," he said, and based on the stream of merchants and sailors venturing past them in either direction, he'd no reason to doubt it was the Lechaeum Road—the road to the port.

"Is that where we go?" Aratus remembered asking.

"No," Naukydes said, smiling with a hard pat on his back. "Port's no place for a boy; 'specially not *that* port."

"I'm not a boy," he protested, and already having three or four inches on his caretaker, he probably had a case for himself. But Naukydes's silence meant the discussion was already at an end, so he didn't persist. Port-bound or not, however, he heard the distinctive sound of rushing water nearby; they were too far from the coast to explain it, and it wasn't until he looked back to his right that he found the source.

A set of stairs descended between two lion statues, at the bottom of which were six hollow chambers of fine limestone, large enough for a man to enter. Indeed, men and especially women queued at the entryway to each antechamber; those exiting the chambers emerged with vessels of water balanced on their heads or gripped with handles on either side. A small stoa of six pillars loomed over the depression to the east, along with an array of statues to the south, the latter seemingly keeping watch over the water-gatherers.

Naukydes must have noticed his lagging, calling back to him, "That's the city's lifeblood right there, the Fountain of Peirene; surely, your tutors have told you—"

"Aye," Aratus replied curtly, fixated on the elaborate craftsmanship of the fascia above each of the chamber's dividing walls. He could also make out a line of thin Ionic columns deeper within the spring.

He felt the man's arm around his neck. "They tell you why it's called Peirene, boy?"

Aratus hated being stumped, but he conceded defeat with a shrug.

"The Corinthians say that Peirene was a lover of the gods; a lover of Poseidon, actually. They say she gave birth to his sons, Leches and Cenchrias, for whom—"

"For whom the city's ports are named."

Naukydes grinned. "Aye. Now Cenchrias was interested in the hunt, see? Begged his father to send him out with the bow, but Peirene begged just the opposite! Said he was too young, wasn't ready. As a compromise, Poseidon sent him out with Artemis, goddess of the hunt, but alas, the fates were still against the lad. One of Artemis's arrows, meant for a beast, found its way into the boy's beating heart instead. When his mother received the news, it's said she came here to weep, but did so for so long and so hard, that she finally dissolved into the spring that still flows here."

As they resumed their march north along the Lechaeum Road, he remembered seeing perhaps the most indelible image of his visit—the Temple of Apollo, the city's oldest structure, rising torch-lit and triumphant under a darkening western sky. It was crude by the standards of his day, yet its twenty-five-foot height atop a spur in the northern Corinthian plain made it look as imposing as any of the great temples that he'd heard of and seen throughout Hellas; indeed, it was said that even Athens aped its design when building their acropolis masterpiece a century later. Six white limestone columns lined the temple's front, fifteen along its sides, while blue, red, and golden paints decorated its pediment and the frieze below it; which is all to say nothing of the giant bronze statue of Apollo said to be housed within.

That's what we were there for, he remembered now, standing on the Ornis. *It was—*

"What the hell's he doing?"

The daydreaming Strategos "awoke," looking over to his companion, Timanthes. "Hm?" he muttered groggily.

"He's—he's walking back toward the city; what the *hell* is he doing?"

"What?"

"Technon! Look! Are you blind?"

Aratus's eyes suddenly scrambled over the Sicyonian Road, finally finding his sweaty servant a hundred yards off—indeed, there he was, walking back to—"Where the bloody hell is he going?" he suddenly roared in shock.

"Aye!"

His heart raced, the view leaving him stunned. He squinted hard, hands shading eyes despite the trees' shadows. "He's got a beard," he said in near whisper, stomach twisting.

"What?"

"The man leading Technon, he has a *gods-forsaken* beard! He can't see the scar!"

"Shit."

His servant was barely sixty yards from the gate.

"Aratus, you can't let whoever that is take—"

"I know!"

Fifty-five.

"Shit!"

"Shall I get him?"

"Not yet... not—"

"Gods, Aratus..."

"He's too bloody smart for this; Technon, you're too smart!"

Fifty yards.

"Let me get him; any closer and the wall guards will—"

"Erginus."

The Syrian he bartered with suddenly moved into view, briskly marching out from beyond the gates toward Technon and his apparent captor.

"Don't you betray me, you bastard…"

The three of them met on the road, a disagreement appearing to ensue. The captor gripped Technon's wrist as Erginus's hands rose in placation.

Gods, I beg of you…

Erginus shoved the man to the ground, dust masking his fall.

"Shit."

His eyes flicked from the men to the soldiers leisurely pacing atop the walls, petrified they'd take note. In a flash, his servant and Erginus were in a dead sprint toward the Ornis, the shoved man giving chase. Timanthes pulled a dagger from a sheath; Aratus did the same. He crouched.

"Kill him outright?" Timanthes asked through short breaths.

"Erginus?"

"Aye."

"No!"

"He's a traitor, are you—"

"*No!* You—"

Before they knew it, they were there, Technon and the Syrian. Both gasped for breath, Erginus collapsing to his hands and knees beneath a tree. The Strategos was too wary to move yet, though he saw the third man had given up the pursuit. Instead, the man paused halfway between the road and Ornis, utterly perplexed.

Aratus exhaled, frantic eyes locking on Technon, who refused to meet them.

"What happened?" Aratus asked with a shake of his head, restraining his anger with all his might.

"It's not… it's not him…" Technon said through pants.

"I can see that."

"He… he…"

"He what? Dammit, I told you to *look* for the *scar!*"

"I did… I thought I… I thought I saw it—"

"You thought?" the Strategos raged. "He has a beard, black as ash, how would you have seen a scar—"

"His ear was cloven!" Technon pleaded, eyes finally raised. "I thought it was him! I thought… I thought that was the scar, or the—or the start of it anyway…"

"They look alike," Erginus groaned, forehead still resting on the ground, chiton soaked through.

Aratus's glare fell to the Syrian. "Who?"

"It's my brother, Strategos."

"*Who?* The man you just bloody ran from?"

"Aye!" the Syrian growled, sneering at the Sicyonian before rolling onto his buttocks, arms wrapping around knees.

Aratus looked to Timanthes, no less confused. "This whole day was *planned* around meeting your brother, why are you now running—"

"*Diocles*," Erginus said, before shaking his head. "*Not* Dionysius."

It felt like he'd been booted in the gut. His gaze drifted over toward the third man, still pacing about some forty yards off. No, the third Syrian, the third—"That's Dionysius."

Erginus only nodded with closed eyes, mouth agape in exhaustion. Timanthes stepped toward him with dagger still drawn, but still Aratus held an arm out to stop him.

"And why is he here? Where the hell is Diocles?"

The Syrian looked askance at his menacing friend before back to Aratus. "I don't know why he was there."

"You don't know?" Timanthes demanded.

"No! He must have—he must have overheard me, or Diocles, or—"

"That's it? That's your only explanation for this?"

"Who are you, anyway?"

"I'm Timanthes, and I hope you'd have a better—"

"Well, what else should I say, Timanthes? If I don't know, I don't know!" Erginus barked, hands upturned. "Strategos, I told you before... I told you Dionysius was a bastard, a rogue!"

"Aye, what of it now? I told *you* to take precautions!"

"I did!"

"Then gods tell me why it's that 'rogue' staring at me right now, and not Diocles? Tell me!"

"Diocles couldn't leave his post today, after all. I waited as long as I could for him, but—"

"When we talked, you never mentioned he might simply just *not* show up!"

"Aye... I did though, I waited for him, and by the time I gave up and walked out the gate, I came across..." The big Syrian trailed off with a sigh.

"A lie of the tallest order," Timanthes grumbled.

"I won't be challenged by *you*—tell me what *you've* risked here?"

"Me? I owe you answers to nothing!"

"Quiet!" Aratus yelled, drawing glares from both men. Grinding his teeth in the awkward silence, he came to his decision. "Go get him."

Erginus blanched, as if he'd heard the command in foreign tongue; Timanthes looked equally baffled.

"Get who?" the Syrian asked.

"Dionysius. Get him, *now*. It's the only way around this."

Timanthes threw his hands out to his side. "Are you mad? This man's idiocy almost gets your servant killed before a garrisoned wall and still you trust him?"

"I have plenty of ways of testing men's fealty, Timanthes, and the first of which starts right now. *Get him*, Erginus."

"You've lost your wits," Timanthes said with a disbelieving smile. "Truly, you have!"

The Syrian rose tiredly to his feet, eyes wide toward the Strategos. "And if I bring him here?"

"*When* you bring him here."

Erginus looked to his feet for a moment. "I can't let you kill—"

"Erginus, you just bring him here. I promised you what I promised you before—hearth and home for you and your brothers, did I not?"

The Syrian warily nodded.

"Well, I *keep* my promises," Aratus said, gaze afire.

He looked no more convinced, but Erginus ran a hand through his beard and started a slow trek back down the Ornis toward his brother.

Timanthes came to his side. "I'm not a murderer, Aratus, but I can justify killing someone who betrayed us," he whispered. "I pray you hope to take them both—"

"Did you believe his story, Technon?" Aratus asked, watch never leaving the Syrians.

A response was not fast in coming. "I did, sire. For… for what it's worth, anyhow…"

"Even so, Erginus *admitted* that his brother 'overheard' the plans! Who else may have 'overheard' this, Aratus?"

"I don't know," Aratus said at length, finding his friend's dark brown eyes. He could barely think. Didn't want to. "Just follow me, brother. I beg of you." Timanthes looked away, sheathing his knife.

For better or worse, Erginus returned with his older brother in tow. The former stared daggers at Aratus, whose own face wore a frozen scowl. His heart quickened again, hand tightening around his blade.

"My friends, this is Dionysius," Erginus with a sigh.

He was right, Technon was. Dionysius's looks largely fit the description Erginus had given him—curly-haired, swarthy complexion; and though he had a beard, it wasn't nearly as heavy as it looked from a distance. His right ear had a grotesque divot cut out of it. The man looked immediately suspicious, a lazy eye lagging behind the other as they danced among the members of Aratus's group.

The Strategos extended a hand. "Welcome, Dionysius."

The elder Syrian didn't move, not even with Erginus's comforting arm about his shoulder. After an awkward pause, it became clear it was Aratus's knife that drew his concern.

"Never mind the blade, I don't mean you harm."

Aratus looked to Erginus, growing tense with his brother's silence.

"Sheath it," Dionysius finally said.

Aratus swallowed hard, but didn't budge. "Why do you think you're here, friend?"

"Not your friend."

"All the same, friend."

"I'm *not* your friend."

"But you should wish to be."

"Should I?" Dionysius mocked, revealing a mouth even more devoid of teeth than Erginus's. Aratus nodded. "And why's that?"

"Because—"

"Better yet, why don't you tell me why the fuck *you're* here? And holdin' a bloody knife at that? This is *my* home!" the Syrian said, pounding a part of a hairy chest his tunic left bare.

Aratus's face darkened. "My friend—"

"I'm not bound to tell you a damn thing, whoever you are or think you are."

"I'll ask you one last—"

"Aye, you want an answer? A talent, there's your answer."

Aratus glanced at Timanthes and back. "A talent for what?"

"A talent and I won't mention whatever it is you're schemin' about doing with Erginus. Whatever *he's*"—he planted a hard finger in his brother's chest—"been schemin' about doing with Diocles. That's my price, because it's *something*... something, someone, somewhere in that city would wanna hear, I'm sure of it."

Yet for all his bravado, the elder Syrian looked nervous, feet pacing, hands fidgety. The Strategos stared hard into his black eyes, trying to summon the depths of his knowledge of their plan.

"Who've you spoken of this to? Anyone?"

"Maybe I have," Dionysius offered uncertainly.

"Well, then why would I bother giving you a talent if the 'secret' has already been told?"

"Because maybe I haven't told the *right* person, yet..."

"Or maybe you haven't told anyone at all," Erginus growled beside him, drawing his sibling's ire.

"Oh, to the crows with you!" Dionysius snapped. "You're beyond a thieving bastard leaving me out of this, ya know that? You're just a flat-out *bastard*—"

With a crack, the hilt of a knife slammed into the back of the Syrian's head. He crumpled into a heap at Erginus's feet; three pairs of eyes locked on Aratus in shock.

The Strategos sheathed his knife. "Bind him, Technon." He looked back at his servant. "Do it."

"That's you keeping your promise?" Erginus said, pursed mouth disappearing into a bushy beard.

122

"He knew, Erginus," Aratus said, pulling his wavy brown hair behind his head with a sigh, to which the Syrian gave no response. "Worse, he knew enough to believe there was *value* in what he knew; so he knew enough to be a threat. Only thing that matters now is *who* else might—"

"What matters is that you spilled my brother's blood."

Patience drained, Aratus moved nose to nose with Erginus, clenching jaw and fists alike. "Will you bloody tell me something? What's more important to you, hm? A lump on your brother's head or your chance to live bloody well? To never have to steal again?"

Cold black eyes stared back at him.

"His blood will dry, his wound will heal, and *you* will still have your chance at riches; your brothers too, should you choose to share it. Now tell me you don't know that's true. *Tell me*, I can wait." He could smell the big man's angry huffs filtering through a sweaty beard.

"And when those wounds heal, what the hell are we supposed to do with him, Aratus?" Timanthes asked, voice incredulous.

"Aegias's. Eck's. Someone will hide him for us—*just* until it's over. Just until I'm dead and gone or he's alive and rich."

He could see his friend shake his head out of the corner of his eye, but the Strategos remained fixed on the Syrian. "When you shook my hand in Sicyon, that's when you told me you understood there's no going back from this, Erginus... isn't that right?"

At length, a nearly imperceptible nod.

"Good."

He finally backed away, moving instead toward the hill's edge again, gaze locked on the monstrosity sticking out from the southern horizon. "Now, you're going to take a moment to gather yourself and then—Diocles or not—you're going to stand here and tell me every damned thing you know about that fort."

* * *

"You don't want to use these gates," the Syrian said, pointing in the direction of the two gates through which the Sicyon Road passed. "Too many guards, even at the lesser one. Too much trade and too many towers."

Aratus nodded, though nowhere on the wall looked particularly inviting.

"Skip those and skip the Tenean Gate—that's the one closest to the fort. There's a gate in between the two, and that one's called the Phliasian. It'll take you in from the southwest at a safe distance from the peak and it's just about impossible to see from there, too."

Before he continued, Erginus took a look back at his brother, propped up against a tree with hands roped behind his back. He sighed. "So there're three garrisons you're worried about, aye? Theophrastus has a few hundred at Lechaeum, though he's probably far enough away not to be a bother... and if they are a bother, it's the gods telling us we're fucked already."

123

Aratus slow-blinked in agreement.

"Bigger problem's the city watch under Archelaus. He's got at least a few hundred of his own, stations them in a barracks by Demeter's sanctuary, just northwest of it. Carry spears, light armor, but they're fully Macedonian. No question of loyalties there."

"How active are they by night?"

The Syrian shrugged. "More so than during the day, patrols out and about," he said, before locking eyes on Aratus. "Waiting for bastards like you to show up."

The Strategos grunted. "So the Sicyonian Gate, except there're more wall guards waiting; the Phliasian Gate, but it's nearest to the barracks; the Tenean Gate—"

"The Tenean Gate and you better get your coin for the Boatman ready."

Aratus nodded grimly. "Some options."

"Like I said, Phliasian Gate and you've got a chance, at least. The Phliasian Road will take you straight to the agora in the north, but you need be headin' south as soon as possible, so when you see an alley taking you that way, take it; it'll be on your right. If ya lucky, you'll pick up the Tenean Road from the proper side of the wall and follow it to the mountain's base."

"And then it's only a two-thousand-foot climb," Aratus said.

"Just be glad you're breathing at all at that point, but aye, it's a bloody miserable climb. Just remember, the Acrocorinth's a bean with its curves facin' north; take the mountain path up along its western side."

"Is it laid with stone?"

"Aye."

"Sandals off, then... too much noise. Torches?"

"None along the path, no... not that I recall, anyway, but I've never done the climb at night to be sure..."

"Yet you're supposed to be our guide in this endeavor?"

The Syrian shrugged. "Diocles would be able to say—"

"Aye, well, he's not here and you won't see me again before the next four days have run," he said, groaning to himself. "We'll just have to be ready. So go on."

Erginus wiped a sweaty brow, skin looking almost pallid aside from flushed cheeks.

"Well, normally as you reached the top you'd head a bit northeast toward the fortress's main gate; that gate, it's centered so it'd split the 'bean' lengthwise, if you take my meaning."

"Aye..."

"But you're not headed to that gate, you're headed southeast for the cleft I've spoken of. Leads you right to a part of the southern wall that's barely fifteen feet high, unlike the rest of it."

"You've taken this cleft?" Timanthes asked suspiciously, earning a Syrian scowl.

"Obviously not."

"But you can see it? You can see the cleft reach the wall?"

"Aye… near enough."

"He'll be there to show us, Timanthes," Aratus said.

"Small comfort."

"My brother agrees on it!" Erginus cried in protest.

"As Aratus said, your brother's not here. Not *that* brother—"

"All right, enough," the Strategos said, sensing tensions rise.

"That one's a complainer," Erginus sniped.

"I said *enough*. Worry yourself with the fort; what's within the walls? What should we expect?"

But the Syrian only confirmed Aratus's worst fears, remaining poignantly silent. He closed his eyes as he dropped his head. "*Can* you tell us anything or is that the province of Diocles as well?"

Erginus clenched his jaw, searching for something. "The grounds of the fort get higher the further east ya go," he offered finally. "The spring's in that direction too, Diocles told me, right along the south wall… and there's the temple at the very top… Aphrodite's temple, with the… with the women…"

"Every man in Hellas knows about those women, Erginus, I'm not bloody worried about the *hetairae*. I need to know about the troops, their arms, their ballistics, their numbers. *Anything* would be a start."

"Well, m'apologies, then, because I've never been inside the gates," he said with a defensive tone. "But I know my brother's one of many Syrians on the mount, probably in the hundreds. And he said they brought in some Gallic and Illyrian fighters too, mixed in among the Macedonians themselves. And they all answer to Persaeus; he's the Archon."

"Persaeus the Philosopher Governor": that was one man Aratus was familiar with. Born a slave of the famous philosopher Zenon, he quickly became one of Zenon's brightest pupils, growing famous as a Stoic in his own right, and becoming a fixture at Antigonus's court. He was said to be among the King's closest friends in Hellas, a man he would verbally joust with for hours at a time. His appointment as Archon of Corinth, however, was a recent development and surely meant as an honorary post for the aged man more than anything.

Aratus looked at Erginus, hoping for more. "That's it?"

Erginus shrugged. "I'll lead you best I can, as I said. Diocles will do the same along the wall."

So that really is it, he thought irritably. The Strategos sighed, eyes searching the western side of the crag from his far off distance, looking for the path that in four days would lead him either to the Styx or to the greatest glory he'd ever known. He was suddenly swept up with the urge to laugh, one chuckle leading to another, soon in a fit of hysterics as the rest of his group watched him with alarm. "What the hell am I doing here, lads?"

The Syrian offered the faintest inklings of a grin from beneath his beard. "Been askin' you that since I met ya."

"I mean, marching blind, no numbers, no idea on their logistics. All to take that damn rock. That damned, cursed, *miserable* rock."

"I'd rather you take some time to ask the Oracle..." Timanthes muttered drily.

His laughter faded, but a smile lingered on Aratus's face. "Gods only know what the proper question is, my friend," he said, before pointing one last time at the Acrocorinth. "But that's the *answer*."

CHAPTER 12

14ᵗʰ Day of Apellaios, Year 2 of the 134ᵗʰ Olympiad
(August 5, 243 B.C.)

The man at the palestra's door beamed warmly when he saw who'd knocked. "*Khaire*, Aratus."

"*Khaire*, Xenocles," he said, nodding back. He was a good man in his late thirties, a trust-worthy man, one of his fellow exiles in Argos who'd joined him to free Sicyon. He'd shown exceptional bravery during the attack, courage which had not gone unnoticed by the city-dwellers. As such, several times since then he'd been elected *gymnasiarkhos*, the official who oversaw the city's gymnasia and palestrae.

"The gods find you well?"

"Well as could be expected given my transgressions," he replied with a smile of his own and a whack on the man's bare arm. Xenocles laughed.

"Haven't had much mind to change over the years, have you?"

"If the gods saw fit to make me a bastard, then who am I to question them?"

They shared another chuckle before the gym master grew quiet and rubbed a chin scruffy with black and gray stubble. He shot a glance behind him into the palestra. "Well, if you've come to relive your past glory in the sands, you're a bit late. Most of the lads have quit training for the day and have gone off to their lessons."

Aratus looked hard at the man with a fading grin. He knew damn well why Aratus was there.

Xenocles looked to his feet. "Though I suspect you're here on other affairs…"

"Aye."

Xenocles just nodded and gave way at the door. "Upstairs to the left, overlooking the terrace."

"Thank you, my friend."

Xenocles grabbed his arm as he passed, face bearing concern. "He's not even bloody trying to hide, Aratus. Just standing there, right in the middle for all to see, should anyone care to look."

"Oh?"

"Aye… just didn't want you to be caught off-guard in case you're seeking to avoid notice… You know how the people talk."

Aratus nodded in mild irritation. "Indeed, I do. Now more than ever. My thanks again."

With that, he passed under the propylon and entered the palestra proper. Aratus's father had built the complex such that it spread out over two rectangular terraces, all enclosed by foreboding walls. The lower terrace was a flat, open space of fine dust, dirt, and stone, the place where the city's boys came to train for boxing and wrestling in the many holy festivals—indeed, the very word *palestra* originally meant "school of wrestling." Framing three sides of the wrestling grounds were lines of Ionic columns, interspersed with life-sized white marble *hermae*—four-sided pillars with only the heads of a god; here an Artemis, there a Heracles. Beyond the portico were arcades for the fighters to oil and powder their bodies for a match or continue training on punching bags hung from the ceiling. The fourth side of the lower terrace was a retaining wall that separated it from the upper and western terrace. A staircase cut through the center of the wall, flanked on either side by elaborate bathing and drinking fountains with Doric columns across their façades.

Though of similar design, the upper terrace of the palestra complex was far less martial. Indeed, in the arcades of these colonnades, youths were taught in the finer things of Hellenistic life—philosophy and literature, mathematics and the sciences; the art of the lyre and other such instruments formed another basis of the ideal Sicyonian. But above all, the upper terrace was the perfect place to observe the scraps of the grounds below, Sicyonians ever excited for the next champion their city may produce.

Another "Bear" perhaps? Aratus thought as he climbed the staircase just inside the propylon, thinking of the largest man he'd ever seen fight. *The unbeaten "Lion"?*

Though for Aratus, it was a tall Megalopolitan that awaited him on the edge of the upper terrace today. *The "Fox,"* he sighed to himself.

Ecdelus looked back at him with hands flung out to his sides in annoyance, preaching punctuality as he was wont to do. "Next time I'll send a servant to fetch you; as if I've nothing else to do but bake my skin all day!"

Despite his antics, Aratus couldn't help but note the man looked more refined than usual. Maybe it was the newer himation he wore rather than the ratty yellow one he was used to seeing him in. Maybe it was his typically wild silver-black hair instead tied off neatly in the back. Regardless, his eyes still breathed the fire they were known for.

"Ah, you speak with Chronos's scorn," Aratus said teasingly with a hand extended in greeting.

"As well I should," he said as he looked back out over the wrestling grounds of the lower terrace. Only two youths remained, hands on hips breathing heavily, joined by a man in a blue wrap offering instruction. From a far-off room behind them, softly strung notes floated through the day's hot air.

Aratus looked him over some more, his appearance bringing a grin to his face. "I'd say you were trying to disguise yourself with this look of yours, if you weren't right in the middle of my father's palestra, clear as the sky above."

"No longer the people's palestra?"

The Strategos's eyebrows peaked. "Of course it's the people's; you knew what I meant."

"Should I stand aside from you, then? No pillars to hide behind this time, so should I stand in the fountains?" he said, an unmistakable tone of anger in his voice as he pointed at the lower terrace's fountains. "Pretend to be a water nymph?"

Aratus had to stifle a chuckle at the thought of the lanky old man frolicking in holy waters. "You're a man of many talents, my friend, but a comely young maiden? That's beyond even your range."

"I'm a fine singer, you know. A fine dancer. No one would ever know it was me; give me the word and I'll jump in now."

The Strategos let a silence linger for a bit. "Are we here to discuss nymphs?"

"Just trying to protect your reputation, lad, lest you be seen fraternizing with a madman."

"I'll worry about that. If I want to stand here and talk to you, then I shall."

Finally, the Megalopolitan turned his blue-brown eyes on him, prominent nose scrunched. "No chance you've wisened, so why should that be?"

Aratus thought about it for a moment, before answering calmly. "Because my life ends or begins anew in two days. Who gives a damn who I talk to today?"

"Hmph," the older man grunted at length, looking away. "I've heard little of the particulars of this event 'in two days.'"

"I thought you seemed irritable. More so."

"Shall I presume my lack of knowledge of those particulars means something about my involvement?" Ecdelus asked, dripping in bitterness.

It was a talk Aratus had been dreading to have, even if he knew himself to be correct without question. "My friend, you know what my decision has to be on this."

"Oh, I do?"

"Come now," Aratus said, gently as possible. "You can barely walk without hobble anymore. You can't expect to keep pace on that mountain—"

"I've no bloody hobble. Was I a burden when we took Sicyon?"

"Ecdelus, that was eight years ago. You have a damned hobble now and my decision's final. On even footing, I'd cast my lot on you without a thought, but this…" Aratus sighed. "*This* is going to be different."

The firebrand shook his head in disbelief. "Greatest gambit of my lifetime and you shut me out of it. Why did you bloody tell me about it to begin with?"

"You've more tales to make the gods jealous than twenty other men combined, I assure you that."

"I don't need your—"

"*And* you've plenty more tales to tell. Just not this one. Not the attack itself, anyway."

"Hmph," Ecdelus grunted again.

"I'd be remiss not to remind you that you've been a massive help to me already, years before and now just as much," Aratus said, hand on the man's shoulder. "You helped give me the courage to even take this chance; you made me keep heart after the debacle in Aegium. Without those things, the attack on Corinth wouldn't happen—assuming we even get that far, gods willing."

"Compliments better given to a mother, a father, a *priest*, not a man like me."

"Well, so be it, it's true all the same," Aratus snapped, growing frustrated. "And I'm glad to hear you're so eager to offer help beyond your words. Just because you won't be drawing swords, doesn't mean it isn't needed."

"And what's that? *Polishing* your sword? Wringing out your armor?"

"*No.* But our surveillance of the wall a couple days ago wasn't without problems."

Still frowning, Ecdelus couldn't hide his piqued interest. He turned his head halfway toward the Strategos, saying nothing.

"It was the Syrian's brother. The *wrong* brother, should I say. We were supposed meet the one that actually mans the damn walls, hear a report about the fortifications, defenses, men, what have you, but through a series of blunders that only Momus could appreciate, Erginus's *other* brother arrived instead, only to start a brawl before the very walls of Corinth itself."

"Hah!" Ecdelus exclaimed.

"We got hold of the man, and as you might expect, he knew enough to be a threat to the whole endeavor. So he's back here now."

"In Sicyon?" Ecdelus asked with wide, laughing eyes.

Aratus nodded.

"*Hah!*"

"Aye, well, I'm glad you're amused, because we need to keep him in a safe place until the task is done. He's been at Aegias's ever since we returned, but it's drawing suspicion seeing his facilities under lock and key and so much needing to be done for the League. We need to move him to your place."

"Oh, I'm to be a jailkeeper! The true calling of a nobleman!"

"For two days? You can manage. Two days, turn him loose."

"Aye, aye," Ecdelus said, irritatedly waving a hand in Aratus's direction. "Two days."

"If it matters, you have my thanks."

"Hmph, I should thank you for putting me to such valiant service."

Aratus looked at the man with a pursed smile. "Well, then I should accept your thanks."

The men fell quiet for a bit as they watched the two youths begin sparring again on the terrace below. After only a moment of pacing around each other, it was clear the young men were training for the *pankration*, a grueling event best described as a hybrid between the wrestling and boxing purists. Outside of eye-gouging and biting, virtually no rules applied to the scrums, although the initial phases invariably held true to a certain formula, as these two were proving. The fighters neither faced each other nor turned away, rather they approached in cautious stances, hands open and raised to their eyeline as they closed the gap.

Though they appeared to be of like age, perhaps sixteen or seventeen years, their size disparity made for an interesting show, the taller of the two whipping kicks at his opponent to keep him at bay, while the latter kept dodging and creeping closer with a cocked fist. Both of them tried playing the sun to their advantage, constantly circling to blind the other.

"Drachma on the tall one," Aratus said, hoping to lighten the man whose ego he'd offended, if not crushed. And despite the silence, he sensed there were things the Megalopolitan was leaving unsaid. Ecdelus was simply too blunt not to leave if his business was indeed done.

In a flash, the shorter fighter grabbed the leg of an errant kick behind the knee and jerked forward, launching his free fist into the other's jaw with a loud pop. The taller boy fell to the ground, whereupon the teacher raised a hand, signifying a point had been won. Soon the teacher was yelling at the fallen fighter, scolding him for not pressing the attack.

"Shit, tall one's falling right into the hands of the little one," Aratus muttered, reminded of his youth. As a taller fighter of some repute himself, he remembered having more difficulties with smaller opponents than those he looked eye to eye with. The latter made sense, there was a balance, a symmetry to the fight that simply wasn't there against the former. His matches against smaller athletes inevitably degenerated into ruthless scrums, though he'd never gone to the level of Sostratus of Sicyon to achieve victory; Sostratus was perhaps the most legendary Olympic champion Sicyon had ever produced, winning the pankration three consecutive Olympiads some hundred years prior. But he was especially renowned for his methods en route to his victories— snapping or breaking his opponents' fingers.

The tall fighter rose, rubbing a tender jaw before taking stance again. First to three points wins, after all.

"He needs to—"

"I'm leaving here, Aratus."

Aratus looked to Ecdelus with a start. "You're leaving?"

He nodded.

"When?"

"Don't worry, I'm not leaving before your little party in Corinth is over, but not much past it. Next day after, maybe?"

"And where, may I ask?" But as he asked it, he already knew, and a glance from the Megalopolitan said just as much.

"I've given it much thought, which I usually see as a bad thing. If perfect certainty is truly elusive, then where's the point in wasting my days ruminating about it?" He grunted. "But this time I did. And I decided I'm going home; going to teach that lad Philopoemen, at Cleandor's request."

The Strategos's heart sank a bit, even if he agreed with the decision. He'd seen the man on at least a weekly basis for almost a decade, and regardless of whether those meetings were enlightening or infuriating, there was no mistaking their friendship. No mistaking their agreement on the fundamental disease of tyranny, on acting first and letting results be what they may.

"Did I force your hand on this today, friend?"

Ecdelus grimaced. "Perhaps. This venture you're embarking on without me is exactly what it appears to be—a venture without me. A venture without me—"

"It's not without you, Ecdelus. I need—"

"Aye, you need a storage space for a mad Syrian, I understand. That does not a necessity make," he said, a sense of sadness to his voice. "You don't need me, anymore, and it is not a bad thing to state as much. But while *I* still walk among the living—likely longer than you, I reckon—I must press on with what I believe to be right. You understand that?"

He did, and he nodded as much, but still, one aspect troubled him. "As I recall, you pondered returning as much an assassin as you would be a teacher."

"I recall the same."

"And?"

"And as you said, I'm trying to return home the right way; problem is what I think is 'right,' most others declare mad."

The men shared a chuckle at the all-too-true assessment. "So that doesn't answer my question," Aratus said, after a moment.

Ecdelus was slow to respond. "If you're asking if I *know* that I will not be an assassin in Megalopolis at some point…"

Aratus rolled his eyes, knowing he invited the man's philosophical wit—the more patient may call it genius—by the very structure of his question. "You are truly maddening. You know damn well whether you have an intent to kill that tyrant Lydiades."

"Intent's not knowledge."

"No? How about a fig shoved down your throat, is that knowledge?"

"Impossibilities. Both knowledge and your fig idea." The two laughed again. "No, lad, after all my thoughts and dwelling on this, I see that what you said a few weeks ago is right in a sense. I helped you back here, you stayed here, planted your seed here, and here it grew. The city's been stabilized." He paused, licking his lips in thought. "*I* can't be the seed, but I can spread them, I think," he said, looking to Aratus with squinting eyes. "Sow them, help them grow, like I did here."

"Ecdelus the farmer, you say?"

The older man looked askance at him with a crooked grin. "Surely, your pending death is what spurs your courage at this hour."

Aratus smiled back. "Some'd say that's the way of it."

The two watched the taller pankratiast pound his foe's stomach with a kick, dropping the smaller man to his hands and knees. As if on cue, the teacher was lambasting the fallen boy for failing to foresee the strike. Aratus smirked, reminded of those days in the sands that seemed never-ending, those days when a rage burned so brightly inside of him that no amount of fatigue could keep him off the sands or his opponents; a rage that led to a winning streak that some thought would never be snapped. Seemed like lifetimes ago now, and while that kernel of rage still simmered, it had morphed into something far more dangerous: a purpose.

"We'll drop the Syrian off after nightfall," he said after a pause. "After that, you probably won't see me again for some time, no matter what happens in Corinth. But I pray you see nothing but good fortune in Megalopolis."

"Wish you well too, lad," Ecdelus offered, and with characteristic briskness, headed off toward the staircase Aratus entered by. He stopped at the top of the stairs and looked back to the Strategos. "And remember—whether you fail or not, whether you live or die, it's a *stand that had to be made.*"

CHAPTER 13

16th Day of Apellaios, Year 2 of the 134th Olympiad
(August 7, 243 B.C.)

Dusk on the agora. Most nights it was the perfect time to enjoy the breezy relief of a setting sun, take in the painted sights of the city's many aesthetic triumphs, be it the colonnades lining the market or the statues by expert craftsmen. Maybe listen to a poet's ode as set to a tune or paired with the strings of a *lyra* or *kithara*, thespians aspiring to Sicyon's theater often taking their gifts to the masses free of charge. Aye, most nights Sicyon was one of the most idyllic poleis in all of Hellas.

Most nights.

Tonight, however, officers from a dozen poleis and soldiers of a dozen tongues kept the city alive and bustling. As Aratus emerged from the *Bouleuterium* with sergeants and League officials in tow, he felt for a moment like he was back in Corinth with all that he saw around him. Mercenaries gathered in groups of fives, tens, scores, sometimes more, adorned in all the varied cloaks and tunics of the places they called home; they hailed from across Hellas, even beyond, but most invariably came from Peloponnesian states. Sailors in sleeveless tunics mingled amongst them, warriors of Achaea looked about the city with a sense of awe, all while a seemingly never-ending stream of carts plodded to and from the port in the east. In fact, to say the city was merely "alive and bustling" was indeed a gross understatement.

"I'd hoped for better omens than those," Mnaseus said in his characteristic dour. Aratus followed his eyes upward and indeed found a patchwork of clouds marring a typically spotless summer sky.

"And I'd hoped you wouldn't take fear over such trivial things as a cloud or two."

"You're not the one that pilots those woodpiles we call ships," the Navarch added drily. "If ya did, you'd find a 'cloud or two' was nothing to trivialize."

Aratus frowned as he took in a sniff. "No sign of the *anemoi* winds; you'd smell the bloody port from here if there were a storm brewing."

"Hmph," the grizzled sailor grunted, folding bare arms of his chiton across each other. "Still don't like it."

Aratus smiled to himself, shooting a glance behind him at the rest of the Hellenes still making their way from the Council hall. Conspicuous enough was Agonippos, but not for his combativeness as expected; no, for his disarming cordiality at the final planning meeting, where he even went so far as to toast the Strategos for his efforts in coordinating the Aetolian campaign. Fellow Achaeans and Timanthes alike had traded looks of surprise, given that most had been bracing for tension. So if Mnaseus felt inclined to see bad omens in the skies above, then surely Aratus was entitled to find good ones on the grounds below.

"Maelstroms and storms aside, how do you feel about the campaign? You didn't say much in there, so I hope that's a sign of your endorsement."

The Navarch's weathered eyes vacantly scanned the humanity before him for a few moments. "Lad, at my age, you just point my ships in the direction you wish them to go, and I'll do my damnedest to make 'em go in that direction."

Aratus chuckled. "Does nothing rattle you as you near infirmity?"

"Not much."

"Should we all embrace our aging so gracefully, then," Aratus said, before narrowing his eyes on Mnaseus. "You truly have no feelings on any of it?"

"Any of what?"

"The campaign, dammit. The meeting. Any of it."

Mnaseus looked at him, hints of bemusement. "How do you feel about it, Strategos?"

"Me?"

"Aye. Do you feel vindicated now, for the way you humbled young Ago?"

Aratus gave him a crooked grin back. "Does it show?"

Mnaseus sneered. "I was embarrassed for the boy. Cowed like a yearling."

Aratus waved off the comment. "He'd be just as embarrassed to hear you calling him a 'boy,' if you're still so concerned for his feelings. In my eyes, I was proud of him, shows he can be brought into the fold. I've always said that—"

"And who'd have thought a tongue-lashing was all it took to get him in line?" Mnaseus asked with eyebrows raised, mouth frowning but for its corners. "Not me."

Their stare lingered for a bit before Aratus broke away. "I'd dare not ask the source of my good fortune; if he's inclined to act with an ounce of respect, then I won't question it, nor should you. Benefits us all in the end."

"Mm-hm."

He started to respond again but caught himself and simply scoffed. "For all the bloody Aetolians we have ahead of us, here we are discussing a petulant Dymean."

"No argument from me, lad. Given the way you left things in Aegium, I'd offer any sacrifice I could so this campaign in Aetolia turns out better than your last."

Mnaseus knew it was a sore subject, to say the least, and he cursed him for raising it, but he knew the old man never pulled his punches. "As a man of reason, you can't possibly blame me for the failures of that campaign. There were problems before I'd even left port, you know that."

"Strategoi must take the blame, that's all part of it," the Navarch said, before shrugging. "But what's the difference if I did blame you?"

"Because your opinion I actually value, Mnaseus. The men of that Council have fallen so far from the League's purpose, it's hard to give their thoughts weight at all, anymore."

The older man looked to the younger with a look of amused bafflement. "Aratus, do you have any idea what Margos has done for the League? Before you were even a thought in your mommy's mind?"

"Of course I know what he did."

"He *is* the League. It's not here today, without him."

"Aye, and he'll be the first to tell you that," Aratus said defiantly.

"Well, just remember you're not the first Hellene to saunter along with a pair of balls, aye?"

"Aye, and to you I'd say that what a man once *was* doesn't make him what he now *is*. *That's* the problem. There *was* no braver man than—"

A horn blew.

A loud one, enough to pierce the din of the agora.

The commanders' heads rose in unison at the sound, eyes widening in alarm.

"The hell was that for?" Mnaseus muttered under his breath.

"Don't know," Aratus replied.

Another horn.

"Shit."

"What is it?" the Navarch asked, face contorted in confused anger.

"Two means there's something going on."

"Where? Within the gates? The port?"

"No, beyond," he said, leaving the man to head west toward the acropolis road. "Stay here a moment, I'll try to—"

"Stay here? What's 'two horns' mean? We being attacked?"

"I don't know yet! It's just—it's just a warning that something is happening, somewhere outside the gates!"

"Who the hell would try anything with a full measure of troops and ships in port?"

Aratus stopped and looked at him. "You're a strategist, Mnaseus—why the hell *wouldn't* you try something with all your enemies in one place?"

The old man blanched as another horn blew. Out of the corner of Aratus's eye, he felt his young Hypostrategos marching toward him, but he pretended not to see him, turning westward once again.

"Aratus!"

The Strategos stifled a smile.

"Aratus!"

Both Agonippos and Mnaseus were following when he felt a pair of hands on his shoulders. "Sire!"

It was Euphranor, a skilled craftsman and one of his lieutenants on the acropolis; his youthful face was struck by fear, despite his linen breastplate and metal helmet.

"Tell me what could possibly have you blowing the horns on the eve of our bloody departure," Aratus growled at him, as his Navarch and Hypostrategos caught up to them. *"Tell me."*

"There's smoke on the northern horizon, sire. A wall of it's gone up—"

"Where?"

"Beyond the valley, er, past the far banks of the River Helisson."

"Beyond the Helisson?" Aratus repeated with furrowed brow. "Can you make out numbers? Can you make out *who* it is?"

"No... no, we can't see much of anything in this light," he said nervously, as Timanthes joined the group. "That much smoke, though, you would think at least battalion strength—"

"Oh, how could that be?" Timanthes demanded.

"Just an estimate, sire, that's all I can give."

"A battalion of *whom*? You're certain it's not one of ours?"

Euphranor shook his head. "Don't know. Some men were suggesting Aetolians, but—"

"Aetolians!" Mnaseus exclaimed.

"—but it's all conjecture..."

"The port," Mnaseus said harshly. "Has anything been seen near the port? The ships are mustered and almost entirely unmanned. One fire ship could—"

"No," Aratus stressed. "No one's breached the breakwaters or the east towers would have signaled as much."

"Well, let's not wait for that to happen, aye?" Timanthes said, eyes transfixed on his friend. "Let's take up arms; we've got more than enough to make a foray, at least see how many we're dealing with."

"Or if it's anything at all," Agonippos added, breaking his silence, expression utterly neutral.

Euphranor's back stiffened, face notably offended as he looked to Aratus, but he held his tongue. It was the respectful move, hard as it may have been given that he wasn't bound to take orders from those beyond Sicyon. "He wouldn't have sounded the alarm if it wasn't called for, Ago, but gods willing, you'll be right, and it's all an exercise in futility."

The young man nodded casually and looked away, taking interest in the rising clamor around them.

"You need to spread word of this throughout the city," Aratus said. "Forget the mercenaries, they'll simply want more coin if we ask them to help, but tell any other soldiers able to bear arms to bear them; instruct them I want two units formed, one to take to the Helisson Valley and investigate whoever the hell it is causing the fire, and another group to muster outside the southern wall by the Asopos Bridge."

"Aye, sire," Euphranor said.

Aratus looked to the Hypostrategos. "I'd like you to lead the northern contingent, Agonippos," he said, drawing a brief look of surprise from the young man. "Mnaseus will be checking in on the ships, when we find Cratinus he'll tend to the horse, and Timanthes will be calling Sicyon's thorakitai to arms; so would you do me that honor?"

Ago looked around the circle of men with a plain face before landing on the Strategos again. "You don't wish to lead your own city's protection?"

"I'm off to grab arms at my home then I'll take control of the south unit and circle around the west to reconnect with you. I have the utmost faith in you and in any event, I don't want you engaging in any fights yet; we're just looking for information, and should you see any sign of a hostile force, you back off and wait for the rest of us."

The Hypostrategos's gaze lingered on Aratus before he responded. "I'm happy to take the south unit instead of the north, if you'd like."

Aratus felt the group brace around him; the ball of fire in his stomach so familiar from his previous encounters with the upstart flickered. He ground his teeth, watching the blackness of the northern smoke mix with the sky's navy blue, before glaring at the man. "The north will be fine for you."

"Oh, what's it matter if he wants the south?" Mnaseus added with annoyed expression. "Let him have—"

Aratus's face flushed red with anger. "What matters is that I'm Strategos of the League and I'm Archon of Sicyon—and now I'm giving orders as to both, and you've heard them, so *go*," he growled, the group dispersing at length. All but one, dark eyes still locked on the Strategos.

What's your game, you bastard?

"Have you misunderstood me, Ago?"

The young man shook his head with a look of dubious concern. "Not in the slightest, Strategos. Off I go."

CHAPTER 14

*16th Day of Apellaios, Year 2 of the 134th Olympiad
(August 7, 243 B.C.)*

A harried crowd gathered on the moonlit street outside his abode, men, women, children, all in various stages of distress. They waited for him, of course, waited for their leader, even as he pushed his way through them as politely as possible, seemingly oblivious to their nervous energy.

"Aratus!" cried those that knew him personally.

"Archon!" cried those that didn't.

Finally, he turned as he reached his door, raising bare arms in placation. "My friends, my citizens, I promise you I've heard the alarms—"

"What're they for? What's been seen?"

"—and I assure you we are deploying the city's defenses as we speak."

"Defenses?" an old man said as he balanced himself atop a cane. "Defenses against what?"

"Ah, that's precisely the question, isn't it?" Aratus said with a grin and a nod. "And likely one with as benign an answer as we'd all expect while the city holds six thousand soldiers looking to wet a spear or two!"

The crowd gave an edgy laugh, buoyed by the Archon's confidence.

"But all the same, we're going to find out—*I'm* going to find out to be sure. I won't rest until it's done, you know that as well as I do."

A clamor rose anew but he wiped the smile from his face and turned away from the crowd, disappearing into his home. The calls of *"When, Archon?"* and *"How will you find out?"* followed his ears inside, but he simply leaned against the closed door with eyes shut, exhaling deeply.

You're doing this for them, Aratus… and you're almost there. When they know what you've done for them, when they see it with their own eyes, it'll all be easier. But for now, just keep moving. So far, so—

His eyes opened to find his wife standing alone beside their courtyard altar, arms crossed, her look stern and searching, at once pensive and anxious. He sighed and wiped a sweaty face. *Maybe there's no threat to my life outside Sicyon's walls this evening, but within them?* he thought, darkly amused. "Tele, my dear," he said awkwardly, breaking a veritable silence between them that had spanned nearly three weeks.

She stayed mute but he'd no time to await a response; likewise, he'd no time to indulge his guilt upon seeing her, much as he'd give almost anything to make her understand, make them all understand. No, that time had come and gone. Instead, he grabbed an oil lamp from a stand and marched straight for his andron, where behind the couch at the farthest corner was the package he'd left for himself in the wee hours that morning, wrapped tight in an unassuming blanket. It was a package of necessity.

It was a package for *war.*

A helmet, its bronze glinting in the lamplight, reinforced through the crown with a feathery plume of black, cheeks protected by dangling metal pieces on either side.

A cuirass of layered linen, shimmering now with silver-gray scales overlapping one another, its lower half cut into strips where the armor fell below the waist.

An oval shield over three feet high and half as many across, the leather stretched over its wooden frame painted white beneath the black of the League's *AX* monogram.

A seven-foot spear of the finest ashen wood, capped by an iron head; a straight-bladed *xiphos* with a pommel shaped like an ear, holstered into a black baldric to strap around the chest.

He ran a hand over the smoothness of the shield, losing himself for a moment as his finger traced its lettering; it hardly looked the way it did the last time it saw battle, awash in the crimson of Aetolian blood. Nowadays, the Achaeans were on standby for Aetolian raids, as they had to be. But even with that vigilance, even with the increased fortification of the coast and riverways through watchtowers and the like, a sizable raiding party came ashore just three years ago. Clambering along with swords, spears, and an appetite for destruction, it landed northeast of Pellene, then moved swiftly up the Sythas River valley, torching and looting outposts and farms along the way. Pellene relayed a panicked message to Sicyon as it battened down its defenseworks, prompting Aratus to speed toward the fray with a small corps of elite thorakitai.

Wasn't hard to find the bastards, he thought to himself, picturing the spires of black tendrils on the western horizon. *Followed the damn smoke.* After a forced night march, they arrived on the Sythasian banks to find the Aetolians seemingly without a care in the world as they headed for Pellene proper, so laden down with booty were they. Achaeans taken for slaves, mostly of the villages surrounding Pellene, shrieked upon sight of the shimmering Sicyonians, their grief overtaken by irrepressible hope. Before the hundreds of raiders had mind to form up, Aratus fell on them in a sloppy melee along the banks, short spears finding flesh in Aetolian bodies entirely barren of armor—armor doffed to make raiding easier, but at the risk of victims that could fight back. Even armorless and surprised, however, the vastly outnumbering Aetolians were able to smash their enemies back and send more than a few to the Styx; indeed, the lifeless faces of his fallen men haunted Aratus to that very day. Nevertheless, they bought time for Pelleneans to descend from their fortress to force a bitter retreat, forming a bond that remained strong with the Sicyonians ever since.

"On my word to the gods, we'll be back!" he remembered a nasty toothless raider spewing at him in his vile Aetolian twang, glowering as the Achaeans gave up the chase. *"Fight us like men and you'll see how—"*

"Shall I stand here in wonder, then?"

Startled, Aratus's thoughts vanished before his eyes. He looked back toward his wife, gently setting the shield down on the couch. "In wonder of what?"

He heard her scoff in disbelief. "Has the city's alarm not been sounded? The entire street's in a panic."

"There's nothing to be afraid of, Tele," he said curtly, turning back to his array of armaments.

"Why not?"

He didn't respond, didn't want to. He kneeled instead and reached for the first of his two bronze greaves, slipping it over his shin and knee before tightening it with garters at its top and bottom. The metal's coolness felt refreshing against his steamy skin.

"Why *not?*" she demanded again, small footsteps creeping toward his room. "Is there any other reason to sound the alarms than to say that there *is* something to be afraid of?"

Moving right on to his second greave, he simply shrugged. "Wife, my word on this issue should be all the reassurance you ever need. If you were in the slightest bit of danger, I would be the first man to tell you and the last man you'd ever see leave your side. And even if there were a danger, your hiding within the walls is precisely what you, what the whole *city* would be ordered to do, so… you're safe."

"Yet here you are suiting up for battle."

I can't have this clouding my mind, he thought to himself as he fell silent again, gritting his teeth. *I need all my wits for this night. You shouldn't have let things fester. She's too smart for it; too undeserving of—*

"Aratus!"

"Aye, Telesilla!" he barked, patience withering as sweat spilled down his forehead.

"You haven't spoken to me in weeks, I'm *scared!*" she cried, distraught. "Must I fight with you like I'm a child to get your attention?"

He rose to his feet in a huff with his cuirass in hand, back still to Telesilla. "I haven't had the slightest inclination you were of mind to talk to me those many days."

"Why would that be so?" she said, before throwing her arms out to her sides. "What is it that you hold so fiercely against me?"

Just as he'd slipped his right arm through a hole in the tube of the cuirass and wrapped the armor around his body, he paused finally and turned to look at her. She was steel, her proud jaw protruding like she was born to seat a throne, hazel eyes dry as if she'd no tears left to cry or never had them in the first place. True, he had no time to spare, but his heart softened upon the sight. "I hold nothing against you, Telesilla. I'm just… I'm just in a tremendous hurry and need to carry on here. I have to… I have to be on my way."

144

But now it was his wife's turn to remain silent, rejecting his explanation as poignantly as if through spoken word. He knew it and sighed.

"Truth be told, I feel horrid for the pain I've caused you. Pain to you, pain to us, pain to the daughter of Naukydes, one of the best men I've ever known," he said quietly, feeling both burdened and relieved as he bared his heart. "And I feel that every time I've opened my mouth over the last month, it's just made things worse. By the gods' witness, you know that's true."

She reached a hand out to his, her cold delicate fingers scraping the calluses of his battle-weary palms. His thumb stroked them back, leaving traces of dirt across her golden skin. Though his hand dwarfed hers, it was misleading to think she was some helpless babe in the woods in dire need of a man's instruction. He'd been more than convinced of that during their marriage, knowing had she been born a man, she would have been as fierce a fighter at his side as Timanthes had been all these years. Alas...

"I'm sorry this has happened to us."

"As am I," she replied softly, eyes on their interlocking hands before finding his somber face. "What's happening right now? Why are we safe?"

He licked his lips as if to respond but words escaped him.

"I've seen the ships in the harbor," she continued with a calm persistence. "I've seen all the soldiers camped here and about, seen some of the League's men. So when I hear you're leaving tomorrow for Aetolia, I *believe* it, but then..." She closed her eyes and sighed. "But then how would you do what you said about Corinth? Have you changed your mind? Did the Syrian you spoke of decide not to lead you after all?"

He shook his head lightly and found her eyes again, which seemed to fear his answer. "You asked once how you've failed me as a wife," he said gruffly, before gathering his breath. "But I say to you now, it is *I* who's failed you as a husband. You're—"

"Let's not speak of who's failed whom anymore."

"*You're* the wife I needed, but I am not the husband you deserve. So my penance for that will be the legacy I seek to leave behind for you, for our family."

She looked hard at him, eyes searching his face for the meaning behind his words but it didn't take her long. Her lips parted with a gasp, though one small enough to suggest she had at least considered the answer. "The city alarms were no surprise to you."

"No."

"It's tonight?"

"Aye."

Telesilla nodded slightly, gaze falling away from his for a moment.

"The gods know I've no desire to hurt you further, Telesilla," he said as his free hand reached up to a belly still only slightly plump. "Hurt our child."

"Aye?" she answered.

"Aye. No honorable man should."

"Yet, you still go."

"I do. And I know that means I *must* do two things at odds with one another, but what's a man to do in that situation? Truly, a drachma to the first philosopher who could give us the answer," he said with a tinge of frustration. After a thoughtful pause, however, he added, "Leaving my legacy behind to you is the only way I see that satisfies both; that you may find pride in my attack on Corinth someday and my child along with you. That the city and maybe even the League will honor you the same… should I fall. That my memory might live."

She looked up at him again and surprised him with a smile. "It's a high fancy you speak of, but I've nothing else to indulge myself with anymore," she said, shaking her head. "So perhaps I will."

He offered an unsure grin of his own in response. "I thought you'd be more apt to despise me."

She shrugged. "If Macedon has made you this way, then it's Macedon I should despise most of all, no?"

Though he'd be ecstatic if she really held the sentiment, he knew she was simply taking pains to cope with his decision; moreover, she *knew* he knew that. Nevertheless, he said nothing in rebuttal, playing along in his wife's fiction with a fuller smile, turning his attention back toward the left side of his cuirass where the armor tied together. To his further surprise, his wife's hands intervened, carefully tightening each cross-stitch that connected the two armor halves as she pushed his muscled arm overhead.

"You know how?" he asked quizzically.

Her eyes gave him the answer before her words did. "Have I not armed you before, Aratus?"

He honestly couldn't remember but she said it with such conviction that he didn't dare debate her on it. "Perhaps so…"

She grunted. "Well, in any event, you'd confess I can work with a thread, and this isn't beyond that," she said, giving the cuirass's stitching a final tug, before pulling the two shoulder straps down to do the same. "If I'm to see my husband off to the Styx, I'd have him presentable."

He chuckled awkwardly as a silence fell between them while her hands stayed busy.

"Think our boy will be a fighter like his father?" she asked finally with the inklings of a grin, slipping his baldric with sword across his body. "A wrestler? A runner? Or maybe a philosopher?"

"Hm," Aratus replied, caught off-guard by the question. "Well, your father's greatest gift to me was the education I received, far more so than the sands I trained in. The body can be taught to grow and prosper, almost in spite of itself. The mind, however… the mind takes constant prodding, constant challenging, but once it's been coaxed into form, it will see you to triumph in all manners of life. Wrestling, writing, what have you."

"So it's the books we should start with…"

"Aye," he said gently, before a final thought struck him. "And gods willing, he won't have the anger that made me succeed on the wrestling sands, either."

"Oh, perish the thought," she said as she clasped his face with her hands. "That was born of something our children—our child—will never know, I pray."

"I too pray that's so," he replied, covering her hands with his. "And what if it's a girl?"

"It's a boy."

"So you've said, my dear," he said, amused at her adamance. "But if it is a girl, I want her your mirror image in fight and spirit and mind; I want her *taught*. Home-running, certainly, but equally so in the arts, the sciences, politics; athletics if she's so inclined. Will you promise me that? Whether I live or die?"

She closed her eyes and nodded painfully. He leaned forward and kissed her forehead. "Good, and you'll promise me too that she'll be named for the strongest woman I've ever known," he said, tilting Telesilla's head up to look deeply into her eyes. "I want her named for my wife, daughter of Naukydes, honor to that legendary woman who fended off the Spartans, aye?"

It was the closest he'd seen her eyes to watering, but still, she managed to hold firm. Instead, she simply shook her head with a disbelieving frown instead. "Hardly feel strong. Not anymore, I don't."

"You are, Telesilla, and I need you continue so. Maybe not 'fighting the Spartans strong,' but strong."

She chuckled through a stuffy nose. "Must we keep talking as if we're saying goodbye?"

"We must, in fact."

"Can't we just pretend—"

"No… or at least for one more moment, no," he said as he pulled a sealed scroll from his "package of war" to place in his wife's hands.

Her brow furrowed. "What is this?"

"It's a letter to the city's *Boule* if I don't return. It has my wishes and instructions, sealed in my name, and no other's. It will help any turmoil caused by my de—well, caused by my absence."

She rolled the scroll around in her hand, staring at it with a growing frown. "And why should I have it?"

"Because if it needs to be delivered, I trust you above all others to see that it's done. It would be your 'Telesilla of Argos' moment," he said with conviction, shaking his head as he pondered Sicyon's aftermath if he died. "Freedom's a fragile thing, especially amidst the plague of tyranny in the Peloponnesus; the weak *will* cave to a strong-willed evil. So it'll be your moment

147

to see to it that the city doesn't come apart at the seams, much as I hope that never comes to be."

Her eyes rose to his. "And you're telling me this now? All these days of silence when I didn't even know which gods to pray to for you, and now—"

He placed a hand along her jaw to quiet her. "I hadn't planned to tell you this before I left; I'd planned to have a messenger ready to tell you should he see the worst happen at Corinth. Instincts told me to tell you now, though. Gods willing, they can be relied on."

She nodded in silence as the pit in his stomach told him it was time. "I have to leave now," he said softly, taking a deep breath before donning the felt cap he'd wear beneath the abrasive metal of his helmet. With spear in hand, he turned to see Telesilla holding his shield. He smiled.

"You told me something else about the Spartans, I remember; an old saying of their women," she said stone-faced, holding firm as her husband reached for the *thureos*. "'Return with this or upon it'?"

He chortled. "Aye?"

"Well, damn the shield—I'll take you without it," she said, without an ounce of jest. "Just win or come home…"

He embraced her body one final time against his metal-scaled chest, swallowed his guilt, then headed for their front door.

"He'll be named Aratus, by the way, this son of yours," she called out, pausing him. "So if the gods take you in Corinth, just know there'll be another of your name waiting, another of your line."

With a smile, he looked back with a lightened spirit. "I would like that."

Pushing the door aside, he was off into the night.

Off to war.

CHAPTER 15

16th Day of Apellaios, Year 2 of the 134th Olympiad
(August 7, 243 B.C.)

By the time Aratus was a half mile out from Sicyon's Sacred Gate, the road had descended nearly 350 feet, with another fifty to drop before he reached the bridge. It'd been chaos getting out of the city, what with horns blowing, soldiers barking orders, priests chanting when they weren't scrambling to secure their temples' valuables. Had the guards of the tower not seen the black plume of Aratus's helmet, they likely would have mistaken him for any number of the thorakitai and thureophoroi trotting toward the rendezvous point at the Asopos Bridge. Instead, they gave him a proper salute and wished him well on this night of unexpected excitement.

Now, as he turned and looked back at the darkened façade of the gate and his city's walls cast aglow under the moonlight, it struck him that it could be the last time he'd ever see the guardsmen again, the last time he'd ever pass through that portal so ornamented with reliefs and bolstered with towers, their torchlight growing fainter with every step he took. In an odd way, it brought him back to the night he'd so improbably first scaled those walls, an endeavor undertaken with little more planning than simply deciding to do it.

He chuckled to himself. *Has anything really changed?*

But he only allowed himself a moment to indulge in the nostalgia. Blinking hard and swallowing deeply, he rapped the sword resting snugly against his chest, gripped his spear tightly, and turned away. "Why think as a dying man should?" he chided himself under his breath. "Of course I'll return."

A crowd had gathered on the western side of the bridge, a modest gray crossing that spanned seventy feet abutment to abutment, planks resting on two stone and mortar piers in between. It was wide enough to fit ten men abreast, but in truth, the river ran so weak and shallow in the dead of summer that it could be crossed without need of the bridge if one didn't mind damp sandals. For the same reason, the bridge was rather lightly staffed with guards this time of year, Aratus preferring to rely on his network of observation towers placed strategically throughout Sicyonia instead.

The men mingling about bore colors from all of the League's cities. There had to be at least a few hundred by this point, and though he was expecting upward of a thousand before he took off, he was encouraged by the early returns. Most were thureophoroi, standard infantry bearing thrusting or throwing spears with little armor about the chest and only helmets and large oval shields for defense; some of those shields had the same *AX* monogram of Aratus's, others a letter or two from their home-polis, and others had nothing distinctive at all beyond bronze bosses in their centers. The rest of the troops were his expertly trained and armed thorakitai, distinguished tonight among the rest by their uniform silver chests of armor. He'd selected each member of his thorakitai corps personally and saw to it that their trainers had everything they needed to keep them as elite as he'd envisioned.

He instantly recognized some of the captains from prior campaigns and returned their curious but friendly gazes with a smile—Agesarchus of Tritaea, Xenophon of Aegium, Oebatus of Dyme, Callicrates of Leontium, Promachus of Pellene, to name a few. They were good men, all of them, and even where he'd quarreled with their cities' politicians, he'd almost always seen eye to eye with the soldiers. On the battlefield or campaign trail, you either trusted the man next to you or you didn't, as enemy spears and arrows cared nothing for politics; if no one else did, the soldiers understood that.

The captains themselves were used to commanding units ranging anywhere from a few dozen men at a time to a few hundred depending on the numbers that had been called to arms and the formations they'd chosen to take. It went without saying that poleis allegiances fell by the wayside when it came to command of the troops; a Tritaean unit was just as likely to fight alongside a unit of Dymeans as he was Tritaeans, just as Ceryneians could align next to Pharaeans, Patraeans, or both. Indeed, the cavalry platoon Aratus had served earlier in the decade was a true amalgamation of the League's poleis. The rationale was simple and accepted as a fundamental tenet of League membership—they were all *Achaeans*, which, save for Dorian Sicyon, they'd always been ethnically, but now politically too.

He extended a hand in greeting to Promachus, a tall man wearing a tunic of light red with a helmet tucked under his arm, his normally light hair made dark by the late hour. Aratus looked over his shield with its ΠΕΛ monogram and gave it a whack with the pole of his spear. "Will you ever add the League's insignia to that piece of wood, Promachus?" he asked with an energetic lightness about him.

The captain chuckled. "Not so long as it keeps me alive, as is. Where's the wisdom in tempting fate?"

Aratus grunted in amusement. "Your family's well? Been too long since I've seen your uncle; thought I might see him among Pellene's ranks this year."

"Family's well, indeed. Though I'm afraid my good uncle's seen the last of his time out here in the fray, I think. His shoulder is so racked with pain that he can barely hold a shield at the level anymore."

Aratus shook his head in disappointment. "A fate that awaits us all, unfortunately; all we can do is hope to face that day with grace, as I'm sure he has. I shall pray for him. A good teacher for you growing up, anyhow, no?"

"Undoubtedly so," the young captain said proudly, before embarrassedly stifling a yawn. "Though I imagine he'd be asking the same thing we're all asking about now—the hell are we doing out here at this hour on the eve of a campaign?"

The Strategos looked at him with a fading grin. "If only the people causing mischief out here would be so kind as to tell us," he said drily.

"Aye, if only," Promachus said with a roll of his eyes. "Just that every poleis within a day's ride has to know how many we have afoot here, so I'm surprised anyone would pick tonight of all nights to start that mischief."

"Their bad fortune?"

"Or our good? But here we are, all the same."

"Aye," Aratus replied without elaboration.

After a pause, Promachus asked, "How many more are we waiting on, then? I can take a squadron and make an initial run over the bridge, if you'd like." An altruistic offer on its face, though his tone smacked of impatience. "I think you see we have the men for it."

Which may well be true, but the one person the Strategos did *not* see was Timanthes of Sicyon, an absence which surprised him. "Not yet, but not long now, either," he said quietly to Promachus as he moved past him on his way to Lysistratos, a burly junior officer of his thorakitai. Upon sight, the soldier straightened his back with a salute, black eyes wide over a pursed line of a mouth.

"Sire."

Returning the salute, Aratus looked back to what seemed like a faraway Sacred Gate now. "Lysistratos, you've seen Timanthes this evening, have you not?"

The man's brow furrowed as if he'd been asked a riddle. "Aye, sire. Timanthes was the man who called us to arms."

"Aye, as he was supposed to," the Strategos said. "I'm a bit surprised he hasn't arrived yet... did you see him long afterward?"

The officer looked down with a frown before shaking his head. "Not that I recall, sire. He disappeared from the barracks after his alert, though nothing suggested he'd be long in coming."

"Hm..." he said, suddenly troubled but quickly blaming his anxiety for this night of nights. Everything slowed down when desire was at its highest, did it not? He knew he'd be lying to himself, however, if he wasn't equally concerned that the stream of troops flowing down the path to the bridge had slowed to a trickle.

"There a problem, sire?"

"No."

"Shall I return to the barracks and inquire? Take a look around the city? Wouldn't take me long to get there and back, you know I wouldn't dither."

"No doubt you wouldn't," he said tersely. "But that would imply there's a problem, wouldn't it?"

The junior shrugged. "Or that you're just curious. Same way I'm curious as to why we were told to bring the scaling ladders..."

Aratus quickly shot him a scolding look. "Being a soldier is a curious lot, isn't it?"

"It can be."

"Why shouldn't we have the ladders?"

Lysistratos couldn't disguise a slanted grin, eyes refusing his general's. "On a cautionary inspection into some folks setting fires here and there? Seems—"

"Like a good idea, aye?" Aratus said, thrusting a few fingers into the man's chest, but allowing his glare to fade.

"Aye, sire," he said with a back that stiffened again and a face that went blank. "Apologies, sire."

Aratus nodded as he looked away. His junior officers, and Lysistratos chief among them, were strong men, confident men that Aratus took pains to keep rapport with; but even they had to be reminded where the Strategos's line was at times. "And it's true we don't know where these 'firestarters' are holed up, so just in case," he continued in needless punctuation to his rationale. "But enough of that; have the men form ranks, files of eight and count off. I need a precise count on where our numbers are."

"With honor, sire."

And I need to know precisely where gods-forsaken Timanthes is as well.

But he'd barely finished the thought, barely heard Lysistratos's boisterous commands to the gathered soldiery, when he got his answer—one that concerned him from the start.

A shadowed figure moved briskly down from the gates—too briskly—toward the men. Dark as it was, Aratus had no doubt the armored shadow was his friend, moving quickly to meet him on the gathering's edge. What he met was a panting Sicyonian, his curls clinging to a forehead slickened with sweat as he bent over to rest hands on knees. Yet despite his gasps, Timanthes's face was nearly devoid of color, his normally relaxed eyes wide with alarm.

Words escaping him, Aratus simply upturned his hands.

"He knows."

A chill ran through him. "What?"

Timanthes swallowed deeply as he rose from his crouch, throwing his shield and spear aside. "Something's going on up there, something's happened. But it's pretty damn clear he knows."

Aratus shook his head. "Who knows? And knows what?"

Timanthes gave him a cock-eyed stare through his breaths. "Agonip—"

"Shit."

"Aye."

Aratus's free hand found his mouth, running fingers over a layer of stubble. "How?" he asked in wonder. "What did he say to you?"

His friend threw his hands out. "I was making my rounds with the soldiers in the city, talking to the captains and the like, telling them to report." He nodded toward the men mustered a few yards beyond them. "A fair number made it down here, but dammit all if that little worm didn't step in after I'd talked to some Dymeans."

"Oebatus is here..."

"Aye, he must have left before I ran into Agonippos."

"Well, that bastard was supposed to be beyond the western gates by now!" Aratus said, feeling a rage swell inside him. "He should damn well have his men beyond the Helisson!"

"He doesn't. And we'd be fools to think that's happening now. He commanded the remaining Dymeans and anyone else who'd listen not to move an inch."

"He *commanded...*"

Timanthes nodded. "Said there was no threat and not to worry any longer and that everyone was to stay put 'til further notice. Looked me dead in the eyes and told me as Hypostrategos, the League's forces were his to command in your absence, that he carried rank at the moment, and if you had issue with it, he'd wait your return in the agora."

The Strategos turned away from his friend, dropping his spear and placing hands on his hips.

"Of course... I told him it was insubordination, that he was in violation of his duties, that—"

"How could he have known?" Aratus muttered, gazing vacantly northward toward the coast.

"I can't say. *He* didn't say."

"But you found him sincere? Genuine, I mean?"

"Clear as we'd both fear, I'd say. Said he knew it was a ruse meant to get him beyond the walls and away from whatever you've planned."

"Did he mention Corinth?"

"No," Timanthes replied.

Not that it matters, I suppose. He'd be a bloody fool not to conclude that, if anything's afoot, Corinth would be the goal. But still...

"How?" Aratus asked aloud once more, turning to look back at Timanthes, but finding the sight of him sent suspicious waves rippling through him. His friend's eyes narrowed in response.

"Come now..."

"You swear to me?"

"Gods watch this, he accuses me! *Me!*" Timanthes bellowed, eyes to the sky.

"Mind your noise!" the Strategos said with a glance back at his troops. "I'm not accusing you of a thing, I'm just... I'm just trying to figure this out..."

"Aye, well, leveling that glare at me is the wrong way of going about it," Timanthes scoffed. "This raid of yours is making you lose sight of things, that's all that's clear. To even hint at such things—"

"You've never approved of what I'm trying to do here, don't deny that now."

"And that makes me turn traitor? Backstabber after I pledged my word in spite of my disagreement? After how many years, how many struggles? Am I so base to you?"

"*No*," the Strategos affirmed through gritted teeth. "So just swear to me, Timanthes; just so I can hear it and put it to rest."

His friend shook his head in disgust. "I'll swear again and I do swear again. Doesn't help us at all."

"All right, then what is a help? There's only so many people that had any inkling of this. Agonippos hadn't a reason in the world to doubt the legitimacy of our alarms unless he'd been told otherwise, and clearly he has."

A tense silence fell between them for a moment, as Aratus's mind raced uncontrollably. "Any of them show suspicions?" Timanthes asked, nodding toward the gathered troops.

"No," Aratus said. "Lysistratos thought it curious we've the ladders, and he's probably not the only thorakites to think so, but he made no more of it than that. And we've kept the ladders covered so we don't alert the rest."

"Ecdelus?"

Aratus shot a look of disbelief in his friend's direction. "Much to your chagrin, I think not."

"You said he was upset with being left out of this..."

"Aye, but deep down he knew I'd done him a favor, despite the bluster. He's made his peace with his decision to leave for Megalopolis and has been holed up in preparation. Accidentally he could've tipped our hand, I suppose, overseeing the Syrian, but... no."

"The Syrian, then? Any of them?"

He pictured the men's faces, pondering whether Erginus or his brother could have possibly played a role, but he had to shake his head at it. "Dionysius was locked solid with Ecdelus since I saw him last, and Eck knew to send word at the slightest sign of trouble. Besides, even if that was the case, even if the Syrian had broken free, what would make the man confess to whatever it is he knows? And to whom? Why would he think it would mean anything to anybody?"

Timanthes grunted.

"And Erginus hasn't been seen near the city in weeks, but even so, the man stands to inherit a fortune win or fail with me."

"Sounds like you trust the Syrians more than me," Timanthes sneered.

"Nonsense. But in Erginus's case, we can pay him far more than I can see any other in the League... as far as I know."

His friend sighed. "So not me, not Ecdelus, not the Syrians..."

"Aye."

"And Xeno obviously came through on setting the fires, so he's..."

But Timanthes's words trailed off precisely as Aratus's eyes relocked on him. A new burning sensation spread over the Strategos's neck.

"Could he have?" Timanthes asked quietly.

The suggestion quickly grew beyond possibility in Aratus's mind, head slowly nodding. "Indeed, he could have," he said gravely.

They briefly fell quiet again, before Aratus offered simply, "He's hedging, that coward. He's bloody hedging."

"On what?"

"On us failing. He didn't think we could fucking do it, that *coward*!"

"So he told Ago, but then set the fires anyway, to—to—"

"Just to see our reaction, Timanthes," Aratus said sharply. "And that reaction tonight surely proved to Agonippos that he was being truthful, no?"

Timanthes grimaced in bafflement. "After Titane and all the protection you've given him? For all the years of favor and coin, you really think this to be the case after the way we left things with him not eight days ago?"

"So maybe he thought about it more, maybe he thought he could woo the rest of the *Boule*, maybe he thought he would sell me out and seek the King's services again after all. I don't know! But it makes a hell of a lot more sense than any other option I've heard. He does this, it either ruins me or kills me, but it would sure make him look good to everybody else, I'd reckon."

"If this is true, I'll have his head on a pike tomorrow," his friend declared after a moment of stunned silence.

But the bandit's fate or the pain that such a betrayal would inflict upon him were the least of Aratus's concerns. More important was that if it was in fact true that he could no longer trust Xeno, then what about the uprising in Corinth? Had he ever even bothered to go and seek out Timodemus? Maybe he did, he thought on the one hand. Maybe Xeno had hedged even further, helping facilitate the uprising to help Aratus in Corinth, should he make it that far. Then if he were to somehow succeed in Corinth, he would reap Aratus's favor; if he failed in Corinth, he would be free to court the League or the King.

"Bastard," he finally muttered with a shake of his head, the various permutations driving him to greater levels of fury. "How could this happen to me on this of all nights?"

"No doubt it's a foreboding sign—"

"But the rest of the omens were so *good*," Aratus protested, recalling the animal's bloodletting he'd witnessed earlier that day. "Omens for crossing the river, omens for fighting."

"The blood always runs the way we need it to eventually, doesn't it?" Timanthes replied coolly.

"Some practice sacrifice that way, but I don't. I take what it tells me. Even still, what about the rest of the signs since this—"

"I don't say a thing about any other signs, I just say that a betrayal discovered on the very precipice of a great endeavor is as *bad* an omen as you'll find anywhere. *That* is what matters now."

"Cowardice is *not* an omen."

"Well, there's no more time for debating this; you need to make a decision," Timanthes snapped with an exasperated look. "Ago said as I'd left that he'd come down here himself to 'talk,' if need be. Maybe an idle threat, maybe not…"

The threat enraged him further as he looked up at the city walls on the hill. "I can't go back up there," he muttered softly.

"Then you'll wait for him here?"

But Aratus was slow to respond, and in truth, he didn't know how, only that he didn't want to. *"Lysistratos!"* Aratus suddenly yelled, his friend flinching.

Footsteps behind him. "Aye, sire?"

"How many?"

"Three hundred seventy-two, plus the hundred thorakitai."

Aratus closed his eyes and bit his bottom lip. *Not even half.*

"Do you have orders, sire?"

"Then you'll wait for him here?" Timanthes's question echoed again in his head, a surreal sensation coupled with eyes that watered in focus upon the city. At last, in near whisper, *"I've waited long enough."*

"Pardon?"

He grabbed his spear from the grass, fixing his gaze upon Lysistratos as he rose. "Prepare to march."

* * *

He could take them only so far before they'd begin to wonder. Wonder why they'd marched in a straight line without pause for almost two hours; wonder why they'd been kept in obscurity as to *what* exactly they were looking for; hell, probably more than a few thorakitai still pondered the damn ladders. So when he came within eyeshot of the River Nemea, he knew it was time. Though it was a "river" in name only this time of year, its relevance was political rather than geographical.

The Nemea was the border between Sicyonia and Corinthia.

In truth, one would never know it. For the same reason Aratus kept the Asopos crossing lightly guarded, the same was even truer for the Nemea; as it was little more than a damp gully-bed dotted with pebbles and healthy weeds, "guarding" its formal crossings would be an exercise in futility. The bridges over the river served mainly as conduits for carts and beasts, but the rest of the traveling Hellenes would be just as likely to tread through the riverbed itself.

All the same, he kept his troops in disciplined silence throughout their march, issuing directions with nothing more than points and nods to his captains. The irony wasn't lost on him, of course, that he looked backward for signs of Agonippos giving chase as much as he looked forward for any Corinthian guards keeping watch along the fast approaching border. To the former, Aratus had requested that his Sicyonian bridge guards "hinder" any pursuit of his troops, an order that left the soldiers mystified; nonetheless, the results thus far appeared to prove their obedience, as Aratus had seen not a trace of the young Dymean, or anyone else for that matter.

"Turning back?" Timanthes asked sarcastically as Aratus's pace slowed to a halt. He'd been surprisingly quiet about, even accepting of, his decision to proceed with less than half the numbers he'd expected to take to Corinth's walls. Timanthes's disapproval had been palpable, but he also knew that Aratus would have marched alone if he'd had to. Aratus was glad he didn't have to.

Even so, the Strategos couldn't fake good humor at the moment, his mind hopelessly fixed on their destination. He knelt down to the grass below, running a hand through dry, crusty soil, and sighed. Despite the days and weeks that led up to this, he had yet to conclude what he'd say to the men, his eyes ever searching the eastern horizon for the elusive words. Finally, he just shook his head and rose.

"Take a knee, lads," he ordered to Promachus and his other forward captains. The men were in a semicircle around him in short order, ten ranks deep at nearly forty a row. Timanthes stood off to the left of the gathering, eyes on his friend with arms crossed. The Strategos scanned them all in poignant silence, even the crickets and nightbirds seemingly quieting before him, his heart thumping the way it had in the Aegian *Bouleuterium* a month ago. "Does anyone know why we're here?" he asked with a raspy voice.

"Been warned of raiders, sire," a soldier offered meekly. "Were told we were out here to look into it."

"No," Aratus replied with a shake of his head. "Why are *we* here? Why are *you* here, my friend? Why not another man? Why were *you* chosen?"

The young warrior looked perplexed. "Sire?"

"Because the gods willed it," he said with conviction. "The gods chose you for this night, they chose me to lead you. They've chosen *us* to attempt something magnificent tonight, something unimaginable just a month ago."

His audience's breathing crawled to a halt. His had too.

"I want to tell you something," Aratus said, hands mounting on hips. "It's a tale of the gods, one you've surely heard before at some time in your early years; certainly every Sicyonian among us has heard it, but I suppose some of my friends from the far side of the Achaean League may not be as familiar." He paused. "But it's about a place not far beyond this river; it's about Corinth. It's about the Acrocorinth, that mountain peak whose shadow nearly blots out the city it's meant to protect.

"You see, at one time, Poseidon had a dispute with Helios about that mountain peak; Poseidon coveted it, he desired it, to the extent that the gods nearly came to battle over it. But Briareos, one of the very giants that overthrew the Titans at Olympus, he intervened in the dispute; he arbitrated between them, and in so doing got them to agree that to Poseidon would fall possession of the Isthmus and the lands surrounding it. But to Helios," he said, eyes nearly watering, finger pointed to the sky, "to Helios, he gave the Acrocorinth, to have and to hold and to do what he pleased with it. And though Helios in turn gifted it to fair Aphrodite, that fortress, my friends—is the fortress of the sun."

He looked to his feet for a moment before breathing deep and continuing. "That fortress has been corrupted. It's been dominated by a man and king that would sooner have the whole of Hellas pay homage to him than win their respect. It's been held by a people that have taken no shame in using it to keep every Hellene, certainly every Achaean, in paralysis and fear, living 'free' only to the extent it pleases 'His Majesty'—*though that is not freedom!* So tonight, the gods have told us to strike back."

The faces around him remained as baffled as they'd been initially, but Aratus felt a surge of confidence rushing through him with every word he spoke. "Lads, we're not out here to chase bandits setting fires. We never were. And you know I'd sooner fall on my sword than deceive my own troops, but a mission as critically important, as critically secret as this one had to be kept that way until the final hours—well, those final hours are here. As we speak, a man at Corinth waits to lead us to a weak point in the Acrocorinth walls, a spot where even the fortress is vulnerable to a surprise attack. Within the city itself lay rebels waiting to rise up with us, if we can only give them the excuse." *And if we can find them*, he thought to himself in a split-second of doubt, the detail that gave him the most concern of anything.

Callicrates of Leontium spoke after a brief moment of silence, no doubt echoing the group's sentiment. "You mean to attack Corinth?"

Aratus smiled at the simple elegance of the question. "I do. I will. And I wouldn't do it if I didn't think we could succeed or that the gods didn't favor this, but for weeks I've been told otherwise. And though I'd much prefer to have them performed before your eyes, I can tell you that even the sacrifices today bled just right."

"Will the rest of the army be joining us in this endeavor?" Callicrates continued quietly, before considering his question and adding, "Does the rest of the army even know?"

Aratus shook his head. "The gods chose you, Callicrates. They didn't choose them. And lest you wonder—*no*, the League as a whole doesn't know about this either. Revelations came to light since the Council last convened and we had to act before this opportunity was lost. And lest you wonder *another* thing—*no*, I am not requiring you to join me. In fact, each of you is free to leave at your choice, to walk back to Sicyon the way we came. But to those so inclined I would beg you consider this before you leave…

"*This* is what your life has been building to!" he urged through clenched jaw. "Every breath, every moment, every step you've taken, every sword you've swung, every life you've created, every life you've taken, *this is it!* This is why! A chance to be remembered for all eternity, and in that, a chance at immortality! Isn't that all any brave man could ask for in his life? That one chance? Well, that chance is here, lads. The biggest gift you could ever give to your family, your polis, your League, it all lies within that fortress of the sun. Control it, and trade flows into the League at levels unimaginable; control it, and our children take breaths of free air they haven't seen in a century; control it, and we say and affirm to the world that we are *free* Greeks, ones not afraid to take a stand against the strongest man in Hellas!"

His chest heaved up and down, eyes wild and wide, voice dangerously loud, but he didn't care anymore. "With the gods' favor, I will lead you tonight. I'll be the first to cross the Nemea, the first past Corinth's wall, the first up the fortress hill; you'll never face a danger that I won't face head-on first. All I ask is that you join me in this feat; join me so that I won't bask alone in the adulation of Helios as I stand upon his mountain and plant our flag in its soil!"

He turned finally, pleased with his message but nervous that his troops wouldn't follow him as he took his first steps into the muck of the River Nemea.

He wasn't a few paces in before Timanthes had returned to his side. His friend whacked him hard in the back and Aratus gave him a stiff nod in return.

"Thorakitai!" he heard Lysistratos call out behind him. *"March!"*

He smiled as he heard the jingle of their armor trailing just behind him. The boots of dozens, then scores, of Achaeans soon followed.

Aye, some left. Some stayed put for a while before they left too. But most embraced the gods' offer, their leader's invitation. Most formed up in their thin column for the five-hour walk, laden with arms, armor, weapons—and ladders. And by the dead of the night, a hostile little army of four hundred was embarked upon one of the most audacious marches in the annals of the Hellenes.

They marched upon the greatest city in southern Greece.

PART III
CORINTH

CHAPTER 16

*17ᵗʰ Day of Apellaios, Year 2 of the 134ᵗʰ Olympiad
(August 8, 243 B.C.)*

Oh, Mnaseus, my friend, Aratus thought as he watched clouds roll in from the Corinthian Gulf, all but blotting out the moon. *And you thought the clouds were a bad sign. Something to fear.* He smiled. *Not on this venture… not on this night.*

He'd fretted about little since they'd crossed the Nemea. The path he'd chosen, the omens he'd seen, the fortune that seemed to smile on him and his men; all served only to bolster his confidence. They'd seen almost no traffic since the crossing, marching over the Corinthian plain with impressive rapidity given the load each soldier carried. Farms and homesteads along the way seemed sleepy and uninterested, bandits roamed out of sight, and trade wagons must have taken the older, more frequented southern path to Sicyon, leaving the northern trail to the Achaeans.

No, there'd been little to worry them yet, except one thing—moonlight. Sharpened spearheads and swordpoints, polished armor and helmets—they made for a handsome army on parade and an intimidating one on the battlefield, but when stealth dictated success or failure, their shimmer could alert the enemy—a death sentence. The clouds that so vexed the sailor Mnaseus in Sicyon had vanished for the bulk of their trek, leaving the sky as spotless and bright as Hellenic summer nights typically were. As a result, every glance at his troops saw his anxiety rise, fearing the moon's reflection as if the soldiers wielded raging torches, just beckoning Macedonian attention, testing the very limits of the gods' favor.

And then, just as they'd drawn to within a mile of Corinth's walls, near enough to catch sight of the very Sicyonian Gate that they were avoiding in favor of the Phliasian, the clouds came in. Instantly, the troops and city were blanketed in darkness, letting the Achaeans veer south in good order and move calmly into the prickly brush of the foothills off the main road. They reached the hill's grove just outside the Phliasian Gate no worse for wear, save for scraped shins and knees during that final stretch.

"So far, so good…" he muttered.

A coo of a bird. Or a poor imitation of one, at least.

Aratus returned the signal as he scanned the blackened grove.

"So where's the rest?" a voice called from behind him.

Aratus about-faced with a wry smile. "What do you mean?"

"I mean I'm no man of numbers, as you well recall," the gruff Syrian Erginus replied, waving a hand toward the soldiers filtering into the grove behind the Strategos. "But you're lookin' a little light to be saying you're a thousand strong."

"Did I say a thousand?"

Erginus scowled, a poor detector of sarcasm. "Aye, ya did. And that ain't a thousand, is it?"

"Thousand or not, the gods walk among us. We may as well have *twenty* thousand."

Erginus shot a wary glance at Timanthes and Promachus, the pair having made their way up the hill to Aratus's side. "Well, if the gods wanted to grab a spear or two, I wouldn't stop them."

"Don't you lose your nerve on me now," Aratus warned, only half-kidding.

"M'nerves *were* built on a thousand men, is all I'm saying…"

"Oh, never mind that," Aratus chided confidently. "Even had I brought a thousand, we would have still been outnumbered, so it's simply a matter of degree. Aye?" he asked with a pointed look.

The Syrian would only grunt, avoiding the Sicyonian's eyes.

"Besides that, we've the people of Corinth as our allies. But look, this night has always been about stealth, and it still *is* about stealth. If we're detected too soon, it won't make a damn bit of difference what our numbers run."

In truth, Aratus wasn't that naïve about any of it. Aye, he'd no doubt the gods favored him, no doubt they'd spoken to him, but he was also no fool to practicalities—their numbers, their odds, their unknown support within the city. And truly, since his suspicions of Xenophilus first took root, he'd grown only more certain that it was he who'd betrayed his plans to Agonippos, and if so, that he'd probably never made any effort in Corinth. But what Erginus needed right now, what all of the men needed, was to hear unwavering confidence, not a litany of the Strategos's doubts.

"Well, while I'm still alive, I should ask you—my brother's well?"

"Your brother's fine. He asks that you do the family proud; that you focus on the task at hand and get your generous leader to that bloody fortress like you planned."

The Syrian let out a phlegmy guffaw that seemed to surprise him, looking back at Aratus with his toothless grin. "Aye, I bet he did. And I bet he's turned painter and singer among you enlightened Sicyonians?"

Aratus kept a serious face. "Sculptor, I believe," he said to another laugh.

"He'd sooner grow hooves and a pair of horns."

As the last of his men had made their way into the copse, Aratus pointed Erginus in the direction of the city. "So then…"

The Syrian simply nodded his head with a vanishing smile, and the two men instinctively crept toward the tree line, followed in toe by Timanthes and Promachus. The copse in which they stood straddled a subtle crest barely 150 yards from the Phliasian Gate, foreboding wooden doors meeting a path sloping gently downward. The portal, bookended by two square towers capped with triangular roofs, was just part of a mile-long wall circuit extending north toward the coastal plain and south up the western rim of the Acrocorinth's crag. Within the wall's shadow and not far beyond the southern edge of the trees was a small, but well-kept temple to Hera, seemingly quiet now but still a potential source of betraying eyes.

Looming above everything, of course, was the mountain itself, its monstrosity omnipresent and overbearing, but it was the nearby gateway upon which Aratus was now transfixed. His eyes scanned blackened ramparts with walkways wide enough for several men to walk side by side, finding a few figures coming in and out of view as they paced between the two towers, nothing more than shadows against a meager torchlight. Even their choice of weaponry was a mystery from his vantage.

Are there two up there? Three? Four?

Regardless of the number, one thing was clear—the gates were sealed and looked unlikely to part ways for anyone.

"So we try the gate first, aye?" Erginus asked, breaking the men's contemplative silence. "Put a handful of us out there as wayfarers to lure them out? Merchants, as we discussed?"

"Mm," Aratus grunted, wetting dry lips. "And at this hour, you remain certain a traveling merchant wouldn't be far-fetched if you're a guardsman?"

The Syrian shook his head vigorously. "In this city? Never. People bloody coming and going from this place all the time; trade coming in from every corner of the world. Shouldn't raise an eyebrow… if done right."

"And you've brought the necessities to make this ruse?" Timanthes asked skeptically.

"Of course I did, as I promised I would," he said proudly, pointing to a worn-down wooden transport almost invisible in the trees' darkness. "That cart will serve us fine; already stacked full of garments, too."

"Where'd you get the wagon?" Aratus asked, eyes narrowing.

"I bought it, how do you think I got it?"

"You paid for it? You bought it within Corinth?"

"What difference is that?" the Syrian snapped. "You didn't say we needed an artisan's finest work, we just needed a damn cart."

"I don't care who made it, but if they've seen you already leave with that cart through this gate, it is something we need to account for. They may recognize you—"

"I left through the Sicyonian gate," Erginus replied briskly. "And I didn't get it in Corinth, I bartered for it… with a man I met along the Phliasian Road, maybe a few miles away."

"You bartered for it?" Aratus asked with a scowl. "Bartered with what?"

Erginus avoided the Strategos's eyes at first, before finally cracking a grin. "His life. I bartered his life for the fucking cart."

The three men of the Achaean League shared glances before it was Timanthes who surprisingly broke out in hysterics. "Cart looks like it's fit for a damn mule," he said with a shake of his head, his colleagues fighting the same urge. "And gods help us if you 'bought' it off any man of import."

"Cart's a piece of shit, so you shouldn't worry yourself. It'll serve our purposes just fine though."

"Agreed," Aratus said, disapproving of his methods but embracing the result. "Hide your weapons under the garments and pray we don't need them right away... though there's at least a handful of guards at the gate, so we probably will. Hard to tell if they're regulars or mercs."

"Could always drop the cart charade and just make a run at the walls," Timanthes said. "Clap the ladders against them and climb as fast as we can..."

"You do that, and run the risk of a guard getting away, sounding an alarm."

"May happen either way. There's probably another batch just inside the gate that are out of sight."

"So that's why we're doing both," Aratus declared. "A smaller group plies the gatemen and once they're preoccupied, the rest rush the walls with the ladders." He looked to his friend. "Aye?"

"Sounds as grand a plan as any," Timanthes said as he looked away, wide eyes locked on the massive walls. "So who's leading what part?"

Erginus met Aratus's gaze, the Sicyonian showing the faintest signs of a grin. "Well, it's your cart."

The Syrian grunted. "I assumed you'd say that. I pray you're not asking me to barter entry to the city by myself?"

Aratus shook his head. "I'll join you. Take at least another six or seven with us; that should give us good enough odds to at least take out the gatemen. Timanthes, you can lead the thorakitai to the walls with the ladders. Promachus will follow with the rest."

The wiry young captain gave a tentative look at the Strategos before he pushed a bush of light hair off his forehead. "You honor me, sire," he said with a tone of hesitation. "But with all due respect, I'd have you let *me* take your spot at the gate."

Surprised, Aratus gave him a sideways look. "And why's that?"

"Gods forbid the ruse goes awry and you're taken captive or... again, gods forbid, but what of something even worse?"

The Sicyonian grimaced and waved away the concern. "That could have happened a dozen times by now and it hasn't. I'll not have others face dangers on my behalf, that's no way to lead." Although the truth was it was his last way of protecting his men against any betrayal by Erginus; no matter how remote he thought that chance to be by now, it was still a chance.

"To the contrary," Promachus said, more sternly and sure of himself, "if you fall, the mission fails, don't you see?"

"Precisely, and the rest of you can fall back in good order, save yourselves."

"But if *I* were to fall, you'll still be able to lead them. Tonight or a night in years to come; to the gate, to the walls, but whichever it is, *whenever* it is, you'll be *alive* to do it. If this is what the gods have willed you to do as you say, then surely they'd want you to do it again if mere chance ruins this time."

Aratus was genuinely silenced and his eyes bounced to his lifelong friend. Timanthes gave a thoughtful frown under thoughtful eyebrows and nodded. "I'd concur."

"Fair enough," the Strategos said at last, hand forced. "You'll join Erginus with six men of your choosing. Timanthes, I will take the thorakitai to the wall; you'll wait to follow with the rest. I'll hear no more argument on the subject."

Heads nodded all around him. "And I want everyone's shoes off save Promachus, Erginus, and their squad, with voices silenced from here on out. Not a whoop, not a shout."

"Shoes off—" Erginus started.

"Because bare feet make less noise on stone paths, don't they? And they grip ladder rungs twice as well."

The burly man grunted again and looked away, hand running through a bushy beard. "Well… let's get on with it, then."

The Syrian and Promachus had their soldiers together in short order, cloaked as common merchants weary from a long night of travel. They lugged the cart to the southern end of the grove, looking to catch the Phliasian Road out of eyeshot of the gatemen; certainly, in the darkness that eyeshot didn't extend very far.

And with that, Aratus knew the time had come. An entire month of anxiety, of excitement, of hope, of despair. A surge welled within his stomach to match a heartbeat he heard crystal clear. He forced himself to exhale, eyes drifting toward the mountain peak beyond the walls that loomed so close, yet so far. *I shall see you soon*, he thought with pursed lips.

"Erginus," he said quietly with extended hand, hoping to will his fidelity. "May the gods be your guides. You're a damn brave man, as I've told you."

Erginus returned the grip with vigor, bearing his toothless grin for what Aratus knew could very well be the last time. "I'm a damn fool… as I've told *you*."

Aratus smirked and gave him a whack on the shoulder. "I shall see you in Corinth."

CHAPTER 17

17th Day of Apellaios, Year 2 of the 134th Olympiad
(August 8, 243 B.C.)

They lay on their knees in an agonizing wait.

Aratus and his closest friend, masked still within the copse, bearing unfettered witness to the Phliasian Gate.

Thorakitai, armed, armored, and with folded ladders in tow, trailed behind their Strategos in a collective crouch, two abreast. The rest formed up in mirrored fashion behind Timanthes.

All waited. All tensed.

Slowly creaked the Syrian and his cart toward the gate, seven Achaeans following closely. Real or not, every turn of the battered wheels seemed to ring out through the night like a blacksmith upon anvil. Every scrape of their sandals a tearing sound enough to make a man cringe. Not a word was spoken among them, not a cough, a sniff.

Aratus forced himself to swallow. "Well, Timanthes," he whispered through dry throat. "You've wished to gauge this man's loyalty for more than a month. You're about to get your wish."

Timanthes glanced at him, Aratus feeling his incredulous eyes. "*My* wish? It should have been yours just as much!"

Aratus only smiled. "May your suspicions be for naught."

"At this stage, at this hour?" Timanthes snickered. "Aye, gods willing." After a quiet pause, he asked, "Did you ever make amends with your wife?"

The Strategos's brow furrowed. "In our own way."

"Good."

"I'm sure I needn't ask you the same."

"You needn't. Nothing to amend."

"A more lovestruck fool I've never known," he said, half kidding, half jealous.

"Says the man with two wives," Timanthes jabbed back.

Aratus chuckled. "I don't chide you for it. The gods blessed you that way."

"To Hera, we've always given thanks."

"And your boys?"

Timanthes smiled. "They were asleep, but I poked them awake to see their eyes. They didn't like it much, but I need to see 'em... I don't think I've ever started a venture since either was born without doing that. Helps me survive, I think; helps me fight. Always will, 'til my eyes fail or the gods say otherwise."

The proud father's gaze drifted toward the gate once more, his friendly countenance morphing into one that could freeze water. Aratus knew the look, knew Timanthes's words were at an end no matter how much they soothed his friend's nerves, his focus thereafter solely on the fight ahead.

And indeed, soldiers stirred atop the Phliasian Gate. It was clear now there were three—at least—surely one the gatekeeper and two tower sentries. The former stood directly over top the gate, arms resting in a gap of the battlement's "teeth," the latter appearing at the windows of their designated stations, torches illuminating shiny helmets and drab tunics. Their positions betrayed their curiosity at the sight of their midnight callers.

Aratus looked back to Lysistratos, immediately behind him. "Ready yourself."

A nod in return.

"Hey!"

A voice called down from the gatekeeper as Erginus closed on the gate. No response.

"Hey, you!"

The Strategos took heart—even two words were enough to betray the man's accent, to tell him that it wasn't Macedonians atop the wall. *Likely dumping the duty on mercenaries... but* whose *mercs?* he wondered irritably, momentarily recalling Xeno.

"Greetings, my good man!" the Syrian finally called back with a hearty wave, voice echoing off the wall toward the forest of soldiers. "Could I trouble you to part the gates for—"

"You can stop where you are," the gatemaster ordered sharply.

The eight men halted with a raise of Erginus's hand. "Well, I've no other path to proceed on with the gates shut, so I s'pose I'll obey," he quipped, still in jovial tone.

"There's a path you can proceed on right behind you, in fact."

Erginus looked around in wonder for a moment, when his hands upturned at his sides, baffled.

"You can bloody turn around, and march right back up that path you approached on, imbecile. Gate's closed to you."

Shit, Aratus thought, immediately regretting his decision to send Promachus in his stead. *Have I really bet on a Syrian bastard's wit to see us through? Fool!*

"And why's that?" Erginus called back defiantly. "We have business in Corinth! We've come from a full damn day and half a night of walking."

"Took eight of you to lug that lousy wagon?" the gateman asked suspiciously.

The Syrian looked behind him. "When a wagon's lousy, of course it takes more'n one to get 'er moving, aye?"

No response at first. "But *eight* men?"

"Aye, eight. Not all at—at once, of course, but... well, must I run through every detail of our bloody journey!"

"Aye, I reckon you must."

Aratus could picture the burly man's face reddening as it had in Aegias's shop not so long ago, all the more poignant against the blackness of his beard. His muscles tensed, sensing the negotiations' imminent failure. Any more yelling could only raise the risk of others taking note, of putting the city on alert.

"In all my years traveling to Corinth," the Syrian ranted, "I've never seen a gateman turn away a convoy of trade! What would the King say to such behavior?"

The three guards shared a chuckle. "I imagine he'd compliment us, my friend! As we are merely following *his* orders, given through Persaeus, the Archon *he* appointed!"

Erginus looked around in frustration. "Accept us this one time, I beg you. We've traveled far—"

"And you can travel a little farther on down the road to the Sicyonian Gate, then!" the gatemaster snapped, any semblance of better humor having vanished. "Sicyonian Gate's the only one taking trade this time of night! If you don't like it, you can nap in your own shit outside these bloody gates until the sun rises, then you can have another go at it!"

Silenced, the Syrian put hands on his hips and paced, meeting Promachus's eyes briefly before finding his feet. Aratus winced, prepared to accept the failure and opt for the far worse of option of charging the wall with the guards fully alert. Lest his frustration overtake him, he forced himself to recall the ode to Apollo he'd learned in Alexandria years ago, a masterwork of Callimachus of Cyrene that had brought him profound calm ever since. He'd recited bits of it to himself in moments of highest anxiety or danger, as closely as his frenetic mind would allow.

Oh, Apollo… he who "sitteth on the right hand of his father, Zeus, king of the gods," as Callimachus writes it. There is no holier place in Sicyon than that of your temple, no god more venerated than your divine being. So too is it in Corinth, before whose walls I now lie in awe. In wonder. Poseidon, your father's brother, your uncle, the very patron god of Corinth, he's given me sign after sign to appear outside these walls. To free it from the tyrant which has wrought it such disgrace, for yea, it's "a wicked thing to fight against the Heavens, to fight against Apollo!"

He gritted his teeth, sealed his eyelids tighter.

Oh, giver of light, you'll guide me by that light, won't you?
Founder of cities, you'll let me find Corinth anew, won't you?
Healer of wounds, you'll heal those lesions I'm sure to endure, won't—

"How much do you want, lads?"

Aratus awoke to find the Syrian staring directly at the gatemaster, not having moved an inch.

"Pardon?"

"You heard me. I started this day with a talent's worth of stock here, and I sold half already. So how much do you want? I'll give ya your due, but I'm not looking to be bled dry."

The Strategos braced for a swift rejection. An admonishment.

But it never came. Instead, the gatemaster looked on silently and skeptically—but not dismissively... not yet.

"Looks like a wagon of ratty garments to me. Eaten through with moths, probably."

"I'd sooner eat a moth myself than let one near these tunics," the Syrian scoffed with believable offense. "No, these garments are of the finest thread you've yet seen in your miserable lives, I can assure you. Golden fleeces, I call them!"

"Hah! They're threaded with gold? And I've bedded every *hetaera* in Corinth!"

"No, not threaded with gold, but they may as well be. Feel 'em for yourself, if ya want. I told you, the folks in Phlious snatched up half my lot before the sun had fully risen!"

"Then why not stay in Phlious?"

"Because I follow the coin. And let's face it, you Corinthian bastards shit gold and silver. You know what the Phlians shit?"

"And what's that?"

"Shit."

The gatemaster couldn't help but chuckle, even as the towermen looked on, less amused. *Hopefully, they're not Phlians...*

"And you leave such valuable stock exposed to sun, wind, and rain, do you?" one of the towermen asked coldly. "Can't even afford a cover?"

Erginus looked hard at the man for a moment before glancing away, seemingly stumped at the question. But in short order, he returned his look with what Aratus could only imagine was his gap-toothed grin. "Well, I hear Corinth has the finest covers in Hellas, so I figured I'd buy one here," he said calmly. "And I'd be happy to buy you one too, if you'd like... or something else." With a lurch, he pulled back a layer of the cloaks at the front of the wagon, revealing for the first time a loaded basket full of gold and silver coins—though naturally, not far enough to reveal the array of swords stashed at the back. Holding it just long enough to pique interests and whet appetites, he let go, leaving the hoard hidden again among the clothes.

"You understand then, why it took eight men to 'operate' this cart," he said. "But come down and take a look, if you need further assurance."

After a silent spell, the man in the southern tower left his window to find the gatemaster's side, where an intense debate followed suit. The northern towerman looked nervously between his colleagues and the Syrian's band of merchants, but stayed put. Aratus, meanwhile, caught his breath, allowed the inklings of a grin, and let his words to Apollo resume, albeit with eyes wide open this time.

"For golden is the tunic of Apollo..."

The Strategos grinned as the south wall grew closer, his ledge thinner. *"Come now, Timanthes,"* he muttered to himself. *"Finish those miserable bastards! Finish 'em and join us!"* Apollo protect you. Apollo send you here!"

Ahead of him, Erginus grunted and swore as his ascent slowed and foot slipped precariously on virgin stone, hands aflail. *"Dammit!"*

The Strategos instantly grabbed the errant limb ahead of him. "Steady up, man—we're here."

And a glance ahead confirmed it—the cleft deposited them at the base of the foreboding wall, one spanning a thousand yards end to end, its earthen tan glowing in the moonlight. It was not as foreboding as it could have been, of course, as the rocky foundation made this portion of the southern wall "short" relative to the rest of its length. A perhaps startling defensive gaffe unless one considered the questions that Corinthians and Macedonians must surely have asked of themselves:

By the gods, who would be mad enough to attack the most impregnable fort in Hellas in the first place, one that hadn't been taken by force in centuries?

And who would be madder still to assault the south wall, that which sat above a near vertical slope?

Indeed, many cities of Hellas chose not to even erect a wall on the most hazardous sides of their acropoles—Sicyon chief among them. A wasted expense, they'd say. "Gilding a crocus," his father-in-law liked to say.

Aratus licked his lips, hearing his heart race with greater clarity. *Yet here we are.*

Above him, he saw no sign of enemies along the ramparts. "Your brother's done his work, it appears?"

Erginus gave a panting nod as he rubbed his swollen shoulder. "I'd hope. But you know it's not stayin' that quiet."

"Just asked for a chance, that's all," he said as his soldiers filed in alongside him, stomachs pressed flat against the wall, feet tiptoeing dangerously along a rim leaving no room for error. But as he looked again at the toothy ramparts silhouetted perfectly against the sky, he grew concerned at an alarming resurgence of clouds. The light that had been his elixir not moments earlier was certain to fade away in minutes, who knew for how long. The shadows kicked him into action.

"Ladders up!" he growled with a scan of his winded, sweating men. *"Get 'em up!"*

As he watched his ladders' feet slipping and sliding, he realized it was easier said than done. At the city walls, the ground had been softer and level, and more of it. Here, there was a foot of space, maybe two, and even that was uneven and strewn with crumbling stone. Worse yet, the ladders—best inclined at an angle for climbing—had to be stood nearly straight up in the air, leaving gear-laden climbers with the sensation that they were in fact falling backward.

"Stay there," the gatemaster commanded with a point to Erginus. "We'll come down to inspect." He fired a glare at the northern towerman. "You keep watch for Archelaus."

And with that, the gatemaster grabbed a spear and disappeared with the other guard down a staircase hidden from view within the southern tower. It felt like an eternity, but sure enough, Aratus heard the distinctive sound of door bars being lifted, presaging the groaning of massive doors hewn of iron and wood.

"For golden is his mantle, his lyre, his bow and quiver..."

The portal was open. There was nary a barrier between his men and the city, tantalizing glimpses offered from his vantage. It was all he could do to keep from sprinting headlong through the breach.

But the gatemaster didn't emerge with just the south towerman—four more joined them from either side of the towers' bases.

The Strategos swallowed hard, eyes bouncing from the men ahead to the lone north towerman keeping watch from above.

"How the laurel trembles at your approach!"

The Corinthians cautiously emerged, two flanking the squat gatemaster's left, three on his right. They bore linen armor, similar to that of his own Achaeans, and their spears were of standard length, not like the Macedonians' trademark *sarissae*—heavy pikes nearly twenty feet long. Definitely mercenaries.

"So why are you so intent on coming through this gate?" the gatemaster asked Erginus with a crooked smile under a spotty beard, voice sounding tense. "Told ya the Sicyonian Gate will take you."

"Because you know damn well their hands will be out at the Sicyonian Gate. Always wanting something before they'll let ya pass."

The gatemaster glared at the Syrian before grunting a laugh and sneering. "You're quite the jester, aren't you?"

"Just a merchant."

The Corinthians fanned out in a semicircle around the cart and the Achaeans guarding it. The gatemaster shoved his hands into the stack of garments, running their cloth through busy fingers, emerging with a gold coin. "Your 'fleeces' look like horse dung," he said, stepping away with a nonchalant wipe of his mouth.

"Aye, but the gold doesn't," Erginus replied. "Coin or fleeces, lads, pick whichever you want. Within reason."

The gatemaster rolled the coin over in his hands, bringing it closer to inspect. His expression suddenly darkened. "I'm only going to ask you this once—where did you bloody come by this gold?"

A blanket of quiet. Erginus looked to the cart and back, tracing a finger along its edge. The gatemaster's face flushed crimson below his bronze cheekless helmet. "What don't you understand about—"

Promachus crumpled him with one punch.

173

The Corinthians froze. They all did.

The only sound was the gatemaster's moans. All watched him writhe, flail. His head tilted up at length.

"Close the gates!"

In a flash—chaos.

Achaeans scrambled to draw swords from the cart as Erginus tackled a guard to the ground. Corinthians leveled spears at the others but were torn as to their target. They were too close to use them to effect, tight quarters always going to the swordsman. Achaeans lunged at chests, limbs, necks, but the spearmen retreated to build distance, holding the shieldless allies at bay.

Erginus found himself on the worse end of his scrum, mounted by a furious and powerful Corinthian. Fists rained down on the Syrian as another hand wrapped around his throat. Until suddenly, a geyser of blood. The Corinthian fell back, dagger planted in his neck.

"How the temples shake upon your approach!"

"Now!"

Aratus was off.

He'd never felt so light in his life.

He had wings at that moment, soaring low over the dry soil, certain his feet never touched it. The shield on his back, the spear, they weighed nothing.

A thorakites raced alongside him, ladder under arm.

In mere moments, they'd passed the wagon scrum to their right. Aratus's appearance shocked the Corinthians just long enough to let more Achaean swords find their marks. One dead, sword through the ribs. Another's leg gashed before his throat followed. A third dropped, a fourth.

"Close the bloody gates!" the pudgy gatemaster yelled again, stumbling his way back toward the doors, blood dripping from his mouth.

"Line 'em up!" Aratus screamed to his troops, smelling the hot stone blocks of the wall next to the north tower. He glanced straight up, the ramparts a toothy gray line impossibly high against a violet sky speckled with stars and thin clouds.

Clack! Clack! Clack!

Siege ladders quickly had their halves snapped into place and slammed against the wall, twenty in a line. One man held it tight underneath, the rest sprinting up the rungs. They were experts in their craft, Aratus having drilled them time and again in rain, in sun, in all conditions. They'd had contests to reward the fastest climber, but the real reward was far less superficial—seconds gained in battle meant the difference between victory and defeat, between life and death.

"Ready, sire!"

Aratus nodded, storming up the ladder like a cat to a tree. Bare feet touched a rung for a split second before they were on to the next, hands moving just as fast. He dared not glance down lest he lose his balance and break the cadence of the man close behind him. They were a single breathing unit, every man doing his part.

He swung his legs over the top of the battlement. Feet planted on the wall's thick walkway.

He was in.

"Begone from Apollo's presence, he who is sinful!"

He smiled through panting breaths, wild eyes taking a moment to scan the view before him—a city quiet in slumber, reddish roofs all a murky brown under muddled moonlight, only a few torches here and there lighting up the white of a temple, the stucco of a home, the bronze of a statue. It was startling to find the city which he'd only ever seen as an anthill with its frenetic pace now as calm as any sleepy town of Sicyonia.

To his left, the wall's torchlit catwalk snaked northward, carving a trail of light as it descended ever lower toward the blackness of the coastal plain. For his purposes, however, he just cared that it was devoid of any guards from the Sicyonian gate some half mile away.

More thorakitai over the wall.

He turned south, drawing his sword before waving an arm in silence for the men to follow, speeding crouched toward the door of the north tower. Leaning against it, he counted down from three on his fingers before he swung it open.

Nothing. A fading torch in the stuffy confines showed his only option was a staircase leading up to the window he'd seen prior, or down to ground level.

"Lysistratos—check the upstairs, see if that second towerman is foolish enough to still hole up there. If he is, kill him."

"Aye, Strateg—"

BOOM.

The tower shook, dust descending from its walls.

He looked into the worried eyes of his captain. "The gates. They bloody closed the gates!"

"Should I still—"

"No! He's already left! Come on!"

He plummeted into the darkness of the descending staircase, air smelling musty, tasting worse. Around and around the spiral he went, the jingling of his armor scales all he could hear beyond his men's heavy breaths. He slammed into the door at the bottom harder than he should have, but he was quite honestly a bit mad, furious that he might get this close and be thwarted before he'd even made it up the mountain.

The door flew open, the Strategos stumbling out onto streets of Corinth. Darkened houses stood not far away, the living areas of this bustling ancient city thrown all the way to the walls in some spots. Nevertheless, it wasn't these that concerned him—it was the barracks of Archelaus and his Macedonian city watch that Erginus had warned him of.

Hearing sounds of the scrum outside the walls, he threw away his concern for Archelaus for the moment, racing silently on the pads of his bare feet toward the gate. He'd unlock the damn thing himself, if he had to, but where was the man who'd closed them to begin—

The north towerman stood in the shadows of the doorway, frantically trying to slide the lock back in place, Achaeans slamming into it on the other side making it all but impossible.

"Gods help me, gods help me..." he muttered in panic.

Aratus looked behind him as he tiptoed forward, finding more and more of his men at his back.

The man stopped, door only half bolted, looking terrified to his rear. His eyes locked on the Strategos, lips quivering. He about-faced to flatten his arms and back against the breach in the doors, as if he alone would hold them together in lieu of the doorbolt. "Gods save me, please don't kill me. I won't tell anybody you're here."

More pounding at the gates, more shaking.

And more worried Aratus became about the noise, about the attention it would bring. "Open it," he commanded in harsh whisper.

"They'll kill me the moment I do."

"*I'll* kill you the moment you say another word. *Open it.*"

"I'll come to you and one of your men can open it, aye? That way—"

"What did I just say!"

"We don't have time for this," Lysistratos whispered.

"He may be able to tell us something about Archelaus."

More pounding.

"Please..." the man whimpered.

"Aratus, just do it, the time's—"

"I know."

"Please! Please! *Please!*" the towerman began to scream.

Shit!

The thorakitai stormed toward the door—

But for naught.

A sword protruded through the man's mouth, silencing him in frozen horror. Arms went limp, knees buckled.

On closer look, Aratus saw it. He saw the sword that had jammed through the door slit from the other side, the split that the Corinthian had so desperately tried to hold together. And as quickly as it appeared, the blade withdrew, letting the man slide down into a lifeless, graceless heap.

He measured the silence that followed as closely as anything he'd ever measured in his life. No sounds of alarm. No sounds at all until...

A coo from beyond the gate.

With an exhale, he rushed to the doors, wrenching the heavy bolt aside with some thorakitai assistance, and throwing them open. A heaving Syrian awaited him, sword as bloody as his face and mouth, tunic torn asunder. Beyond him lay a grislier scene, every Corinthian splayed out in the manner in which they died, some bleeding profusely from the back, others the neck, the throat. The portly gatemaster gushed blood from at least a dozen wounds, face planted in the ground, hands reaching lifelessly for the doorway before which he fell.

"That one wouldn't die," Erginus said coldly, having followed the Strategos's eyes.

"No, I guess not… did we lose any?"

"Couple wounded, one of 'em serious. Otherwise…"

Aratus nodded. "Thank you," he said in full sincerity, taking the Syrian's crimson hand in his. "Somehow my blade's still dry."

"If it stays dry all night, we're—"

"It won't."

He looked for his young Pellenean captain, finding him too covered in blood. "Promachus, well done. Now go to the grove, get your armor, and tell Timanthes to leave the injured with one other; put one more in each tower as lookouts for the rest. Everyone else should follow us as fast as possible. Just a few paces east inside the gate, then a hard cut south 'til you hit the path to the Acrocorinth. Keep pace but keep quiet!"

"Aye, Strategos. Stay alive, will you?"

Aratus chuckled darkly and turned away. "Syrian, catch your breath. The night is young," he said, eyes finding the mountain so tantalizingly close now. "Still two thousand feet to climb."

"For surely, Apollo, you do knocketh at the door in all your splendor!"

CHAPTER 18

17th Day of Apellaios, Year 2 of the 134th Olympiad
(August 8, 243 B.C.)

The Achaean snake slinked through the city. Two by two they marched, shields up, helmets down, swords at the ready, backs gray with dust from sliding along homes on either side of the Phliasian Road. Though by daylight, those houses surely burst with colors along their edges and bases, the street was still deep in shadow by the blotting of the moon, and few torches burned anywhere nearby. Just as well—less light meant less reflection and less reflection meant less detection for the thorakitai and the three hundred Achaeans surely not minutes behind them.

Oh, how one curious glance from these abodes could ruin them all! Aratus couldn't help but think as he trotted upon the warm stones. But despite his worst fears, there'd been no sign, not a breath of opposition. And though he knew it wrong to feel the slightest bit of elation for a job not even halfway done, he couldn't help but allow a sweaty grin, teeth clenched and muscles tense with adrenaline. *Oh, how he'd roar if they'd dare look upon him and his men of Apollo!*

Once through the gate and its small courtyard, the Phliasian Road quickly veered north off its easterly track. Followed to its end, the Achaeans could be in Corinth's agora in ten minutes' time; instead, Aratus waited patiently for a gap that would take him south toward the mountain—the gap Erginus told him to expect.

"Thought you said we'd see an outlet by now," Aratus whispered to the huffing Syrian at his side.

"Thought we would too," he heard back through deep breaths.

"We need to get off the streets, too obvious."

"Soon, I reckon—"

Aratus's hand instantly went up, freezing the snake in place.

Sure enough, an outlet had appeared—though not a mere alley to sneak through, but a road cutting directly across their path just ahead, leaving a small square at the intersection. From his vantage, it looked to shoot southeasterly, but how far southeast? To the Acrocorinth? What if it veered again?

"Crossroad up ahead," he declared to his guide. *"Is that the damn route we take?"*

Erginus glanced around him, searching for a reference point, a sign.

"Well?" Aratus demanded, anxiety building.

"I reckon, but let's get closer yet… ne'er thought it'd be such a tough find in the dark like this!"

The hint of an excuse sent Aratus into a silent fury, but he quickly squelched it. His hands gripped his shield and sword tighter, sweat dripping off the tip of his nose.

"Anything?" he asked again as the troop tiptoed ahead toward the intersection, finding a small fountain in its center. But Erginus only shook his

head. Aratus sighed as he threw his back flat against the home on the corner, angling his head to peer southward around the edge.

It goes southerly, he saw, suddenly lightened. No doubt the road had a few curves here and there, some buildings too, but there was no question where it headed—up a steep, slippery slope to the road ringing the mountain.

He looked in the street's opposite direction and found it equally desolate, finally glancing back to Erginus. *"This'll have to do..."*

The Syrian wet his lips. *"Gotta confess, Sicyonian, I don't recall it..."*

Aratus scowled. *"Look around the corner, are you certain?"*

The guide obeyed, leaning just enough to—

"Shit!"

"What?"

"They're up there."

"Where? Who?"

"Soldiers, men, I dunno!"

Impossible! He'd just looked and—

"Shit!" he muttered as a second peek proved the Syrian right.

It was unmistakable. Two torches, barely a hundred yards up. Was it two men or—

"Four," he said, stealing another glance. Four fingers went up at once, Lysistratos and the men behind him mirroring his move. Aratus leaned his shield against the home and dropped to his belly, showing as little as he could to survey his foe drawing ever closer.

Four indeed, one with a plume—had to be a captain—while the others wore crested red helmets with flaps guarding cheeks. From their torches' glow, all appeared in red tunics under golden linen cuirasses, bronze shields emblazoned with the King's "ANT" monogram. But despite clearly hailing from Macedon, their spears were well short of *sarissa* length, likely a practical choice to better patrol the city's crowded narrow streets—and keep watch for intruders.

On they came, close enough to hear their voices, sounding light and merry.

"We can't avoid them," Aratus concluded as he leapt to his feet. Tactile as they were, a hundred men simply couldn't go unnoticed, whether they stayed frozen or tried to about-face.

"Lysi," he said quietly, eyes wide. *"Soon as they hit the fountain, you seal off both ends of the crossroad. Two more where the Phliasian Road resumes. We gotta box 'em in— no one escapes, aye?"*

His junior officer nodded. *"And you?"*

"First one I see gets the spear. Second gets the sword. Others can get the rest—"

"One's mine," Erginus said.

"— but be careful, they've full armor and shield."

"Aye, sire."

Orders relayed in seconds, anxious whispers followed. He drew his spear as he holstered his sword.

A glow on the ground just around the corner.

They were closer.

Breathe, Strategos. Spear 'em first, then the sword… spear 'em first, then the sword…

"… that wine's barely drinkable."

"Ah, you'd have drunk it in a pinch, I bet."

"On my dyin' days, maybe—"

Aratus's spear went straight through the young soldier's neck. He fell toward the fountain, pole still lodged in place. The Strategos drew his sword and immediately swung at the next man, but the man contorted in time to throw his torch arm up in defense. The hand was severed clean, falling with flames still gripped and flickering bright. Erginus bull-rushed his shield, knocking him to the ground before a thorakites ran a spear through his gut.

Aratus's head swiveled, square barely alit with the fallen torch, looking for the plume, the captain—and there he was: standing at the crossroad now with his last guard at his side, a torch betraying their utter disbelief. Their eyes met.

"Sound the bloody alarms! Go, go!"

Without hesitation, the guard was back running up the road whence he came, while the captain dashed toward the Phliasian Road that led to the agora, the opening that Lysi's men sprinted to seal off.

"Someone get the bastard up the hill!" Aratus roared, dangerously loud—but quieter than an alarm, no?

A flood of thorakitai stormed after the guard, while the Sicyonian and more made for the captain, still roaring in his own right.

"Sound the alarms! Corinthians, wake up! Enemies within the gates!"

But the captain was more than just words, whirling around at the end of the square to parry a spear thrust with his shield, launching a blast of his own that sent the thorakites's armor fragments flying into the air. The Macedonian slammed his shield into another of Aratus's men to send him back, gain some space.

Aratus closed on him, but another spear thrust forced a swerve that sent him off-kilter, the strikes looking like blurs in the dim light.

"Sound the alarms!"

Dammit, die, you bastard!

A thorakites's spear found the captain's shield once again, but this time hard enough that the great bronze plate dropped with a thud upon the street stones. But it only seemed to make the Macedonian angrier, stabbing at the intruder's vulnerable leg and finding his mark.

"Wake, Corinthians! Wake! Enemies within!"

Lights from within homes.

Doors creaked open.

Curious eyes peeked out.

No!

Aratus threw his shield toward the man, who deftly swatted it aside, but in so doing left a head open to a Sicyonian blade. It caught him flush down the middle, plume hairs flying all around them. The captain stumbled backward onto the Phliasian Road, divot deep in his helmet though not quite to the bone. But he refused to fall, instead staggering away from the fray. The Strategos started after him—

When he heard it. When he saw it.

The screams.

The people.

Corinthians appearing from their homes. A trickle at first, then a stream, then a flood. The anthill he remembered.

Aratus stood, paralyzed, watching the captain stumble on toward the city center.

"Sire, shall we chase?"

Shall we? Shall we?

"*Send for help!*" the Macedonian slurred again, moving ever away.

The screams grew as the people saw his pursuers, baffled, fearing the worst.

"*Sire!*"

"No," Aratus said firmly. "Back to the square and head south!"

"South, sire?"

"*We're going for the cursed mountain! Now, go! GO!*"

After one last unbearable look at the Macedonian retreating into the panicked masses, he was back through the square, grabbing his shield but leaving his spear behind.

"*Everyone south, now!*" he commanded.

And off they went, thighs quickly burning as they made their ascent. Along the way, he passed the body of the third guard that his men had run down, rivulets of his blood trickling back toward the square. Lysistratos was soon running at his side.

"You get the cap'n, sire?"

"No," he said between breaths. "Doesn't matter now, the people've been spooked. Bastard did his job."

"Shit," his captain said.

Aratus couldn't rebuke him. The one thing that couldn't happen, happened. Only a matter of time until the full alarms sounded, and it was the gods' mercy every step they took without them. Even worse, Timanthes was still to follow—would they even make it? Would they see the people's tumult and think the worst? Would they turn back—

No, he thought firmly. *Timanthes would sooner wash Ecdelus's feet than he would leave men behind. He'll come. We'll have our day.*

Homes grew scarcer the farther they climbed onto the Acrocorinth's steep base, Aratus trying desperately to follow a path which turned to dirt and brush as it snaked toward the mountain road above. About a quarter mile to the east, he saw the top of Demeter's Sanctuary that had so awed him a decade prior, façade still alight. But just northwest of it was the building he feared. Rectangular and unassuming, it had to be the barracks of Archelaus, base of the city watch Erginus warned him of, its position on the slope perfect for observation and quick deployment. It had to be where that Macedonian commander headed, that bastard with the plume. Half a plume, anyway.

Aratus winced and shook his head.

On they climbed, the sounds of the frenzied city fading, replaced instead by the steady beat of bare feet and heavy breaths.

"You still with me, Syrian?" Aratus called to his guide, whose feet beat harder and breaths sounded louder than any of them.

"No… talk," he wheezed back.

Aratus allowed a crazed grin. "Just as well, we still have—"

Trumpets.

Shit.

Just one at first, but it was soon answered by another, then another, then another, all resonating deep into the summer night. More city lights appeared, even as far away as the Lechaeum docks at the port. Perhaps worst of all, lights appeared along the forward wall of the Acrocorinth, still looming more than a thousand feet above them.

No time to worry, Aratus finally told himself, legs burning as they churned even harder toward the path ringing the citadel. When he'd at last reached it, his body forced him to his hands and knees upon the stones, lungs begging for air after more than a quarter-mile sprint on terrain feeling vertical at times. His head roasted inside his helmet, defying a thick layer of sweat. He was more tired than he expected, but he took comfort knowing the rest of the ascent would at least be gradual as the paved road gracefully arced around the mountain to the summit—leaving aside the hundreds of hostile Gauls, Illyrians, Syrians, and Macedonians awaiting him, of course.

More thorakitai plowed through the brush and piled onto the road as he rose to his feet. "Take a few breaths, men," he said, indulging his own order. "Take 'em, but only a few, aye? Those trumpets aren't for festivities' sake."

Some tired chuckles, but most graciously took the offer in silence. For his part, Aratus looked about in a fervor before his eyes were drawn to the brightening town square from which they'd run, one that even from this distance had swollen with townsfolk and the like, all surely intrigued by the three dead Macedonians left in their wake. Beyond the square, he searched desperately for a sign of Timanthes's three hundred, his view of the gate obscured by the homes and buildings nearby. He wondered anew how—or if—his closest friend would avoid the gathering crowds below.

"Sire," Lysistratos said to him as his hand met his shoulder. "We should probably move, should we not?"

Aratus followed his outstretched finger toward Archelaus's barracks, a building he could barely see past a bend in the road, but how he found it was his worst fear confirmed, indeed—fully alit with a stream of troops pouring out, storming toward the mountain path.

"Consider a fallback, perhaps? An ambush? No way we can attack the walls without the rest, sire. Not with those bastards on our flanks."

"We can't wait any longer to move on the walls; they'll be too alert," Aratus replied, stomach twisting in knots.

Lysi pointed at the barracks again. "Sire, *they will be on our flank within min—*"

"Brother, I've heard you," Aratus growled. "And you're right, we can't win without Timanthes's men—"

"Aye, so—"

"And we're not *going* to do it without Timanthes's men. They're coming. They're not here yet, but they're coming."

The junior officer looked away, looked farther along the path where it took a sharp southerly turn around the western end of the Acrocorinth's "bean," climbing toward the top. "I'll follow you to the ends of the earth, sire, I've never hinted otherwise and never will, gods willing. But once we take that turn right there, we'll have no idea what's happening behind us. We'll be completely blind. We should at least set up a rear guard to ambush them at the bend, buy the rest some time. I'll lead it, if need be."

Aratus followed his gaze until he looked upon him again with a shake of his head. "And there may very well be Macedonians from the fortress descending toward us as we speak, in which case we'll need every swinging sword we have, will we not?"

Lysistratos's face was wrought with concern, betraying his words before he said them. "Then—"

The commander whacked his officer's arm. "We can't retreat at this point; you know that as well as I do. Tell me you know that."

The younger man offered no response, which was in fact all the response Aratus needed. "Wipe it from your mind, then. Grab your shield, grab your weapons, grab your ladders, and march with me, aye? Timanthes is going to come, Lysistratos. And by the gods above, we are going to the walls."

Lysistratos smiled weakly and nodded, lifting his gear from the shrubbery in which it lay. "Sire."

Aratus had little time to dwell on the man's nerves, moving instead to find his Syrian guide still huffing in a squat, arms resting on knees, hands cradling his face.

"It's time," the Strategos said, placing a hand on the other man's back. "We've only a few minutes 'til Archelaus gets here."

"Only if he runs as fast as we did," Erginus said without raising his head. "No one's that crazy."

"You've a better reaction to a city waking to a fear of invasion?"

"Aye. I'd have said grab a drink, toast to life, and pray ya go quick."

Aratus laughed. "My morbid friend. On your feet, let's go."

The Syrian finally stood with a groan and a bit of help, revealing a face still caked in blood from the battle at the gate. He looked more a bear than he did a man, his eyes black pools as Aratus's bored into them. "Your brother's ready, is he not? He's on the wall, cleared it out?"

A silent, panting nod. "That's what he promised me." Aratus started to turn away when Erginus stopped him. "That's not to say he's cleared *all* of the walls..."

The Strategos looked at him briefly before slapping the blazon of his shield. "I'd no doubt we'd need these in one way or another." He smiled. "Men! Fall in line, four abreast, laddermen in the middle! On my sign, we quickstep!"

His hand went up as he watched behind him, watched the intrepid one hundred fall into place along a path fit for eight if one didn't wish to hug the mountain's edge. *It will be these men*, he said to himself—though perhaps too to his parents, his wife, his fellow Achaeans, his unborn. *These men and gods willing, those with Timanthes, that will bury an era... or see me buried.* He smiled again, silently giving thanks to the gods that they'd allowed him this far at least, far enough to let a Sicyonian orphan stand upon the precipice of the greatest fort in southern Hellas.

Far enough to let Macedon hear him roar.

His hand came down.

They were off.

CHAPTER 19

*17th Day of Apellaios, Year 2 of the 134th Olympiad
(August 8, 243 B.C.)*

When he finally saw him, Aratus swore he was a wraith.

Though he'd kept his men's profiles low, bodies close to the ground at a steady pace, he couldn't help but shoot glances over his shoulder every few paces or so. Looking back at the bend as they ascended the mountain, looking for the source of those shouts, those blaring horns and trumpets he heard drawing closer.

Looking for Archelaus.

But march on he did, the path before him beating steadily south as it hugged the mountain on their left, a precipitous drop to the right that surely offered magnificent views of distant farmlands below by daylight. A short stone wall traced along the mountain as well, small carve-outs bearing lanterns for lighting the path. But the lanterns now were black as ash, and with the restless set of clouds still blotting the moon, the curious enemy lining the walls above them must have found it impossible to see his barefoot brigade hustling along. So he hoped.

The path abruptly swung out two hundred yards west in a semicircle, swooping by the Teneatic Gate before making its final eastward ascent toward the fortress's massive main gateway. But at the risk of a healthy squadron of men atop the Teneatic, Aratus continued his southerly climb instead, opting for the bruises and scrapes of the dry grass and bushes to pick up the path again. He could hear his men cursing his name behind him as thorns pricked tender flesh, but friendly profanities were much preferable to hostile detection.

Even still, it wasn't gatemen or those along the walls that had him worried. And on what had to be the twentieth time he looked back, there he was, plain as day. A dreaded image, a wraith—only all too real.

"Aratus," Erginus muttered.

The Syrian saw them at the same time. Saw the river of Macedonian red pouring around the bend, spears pointed skyward, horns as piercing as if they were right at his side. They stuttered a bit as they saw the Achaeans through the dimness, minds surely failing to believe what their eyes held as true—*this paltry band of scrappers not five hundred yards away attacks the Acrocorinth?* In that moment, an eerie calm took hold, a quantum of peace that betrayed nerves, fear, courage; a fundamental confrontation of mortality for Aratus and his men.

"I know."

"Sire..." a young Sicyonian breathed to his left.

"Aye, lad?"

"Shall we... shall we charge?"

Erginus quickly glared at the Strategos. "No, no, you bastard. You're not dying here, you at least make for the damn wall you brought me here for!"

"I beg you, sire," Lysistratos intervened with urgency. "With a handful of men I can at least block their path for a moment while you rush the walls. At least make them earn it."

Aratus stared into the creeping red abyss, seeing nothing but grim options, and only one that bought them even a few more minutes of life. *If we can mount the wall, if we can just get some up there, we've a chance.* He nodded to himself. "To the walls—"

"Fire, damn you!"

The Achaeans blanched in response to the sudden bellow of a Macedonian ahead. Shields instinctively raised, bracing in place.

But nothing. No bows leveled, no slings.

"Aim for the damn path and fire!"

Aratus looked about in confusion, opposing armies frozen in place.

"Shall we still move, si—"

An arrow shot straight through the Sicyonian's neck. He crumpled at his commander's feet.

The walls, you fool!

A deafening hail of arrow and stone erupted from the fortress walls above, clipping path, armor, and flesh alike. Their angle was still poor and visibility worse, but their order had been loud and clear. And at least one thorakites had paid the price.

He angrily grabbed Lysistratos, who desperately angled his shield overhead. "We're going to be chewed up here if we don't move, so get the back of the column going! Let Archelaus's dogs give chase, they can't come too close with this storm around us! But we have to reach the gods-forsaken walls so *follow me!*"

A chunk of mountainside exploded before them, spraying dirt and pebbles. Lysi looked up with wincing eyes and a sharp nod. "We'll buy you time," he said simply, before peeling off toward the column's tail.

Aratus watched him but with growing alarm—he watched him like a lamb going to slaughter. "You bring up the rear, Lysistratos! You promise me—"

"Just run, sire! We'll hold them back, but run now!"

"Lysistratos! You—"

Another blast found the boss of his shield, staggering the commander.

"Aratus, we go for the wall now!" Erginus yelled into his ear with a steadying arm around his waist.

"Lysi—"

"He's bloody made his decision! He comes or he doesn't! You lose him, you lose a sword; you lose me, *you lose the night!"* The Syrian launched him forward toward the fortress. "Now follow me close, it's going to be hard enough findin' the path without any moonlight!"

"Damn it all, Lysi," he seethed through gnashed teeth, eyes watering, finally turning away from the image of his young officer taking five compatriots to match arms with the best of Archelaus. Swallowing deep, he bellowed back to his troops, "Shields high, lads, we march!"

Or crawl like rodents, as it were, shrubs and dust of their ascent making it impossible to gain solid footing and ward off missiles at once. Their shadowed assailants found even easier targets when they clambered into the open over the path leading to the main gate, the deadly rain picking up ferocity and volume, the sucking sounds of arrows hitting home never ceasing to appall. But all they could do was press on with their climb.

"Follow tight!" Aratus yelled, as much for himself as his men.

But to where were they following? he thought, concern growing as he tailed the meandering Syrian across the path, ground deteriorating into mere stone and dirt on the other side. There was no discernible trail whatsoever, certainly no cleft, and certainly not one within eyeshot on this night of shadows and shaded moon.

After what seemed an eternity, Erginus abruptly stopped. "Dammit!" he yelled, head swiveling back and forth, posture descending into a defensive crouch.

"What the hell are you—"

Shwoosh.

A bolt screamed by the back of Aratus's head. He instinctively fell forward into the Syrian.

"What the hell are you doing?" he raged again, scraped hands and knees burning. *"Why are we stopped?"*

"It's back there, I think!"

"What? We missed the pathway?"

"Aye, it starts with a cleft and I—I—I bloody can't see it! Thought it was over—"

Crack.

"Argh!" Erginus bellowed as a stone smashed into his shoulder. He writhed onto his back in agony, losing grip on his shield.

Helpless, Aratus flattened his body on the ground, looking back to beckon his men to do the same, but to little effect in the end—the wall looming above the side of the cliff on which they huddled had a direct line of sight now. Indeed, they were too far out from the wall base to use the cliff as protection, yet close enough to provide targets. "Erginus, we can't just lay here! Let's circle back if need be, but they're bloody looking right at us!"

The burly Syrian nodded through a grimace. "Back. Back the way we came."

"Aye, then," the Strategos said, before meeting eyes with the Sicyonian behind him. "About-face! Relay the order!"

And soon it was echoed down the Achaean column. But the moment even a few of them rose off the ground, another squall of buzzing shafts erupted along the wall line. Arrowheads clinked off armor scales, followed by more cries of agony. The incessant whining of yet more fletching, the interminable pelting of the stones, it maddeningly drove them all back to the dirt out of sheer reflex.

There was no relief. They were pinned. Defenseless beyond their inching crawl back whence they came, the injured making even that a slow task.

One elbow after the other, that was all he could tell himself. Face down in the earth as he plodded, he saw only blackness, smelled only the soil and sweat and spit stewing beneath his gaping mouth; the sounds of battle—of slaughter—echoed relentlessly in his helmet.

One elbow after the other.

A slinger stone screamed down and scalded the back of his leg, shin greaves rendered useless. His eyes misted in pain, teeth crunched to their breaking point. But still…

One elbow after the other.

"Keep moving, dammit!" he yelled to an unknown audience. *"Keep mov—"*

Light.

Can't be, he thought.

But it was. As he forced his eyes open, the shadow of his helmet appeared then grew darker and darker as it blocked rays of moonlight that were less and less obscured.

Moonlight! Bloody moonlight!

He cautiously looked overhead and sure enough, the night's fitful clouds had retreated before the moon again, leaving a gaping window into the immaculate void of the night sky. Selene shone beautiful and bright, marred no longer.

Whoosh.

A nearby arrow cut his admiration short, but his spirit was ascendant. *"Look around, Erginus!"* he screamed, looking to his rear. *"Do you see it any better? See where we went wrong?"*

For his part, the Syrian was worse for wear, head rolling about but gesturing eastward and upward. Hardly a beacon of certainty.

"Do you see it or no?" Aratus growled back in frustration. Time was short—better light cut both ways, both for Macedonian bowmen and Achaean thorakitai.

"I can't tell unless I stand, and if I stand, I'm dead!"

"No one rises 'til we know! You should be able to tell from where we might—"

"Stay with me, brothers!"

The cry rang out through the night. Aratus looked about, not quick to place its source.

"Stay with me!" it came again. *"By Apollo, do we live or die!"*

And this time, he had no doubt. *Lysistratos.*

He propped himself up onto his elbows despite the danger and saw him, not three hundred yards distant—Lysistratos standing in the middle of his intrepid band of five, still down on the mountain path, still awaiting the onslaught of Archelaus's warriors. The latter continued surging around the sharp southerly elbow in the path, their hundreds dwarfing Lysistratos's few to the point of absurdity. The Sicyonians had cautiously retreated back in lieu of throwing themselves upon the mass of Macedonians, clearly seeking to use the narrow mountain path to a Thermopylae-effect as in the hoplite battle of yore.

But thorakitai weren't the hoplites of yore. In fact, they weren't hoplites at all, neither in armament nor design. Thorakitai were meant to be nimble, notwithstanding their armored shirts; meant to get around flanks and rears, not stand in a line and scrum. Alas, there they were all the same, screaming loud enough to be heard over Archelaus's trumpets and taunts, thumping their shields with spears in rage—for they retreated no further.

They'd drawn their line and waited.

Archelaus did not disappoint.

The first few lines of reds raced forth at a plumed man's order, bronze shields flashing in the moonlight, spearheads bobbing. The Achaeans braced, oval shields leveled with spears held tight underarm. None quivered as the enemy closed the hundred-foot gap.

Aratus remained transfixed despite the aerial carnage around him.

Fifty feet.

Twenty-five.

When suddenly, the thorakitai flipped to an overhead grip and fired the spears like javelins. The front line had no time to parry, three dropping instantly, punctured through neck, arm, and thigh. Another clanged loudly off a helmet, while yet another sailed harmlessly overhead. The charge stuttered from the volley, at sight of its victims. Before it could resume, Lysi's men had drawn swords and sprinted forth in their own right.

Oval shields slammed into round. Macedonians staggered back, swords inside the range of their spears and thus far more dangerous. One fell slain in his place, cloven neck spraying like a geyser. But the rest quickly stiffened with superior numbers, locking shoulders to force the furious Achaeans backward. One Sicyonian tripped en route—he was gored at once.

The resurgent Macedonians now lunged and lunged and lunged again, ashen spears seeking weak points past the big shields. The Sicyonians could do little but huddle, their swords now an unfair match for a pole at length. Sure enough, another swordsman crumpled with a point through bare foot; his retaliatory slice back was stopped with gored shoulder. Failing balance sent him tumbling over the path's steep western precipice.

Lysi did his best to tighten ranks with the remaining men, this last standing band between Macedonians and Aratus's pinned down thorakitai; but even as tight as the mountain path was, three could only do so much before being enveloped.

191

"By Apollo, do we live or die!" the young officer roared again through cracked voice, readying for the final charge.

His commander could barely keep watching, but felt he owed him as much. *"I'll tell them all you died well, my friend,"* he whispered to himself.

But at that moment of finality, his eyes were suddenly drawn to the Macedonians beyond that forward dozen—a ripple had gone through Archelaus's line. Imperceptible at first, yet certain.

His brow furrowed, squinting as a stone kicked up clouds of dust to his side.

Again the Macedonian line shook, before its entire length came to a halt. Trumpets stopped. War cries ceased.

The hell is Archelaus doing?

But the image before him only grew more surreal. Macedonians began to about-face, scurrying back toward the path's elbow whence they came—all but one.

One raced forward and shouted, *"We're under attack!"*

And there it was. A ghostly colored mass carved its way into the river of red, storming over the edge onto the path—a colored mass that could only belong to one man.

"Timanthes, you bloody bastard!" Aratus roared with glee. "Syrian, do you see this? Can you believe this?"

"We're under attack!" the lone Macedonian cried again in panic. *"Archers, archers to the forward walls!"*

Indeed, in a matter of seconds, a vicious melee had exploded on the narrow walkway, Achaean warriors wedging the enemy column in two. Some Macedonians plucked Achaeans off as they scampered up the slope, sending dead and wounded backward in graceless free falls. But Timanthes's brigade steadily got the better of the clash. Many Macedonians had no room to reverse course in their tight ranks, leaving their sides and rears open for quick impalement. The bigger issue soon became the mounting volume of corpses to negotiate among the terrified living.

The forward dozen Macedonians nearest to Aratus had paused, then fallen back upon hearing the tumult to their rear and the calls of their compatriot for help and archers. Lysistratos still faced them without flinching, sword at the ready, testing them—daring them—by his inaction.

"Archers to the forward wall now!"

And hearing it again made Aratus realize—the deadly hail of bolt and stone had lightened. Archers and slingers alike were heeding the panicked Macedonian's call, the Strategos watching them sprint along the wall walk. Sure enough, when he looked back at Lysistratos, he found his junior officer staring at him square in the eye.

"Go!" he bellowed simply. *"Go!"*

192

In a flash, Lysistratos and his men were engulfed in vengeful spears. None of them had a chance, limbs run through from a bevy of angles, before their bellies met the same fate. He died with a blade still in his hand, although save for a glare in Aratus's direction, the Macedonians didn't stop long to admire their work. In moments, they were running back down toward the crisis at the bend.

Aratus's vision went white with rage. "Thorakitai, on your feet!"

Not a moment later, a brisk shove nearly toppled him.

"I see it now, I bloody see it," Erginus growled in frustration, pointing eastward. "Keep low and follow me."

"Move out, then!" the Strategos barked. "And laddermen, you be ready, dammit! You need to be next to me as soon as I say the word!"

"Aye, Strategos!"

And at once the Sicyonian snake slithered single file up a slope becoming increasingly rocky and barren, slowly working their way toward the southwestern corner of the Acrocorinth's bean. The terrain grew steeper and more foreboding, but with the shining light and waning projectiles, the men could cautiously place each step. It wasn't long before Aratus laid eyes on what had become the target of his fascination—his obsession?—the mythical cleft in the rockface.

Sure enough, it was masked. Camouflaged perfectly behind a tuft of grass, a fissure in the mountainside weaved southeasterly up the slope, the "path" a mere ledge at two or three feet across at best. Of course, nothing protected a climber from the near 1,900-foot sheer drop off the barren side should a step miss its mark.

No matter, Aratus thought, swatting away pebbles left in the wake of the burly Syrian's climb. Try as he might, however, he couldn't help but glance over the edge at one point, eyes tracing the seemingly infinite plummet of a stone or two. He swallowed away the ball in his throat and looked upward instead, hands seeking a steadying grip in the rock wall to complement his feet. The peak of the southwestern tower loomed high overhead, but just as Erginus had promised, their trek was for all practical purposes totally hidden at this angle; he could only hope that the fort's archers hadn't kept track of their progress in lieu of the panic that Timanthes's charge had caused. The quiet on this side of the mountain proved more eerie than comforting.

Timanthes! he reminded himself, casting one final glimpse of his friend's battle on the mountain trail. At his distance, little detail was evident except for perhaps the only one that mattered—the Macedonian corps decisively split in two and scattering backward. To their credit, at least some reds had fallen back in good order under the protection of their archers and slingers.

"Split like a log, sire!" an excited cry came from the man behind him, who had followed his leader's gaze. *"We've got 'em running!"*

"Gonna need two men to hold these damn things in place, sire," a young soldier named Pythocles said to him with wide eyes. "No way one's gonna do it."

"So it is, then," Aratus said through a deep breath, before smiling grimly. "Just hold on tight, please, aye?"

Pythocles smiled back. "Of course."

"When the last of us is up, someone needs to return to the main path and wait for Timanthes, aye? Gods willing he will be entering through the front gate and have no need of this approach. But if he does…"

"We'll be there to guide him."

"Aye, then." And with that, he grabbed the side rails of the ladder on his left, Erginus lining up on the one to his right. "You ready, Syrian?"

But the burly man clearly was not, face wrought with pain and despair.

"Erginus?"

"Somethin's wrong," he said through clenched teeth, hand rubbing his wounded shoulder once again.

The Strategos's bloodrush morphed into a weight in his stomach. "Can you climb or no?"

The Syrian mounted the ladder again, but his hand on his injured side quickly slipped off the rung it clung to. He tried to climb it with his one good arm, the other hanging pathetically limp, but his pace was glacial and laborious, his figure one that appeared ready to plunge backward off the cliff to certain death.

"Dammit, get down from there," Aratus barked in frustration.

"No!"

"I mean it, Syrian, I need men who can fight! I don't need liabilities right now!"

"We had a deal and I'll not give you purpose to renege on it!"

Aratus nearly reeled in disbelief. "The deal bloody stands, I didn't say you needed to dance upon the walls to collect your reward! You've gotten us here, it's enough! The gods will do with us now what they will."

The exhausted Erginus wouldn't look at the Strategos as he descended back toward the ground. "Promise me."

"Oh, gods above, we need to—"

"Promise me!"

"Promised! And if you are so inclined to help us survive, you'll get off the damn ladder and wait with Pythocles to help guide Timanthes here if we need him."

The Syrian snorted in assent, before glaring at Aratus. "Aye, but you can send the young'n up with you. A pup can't do this climb again, let alone in the dark. No need wasting a good sword down here."

Pythocles leaned toward Aratus's ear. *"You trusting this bastard? Now all of a sudden he's hurt?"*

195

"I saw the stone smash him. And he killed his share outside the—"
"One of us should tail him at least, even if we say we aren't."
"He could've betrayed us a hundred times by now, if he'd wanted."

"We're fifteen hundred feet up on one of the most gods-forsaken rocks I've ever seen," Erginus growled. "No need for whispering now, boys."

The Strategos smirked, before giving the slightest shake of his head he could give in Pythocles's direction. He knew the young warrior could be right. He knew he could be wrong. But despite the setbacks, despite the obstacles he'd overcome to end up on this side of the mountain, and despite the resistance he'd faced from his confidants, his instincts had propelled him forward, closer and closer to his dream. And as he looked at Erginus now, he couldn't say he felt any doubts. Even still...

"Your turn then—promise me, Erginus. Promise Pythocles."

"Promise what?"

"You know precisely what."

The Syrian chuckled darkly. "I coulda killed you a dozen ways already, and I haven't. But dead men don't pay their debts, I don't care what you pledged to me in that banker's hut. So of course I'll see your friend to these walls if it comes to that."

Aratus gave the hint of a smile as he knew the men understood each other. "It's going to be hell up there, I know it... so don't waste time once we're up."

He pulled down on his helmet, securing it tight, checked the straps of his armored shirt. The welt on his leg from the slinger shot throbbed but he dared not look at it for fear of dwelling on the irrelevant. If he was headed to the Styx in a matter of moments, what's the difference if he goes there with a silly welt?

"Doubt they'll pay the Boatman, will they?" he asked as his hands found ladder rungs once again.

"Who? The Macedonians?" Erginus replied with a surprised chuckle. "They'll gut the first man that fetches their coin purse. Your limbs will be on every corner of these walls if you fail; your head will find a place of honor among the crows, I'm sure."

Though meant in jest, the comment sobered them both; Pythocles too, who looked to the ground in solace, both surely pondering the fact that their bodies may not be recovered, not given the rites. And the crows... in his failed Boeotian campaign, Aratus had seen firsthand what ravages a murder of crows could inflict upon the dead and dying—including human heads, be they severed or attached. Lips torn away, holes punched in flesh left to fester with maggots, eyeballs ripped free or left dangling in grotesque futility. The vile birds painted the skies black over the battlefield of Chaeronea that day, the ground a muddy red with blood—

The Strategos shook his head free of the horrible memories, his tired mind choosing to remind him of his worst failure at the worst time. "Aye," he said simply, legs propelling his body skyward.

With a look away, the Syrian offered, "Remember, Sicyonian—you keep watch for the officers! Archelaus has fallen in with Timanthes, no doubt, but look for Persaeus—"

"A gray old man, as you called him," Aratus hissed back down the ladder.

"An old man, but as city Archon, surely one surrounded by the city's finest! And Theophrastus—"

"I thought he commanded the port!"

"Aye, but he uses this rock to get a better vantage of that port every so often, remember? Put a spear through 'em all, Strategos, and the garrison may—"

Aratus stopped midway up the ladder, firing a glare back down to the suddenly nervous Syrian. Without another word, he placed an index finger to his lips, holding his look until Erginus gave an obedient nod, followed by placing a fist over his heart.

I hope I see you again, Aratus thought, nodding back in kind. Whereby his eyes fell to Pythocles, the man immediately beneath him on the ladder; to him, he held up four fingers, not one, and the young soldier knew precisely what was meant—the men were to form a wall of steel on the wall's walkway, four men abreast, shields interlocking. After that, the plan was clear: a mad sprint west then north toward the main gate. If they could take that, if they could force the entryway...

A final deep breath. *Off we go...*

CHAPTER 20

17th Day of Apellaios, Year 2 of the 134th Olympiad
(August 8, 243 B.C.)

Six rungs to the top. His body felt light, legs heavy. Fatigue gnawed at them, burned them, defied the adrenaline coursing through his every limb.

Four rungs. Arms felt jittery. Mouth dry.

Two. *Apollo guide me. Father, Mother...*

With a final heave, he launched his body upon the tooth of the battlement, rolling quickly and noisily onto the poorly lit walkway. He crouched low and wide-eyed as he waited for the rest of his men to pile on next to him.

For as calm as this portion of the walls seemed to be, the fortress grounds below were a frenzy. Torchbearers flitted about like fireflies upon gravel paths, some carrying bows, some carrying armor, others seemingly running without purpose. Troops scurried back and forth out of barracks, armories, warehouses and the like. Fevered shouts betrayed the men's fears, the sounds of swords unsheathing their martial serenade. There were far more shrines and sanctuaries on the acropolis than Aratus expected to see, his knowledge limited primarily to the infamous Temple of Aphrodite and underground freshwater spring, which crowned the mountain's summit in the east. From so far away, only the top of the temple was visible, the torchstands beneath its four-pillared pediment providing an eerie glow.

A glance behind him showed no wall activity as far as he could see—he only prayed it was as a result of the Syrians' good work. Less than a hundred yards ahead of him stood the southwestern tower, the first target of their assault, the hinge upon which the wall line shifted due north. Multiple torches revealed quite clearly that it was garrisoned, but it seemed just as clear that their attention was drawn to the battle raging on the grounds below.

Have they truly lost track of us? he thought cautiously to himself. *Surely, they know there is a column they haven't accounted for, even as dark as it was...*

Two dozen thorakitai had fallen in with him. He slung his shield to the fore and pulled his spear from its backstrap, settling into his position furthest right, just along the interior edge of the wall. He glanced to Pythocles on his left.

"Another dozen and we push—"

"Hey!"

Aratus looked up.

A torchlit face in the second floor window of the tower. Then another, and another.

"Hey!" the shout came again, more frantic. *"Hey, we've a breach! We've-we've a breach!"*

A Macedonian accent. Macedonian bows leveled at them.

"Shit, shields up, men!"

A horn rang out from the tower, a nauseating sound. Dull, nasally. A harbinger of death.

"There's no more time, sire!" Pythocles cried.

"Aye! March low, shields high. Shields high! Cover each other and make for the door just ahead!"

"Just ahead." The two hundred feet between them and the tower entrance may as well have been a mile as shields in the front rank interlocked, shields in the second rank offering cover overhead.

The first few bolts came screaming in, blasting divots into the centuries-old walkway. Dusty clouds blinded Sicyonians huddled tight in formation.

More faces appeared in the window. More bows. More arrows. More horns.

The dust and dark proved less helpful on the wall than it did during their harrowing climb. Now shields thudded repeatedly upon impact, some split width-wise and made useless. Even then, rear soldiers would offer new ones to keep the push going.

"Agh!"

The man on the far left of the front crumpled, hands grasping a punctured foot. The Sicyonian column rippled along its shield wall.

"Hold form, lads! Let Pausias to the back!"

THOK.

An arrow crumpled the ground beneath him, foot slipping over the edge, body falling uncontrollably backward into the warrior behind him.

"I've got you, sire!" the brave man shouted above the din, arms acting as hooks under his armpits. But still his leg dangled precariously in the air, torso too. *"Help me with the Strategos, dammit!"*

From the impact, he could tell the shot didn't come from the tower. In his frustrated scramble, he looked at the grounds below and his blood curdled. The "fireflies" he'd seen racing about without purpose had seemingly found one—the Sicyonian surprise party. Lights surged toward the wall in growing numbers, those closest already loosing arrows.

"We've got shooters on the right side too, boys!" he heard Pythocles yell, seeing the same disturbing thing. *"On the grounds below, watch yourselves!"*

"Grab the Strategos's other leg!" Quickly now, so he—"

THWIT.

A bolt between the eyes silenced his rescuer. Aratus saw it go in just as he'd been hoisted to his feet and the arms went limp; a foot lower and it was his forehead painted crimson. For all the death he'd seen in his life, it was among the worst sights he could remember, made worse as the young man's body tumbled helplessly over the edge.

"Shit-eating cowards!" he yelled in agony, watching the body land face down as shots poured in from seemingly everywhere.

"Defensive formation's not going to work anymore, sire!" Pythocles said as his spear arm steadied his commander, shield arm swung around them both. *"Too slow, too vulnerable! Permission to charge?"*

"Aye!" the general roared, fury rising, hamstring tightening from his awkward tumble. *"A bloody talent to the first person with a spear through an archer!"*

The harried line broke into a furious charge toward the tower door not twenty yards distant.

Then the door swung open.

The blackness within spewed forth a mad scramble of enemies with swords in hand, throwing spears strapped to their backs, circular shields anchored to their wrist. In an instant, Aratus could see the tell-tale signs of Illyrians—disc breastplates covered in swirling patterns, their crested, chinless helmets covering braided locks, their distinctive *sica* blades, curved for precision stabbing. They were tough non-Greek mercenaries hailing from the lands west of Macedon, north of Epirus—and though they were notoriously unreliable, these men seemed loyal enough.

The thorakitai slowed to a startled trot.

All but Aratus.

"Follow me, dammit! Shield cover along the side!"

The Sicyonians picked up the charge. The Illyrians lost not a step.

"For Sicyon by the gods! For Achaea!"

The two forces collided like rolling boulders. Aratus gutted one right away, his spear entombed in the man's body. On balance, the Illyrians had the better weapons for close combat, but this was beyond "close." Indeed, shields clanged against shields, bodies against bodies, maneuvering room all but nonexistent. The rear ranks of the thorakitai formed a protective dome over the front ranks, doing their best to shield fronts and sides from relentless archer fire.

The fight was quickly nothing more than a pushing match, about a dozen Illyrians wedged between the Sicyonians and the tower. Aratus could hear the grunts and growls and curses of the foreign tongue, occasionally mixed with crude Greek here and there. One of them stared daggers at the Strategos, his mouth an open, toothless maw of frothy spit—until a friendly spear ran straight through it.

The rear ranks had seen openings to send spears over their comrades' shoulders. Indeed, the Illyrians were really sitting ducks, crammed in tight as they were. Aratus's eyes widened with delight.

"Again! Front ranks, pin 'em down! Press 'em!"

The more they pressed, the more Illyrian heads presented themselves as targets, the wide slit down the middle of their helmets offering no protection where it was needed most. Sicyonian shafts shot over shoulders again and again, jabbing at eyes and faces like they were spearing fish. Blood slickened the floor of the old stone wall, and it wasn't long before Aratus realized the enemy hadn't even the room to die in place.

"Front ranks, release press!"

On command, they let up on their pressure, and like a stack of dishes, the dead Illyrians tumbled in succession over the edge of the wall, some aided in their descent by shoves and kicks. The doorway was visible once again, as were a handful of now terrified Illyrians within the tower. Momentarily frozen, they suddenly sprang to close the door.

Aratus grinned, face drenched in crimson, and drew his sword in lieu of his spear. "Thorakitai—*get* those bastards!"

He needn't say it twice. In moments, his men were hurdling their shoulders into the door—once, twice, three times until it swung open in violence. Vicious *sica* slashes immediately dove deep into the arm of one of the Greeks, but Pythocles, Aratus, and the rest surged past him with slices and stabbings of their own, the cries and screams and clanging of metal echoing maddeningly off the walls of the tight quarters. In the darkness of the cell, more and more Illyrians dropped until finally—

"Stop! We surrender!"

An Illyrian man pulled fellow troops back from the fray, back toward a corner. Many of his comrades were loath to follow, weapons still leveled, even as their bodies instinctively retreated against the surge of Sicyonians filling the chamber. Nonetheless, the vocal man clearly carried some weight, surely the mercenaries' captain.

"Men of Ardiaei, *stop!*" he roared again to the resisting few, calling them out by their tribal name. The Ardiaei were indeed one of the fiercest and most dominant clans of Illyria.

"Please, Greek!" he said with hands raised now, staring straight at a heaving Strategos. "We surrender to you, yes?"

His tongue was spot on, meaning he hailed from among the wealthy of his native lands. While most Illyrians had picked up at least some of the language due to their proximity to Hellenic neighbors, true fluency was limited to the upper strata.

Aratus's eyes danced warily between him and the stairway leading to the second story, a quiet thick as soup taking hold. *Is this a trap? By the gods, how could he think we are in position to take anyone's "surrender"? How could we take prisoners in the beating heart of an enemy's fortress?*

"Drop your blades, *now,*" he finally growled.

"Sire, we kill them now, aye?" Pythocles hissed through exhausted pants.

"Pythocles, enough—*Illyrian, drop your gods forsaken weapons now!*"

"We surrender to you; we not fight you anymore, no?"

"Drop the weapons and we'll discuss!"

"Swear to our safety before the gods and we drop them, not before!"

"I'm not swearing anything! You drop them now, then we'll discuss, and you'll tell us about Theophrastus and Persaeus and whatever the hell else we demand!"

"Theophrastus? Persaeus? No, no, you swear—"

"Do it!"

"— to our safety and we drop them! We kill Macedonian—"

Archers from the stairway appeared out of nowhere. Their volley dropped two thorakitai on the spot.

"You bastards!" Pythocles roared, charging the cornered Illyrians.

Fellow Sicyonians followed suit. The mercenary captain kept his hands aloft, eyes frantic. "No, no! We stand down, we—"

It was a fearsome butchery, one the Strategos knew he was powerless to stop. Instead, he pulled his wounded to a side free of the melee, sending others to clear out the brazen archers plaguing the stairs and second floor. When it was done and they'd brought their injured in from the wall and sealed the eastern door, the Hellenes were left gasping for breath in the cramped tower room, the paucity of candlelight betraying little of the carnage they'd wrought. Beyond their own breathing was the innocuous sound of dripping—its source the stream of blood cascading down the stairway steps.

"I'd always heard the Illyrians were dastardly, *dastardly* men," Pythocles said, hands on hips beneath an open mouth, glare fixed upon the heap of slaughtered mercenaries. "But *bastards* they are. Every last one of 'em."

"In truth, I think he meant to surrender," Aratus said, his body reduced to a squat with eyes closed and head hanging loose.

His soldier looked at him cockeyed. "Surely, you do not, sire?"

"I do, I do think he meant to surrender," the Strategos offered, shaking his head. "Saw it in his eyes, whoever that man was."

Pythocles grunted his defiance. "Saw we had numbers on them. Bought time for their archers to save them."

"Aye, well..." Aratus started to rebut again, but petered out. "Well, we couldn't have taken prisoners in any event, and we surely couldn't have advanced with them in our rear, weapons or no. Though it would have been nice to know about Theophrastus and Persaeus."

Pythocles pursed his lips and nodded in concession.

At last, the Strategos let out a deep exhale and rose to his feet, the majority of his troops still in squats, their sweaty helmets doffed aside, others tending to the wounded. "We should have marked the stairway," he said quietly, looking toward the men who'd suffered as a result of the oversight—one had taken a bolt to his leg, which his mates were keen to leave be for the moment, holding in vital fluids as it was; the other was left with a shaft protruding askew from his chest. Neither injuries looked to be fatal, not immediately, anyway. "That is my failing, certainly not yours. As usual, you've outdone your commander so far by three-fold. You've done magnificently, lads," he said plainly, receiving sounds of approval in response. "You've honored the gods with your strength, your valor. Simply take a moment and ponder where we stand! Ponder where we are and what we've done and remember we've not yet *begun* to act this night!"

203

He could feel his blood catching fire again, his body needing every ounce of it. "I told you on our march that the gods willed this mission, and surely you've done nothing to lose their favor, have you?"

"Aye, Strategos."

He nodded decisively, pacing toward the northern door. "Gather yourselves, check your armor, your blades. When we pass through this doorway, we'll have two hundred yards to the main gate, and we'll have to cover it quickly. Gods only know who awaits us, but with fortune, it will include Timanthes and his three hundred."

"To Timanthes!" some chanted with a raise of their spears.

"And the wounded, sire?" Pythocles asked, throwing his bloody helmet back atop a head of drenched hair.

"Aye, the wounded," Aratus echoed, trying to distinguish the lamed from the tired. "How many can no longer run with us?"

He immediately regretted the question, as of course no one wanted to concede their debilities before his colleagues. But boiled down, he had seven that would prove more hindrance than help, as much as he hated the thought of his troop reduced any further. But what to do with them?

The plop of yet another blood drop from the floor above brought him clarity. "We've got a bunch of dead bowmen upstairs, don't we?" he said, looking around the room. "Any of you wounded fools feel like working bows?" He had trained them in archery in Sicyon, but only minimally; marksmanship with their throwing spears took far more precedence. Nevertheless…

"Well, you'll work them, anyway. Some of you can sweep the grounds below, some of you the northern wall. Apollo guide your shots, but even enough to make a Macedonian or two piss himself will do the trick. At the very least, don't hit us…"

The soldiers chuckled and the makeshift archers were soon at their posts, though not before hurling the slain Macedonians from the tower windows. Some of the Sicyonian shooters looked helplessly impotent, so overcome with pain. Pausias, the poor soul that took that first arrow to the foot, stuck a wooden bit between his teeth—anything to ward off the agony and steady his arms. Anything for one more chance to make an impact on this night of nights.

Apollo watch me, he thought to himself, wincing as his men braced behind him, waiting for their commander to swing open the portal to the northern wallwalk. *Father, watch me. Mother. Naukydes. My blessed son, my unborn.* He gritted his teeth, eyes misted beneath closed lids, hands gripped a fresh spear tightly. *I do this for you… that my actions may pay homage to your memory, to remember you and so make you immortal. For if the gods so will it to be and I succeed, your names will bask equally in any honor I reap. I will see to it.*

"Ready, lads?"

"Aye, Strategos."

"Four to a rank, just like before."

"Aye, Strategos."

"Watch your sides. Don't stop until you hit the gate or hit an enemy... whichever's first."

"Aye, Strategos."

A deep breath.

They were off.

The air was cool and refreshing versus the dankness of the tower, filling their lungs as they raced along the walkway. They ran under cover of darkness, the sky still a murky violet as the moon wrestled with blackened clouds. The only light to his left came from homes or temples or sanctuaries in the valley hundreds of yards away; to his right, the fortress grounds still abounded with "fireflies," panic still alive and well, their uproar a stark contrast to the Sicyonians' silence. Aratus knew they had only moments before they were picked up by archers and slingers.

And he was right.

Seconds later, the bolts returned, first at a trickle, increasing quickly to a steady hail. The attacks were all the more unnerving by the absence of light, so one had no sense who was firing and from where. One simply ran, hoped, and prayed.

There was commotion up ahead. Torchlights grew in volume the closer they came to the towers of the main gate, though it was still too dim to tell who blocked the walkway. His back was to the thorakitai, his hands frantically waving at what appeared to be a growing mass of soldiers in front of him.

"I'm seeing a healthy number of Macks straight on, lads!" he yelled, his voice drowned out by a pandemonium nearer and louder. "Three, maybe four dozen, I think."

The shadowy man looked back quickly, certainly seeing the Strategos this time, but again he stood with arms to the side, ranting to the Macedonians at length. *"Stay at your bloody posts below! You're not needed here!"*

Perplexed or no, the Sicyonians drew closer.

"Syrian, they're due behind you! Stand down or by the gods your head will be on this pike by morning! Step aside!"

Syrian?

"Diocles!" Aratus exclaimed aloud. "Diocles, that mad son of a whore! He's mad as his brother!"

"Stallin' 'em?" Pythocles asked through pants.

"Gods willing!"

"I will not step aside, this is—"

But the Macedonians decided the matter for him. The Syrian was hurled unceremoniously off the wall to the grounds below, his landing thud obscured in the light and a cloud of dust. Aratus's shock had no time to linger as spears leveled at him and his men, enemy breaking into a trot. Even in the dimness, he could make out the shiny bronze shields, though their red tunics and helmets were nothing but blackened silhouettes.

The distance closed impossibly fast, but the Macks slowed at the moment of impact, refusing the Illyrian approach. Instead, they ferociously brought their spears to bear. They weren't *sarissae*, but they were longer poles than the Sicyonians', and the enemy knew it. One thrust after another kept the thorakitai at bay, probing, clipping, stabbing away, leaving little opening to retaliate. Worse, they forced rank upon rank back into each other, dangerously compressing the troops.

An arc of Sicyonian throwing spears soared overhead, finding Macedonian marks, groans erupting. The strikes startled their advance, but didn't break it. Friendly arrows from the tower didn't either. These were professionals that the King kept on a war tilt year-round. No one else in Hellas could afford to do that, no one else could match their training, their conditioning.

Their aggression, their form, their cold, single-minded fury was pressure enough to break a fresh man, let alone a spent one. Were it not for the narrow walkway on which they fought, he knew it would have been impossible to resist the onslaught. He'd underestimated the fight; his flesh was weak even if his mind was strong.

On they came, the thrusting, the pounding of iron heads like waves upon beach. The thorakitai held up admirably, but soon Mack spears blasted through wooden shields, splintered others. They reeled further, the second ranks doing their utmost to keep them upright. The left side of the front rank was mauled and bloody, only Aratus and Pythocles resisting on the right. Arrows from the ground below flew unabated, clanking off the stone wall or whizzing by, if not.

"Cowardly dogs!" the lead Macedonian yelled in a rage, sensing blood. *"Who the hell are you?"*

More pounding. A slice through Aratus's spear arm.

"You cowards dare come here? You dare insult the King and gods alike?"

Aratus's foot slipped. He dropped to a knee. His shield was nearly torn to pieces. Only the spears of the second rank kept a death blow at bay.

"Answer me!"

Pythocles took the captain's lance in the chest. The Strategos could only pray that his chain mail did its job. The lad's body lurched into his regardless, sending him precariously close to the wall's edge. Remnants of his shield parried blows from his crouch, spear hand planted to floor.

"How dare you come—"

"Enemies at the gates!"

A pause. A soaring cry of alarm.

"All men to the gate, hurry!"

It was the sweetest sound Aratus had ever heard.

Macedonian cries of panic. Even Aratus's assailant took note, stopped pounding, looked around. *"Shit,"* he muttered.

The moment was all Aratus needed.

The Strategos exploded from his crouch. Before the Mack could flinch, a spear was through his jaw. He stumbled back against his own men, gurgling pathetically.

The success surprised even its achiever. More so when he saw his bloody spearpoint again, shimmering bright red.

It shimmered under the moonlight, unvexed yet again. *"Ha!"* he yelled maniacally. "Selene blesses us, that's why we're here! That's why we dare!"

He lunged again with his spear.

"Helios blesses us!"

And again, followed by a kick against an enemy shield.

"And Apollo!"

"For Apollo!" the second-rank Sicyonians yelled, surging forward against stunned Macks. They were united for sure, defensively sound, warding off the thorakitai's strikes. Even still, Aratus could see their shaken focus, eyes nervously drawn behind them, back toward the gate—and in a moment, he could see precisely why.

Three hundred Achaeans.

Bloodied, tired, but triumphant, Timanthes led them in a brazen march straight up the path to the Acrocorinth's western portal; the gate was sandwiched between two massive towers, the southern of which being Aratus's target. Timanthes's march was only part of what left Aratus speechless, though. No, beyond their motley of colors, beyond the insignia adorning their shields, it was their spears—the brightened moon shone down upon them, rendering their tips as bright as fire; some of the men still had throwing spears to boot, adding more "torches" to the eye. Combined with the length and bellow of the Achaean line, it looked as if Timanthes fielded an army of thousands. This impression, this fortuitous trick of the eye, wasn't lost on Aratus—nor the fort's defenders, it seemed.

Emergency horns. *"Every man to the gate! Now!"*

"Listen to your friends, O Kingsmen!" Aratus cried with great malevolence, recklessly striking at the Macks. "Our numbers are vast! The city below has fallen, I promise you, and this fort's not long for it! You will *not* be spared our vengeance!"

More horns. Screams.

"You're too late, Kingsmen!"

"Don't you listen to a word this vermin speaks!" the enemy captain roared back, having found his voice. "The gate will hold, now—"

An arrow shot through his thigh. With an agonizing shout, he dropped his shield and fell to his hands and knees. Others in the Macedonian column fell likewise.

But the shots hadn't come from the front. Perplexed, Aratus looked about like the rest of them until his gaze found a wounded Diocles directing a small contingent of Syrian bowmen from the ground below. The Mack saw them too.

Aratus smiled. *Oh, Erginus, you failed to tell me your brother worked the bow—or would work it now.*

"You're too late, Kingsman," he said coldly to the captain.

His enemy barely had time to look up before Aratus's boot kicked him off the edge. Diocles was on him like a jackal, quick to cut his throat, while his bowmen drew back on their strings again.

"Aim for their fucking legs!" Diocles raged, one of his arms obviously broken.

The infamous Mack resilience was put to the test—pressed from the front by Sicyonians, assailed by traitorous Syrians from below, a veritable horde gathering just outside their wall, all while their captain lay in a blood-choked heap.

"Stand down and you may yet live, Kingsmen!" Aratus roared.

The second volley launched.

More Macks dropped.

They broke.

Their first few ranks had fought on as long as they could—they had no choice—but those behind them peeled back, one by one. They fell back toward the tower, and the thorakitai followed closely on their heels, as fast as their wearied legs would carry them. They plucked off several more, but the majority escaped to scramble down the tower steps, their fatigue hardly a fraction of their pursuers.

"Tell your Syrians to stand down against us!" Aratus barked down to Diocles just before he entered the tower, unsure he was heard over the pandemonium. *"All of 'em, tell them I mean no Syrian any harm, now or afterward!"*

Please be heard. Please listen.

Because the gateway's towers were still infested with archers—some Macedonian but the overwhelming majority Syrian mercs—it'd be suicide to keep after the enemy spearmen without bringing them to heel.

For their part, the bowmen in the tower were terrified. Some couched by arrow slits, others atop the walkway connecting the gate to the northern tower, but none could believe their eyes when the frenzied Sicyonians appeared. A few immediately threw down their bows and prostrated as if before an idol. They knew their reckoning for a night of showering death upon his troops was nigh.

In truth, there were too many for the exhausted troops to kill and Aratus knew it. *"Drop your bows, now!"* he gambled instead, to which a surprising majority obeyed. "If you're Syrian, you may leave by this staircase, but do so now."

After a hesitant pause, a large body of men, mostly bearded thick and adorned with simple tunics, filed out of the room between thorakitai spears and swords. Aratus's eyes turned to those two dozen left behind, apparently honest Macedonians.

"Kill them all."

Their swords made short work of them. The crosswalk was likewise culled, the bowmen helpless with no infantry to protect them. The stunned Achaean column below cheered wildly as they watched, having suffered a withering fire that to that point seemed never-ending.

As he stood upon the gatewalk between the towers, as he saw the brave column snaking its way up the hill to the massive wooden doors beneath his feet, as he saw his closest friend Timanthes and the intrepid Erginus bathed in moonlight among his men, it was all too surreal for the Strategos. For a moment, the sounds of the attack and panic faded, his eyes blinking away his disbelief before a vista painted in hills and valleys, punctuated by the twin peak at Mount Penteskouphia a mile west. At last, he simply shot his hands above his head despite the pain.

"Achaeans!" he roared to them, and to him, they roared back. *"I shall see you inside!"*

The northern tower was devoid of archers or slingers when they entered, perhaps taking heed of their comrades' fate. It didn't matter. Now, it was but a race down the steps to the gateway door, that final barrier between fort and Achaeans.

The staircase spat them into the fort at the end of the forty-foot corridor beneath the crosswalk leading from the gate—and it was chaos. The Syrian archers Aratus had pardoned were still pouring out of the southern tower, their simple gray tunics in contrasting with the red and bronze of onrushing Macedonian reinforcements, Diocles calling to them all the while. The morass of humanity left Syrians penned in for slaughter, with neither Macedonian nor Sicyonian able to get at the other. The bowmen began to fall like grain to a scythe.

"The Syrians are not to be harmed!" Aratus yelled over a fray made deafening by the narrow corridor. *"Fall back with me to unbar the gate!"*

Down the corridor they retreated, the Macedonians' merciless butchery of their own mercenaries echoing as they did. It was a risky gambit—the gate had three massive bars to undo and the thorakitai had little time, space, or energy to do so. A hobbled Pythocles led part of them in a rearguard while Aratus and the rest went about dislodging the locks. He could hear his friendly troops just on the other side, the very sound like rain after years of drought.

One bar down.

At the opposite end, the Syrian massacre went on without abatement. Soon the option of retreating further into the fort seemed impossible to the sorry lot, so the frantic bowmen turned toward the corridor for safety, thinking the gateway to be an option.

The Macks followed suit.

"Brace yourselves, lads!" Aratus could hear Pythocles cry, a stampede of Syrians and Macedonians imminent.

A grunt. A pull. A stabbing pain through the Strategos's back from the strain.

Two down.

The third was the highest—so high that only the tallest could reach it, Aratus chief among them. On his tiptoes he pushed, teeth gritting, eyes clenched, helmet feeling a thousand degrees. Others tried jabbing it with their spears, all while a veritable battle took place at their backs, all in a nearly blackened space barely wide enough for four people. Thorakitai jabbed at Macks from around Syrian bodies, Macks did the same, sometimes hitting, more often killing a merc.

"Free us!" Syrians yelled. *"Open the gate!"*

"Help us fight 'em, you bastards!" Pytho said. *"There's nowhere to go!"*

Aratus's head smashed into the gate. His vision went yellow. "Agh!" he mouthed, but nothing came out. His body pancaked against the door, his fingers still tickling the bottom of the top bar. The flood of Syrians had found them, panic-stricken and clawing for the gates like dogs.

The Strategos could barely breathe. The whole passageway reeked of sweat and blood and piss and shit. The air was as thick and hot as the most humid day he'd ever known. And they just kept coming. On and on, the crush of men all but paralyzing the Sicyonians, squeezing their lungs, bowing the doors. And who knew how close the Macedonians were getting? Was Pytho alive? Had the rear guard fallen? Couldn't see, couldn't hear anything.

"Get... them... back..." Aratus creaked.

But Pytho was right, there was nowhere to go. The luxury of two options all night—death or keep pushing—rapidly seemed headed toward one.

By the gods, find a way... You won't die squashed like a worm... bloody MOVE, Aratus!

And so he did. One foot, then the other. Lifting them up only to find the space beneath them filled instantly by another man's foot, another man's leg—perfect platforms to launch himself upward, upward into the bar.

THUD.

He hurtled his body straight up off of random knees. The pain sent shockwaves through his body, shoulder most of all.

"Come on, gods hear me! Come on!"

Another hurdle. Blinding pain. Fragments of his armor pinged everywhere.

"Come on!"

The knees of the man next to him buckled, body short of breath.

"Sire, they're getting close!"

Aratus didn't know who said it, the delirious lightness in his head and tingling in his limbs overtaking him. The impossible loudness of the carnage only added to the effect. The doors suddenly shaking as if in an earthquake.

"Sire, here they come—"

THUD.

The bar shook free, fell. The doors exploded open. Aratus collapsed forward—into the arms of an Achaean—gasping for air like a dying fish.

"Sire!" the soldier cried in shock.

A torrent of freed Syrians stormed through the Achaean crowd, oblivious to the sight of more spearmen. The Macedonians in pursuit halted upon sight of the hostile force, the company falling back as fast as they'd arrived once a few had been slain.

"Achaeans, halt!" he heard Promachus bark at the Achaeans giving chase into the fort.

"Syrians are to be spared…" the Strategos said with as much vigor as he could muster.

Steps behind him. "Aye, well, gods' blessings!"

He recognized the voice. When he looked up, Timanthes was at his side, bloodied, cleaved, and helmetless. He took the Strategos's weight from the soldier. "Stand up, you lazy bastard!"

Aratus gave a woozy smile. "Took your… bloody time… didn't you?" he said, embracing him in a painful hug.

"One day I'll grow tired of saving you from yourself, Strategos," his friend responded with a grin.

The pox on his brain dissipated, vision cleared as wobbly eyes found balance. "The job's not done… not yet."

"No, it is not," Timanthes said, face tired, pale, and worn in the light.

"Archelaus?"

"Captured. Bound up at the bend."

"Bound and tied in his own domain?" Aratus said, as he freed his body from Timanthes's support. "Well done."

His hand was wet. He looked at it, then looked to where it had been on his friend's waist.

Timanthes's mail was shattered. A pang struck his gut. Their eyes met.

"You hurt?"

"We all are."

"Are you *hurt?*"

Timanthes's face flashed the pain he was hiding. "There's no time for hurt right now." The stout Sicyonian grabbed a fallen spear and shield from the ground and shoved them into the Strategos's hands. "Come on, now. You were right, the gods will this. You're always bloody right."

The taller man's eyes lingered for a bit, but at last he pulled away. *If I'm a terrible liar, then what does that make him?* "No time to waste then," he said after a whack on the man's shoulder, trying to squelch his own concerns.

"Achaeans!" he called out to the gathering mass outside the gates.

"Strategos!" they called back in salute.

"Stay tight and follow closely! Macks, Gauls, Illyrians, maybe more waiting for us. Don't know how many… but the gods know there aren't as many as there once were!"

Some tired laughs, cheers.

"We make for Aphrodite's temple—and if one of you miserable curs gets lost, it's the highest bloody point on the mountain! And remember—the Syrian lights are to be spared but let 'em *know* they're to be spared!"

"We march!"

Another roar, and within moments they were on the move, funneling toward the doorway at the center between the two towers.

"Why the hell are we sparing any Syrians?"

Aratus looked behind him to find Erginus's quizzical face. The Sicyonian gave a maniacal laugh and gripped the man's bloody beard. "Because that brother of yours is even madder than you! He's turned a good lot of 'em traitor, had them shooting down Macks like fowl."

Erginus guffawed. "By the gods, he did?"

"Broken arm and all. Some Mack bastard threw him off the wall as we approached."

The Syrian darkened. "Aye?"

"Aye. Though he paid his debt in the end, I saw it."

Erginus's honor was hardly assuaged and he simply looked ahead.

"Anger's blinding. Keep your wits just a little longer, will you? This is it."

CHAPTER 21

*17ᵗʰ Day of Apellaios, Year 2 of the 134ᵗʰ Olympiad
(August 8, 243 B.C.)*

The fortress was like a tomb as they entered. Footsteps echoed hollow through the corridor, then crunched on the dry, rocky path leading to the summit a thousand feet further and four hundred feet higher. Gone were the sounds of shouts, horns, trumpets, replaced instead by the somber moans of the dying, the whistling winds that caressed the living. Barracks and quarters and eateries and storehouses and sanctuaries—all were empty or unattended as the Achaeans passed through.

But he knew "they" were somewhere. He hadn't counted the number he'd slain, but he was sure it wasn't close to the fort's full garrison—*it couldn't be*—with or without the Syrian bowmen. His own troops had been pared by about a quarter, the bulk of the losses coming from Archelaus's fierce resistance at the bend. "Fought like a lion," was how Timanthes phrased it.

Diocles met them and Aratus watched the brothers embrace. They muttered words to each other that Aratus couldn't hear before turning to him directly, a force of two or three dozen archers arrayed behind them.

What had once been a light tunic on Diocles was now soiled in dirt and blood. He was of smaller stature than Erginus, but somehow more menacing with a scarred, beardless face and a full head of dark curls. His right arm hung pathetically, his elbow a grotesque shape, broken bone pushing hard from beneath the skin. Nevertheless, to Aratus's shock, it was that hand he began extending in greeting, baring his teeth in pain.

"Friend, you needn't worry about such pleasantries. You've done more than I ever expected, more than your brother ever prom—"

"Take it."

Aratus looked at him and his crippled limb once again, his lips quivering to stay together to conceal his strain. It wasn't until the Strategos obeyed that he realized the monstrosity of his own arm—the slice through his shoulder left it caked in a crimson sleeve. He twitched his lips as he took the man's hand.

"You could tell the story of this night just by looking at our arms."

Diocles's mouth curved ever so slightly.

"And his beard," Aratus added, nodding at Erginus. His expression became serious. "And lest you wonder, your other brother is in my friend's care, and will see to it—"

Diocles interrupted with a scoff. "Dionysius is a dog."

"He's our brother still," Erginus groused.

"I heard what he planned to do; he wanted to turn over everyone, everything—including you, including me. Pshaw! Dog's a dog! The only man who's ever mattered to Dionysius is Dionysius."

"All right, lads," Aratus said in placation, regretting his decision to mention him. "Well, the gods will have special rewards for the courage you've shown tonight, and for that, I thank you."

The man is a traitor, Aratus thought quickly, not without irony. *Can I really refer to him as courageous? As noble? As if his motives have even a façade of altruism?* He shook his head in silence, too tired to dwell on it. *Who's to say what other motives he has? And why not engage in the fantasy that he has them, in any event? The ends and the means...*

For his part, Diocles didn't appear moved by any sentiment. "They've fallen back to the summit. I watched 'em. About five hundred yards yonder."

"As I expected they would. Any sense of their numbers?"

"More than there usually would be."

"And why's that?"

"Theophrastus, the man who commands—"

"The garrison at the port..."

"Aye—he joined the Archon Persaeus with a few dozen of that garrison last night. Had themselves quite a drinking party."

Indeed, he'd seen countless empty jugs of wine strewn about the grounds along with the rest of the detritus. Aratus tried to conceal his grin, glancing at Timanthes. "Both of those bastards are here tonight?"

Diocles frowned in thought. "Think so. But I can't see either of them standing down at this point. And General Theo would be a fool if he hasn't already called for the rest of his garrison."

Aratus nodded, and though the port was nearly three miles away, the message was self-evident—time was as short as it ever was. He eyed the bowmen behind Diocles. "Will your Syrian friends fight with us in taking the summit? Will you?"

"I'd only be a burden; I can lead you there and no more. The rest can choose for themselves," he said, nodding at them. "But they have my every encouragement."

The encouragements worked. The final climb began with a bundle of Syrian archers on either of the Achaean flanks. An unexpected benefit on this night of the unexpected.

As they moved through the silent darkness, his legs felt like anchors, shoulders throbbed, armor hung half-broken in most places. His head still rang with the cacophony of the entryway scrum, which frankly helped keep his thoughts from settling in worry upon Timanthes's wounds. He'd always been a stubborn one, that Timanthes, and the glances Aratus had stolen in his friend's direction showed a face irrepressibly placid, a gait with hardly a limp—which to Aratus meant signs of grievous injury he was desperate to conceal.

What had he said? The Strategos tried to recall through his jumbled thoughts. *"We're all hurt,"* was that it? That he—

A block of white upon the ridge ahead.

Aratus blinked for a second before it became clear it wasn't some monolithic block, rather a line of pale silhouettes, Temple of Aphrodite rising triumphantly behind them. They were naked from the waist up, short swords in one hand, ovular bucklers in the other. Bearded through and through, with wild long hair spilling out beneath conical helmets. They were a menacing sight, their image tonight matched only by their ferocious reputation.

They were Gauls. Barbarians, unfit to live among the Hellenes, their ancestors among those that tormented Hellas a generation prior. The most dangerous and unpredictable mercenaries a leader could ever barter for. The same that had defiled many a holy site in victory despite their payors pleading otherwise.

"Careful, lads," Aratus whispered, as much to himself as to Erginus and Timanthes on either side of him and the ranks they led up the last slope. *The King really dared bring these beasts to his most important possession in southern Hellas?*

A figure appeared from behind the ghostly line. A second. Squires followed with torches at their sides as they moved to the crest of the hill, a hundred feet distant from the Achaeans. On the left, a tall, cuirassed young man in a plumed helmet stood poised, sword drawn, lavish circular shield resting against his leg. On the right, an old man in a flowing chiton entirely devoid of battlefield regalia, his bald scalp reflecting moon and torchlight alike.

The two forces froze in place and eyed each other, silence thick.

The man on the right took a tentative step forward, though not without a hand on the left's shoulder. "Who are you?"

Aratus licked his lips, heart racing yet again, every word measured. "Are you Persaeus?"

A pause. A glance at the young Macedonian on his right. "I am Persaeus," he said, voice gravelly and tired. "And who are you?"

"The man to your right—you're Theophrastus?"

"I don't answer to dogs," the tall man said coldly, body still immobile.

"As is your right, Commander," Aratus said, feigning subordination.

"*Who* are you?" Persaeus demanded again.

"That's not important."

Theophrastus sheathed his sword, posture threatening. "Are you so embarrassed by your dishonor this night that you won't even share your name?"

"Oh, I take no shame from this night!" Aratus said, smile eagerly emerging. "To the contrary, 'my lord'—this is the greatest night of my life."

"Why?" Persaeus asked plainly, almost pityingly. "Whoever you are will be revealed; whoever you love, whatever you hold dear, it will surely be destroyed and for what?"

"For what? For this fort, Persaeus. For Corinth. You're going to stand down and surrender them both."

The older man stifled a nervous laugh. "Pardon?"

216

"You're going to stand down *now*," Aratus said, stepping forward. "The gods, the omens, even the Corinthians themselves have brought me here. And as they watch me now, they know I speak the truth when I say I harbor no ill will toward any Macedonian—"

"Well, that bodes well for the Macedonians, but I'm a Cypriot." His retinue snickered.

Aratus frowned at the mocking tone. "Has Antigonus not made you ruler of this city on Macedon's behalf?"

"He has."

"Then there's no need for distinctions or games, is there? And I was saying that I hold no ill will toward any Macedonian but one—none but the King."

The older man pursed his lips. "Now there *you* are making distinctions—the King and his soldiers are one and the same, I'm afraid. Indeed, you've struck the King this night as much as anyone."

"If only that were true," Aratus said, relishing the suggestion.

Persaeus nodded in silence for a bit as searching eyes jumped to his companion and back again. "Well, 'sire,' I will offer you this," he said, stepping yet closer down the hill, hands folding behind his back. "I will let you walk from here and you can keep your name, your secret. I won't promise we won't find out anyway, I can't promise protection from reprisals. You've done far, far too much for me to promise that, which I'm sure you understand. But I won't ask that you tell me—"

"My name is Aratus of Sicyon, son of the murdered Clenias."

Persaeus fell silent again, mouth half-open. Theophrastus shook off his shock first. "Sicyon?" he repeated in disgust. "You're as bloody dishonorable as we thought, then. Corinth has no quarrel with Sicyon; the *King* has no quarrel with Sicyon."

"The 'King' made quarrel with Sicyon when he sponsored my father's murder," Aratus said, anger rising as repressed emotions came to the fore, spear pointing at the men above him. "My *father*—the duly elected, freely chosen leader of my city!"

Persaeus's brow furrowed. "And your father's death you lay at the King's feet? You now condemn your people to ruin for some-some personal blood debt? Your father surely knew the stakes of leadership, the—"

"You mistake me. My tale is one of many across Hellas, across the Peloponnesus; one that I've heard over and over and over again. So I lay my father's death at his feet not for my own sake or vanity, but for the tyranny he's orchestrated, the tyranny he's spread, the tyranny he's used to keep how many Hellenes under lock and key? *How many?*"

"Aratus of Sicyon, son of Clenias," Persaeus responded in measured tone. "I was sent to his court thirty years ago. So I've known King Antigonus a very long time. I've lectured him, debated him, given him counsel; wept with him over losses, toasted him over successes. And as time's gone on, I've grown to appreciate what it is that he has done that the rest of Hellas does not—"

"Pray tell what that is."

"He saves the bloody Greeks from themselves. Their squabbling, their bickering, their wars, their feuds. And beyond that, he thanklessly throws back the barbarian hordes that batter the gates in the north, the hordes you never have to see. *He keeps the peace for your sake.*"

Deep down, Aratus respected Persaeus, much as most Hellenes did—but that only served to make his comments this night that much more tragic. "You're said to be a wise man, Persaeus, and I have no reason to doubt it. But it seems your familiarity with the King has blinded you as much as anything. You've let him infect you with the idea that he acts in anyone's interest beyond his own. He offers a 'peace' that no Hellene asked for, a 'peace' defined by the King and the King alone, and uses this 'peace' to justify any type of oppression he sees fit," he said with a shake of his head. "But those times are over. Gods willing—and I think they are—Hellas is to be free of his tentacles if it costs me my very life to make it so."

The old man sighed and rubbed a wrinkly face. "And you've convinced your fellow Sicyonians to multiply your folly, I see," he said, perusing Aratus's men again. "Or does your little League join your treachery as well?"

"It doesn't matter. All that matters now is whether you are standing down or you are ready to perish here."

"That's a 'yes,' Persaeus, Achaea's joined him," Theophrastus intervened, moving to Persaeus's side.

"Theophrastus, you have the misfortune of abandoning your post at Lechaeum for this fort," Aratus said with confidence, before pointing at the officer again. "You know your King would have your head for failing to secure the royal fleet—a fleet we're about to seize. But if you can, take solace in the fact that you were *fated* to be here. Aye, you were! So unless you intend to claim asylum in Aphrodite's temple, you have one choice—"

"I've done no wrong for which I need the gods' protection!" Theo yelled, voice carrying in echoes. "I'm not cowering in any temple! And allow me to make this brief—to those of Achaea that were duped by this madman, we offer you clemency now, no caveats given; the wayward Syrian bowmen among you included. Those of you that do not, I want you to hear me—you will be defeated, today or tomorrow or a month from now, it doesn't really matter when. But you *will* be defeated and the lucky of you will die. The rest will be captured, and your family and your little villages will then hear your womanly cries from this mountaintop as we roast each and every one of you alive. EVERY. ONE. OF—"

"And allow *me*, then! To every Macedonian at your side, I repeat, I have no vendetta with you! But understand if you stand with these bastards, you will leave us no choice! Understand that we have hundreds here, that hundreds more are marching up from the city, thousands more from Sicyon—go to your walls and watch them, if you'd like!"

Please do not...

"But you know that, don't you? After all, that's why you've retreated up here, isn't it? That's why you surrendered the gate to us! You know we're coming! So I'll ask you, do you really want to die on this rock hundreds of miles from home? Before your graves have even been prepared for the afterlife?"

He knew of the Macks' peculiar beliefs in a vigorous afterlife. One that had to be prepared for well in advance, such that they had proper provisions in their tomb to take with them into the realm beyond. The Macedonians were so vain as to think that Persephone herself would greet them, to guide them amongst the trees and water to Hades.

"It wouldn't matter," the Strategos continued. "No one will retrieve your bodies, I'll never allow it. Not yours, not your leaders, none of them. So I beg you, *lay down your weapons!*"

The royal general looked to the city's Archon, and after a nod, the latter simply turned his back and walked away from the crest, disappearing behind the Gallic line of white. For their part, the barbarians looked puzzled, their feet antsy—more so when a column of Macedonian soldiers spread out behind them.

"What is your answer, Theophrastus!" Aratus barked, antsy in his own right as Persaeus vanished from sight.

"Aratus," the general replied in a less combative tone, almost calm, "even if I were to surrender the very last shreds of my dignity and concede this hill, concede this night to you, you said it yourself—the King would sooner have my head than he would yours."

The answer surprised Aratus. "So don't return," he said quickly, licking parched lips. "You can take refuge with us, if that is the price to end the bloodshed this night."

The commander chuckled and shook his head. "I must correct myself— *that* would be the very last shreds of my dignity."

He drew his sword, lifted his brazen shield. "So forgive me while I enjoy these last few moments of peace, as I stand here on the high ground and await your 'thousands' en route."

Aratus let his glare linger on the Macedonian, resenting his every breath now. Resenting him for forcing the sacrifice of yet more Achaean lives, these the most bitter of them all—right at the very precipice of victory.

If the gods will my success here, I will memorialize those men most of all.

"Fan out, lads," he called out to his men. On either side of him, a disorderly line of men took shape, about thirty wide and ten deep, Promachus on the right end, Pythocles on the left; archers flanked both sides. A look afore showed a climb ahead of them, and though it was but a gentle slope, it was still

219

a slope, which by default conceded the advantage to the men at the top—especially fresh men, fanatical men in the Gauls' case.

Slow approach, he thought to himself, summoning what was left of his concentration to squelch his pain, his weariness. *Need to be careful, march shoulder to shoulder for now. Watch the Macks they're holding in reserve behind the Gauls… watch for a flank by Pers—*

"Ugh…"

Timanthes collapsed into him. Aratus dropped his spear as he tried to catch him, but instead his friend fell awkwardly to one knee. As he bared bloody teeth, his hand clutched his side, covering the wound he'd tried to ignore.

Aratus looked warily at the hilltop. No movement. Not yet.

"Timanthes? My friend, can you stand?" he said, trying to steady him.

"I can stand, I can… I can stand," Timanthes said, rising slowly, using his spear more as a cane than a weapon of threat. An Achaean came to his side in support.

"Stop!" Timanthes scolded the man. *"Don't let them see a bloody second of weakness…"*

Aratus's heart sank as he watched Timanthes's agony. "Fall back in the ranks," he urged gently. "I beg you! You fall back and we'll force the fight, bring them to heel, and find a healer in the city. There must be one—"

"No weakness," Timanthes replied simply. "None."

He knows he's to die. He's too damn stubborn and practical to stand on principle…

Aratus swallowed a ball in his throat, blinked at welling tears. *Haven't you asked for enough, my gods? You didn't show me this in the omens… there must be a healer who can help or you would have shown me…*

"No weakness!" Timanthes growled at him, eyes wide with pain and fear.

But as Aratus looked about, it was clear that Timanthes wasn't the only one in bad form. His men had obeyed with vigor, but they were obviously spent and couldn't hide it. Not from their commander, not from themselves—

And not from Theophrastus.

"Damn the wait, these men are rotten! Gauls, charge!"

It reminded him of snow avalanching down a peak. The Gallic line screamed a horrific war cry and stampeded down the slope, a blur of pale skin, frenetic hair, and lethal blades poised; indeed, a wall of wraiths. The Achaeans, half in formation, half not, simply braced themselves.

"Stand together, men! Tighten up!"

With the Gauls, he'd always heard you just had to weather that initial surge. Easier said than done when failure meant your head on a blade to be paraded about. Easier said than done on the wrong side of a bloody slope…

"Stay tight! Archers loose!"

The ground shook. A rolling thunder, not unlike that which awoke him the night of his father's murder.

He glowered.

"Brace and push back! Brace, then push back!"

Teeth rattled, helmet too. The gap closed.

He picked a "wraith" out of the pack, who'd picked Aratus out in turn. Gallic sword raised, buckler lowered.

Aratus thrust.

A perfect strike, straight through bare sternum. The Gaul's sword still plunged down, lodging itself in the rim of Aratus's shield, the Gaul's body shimmying further onto the spear. He stopped barely an inch from the Sicyonian's face, his mouth a bloody maw of blackened teeth, breath and twisted beard reeking of alcohol, light eyes afire but flickering.

"Back, you beast!" Aratus yelled, spear caught in the guts of the barbarian, body pressing.

A thunderclap as the rest of the Gallic line slammed home, Achaean bulwark rippling like a pond in the rain. An uproar of swords upon shields and helmets, of spears upon flesh and bone, of wounded cries and warriors' yells, of feet scraping at grass.

"Fire!"

A volley of arrows crisscrossed through the Gauls from either side, Syrians finding ample targets. Heaps of Gauls fell, even more in a second salvo, though their brothers-in-arms quickly sprinted for the bowmen screaming vengeance. The light troops fled behind the safety of Achaean thureophoroi, but some fell nonetheless, their tunics helpless against razor-sharp swords and blind rage. More than one Syrian head rolled from its body.

On either side of him, Erginus and Timanthes fought for dear life. The Syrian opted for the sword and buckler, and though he could barely wield the latter, he lurched into his Gaul and stunted his wailing charge, smashing his fist—sword in hand—into the barbarian's jaw. The Gaul swung back, but not before Erginus sliced his shield arm from his body. The barbarian howled and reached for the Syrian's throat, but Erginus headbutted him back, finishing him with a stab to the belly.

Timanthes was being hammered, and Aratus was powerless to help him, spear stuck in place within his dying Gaul.

Stubborn Timanthes! he thought angrily as his friend teetered upon impact from the charge, thrown backward into thorakitai ranks behind him, dangerous breach opening in the Achaean line. He was forced to his knees in a desperate series of shield parries, the Gaul hacking all the while, kicking him like a dog.

"Timanthes, get up! Someone help him!"

A thorakites's spear pierced the attacker, but he just yelled louder, scent of sour wine permeating the air. More barbarians poured into the breach, Aratus's right nearly enveloped.

Timanthes went low. First, slices through prone knees—one man, then another—then a stab through the groin of the next in line. He staggered to his feet with a thorakites's aid, barbarians collapsing on top of each other.

"Aratus!" his friend yelled above the din. *"Their left is prone—get all the archers to hammer their cursed left!"*

Aratus could see nothing of the Gallic left, only that the Achaean right fought them tooth and nail. But Timanthes had always had the better military mind, and there was no time to question him.

"Erginus—get all the damn Syrians back and hit the Gauls' left flank! Let Promachus roll 'em up if he can!"

The burly man could only nod in a voiceless exhaustion, carefully slipping back through Achaean ranks.

"AGH!"

A blade shot through Timanthes's shoulder, armor useless. Blood poured out as his shield dropped.

"Timanthes!"

His friend reeled again, this time his head wobbling back in Aratus's direction. His helmet slipped off with a clang. *"By the gods, my friend—make this matter."*

"Timanthes, dammit—"

He was undaunted, thoughts and eyes turned elsewhere. *"Forgive me my love, my sons!"*

The stocky Sicyonian spread his arms wide before launching himself at the surrounding Gauls. For a fleeting moment, it was the sight of all sights, one man holding back a half dozen. Thorakitai surged back into the gap, spears finding armorless chests with greater ease. Aratus too dropped his spear at last and drew his sword, ready to begin the counterpush.

But it was too late for brave Timanthes. One sword found his throat, another his side, another his guts. He was dead before the barbarians let his body hit the ground.

Heart torn from his chest, Aratus wanted to collapse at the sight. But battle doesn't let one mourn. Instead, he simply had to watch his friend's body disappear into the Gallic mass as the rival lines smashed into each other yet again. The crush of fighters was nearly suffocating. He fought on, desperately trying to get through to Timanthes; he'd protect his body with his own before he'd let the barbarians defile it.

"Fire!"

A combined volley lit into the Gallic left. A second volley, a third, all while Aratus's center and Pythocles's left tried not to give ground.

"Hit 'em again!" Aratus railed maniacally. *"Fire, dammit!"*

More volleys. The Gauls started crumbling against the Achaean right. Promachus, ever the wolf, smelled blood—quite literally.

"For Achaea!" he yelled, before leading a sweep around the barbarian line, straight into the enemy's backs. The Achaean war cries were tired but fierce, and ones that even Gallic fanatics weren't immune to.

"Press 'em!" Aratus begged, pounding away with his own sword.

The Gauls broke.

From right to left, they peeled back as fast they could. They dropped their arms and ran, a potent reminder that, at day's end, mercenaries were paid a handsome sum to fight—but not always handsome enough to die.

"Achaeans, do not give chase!" the Strategos yelled. *"Stay in line!"*

He watched the Gauls flee in every direction—every direction except up the hill. There stood the line of four or five score Macedonians, fronted by a flailing Theophrastus, exhorting them to follow his charge. He marched with grim purpose and sword drawn toward the Achaeans, his shadowed face one of eerie complacency.

But only a half dozen Macks joined his side. The rest of the Macedonians remained in place, and even those with the commander flicked glances behind them.

Aratus's eyebrows raised. *Is this a feint? Why hold them back? Why didn't they join the Gauls in the first place?* His body was drained of any ability to answer. "Watch them," he called out instead, rather redundantly.

As Theophrastus drew closer, it was evident that he had no expectation that anyone else would be joining, the rest still standing like statues on the crest.

He's come down to die.

"You needn't do this, Theophrastus," Aratus offered. "Bloody surrender, lad."

"I've gotten Persaeus out of this disaster to safety," the Macedonian called back coldly, ten yards out. "With that small bit of honor, I pray to leave my life free of the shame this night darkened it with. If those cowards behind me prefer to await their slaughter, then so be it."

"It's a waste of—"

"Silence!"

He charged.

"Fire!"

A sloppy volley surprised the brave seven, tearing into prone limbs, ignoring chests of armor; the one that avoided damage was soon cut down. Aratus immediately raised a hand.

"Halt fire!" he barked, surprisingly annoyed at the impromptu bolts. "If they want an honorable death, we'll give it to them."

The Achaeans soon enveloped the wounded company. Theophrastus had been hit in the shoulder and calf, drooping his left side, but still he swung his sword with a wild fire and vigor, betraying eyes that showed mounting fear. Even so, Aratus dodged a swipe and countered with a chop to the commander's neck, a geyser of blood spraying forth; the Mack fell to the ground, face to the sky, tongue dangling to the side. As he stood over the dying man, their eyes met.

"The King... he'll never let you sleep again after this..."

In a way, he admired his conviction, dedicated right up until his expiration. He didn't pity him, as he at least had a cause to die for, which many lived their whole lives without. In the end, Aratus simply smiled as he mercifully plunged his sword down through the Mack's throat.

"I haven't slept in twenty years because of him."

When the gurgling ceased, he forced his gaze upward, too tired to be worried about the Macedonian line still at the summit. Indeed, many of his own men involuntarily fell to their knees, every muscle, every fiber of their being stretched to the limit. No, at this point, the Macks would either fight or they wouldn't.

"So what of it, then?" he yelled out to the summit.

Silence at first. Finally, one man spoke. "Were you sincere in offering clemency in exchange for surrender?"

Aratus blanched. "Aye. You throw down your weapons, you submit as prisoners, and you'll be spared."

"We will *not* be slaves," the man quickly rebutted. "We'll fight and die here before we'll taken as slaves."

Aratus shook his head. "No slaves, you have my word."

"And you will not ask us to fight for you."

"I will not. But you *must* submit to us; we'll let you go when all is in order."

Silence again. Aratus could hear his weary heart begin to pound again, dreading the prospect of fighting one more moment.

"What gods can I swear to, lad, that'll convince you of my sincerity?"

"Zeus."

"Aye, then by Zeus, by Apollo, by Helios, whose grounds we tread upon and who bequeathed it to sacred Aphrodite, by Poseidon, patron god of Corinth—I pledge to you your safety and freedom—so long as you submit."

"Aye," the man said. But nothing afterward. No disarming, no anything.

A glare spread across Aratus's face, body anxious. "We're coming to the summit now," he said quietly but threateningly. "We mean you no harm."

With a nod to either wing of his line, the Achaeans lurched forward, every step a burden, an ache, a pain. Frankly, the Strategos wasn't certain that the sight of his men any closer would prompt compliance or compel resistance. Nevertheless, his die was cast.

Fifteen yards out. No movement.

"What of it?" he snarled.

Ten yards.

His hand tensed around his sword handle. "I won't ask again! Achaeans, ready for ch—"

One spear dropped.

Then another, and another, wood striking rocky soil with a rattle that echoed through the night. With a signal from the same Macedonian who'd spoken for the group, they then neatly laid their shiny shields down on their weapons.

"We concede," the man said simply, hands out to his side.

Aratus paused his climb, though suddenly, his feet were light as air again. He scanned the Macks' line left to right. "Your name?"

"Bithys."

Aratus nodded. "Gods bless you, Bithys. Now you'll kindly tell your men to step back and sit before the temple steps."

The Macedonians looked to their apparent leader, and after a nod from the bearded man, they obeyed.

Could this really be happening? he asked himself, unsure of anything at this point. He looked to Promachus, to Erginus, to Pythocles, all of whom returned the favor. All of whom nodded in encouragement.

He smiled, breathing deep. Took the last few steps to the summit, line in tow. Then took his first views of the world from the top of the Acrocorinth.

They were the most wonderful sights he'd ever seen.

To the north lay the entire chaotic outline of the city, torchlights darting up and down the faraway streets, temples popping out above homes, most especially the agora's ancient Temple of Apollo, where he'd stood in awe with Naukydes those many years ago. Far beyond that, he could see the lights and lighthouse of the port of Lechaeum and the churning waters of the Corinthian Gulf, a full fleet bobbing at the docks.

To the east, the sky was brightening with the first wisps of morning light, but immediately before him stood Aphrodite's temple, its pediment showing swathes of red and blue in the torchlight. The goddess's statue inside the main chamber could not be seen, though it was said to be adorned with armaments; visible on either side of the chamber, however, were bronze statues of Eros, her son, armed with his perennial bow, and the sun god himself, Helios, bearing a crown of his rays. A handful of *hetaera* priestesses huddled together near Eros's statue, each wearing a sleeveless body-length himation and hair pulled into a bun.

Aratus saw Helios and smiled, dropping to a knee and nodding in deference. When his eyes opened, he ran his hands through the soil, letting its sediment trickle through his fingers, mouth falling slack-jawed in disbelief. He rose, no longer feeling his fatigue, instead sensing that he'd entered a dream.

His men moved about the grounds in near silence. There were no whoops, no yells, no cries of victory, no looting. Perhaps it was their tiredness, but it was equally likely that the group was as stunned by their victory as the enemy they'd defeated. Certainly, they'd heard their commander's words at the Nemea crossing, heard he'd wanted to strike a blow against the most powerful force in Hellas, but talk was one thing; it was entirely another to stand upon the crag that had marked Sicyon's eastern vista for time immemorial.

An arm slid around Aratus's shoulder. It was Erginus, bloodied and battered, face as blackened as his filthy beard, every bare piece of skin about him caked in sweat and dirt. His mouth hung open as if he was about to speak, but when he met Aratus's eyes, he just smiled his toothless smile.

"Aye," the Strategos said, smiling back.

Footsteps approached on his left, and when he turned, his mind was ready to see Timanthes, his arms ready to embrace his friend and thank the gods together that they'd seen them through yet another impossible peril. Just as they had so many times before, be it Sicyon, the high seas, the shores of Locria, the Egyptian court of the Ptolemies.

But it was Promachus, red tunic darkened, tips of his light hair dripping upon the dry ground at his feet. And as if deciphering the disappointment evident in Aratus's searching eyes, Promachus's mouth formed a firm line, and he removed his helmet and placed a comforting hand on the Strategos's shoulder.

A pang went through Aratus's stomach. *Timanthes is dead.*

It can't be, he thought, looking for his body down at the base of the hillock. The search made him woozy, knees buckling, forcing Promachus to ease him to the ground.

"Sit, sire."

"Thank you," he said with a suddenly heavy heart, looking up to give a nod of approval and distract himself. "You were magnificent today."

"You honored me by giving me this chance," the young captain replied, kneeling to a crouch with him. "If I never fight again, I'll live forever off of this battle."

"Oh, you'll fight again," Aratus replied with a dark chuckle. "Have no fear of that. But you were a gem when Achaea needed you most this night."

"As was Timanthes," Promachus added softly, shooting another stab into the Strategos's gut. "Without him leading the way, we'd have never made it close to the mountain; we'd never have won at the path... I've never seen anyone fight the way he did at the bend; not a moment's hesitation on the attack, not a moment's hesitation in throwing himself in harm's way." He paused. "He took that stomach blow shielding me, sire."

Aratus looked at him, finding eyes of anguish and respect.

"That spear was meant for me."

"No, Promachus," he said, firmly as he could muster. "It was for precisely who it was supposed to be; your stories of him will do him the best justice of all." The Strategos sighed and ran a hand over his face. "By the gods, I'll miss that man."

"So pray tell, Aratus of Sicyon," he heard from the line of seated Macks. "When will the rest of your 'thousands' make it to this fortress?"

At length, Aratus turned a tilted head in Bithys's direction. "What 'thousands'?"

The Macedonian's brow furrowed, but only for a moment. The expression of a man not entirely surprised by what he'd heard. "Did we concede too soon?" he asked blithely. "Did Persaeus?"

"You'd have all been dead to the last man," Promachus growled as he rose. "And what of Persaeus?"

"Persaeus doesn't matter," Aratus said. "Let him run, just a gray old Cypriot who probably thought he'd never fight another day in his life."

"Hm... so are we to sit here all morning?" Bithys called. "All day, too?"

"No," Aratus said. "First, you're going to go with the captain Promachus here and confirm we've safe passage through the gate just outside the main gateway—the one that leads straight off the mountain into the valley below."

"The Teneatic Gate?"

"Aye. In the event your cohorts still take up arms there, they'll need to be—persuaded otherwise. If they resist, then at least some of you will have to be made examples of."

"That is a breach of—"

"You surrendered on behalf of all the remaining Macedonians on this mountain," the Strategos snapped. "The Teneatic Gate guards included. If they fail to surrender, then it is not the Achaeans who have breached anything!"

The Macedonian pursed his lips.

"So, you will deliver the gate to us. Then you're going to provide us with steeds. I presume you keep at least some of them up here, no?"

"We do. But after all this mess, you intend to simply ride out of here?"

"Some of us will. Promachus will find our fastest riders and send them on to Sicyon."

"What should they say when they arrive, sire?"

The Strategos rose upon creaky knees. He scanned the western horizon for vestiges of the city he claimed home, but despite the steady lightening, it was still too dark to see far beyond the mountain. Too dark to see more than a morning mist blanketing the valleys. Even so, a smile crossed his face in thinking of the reaction of the men and women of Sicyon; of the generals and soldiers of the League cities; of his father, his mother, Telesilla, Timanthes. "Tell them to send the army," he said calmly. "All of it hopefully, but at least the Sicyonians."

He sighed. "Tell them that Corinth has fallen."

CHAPTER 22

*17ᵗʰ Day of Apellaios, Year 2 of the 134ᵗʰ Olympiad
(August 8, 243 B.C.)*

They arrived faster than he expected. Impossibly fast, really.

Aratus knew a fit horse and a strong rider could make the Corinth-Sicyon trek in an hour. This morning, of course, saw Achaean riders that were utterly spent from a night of battle, atop Macedonian mounts that were surprisingly unimpressive. Nevertheless, even horsemen moving at a leisurely pace, followed by a three- or four-hour return march from Sicyon—if the army came as requested—meant he shouldn't be seeing reinforcements before high sun.

Instead, it wasn't halfway to that point when he, summoned atop of the walls by Pythocles keeping watch, saw the dust clouds kicking up on the western horizon. Which could really only mean one thing.

"Agonippos followed me, after all," he said aloud, too tired to scoff at the impetuous subordinate—or insubordinate, as it were.

"So he tailed us but refused to join us?" Pythocles asked, standing at his side.

Now Aratus scoffed. "In fairness, he wasn't invited," he said, rubbing a stubbly face. "Must have been waiting for me at the Nemea for him to make it here this quick." *Waiting to show me up, no doubt. Maybe gloat, maybe worse. Oh, to have been there when the messengers arrived!*

He'd almost immediately regretted the decision to demand the rest of his army. In the grim aftermath of the battle, Achaeans took turns descending the dim, damp steps of the Upper Peirene chamber, the mountain's underground spring and lifeblood, the one feature above all that made the fort virtually impervious. Within the stone confines of the spring, they found an infinite supply of crystal clear water to slake equally infinite thirst, some even sneaking a nip of watery wine while they were down there. Even still, some of the men were so racked with post-battle tremors or utter exhaustion that they vomited on the spot, others collapsing into a deep sleep, nodding off in the cool dankness.

Those that were spared such ailments went about their post-battle duties. Some of them, behind Erginus and Diocles, were in charge of recovering the treasure and coin which the King maintained here—the same that the enterprising siblings had been pilfering for months. Other men carried the sullen responsibility of separating their dead from the enemy's, to which some Macedonian captives even offered to help. Indeed, the Northerners worried for their brothers that may not have properly prepared for the afterlife, or if they had, feared that their bodies could become defiled in the interim. For the Achaeans, like most Hellenes, they simply wanted to keep track of all who had fallen, so that their families could prepare their bodies for the appropriate rites. It was the greatest fear that a body may go unclaimed and somehow forgotten, their station in Hades ever tied to the memory of their spirit.

For Aratus, the peaceful look upon Timanthes's ashen face was almost too much to bear. His friend's lips pulled back and teased upward, his eyes open still as slits; considered in context of his splayed position, a passerby might mistake him for a man in leisurely repose. In his delirious state, Aratus almost indulged in that fiction, that idea of a murky divide between the quick and dead. Finally, however, he dried his eyes and simply kneeled to Timanthes's side, closing his lids and mouth with clinical precision, in an instant ceasing any such delusions of vitality. After a kiss to his cold forehead, Aratus dragged him over to the rest of the allies that had fallen in the assault, pledging that his honors in Sicyon would be unmatched.

It was then that he started to conceive of the true immensity of what he had done. Not in the military or tactical sense, but what he'd actually committed himself to, and by association, the Achaean League. Within the span of half a day, he'd gone from seeing his plans betrayed, his attack uncovered, his troop numbers only a fraction of what he expected, to standing on the apex of southern Hellas… but now what? In his thirst for the attack, he'd ignored what his sentiment was to be afterward. Most importantly, he had no sense of the tenor of the city folk below; he had no idea whether Timodemus had ever been contacted—though certainly not—or whether he marshaled them, or worst of all, whether he even was who he said he was. The very basics of the tongue-lashing he'd received in Aegium more than a moon ago remained unanswered—*who is Timodemus?*

It was in that light, in looking at the wretched state of his troops, in recognizing the uncertainty of his position, that he regretted calling for the rest of the League's army. Sixty thousand people resided in the city below. Sixty thousand. Even if more than half were women and children, the old and the crippled, it was a formidable number by any measure, one that made absurd any notion that having the full six thousand from Sicyon would make a difference compared to the mangled three hundred he already had. In the end, he would have to descend into the city proper and make his case for the presence of his men; and they in turn would pass judgment. It was that simple, thus making any wait for the troops' arrival largely irrelevant and ultimately serving only to surge the Strategos's own anxiety.

But now, here they were all the same.

"Shall we send another rider, sire?" Pythocles asked as he leaned into a gap in the gatewall's crenellations. "Tell them to make for the Teneatic in lieu of the Sicyonian Gates?"

"No," the Strategos said quickly. "You'll send them a rider telling them to stay put. I don't know the slightest about their intent."

The soldier looked amused. "Surely, they come in peace, though?"

"One would hope. But I've earned the rancor of some of those men, some who scoffed at the very notion of this venture, let alone its success," he said bitterly, pondering how much easier the night might have been had he received even the most basic support. "And in turn, I don't know how we're being received within the city, so before I put more men at risk, we settle that point."

Pythocles's expression fell serious. "Settle it?"

Aratus's brows peaked. "You didn't think we were staying up here for all eternity, did you?"

"No... but..."

"Then we need to settle this with the people of Corinth."

"And how's that?"

The Strategos gave a loud exhale as he peeled away from the walkway. "We're going to ask them."

* * *

There were eleven of them in total. One from every city of the League.

Some were more battered than others, some more frightened than others, but it was imperative to present the proper image before the Corinthians. They needed to see that this was not the raid of some soldiers of fortune, or conquerors built on exploiting the Corinthians, or adding them to some sort of an empire. They needed to see the unity of the League at work, who it was that could stand up to the most powerful man in Hellas where others had failed. Hell, even the Ptolemies had failed, despite their overwhelming grain and coin.

All assuming the Corinthians even cared for such distinctions, of course.

Strewn along the path from the fortress were reminders of the scraps from the night before. Lysistratos still lay prone and lifeless, even in death still gripping his sword. Further down, the battle at the bend left the stone walkway littered with bodies, broken spears, shields, and arrows among them, all to say nothing of the blood that caked every inch of it and the mountain wall to their right. The day's rising heat beneath a cloudless blue sky was quickly turning the red to a rusty brown.

Aratus silently prayed for the casualties as they hobbled by, but as the city came closer and closer into view, as the buildings grew larger and larger accordingly, his thoughts locked on the here and now. He could see the crowds gathering at the end of the mountain path, where it met the main crossroads headed into the city.

Just breathe, Aratus.

"Full night of fighting and I'm fine," Promachus said, wounds surprisingly light. "Yet now, I can barely breathe."

Aratus laughed as the man read his mind.

"Might not have come if you'd told me about this part..."

"Ah, you still have your lucky shield," Aratus said, half in jest. "All the protection we'll need."

They'd descended probably 1,500 feet, well past the back of Demeter's Sanctuary, the clamor of the masses ahead rising with each step. Their commotion rolled like a thunder up the slope, their energy almost palpable even from the distance. Hundreds of eyes locked on them, searching their beaten faces, their filthy attire, their worn-down weapons, their limping gaits.

"Well, if they tear us to pieces, it's been an honor serving you, sire," Promachus said, hand sliding to his hilt.

"And you," Aratus said, wiping his brow. "But let's pretend we're surviving this. Chin up, now."

And that's when he saw him.

Just as they'd entered the crossroads, a tall, grinning fellow strode out of the human maw, flanked by a dozen on either side of him. They wore short-sleeved tunics of different shades, each overlaid by a sword and baldric. Save for the friendly countenance, the gang moved as if they came to arrest the Achaeans. Instead, the man in the center extended a hand in greeting, his close-set eyes beaming over a squat nose and full lips.

Aratus took the man's hand with grace. "I am Aratus—"

"Of Sicyon, aye," the man said, without missing a beat. The crowd of people behind him watched on in curiosity, though some retreated just a bit, still wary of this alien band of warriors in their midst. To his end, the man simply looked the Achaean crew over one by one, before returning to Aratus's eyes with a satisfied nod, saying nothing.

The Strategos flicked glances back and forth, the crush of people tweaking his nerves. "And you are?"

"You know precisely who I am," the man said, grinning still. "And you should have told me you bloody accepted my offer."

A weight lifted from the Strategos's shoulders, suspicions confirmed. "Timodemus?"

A nod. "So why? Why did you do this without my knowledge? Did you think I misled you?"

Aratus could only laugh. "Lad, if you only knew the extent to which I tried passing word to you. Though I must confess, I scarcely believed you were real half the time. I scarcely believed our *talk* was even real after a while."

Timodemus offered a giddy laugh of his own. "All too real, my friend, though I must confess as well—I thought you'd given up on the idea. When I heard the alarms last night, I thought surely it was a fire that had broken out, or a band of thieves. Wasn't 'til my mate Stachys here told me it was an attack, that I knew it. I bloody knew it, ha!"

Aratus smiled as the man grabbed him in a rough hug. Even with the camaraderie, however, he still felt ill at ease. "You're certain we're safe here? There are no more Macedonians about?"

Timodemus's face turned cold as ice as he released the embrace. "Your lads destroyed the city watch and you overran the fort. Beyond that, it's only the port garrisons that needed watching, and my men and I have them well in hand."

"My thanks, then. We'd been warned of the Lechaeum contingent."

"Aye, rightfully so. Theophrastus is the bastard that led them, and by all accounts, he's tough as steel and trained his men to be the same. So if there's any worry, it's that he was nowhere to be found at the port. Means he either left for Mace—"

"He's dead," Aratus said briskly, glancing at Promachus. "He was on the Acrocorinth. Died in the Macks' last charge. Persaeus fled, but took little in his flight."

The Corinthian's irrepressible grin resurged, body frozen in place. "Praise be to the gods," he finally said, shaking his head. "And to think your Council approved of all this without even asking to see me first!"

"Aye, well," Aratus said, uncomfortably shifting his eyes away. "You should know that the Council was not in favor of this."

Timo's brow furrowed. "Yet your army gathers in force outside our gates, no? They released them even though—"

"The army only just arrived," the Strategos said, too tired to mince words or spin stories. "They'd only come after I showed them it could be done."

The Corinthian looked baffled. "So—so then, your men here? You surely had some to take the fortress somehow?"

"Four hundred."

"Four hundred men?"

"Four hundred. Only those who recognized this to be as tied to fate as I did."

"Ha! Four hundred men! Did you hear that, mates?" Timo asked aloud, looking at his comrades on either side of him. "With bloody four hundred men, this man's done what no one has in centuries!"

He threw his arm around the Strategos's shoulders and turned him toward the mass of humanity crowding the streets. *This man!*" he bellowed. "*This man here* kicked *the bloody Macks out of the Acrocorinth!*"

Timodemus forcefully paraded Aratus straight into the sea of people. *"Aratus of Sicyon! The man who took the Acrocorinth with four hundred men! The man who killed Theophrastus! The man who saw the King's archon tuck tail and run!"*

The crowd caught the fever of the moment, rapping the Achaeans' backs and shoulders, beginning raucous chants of their own.

"Cheers to Aratus of Sicyon! Praise be to the gods!"

Men and women crushed on either side of the Achaean column, showering them in adulation. The noise, the fervor, the revelry, it was all hypnotic, the sensation one that washed away the pain in every limb of his body, the fatigue that devoured his legs most of all. On and on they plowed, Aratus nodding and smiling and nodding again, white stucco facades of houses arising behind either side of the horde.

In the midst of the chanting and joy, Aratus looked over at Timodemus, studied him, his profile so familiar now from the Games, his youthful exuberance infectious. "So who are you, then, Timodemus of Corinth? Who

233

are you to promise me the things that you promised at the Games or to even lead this damn parade?"

The other man laughed. "Son of an old family, one that used to be important. But truthfully, just a Corinthian who'd had enough, my Sicyonian friend. Tough to speak publicly against the Crown in this city, but it didn't take long to find others that felt the same—a *lot* of others, enough to make ya wonder why we hadn't done something sooner," he said, pausing to wave to more ebullient onlookers, before leaning in to whisper in Aratus's ear. "But don't kid yourself—Antigonus keeps a solid lot of the high-borns here fat, rich, and happy. They won't be pleased about this in any sense, one of the very reasons we needed outside help."

"Ah, it's the same in every city, lad."

"Perhaps, but with due respect, every city isn't Corinth. If coin is merely enticing in other cities, it is a veritable infatuation here; an infection, even. Men like my father and my house are the exception, if our voice even matters at all."

Aratus met his dark eyes, which only underscored his sincerity. Alas, the Strategos shook his head in a frown, soaking in the crowd again. "Well, whatever voice you think your house lacks, your kinsmen certainly seem to make up for it."

"Indeed they do," Timodemus said, smile returning.

"I need to address them, you know."

"You surely do. Oh, I promise you there's an end to this stroll! You'll see soon enough!"

And there certainly was an end. After they'd passed through the city center, passed the landmarks, temples, and stoas he remembered from his youth, they arrived at a *parodos*, an arched doorway on the northern fringe of the city that led into an immaculate stone theater. It was semicircular in shape, its wedges of seats radiating two hundred feet outward from the flattened *orchestra* space, upward nearly sixty. Much like Sicyon's, the seat rows were built with stone blocks laid into the side of the hill, and spaced so precisely, angled so exactly, that those farthest from the stage heard just as clearly as those in the front. Framing the farthest row stood a portico bookended by tall statue-bearing platforms, the soft gray of both a striking contrast against the sky's bright azure.

The *orchestra* was a terrace about eighty paces in diameter, inlaid with large colored tiles in checkered fashion, a space typically reserved for the singing and dancing of the chorus. Behind it was perhaps the most magnificent portion of the entire venue—the *skene*, a two-story structure nearly two hundred feet long, its painted façade a stunning backdrop of pillars, patios, murals, and statues. Two false towers framed either side of it, each capped with its own triangular pediment. Various doors in the façade allowed actors to come from behind the *skene* to the attached stage.

As Timodemus led him into the hidden backdrop of the *skene*, Aratus could see that the theater had already swollen with Corinthians, its 15,000 seats quickly nearing capacity. Though the chanting of their city walk had waned, the buzz in the theater remained palpable, the attendees seemingly just as aware of what had happened as those he'd seen prior.

Despite his exhaustion, Aratus felt his adrenaline surge. "Will you introduce me?" he asked, growing nervous.

"There's no need," Timo said matter-of-factly. "You've already received all the introduction you could want; but we have guards stationed with your men at both of the theater's entrances, lest you worry. Now simply go out there and say what you'll say."

"And you're certain they're receptive to what we've discussed?" he asked, eyeing the Corinthian. "To what I'm going to propose?"

Timodemus frowned. "Reasonably so. You'll have your answer, in any event. Mine too, I suppose. And what about you?" he asked with an amused look. "What will your Council say if the people's answer is what you hope it to be?"

Aratus shrugged, concluding with utter dismissiveness, "Let them turn away the greatest city in southern Hellas." Then he added, "And if I'm wrong, they can crow how they were right all along. Either way, they prosper."

The Strategos took a deep breath, before a memory came to him that he was surprised to only just now recall. "As the day broke after I freed my own city, I addressed the people from our theater," he said quietly, grinning ever so slightly at the parallel. "Here I am, in a theater yet again."

"The gods delight in symmetry, do they not?"

"So it seems."

"Ah, but they love dichotomy, too, I suppose. A year ago, the King gathered in this very spot for the wedding of his son and crown prince, Demetrius."

Now, the Strategos could only grunt.

The younger man grinned and patted the Sicyonian's armored shoulder. "I'll wait for you here—remember, 'the man from the Games chooses everything.'"

Aratus smiled. "Aye, he does."

With a nod and a final exhale, he was off. As he emerged from the darkness of the *skene* onto the bright stage, the crowd roared at his appearance, sending vibrations through the ground and his body alike. With genuine humility, he nodded and raised a hand in acknowledgment of their praise, taking in the sight as well as his tired eyes would allow. Though creeping shadows blanketed the eastern half of the gathering, he could see that the seats were almost full, even as more people jammed the *parodoi* seeking entrance. Those already seated revealed citizens of all ages in every shade of tunic. Beyond the people, Aratus watched as a line of birds mounted peacefully on the stoa behind the last row of seats, a sight of poignant contrast against the growing flocks of vultures circling the Acrocorinth in the distance.

As his mouth opened, the cheers grew louder, the people rising, beckoning him into the *orchestra*. With this, his nervousness faded away, his weariness returning in its wake. Using his spear as a crutch, he hobbled down the steps of the stage and into the circular terrace, drawing him close enough to the people to hear individual accolades. When at last the clamor had waned, he found himself glued to his spear in order to stay upright.

His eyes scanned the multitude, who eyed him right back. At last, he smiled.

"My name is Aratus of Sicyon," he said plainly, pausing for another roar as his voice reverberated around the theater's perfect acoustics. "And you honor me with your words and acclaim, much as the gods did in blessing this venture from the start. I came here today upon invitation of some of your bravest citizens, men who believed in what many thought impossible; men who believed in what many of *my* colleagues felt impossible, and perhaps many of you as well—that Macedon could be beaten; that Corinth could be a free state once more. That she could reclaim the position of preeminence she had for centuries before northern kings descended upon it."

His eyes stayed busy despite his tired body. "With the coming of Alexander a century ago, a curtain fell upon the Hellas of old. We all know that. Autonomy and freedom and democracy were no longer inviolate, no longer subject to the people's will—they couldn't be while tyrannical power grew like a tumor upon the body of free Greece. And all these years later, still that remains true.

"You see, Macedon is a plague, my friends. It is a blight whose ills you've tasted all too precisely, all too frequently. Aye, there are days when you may walk about your city, days when you sit down in your homes or those of your friends and family and eat your bread, your fish, your cheese; when you'll consume your wine; when you'll kiss your child's head and wish them restful slumber; when you'll give thanks to the gods in total tranquility. On those days, everything seems as it should, as if that overarching fog of tyranny isn't there or doesn't exist or never existed. Maybe, in those moments, you even feel as if you're a *free people*.

"But you're not free. And you *cannot* be without acknowledgment of that, that your every breath of air, your every moment of 'peace' is merely a 'gift,' a fraudulent gift, an *illusion*, perpetrated by the King of Macedon. Then you must acknowledge that freedom is *earned* from tyrants, not *gifted*, and it is obvious enough why—*every city's freedom* is a threat to their illusion! Because if one is free, others should be free, and if others should be free, then Pella will soon have the whole of Greece with spears pointed toward them.

"Forty years ago, a group of city-states took that tenet to heart. They cast out the tyrants and the garrisons blessed by that bastard in Macedon. They banded together in pursuit of something greater—protecting freedom of the many through the power of a single union. The Achaean League was reborn, an alliance which cared not for the distinction between Dorian and Achaean, but only that of the free and the shackled. It was this which I knew to be the answer to the power of the King; it was this which I was all too happy to unite my city of Sicyon with some eight years ago."

He took in a deep breath and let it leave, gaze finding the birds atop the back row's stoa. "Corinthians, I come here not as a conqueror. Though my army waits outside your walls for your protection, I am too tired to conquer and you've too many, in any event," he said truthfully, to a chorus of laughter. "Nor do I come to demand tribute or beg your submission. No, it is *I* who wish to pay tribute to *you*—tribute to the long and proud history of your ancient city. It is *I* who wish to submit to *you*—I wish to submit to you an invitation to join the greatest venture the Peloponnesus has ever seen. Join a union forged not by blood and steel, but by the unity of man, the humility of man, the love of man, and the knowledge that individually we serve only to squabble and destroy one another, to serve ourselves up as victims to Macedon's predator—but together, as free men, we face no limitations; we need fear no man, nation, or king. Where we can stand and say in one voice, one loud, determined voice, one indomitable spirit, that we will not stand idly by while our neighbors taste fear, we will not rest while our neighbors lie in chains, we will not bear witness to the sufferance or indignity of occupation or tyranny!"

Aratus's voice had risen to a shout which sent a stabbing pain throughout his body. He winced as his chin dropped to his chest, trying to swallow the sensation and carry on. The crowd's silence morphed into a murmur as they observed his face of agony, his desperate grip on his spear. Finally, he opened his eyes and forced his back straight.

"I told my friend, my *dearest* friend, that when this started it was about freedom. Freedom and nothing more. He lies now upon that mountaintop," Aratus said with a sigh, finger pointing to the Acrocorinth. "Lies there in everlasting repose along with dozens of Achaea's bravest, men who fought and died just to bring you this message, this invitation. This moment."

He paused to let the mist over his eyes subside. "So what does this have to do with you, Corinthians? Well, I'll tell you as your own brave Timodemus told me when I asked him the same question—everything or nothing. To me, your city is too strong and too proud to spend another moment under the Macedonian yoke. To me, Achaea is Corinth and Corinth is Achaea, if you'll only choose to make it so. I pledge my word to that, but if that's not enough, I will offer up the keys to your city, controlled by Macedon for far, far too long.

"But in the end, this is not a question for me. It's not a question for the Macedonians. It's not even a question for your own magistrates—it's a question for you, the people of this great and ancient city with whom my own has shared its border for centuries." He licked his lips. "So I ask you now—will you join me? Will you join the Achaean League?"

A silence ensued that left even the birds at a loss. The breeze that had whisked away the morning's rising heat ceased as well, slowly searing the remnants of Aratus's metal armor to a burn on his shoulders. His eyes scanned the gathering left to right, right to left, waiting for a sign, any sign, anything that would betray a verdict.

And then he heard it.

"Aye, Aratus."

One man, then another. Like the opening drops of a coming storm, sporadic here and there, a mere sprinkle, before a crackle of thunder hearkened the downpour. Soon the crowd had risen to their feet in approval, stomping in place, clapping boisterously, bellowing loud enough for Zeus to hear them.

"Aye, Aratus!"

"Aratus! Aratus! Aratus!"

"For Corinth!"

"For the Achaean League!"

For his part, Aratus could only smile. He looked to the heavens and raised his hands in thanks, spear in hand. *Mighty Apollo, it is by your will that I am here. It is by your grace and those of your brethren that I am able to pay homage to your names and those of my family, those of my friends that precede me in death. I shall visit your temple and offer as great and numerous a sacrifice as the priests will allow, I promise you!*

"For golden is your mantle, your lyre, your bow and quiver,'" he muttered to himself, eyes closed to the frenzy around him. *"'And now you bathe me in gold, you rinse me in silver.'"* His teeth gritted in furious, exhausted joy, eyes open and bloodshot to the world.

"And for so long as Macedon fights against the will of Apollo, I pledge to be thine wrath and thine mercy."

* * *

Aratus greeted his army at the Sicyonian Gates. It wasn't the entire army, and in fact appeared quite light in mercenaries, but there must have been at least four thousand men-at-arms nonetheless. Agonippos was indeed at its head, flanked by the Hipparch Cratinus, though any fears Aratus had of the former's insubordination were quickly cast aside when he saw the young man's expression: sheer and utter awe.

Awe from the gates of Macedon's most important possession freely swinging open to an army of Achaeans.

Awe from the rowdy and musical revelry gripping the city streets within, the flower petals cast upon the Achaeans and their leaders, the townsfolk swarming the army with cheer and praise.

Awe from the sight of the Strategos, standing tall in the middle of it all, bruised, battered, bloodied, and barely upright, his countenance hardly swayed by the tumult. His Achaean representatives to the Corinthians flanked him, looking equally worn.

The Hypostrategos approached him through the crowd in his shiny cuirass and light blue tunic, his jaw slack, eyes wide. The column trailed behind him, equally astounded.

"You traveled fast," his commander said drolly.

But the young man hardly reacted, instead eying the Strategos up and down, extending tentative fingers to touch his bloody marks, his shattered armor scales. "What have you done here?" he croaked out.

"You know what I've done. You know exactly why I'm here."

"Tell me."

Aratus sighed. "We stormed the Acrocorinth, Agonippos. Slayed one of the Macks' generals, captured another."

The eyes of the Hypostrategos narrowed. "Y-you've… succeeded?"

"This would all be a merry waste of a celebration right now if I hadn't. Though it would have been better to have had the entirety of the force I'd planned to have."

Agonippos blanched, eyes falling away in embarrassment, finding the Hipparch at his side. "Well, in due candor, we wouldn't even be here now if it were not for the imploring of Cratinus. We waited for you at the Nemea, but… I never expected the messenger that we got from you. The one that said… that said this had happened. But Cratinus didn't waste a second; he organized the army, got it on the move, so I will not seek to steal his initiative and call it my own."

Aratus was too tired to challenge the sincerity of the man's humility. In fairness, it seemed authentic. "Thankfully, you came, whatever the circumstance. My message would surely have been weakened were you not within eyeshot of the walls."

"You've spoken to them?"

The Strategos nodded. "After the battle, I asked the people for their loyalty and commitment to the League, and by the gods, they gave it."

"Their *Boule* allowed it?"

"Their *people* allowed it. Their *Boule* will have to fall in line."

"Aye, but don't—" The headstrong lieutenant caught himself in mid-protest, mouth half-open. "Aye…" he finally said, looking around the street at the crowds. "And what of the *League's Boule*?"

Aratus smiled. "That one will be more interesting. I'll have riders out by nightfall to call an emergency meeting. Think it's warranted?"

The hint of a grin appeared on Ago's face. "I don't know what to think anymore. This is the most astounding moment of my life," he said, arms flopping at his side, gaze finding the crag of the Acrocorinth to the south. "To think that… to think that…"

Admit it. To think that you *missed your chance…* "You don't have to be on the wrong side again," Aratus said, as much a threat as it appeared innocent. He could never forgive the man for sabotaging his plans, for making the night harder in ways that could never be measured. But the truth was that Agonippos was the son of an old Dymean family, thus carrying favor in western Achaea, and if Timanthes had begged of Aratus one thing, it was that he couldn't afford to alienate any more men of importance in the League and expect to be followed. Ago was impetuous but had such a thirst for glory that he may yet be moldable into something better than he'd shown to date. "But you'll have to make that decision for yourself."

The lieutenant flashed a look of annoyance, clearly not looking to reconcile his old loyalties with new realities… not yet.

City folk swarmed around them in joy, offering drinks and more adulation. Aratus grimaced as another pang shot through his body at the touch.

"Are you hurt?" Agonippos asked.

"Nothing I won't survive."

The Hypostrategos nodded in a daze. "Even still, you should be, uh… you should be inspected by a healer of sorts. They could lance some of these welts on your legs… your arms. Patch up some of these gashes."

"Aye, perhaps I'll do that," Aratus replied tiredly. "But later."

"Then what comes now?"

"The Port of Lechaeum, to sort out the spoils there. The Macedonian garrison is entirely under arms and twenty-five of her ships sit captured in the harbor."

Ago's eyes widened. "Twenty—"

"Then it's to the Acrocorinth again to staff it with fresh troops and make a judgment as to our prisoners there. There's also the matter of seeing to the dead men's rites."

The lieutenant's eyes widened further. "How many—"

"Then I must give my thanks and offerings to the gods that presaged and bore witness to our success. And pray for our continued protection—we have a week or two at the most before the King realizes what's happened here. A few weeks or so more that we learn his response." His stare fell upon Agonippos. "We have to be ready."

The Hypostrategos was silent for a moment, before asking mockingly, "And then?"

Aratus chuckled. "And then I shall have some wine and pass out on the nearest cot."

The men shared a fleeting smile, before succumbing to the distractions and noise of the festivities around them.

"Come on," Aratus finally said, nodding behind him, where the road led eventually into the heart and mobs of the agora. "The hard part begins now."

EPILOGUE

14ᵗʰ Day of Phoinikaios, Year 2 of the 134ᵗʰ Olympiad
(September 4, 243 B.C.)

The rains had cleared out almost all the denizens from Sicyon's agora. It had been a torrential downpour, a violent late-summer storm that uncharacteristically overstayed its welcome, pounding the stone and earth of the grounds.

But to Aratus, the beat of the raindrops upon the stoa's roof brought him nothing but peace. The thunder which had haunted his being for more than twenty years now hardly caused a flinch. He laughed at it—reveled, even—as he leaned casually against a pillar, listening, watching, thinking in solitude. No, after what he'd experienced over the last month, everything else seemed trivial.

For the fall of Corinth had brought immediate rewards.

Within a matter of weeks, envoys from three poleis arrived in Sicyon, each swearing alliance to the League if it would have them. Megara, Corinth's neighbor in the east over the Geraneia Mountains and perennial buffer against Athens; Epidaurus, a small but renowned realm on the Saronic Gulf, due east of Argos; and Troezen, a day's ride southeast of Epidaurus, farther down the Argolid Peninsula. Taken with Corinth itself, it was a coup for the League in every respect, be it wealth, manpower, or strategic positioning—hopefully, the Council would see it the same way.

The weather had delayed the League's gathering. It had been one of the few points of frustration Aratus had experienced, but in truth, it may have been a blessing. His body took many days to heal, from his mind to his flesh, and he still had more weeks to go before he'd be whole again; *if* he could be whole again. It also let him see to the proper burial of his fellow Sicyonians who had fallen on the mountain, including good Timanthes. His wife had been devastated, her grief palpable through the *prothesis*, or laying out of Timanthes's prepared body so that family and friends could pay their respects, all the way through his final interment in the cemetery just outside the city walls. Aratus's own wife, Telesilla, was of great comfort to the widow at a time when she was euphoric to have her husband back—a euphoria she at first tried to mask behind a guarded grin in Telesilla's typically stoic fashion. But when they finally came together, they exchanged a wordless embrace, each weeping on the other's shoulder for reasons they could not and need not say.

And aye, there was still much left to be addressed beyond the League and Timanthes, both new and old: a dangerous dispute between the two kings of Sparta left the southern frontier with Laconia unsettled; Aetolia was certainly plotting attacks to offset the stunning gains accrued to the League; and of course, the heavy crown in Pella had yet to reveal the form that his revenge would take.

But he didn't care about such things, or at the very least he didn't fear them. He had been vindicated. His focus, his prayers, his omens, they'd all been justified, albeit with great sacrifice. Moreover, Corinth, Megara, Epidaurus, and Troezen were simply the beginning; springboards for moves beyond. From Megara, Athens and the isle of Salamis—both manned by Macedon—were within reach; from Epidaurus and Troezen, the sea routes along the eastern Peloponnesian coast could be monitored, and together with Corinth, they kept Argos and its tyrant Aristomachus hemmed in on three sides.

These were the thoughts that eased his mind, these visions of battles to come in a seemingly endless war against tyranny, these promises of more chances to set things right, of another day blessed by the gods. And so instead of the nightmares and panic he'd suffered for so long, his head now fell to the pillow each night with the carefree spirit of a babe.

It was the best he'd slept in twenty years.

ABOUT THE AUTHOR

E.M. Thomas is the author of two novels - an epic fantasy (*The Bulls of War*) and a historical fiction set in Ancient Greece (*Fortress of the Sun*). He was born in the United States but is a world traveler at heart. He caught the writing bug early on and has a passion for all good fiction, but especially that of the fantasy and historical variety. One of his favorite moments as a writer thus far was drafting a chapter of his book about ancient Corinth - while sitting amidst the ruins of ancient Corinth.

For more information on *Fortress of the Sun* and E.M. Thomas, visit my website at emthomas.com and sign up for my newsletter.

You can also connect with E.M. Thomas and leave him a message at:

twitter.com/EMThomasAuthor
facebook.com/EMTHOMASAUTHOR1
amazon.com/author/emthomas

If you enjoyed the book, then please leave a review at its Amazon link: https://www.amazon.com/dp/B07MN3DYTR. Word of mouth truly is the lifeblood of an author.

To the extent you would like to take a look at my other work, my epic fantasy *The Bulls of War* is currently available for purchase at the following link: https://www.amazon.com/dp/B01J0AXB74.